This book belongs to

SLIEVELEA

GENEVIEVE LYONS
SLIEVELEA

The
Leisure
Circle

Typeset in Goudy Old Style by Leaper & Gard Ltd, Bristol,
England

Reproduced, printed and bound in Great Britain by
Hazell Watson & Viney Limited,
Member of the BPCC Group,
Aylesbury, Bucks

This book is for Mary,
who inspired Slievelea,
and for Michele and Theresa, who
gave me such much-needed support.

ACKNOWLEDGEMENTS

I would like to thank David Stopp for permission to use the original ballad 'Backstreet Morning'.

I am eternally grateful to Robert Kee for his brilliant and comprehensive *History* of my country which I used for reference.

PART ONE

Chapter

1

BIG Dan Casey was dying. His body was eaten up with cancer and his mind with jealousy. He sat at the French windows overlooking the lawns at Slievelea, gazing out at the misty morning, his mind in turmoil. He had got Devlin to dress him, against the doctor's advice — no, against the doctor's strict orders. But what mattered a day more or less in the painful business of dying?

He had always been afraid of dying, of death, and his ego could not envisage a world without Big Dan Casey in it. He had not had much time to contemplate death before. He had been in such a hurry to become rich, to become important, to make his mark in this world. Well, he had achieved all he had set out to do and more, and now he was dying. And it didn't matter.

He was alone. He had asked to be left by himself. He didn't like them fussing over him, fidgeting at him, irritating him, interrupting his train of thought, which, although disturbing, obsessed him so that all the other mundane details of life were vexing intrusions into his endless internal interrogation. Who was Alain? Who in God's name was Alain?

He looked out over the sloping lawns to the sea. It looked bleak on this February day. A wind blew the bare branches of trees etched against the ice-blue sky like a Japanese print. Spring had not managed to tiptoe across the land yet — but soon, soon. Any day now the first snowdrops would cluster around the elms, and the crocuses, in drifts of purple, yellow and white, would begin to appear at the base of the apple trees in the orchard. Dan closed his eyes as he imagined the orchard a mass of cherry and apple blossom — yes, it was painful to take

3

leave of that. They said most old people died in February. The body was at a low ebb after winter. Well, it didn't matter to him any more!

He wondered if she would come. The doctor had insisted that Aisling be notified. She was in Gstaad skiing. He sighed. He would have preferred to die without her. He did not want to see once more the accusation in her eyes. He did not want to have to face her terrible resentment. He did not care to be too close to her hatred. It was all too painful. If *he* had aspired, against all odds, in that Dublin slum, to become rich, his daughter by a casual marriage became richer! Did she love Ali, her oil rich husband? He doubted it!

Yes, she hated him, her father, hated him with a barely concealed passion. All because of Alexander. And she still didn't know the truth of it all. Only he did, and when he died it would be buried with him.

Had Livia ever guessed about Alexander? He was sure she had not, but then, he asked himself, how could he be sure of anything any more? He shivered under the rug that was tucked around him. He remembered his despair, his tears, his inability to contemplate life without her, how he had been summoned to her room to be with her at the end. His love, the one pure, good thing in his life. And he remembered that her last words had been, 'Alain, Alain, at last.'

He had not known any peace since that moment. Even now his mind shied away from the laceration his heart had received. He had come to doubt everything since that moment, he who had never had any doubts about anything in his life before. People said his wife's death had destroyed Big Dan Casey, and it was true. It had shattered him, but he would have recovered from an understandable, heartrending grief; time would have softened though never erased it. What had really been the undoing of Big Dan Casey were those awful parting words. The enigma had truly destroyed his confidence, knocking him off balance so that his mind had lost its perspective and his body its health. How could you be married to a woman for half a lifetime and not know her? A woman, moreover, you had loved, cherished, adored and trusted? How could she die with another man's name on her lips? It was beyond his comprehension! And who was Alain anyway? He had never known or heard of anyone of that name. Like tides the waves of physical pain ebbed

4

and flowed, but the pain of his thoughts was worse, giving him no rest. Livia and Alain, Alain and Livia. Aisling and Alexander, Alexander and Aisling.

Big Dan listened to the workings of his body as he sat at the window and thought of the past. How he had fought and cheated, murdered even, to have this view in this house, once the residence of Lord and Lady Rennett. Then his grandparents had lived in the gatehouse. Now he was 'Lord of the Manor', lord of it all: the beautiful grey stone building; the verdant lawns rolling down to the sea; the bluebell wood leading to the misty waters of the lake; the rose gardens; the herb and physic beds; the stables; the orchards; all, all of it his. A far cry from the slums in Foley Place, that noxious little street where he had spent his childhood. He had come so far, had become so powerful, yet he had no power now over this enemy — his own body.

It had never dawned on him that his body would let him down. People, yes! He was always prepared for that, but the possibility that his own body would play the traitor was something he had left out of his calculations. He had trusted no one in his life except the women. His harsh childhood had erected a wall between himself and all others, except Jessica, Livia and Aisling, the three women he had adored and lost. His childhood had trained him never to leave himself open to rejection. By giving him no love, his parents, cold Conor and Aideen, aloof and remote, frigid as the snows on the breast of the Wicklow mountains in mid-winter, had bequeathed him an inability to communicate love on any deep level, and he had been unable to feel it for anyone of his own sex in all his life. He had a built-in aversion to his sons which he could not understand and therefore felt guilty about. I never knew you and still don't and I don't understand why, he thought.

Then there was Diramuid. Hate there. Hate I understand very well. Hate and the pursuit of power and money.

It had been enough to love the women. Irishmen, he mused, idolize women, while their fellow men they tend to be wary of unless in the throes of intoxication, and he had never been drunk in his life. He knew himself to be incapable of that kind of abandonment.

He had never looked for love, never asked for it, never sought it. Deirdre had found him, bestowed on him all the richness the earth had to offer with breathtaking generosity. Jessica had seduced him. Livia was presented to him. She might as well have been gift-wrapped in cellophane, tied with a bow and handed to him on a plate. Perhaps if he had had to seek love he would not have committed such crimes against the people he loved and therefore against himself. He really did not know.

Now as he sat feeling the pain, knowing he had no control over the decay eating him up, the fungus galloping through him on its final path of destruction, he thought of the past.

He was not sentimental. He had lived his life on a forward-looking plane of thought. Very early on, he had acquired the knack of erasing from his memory many of the unpleasant things he had had to do in order to gain and maintain his power and position. But now, weakened by pain and his aloneness, his thoughts took refuge and a kind of comfort in the old tales from the past. They had always said that the Caseys were survivors. Sometimes, as he knew only too well, you had to do terrible things to survive, things that could prey on a man's mind if he let them. But wasn't it better to live at all costs than to turn over and die honourably? What use was a dead hero? Dying in battle was a different thing, he supposed. Posthumous fame and distinction could be sweet no doubt, and useful, as his father's had been to him, but to die unsung, unapplauded because you would not do the bad thing that probably no one would find out about? How many people hung back because of the fear of discovery? he wondered.

Yes, the Caseys were survivors, he thought. Conor, his father. He remembered the gaunt joyless man who had raised him. Michael Casey, his grandfather, who had started the whole thing off by managing to get to Dublin from County Cork at the height of the famine. No mean feat in those days, and he wondered what crimes his grandparents had committed to survive. He chuckled. If there was an afterlife, which he doubted, he would have a fine time finding out about that. He realized he had never asked himself that question before. He had just taken it as history. Michael and Siobain Casey, penniless cottage labourers from Barra Bawn near Skibbereen, County Cork, had reached Dublin against all odds, and gone to work for Lord and Lady Rennett in their stately home, Slievelea, in the County of Wicklow in the year 1847. How in God's name had they managed that?

Chapter

2

MICHAEL Casey had known Maureen all his life. They were cousins and had grown up together, but it wasn't until the night of the barn dance that his eyes were opened and he fell in love with her.

The Casey family had always lived in Barra Bawn near Skibbereen. Stories told that in the great time of the Island of Saints and Scholars, the Caseys had been warrior chiefs and, some said, direct descendants of the High Kings of Ireland. But, sure, didn't every Irish family claim that, and who was to know whether it was true or not? Mind you, looking at the beauty of the menfolk — their nobility of head and their grace of movement — you wouldn't put it past them!

At all events, the Casey clan had been labourers and workers on the estate of Sir Jasper Lewis as long back as anyone could remember. Michael's family and his aunts, uncles and cousins all lived in small one-roomed cottages surrounded by tiny plots of land on which they were allowed to grow potatoes. They were not allowed to grow any other form of food and they paid enormous rents for their tiny homes. In the lush, verdant countryside around them were grown all manner of vegetables, fruits and grains which went to the English landlords who tolerated the labourers' bare survival on the land. It was a feudal existence where men, women and children worked the beautiful agricultural country for long hours and for the sole benefit of their owners — for the landlords owned them as surely as they owned the country. Yet, it was rich land and most were happy enough.

Sometimes Peader, Michael's father, shot a rabbit and they ate like kings, but it was a fearful risk and a chancey thing, for,

7

if caught, the penalty was exportation or even death, depending on the Lord of the Manor. Michael and his cousin Maureen had grown up knowing no other life and, being still young, were quite content with their lot. Life, as the people of Barra Bawn knew, was a hazardous affair, a tricky business, at times a daily life-and-death struggle, and they accepted it so.

But Michael sometimes saw the fear in the faces of his parents and the resentment that would flare up as Sir Jasper's carriage thundered past — like the day they saw Hunchback Johnnie beaten half to death. Johnnie had run across the lane in front of the carriage and frightened the horses so that they reared. But sure the coachman had them well under control and isn't Hunchback Johnnie as deaf as a post as well as being a physical disaster? So that was not enough reason to strap the skin off his poor deformed back so hard that afterwards he shivered and shook every time Sir Jasper's carriage clattered along the lanes to the great house. An' the time Sir Jasper raped Katie Flanagan ... God, many's the one he'd seduced, and the land was littered with his bastard offspring; and some were more than willing to be his doxies and cavort about on the sheets in the big house for a night (or two, if they were lucky). But poor Katie hadn't even a lilt in her hips like Mary Kenny or Maureen Casey or Siobain Mulholland whom nature had endowed to drive a man wild. No, poor Katie was almost a half-wit; and didn't she have to carry her shame with her in the form of a sickly brat she produced under a hedge near Lewis's wood nine months on, and lose the few wits she had in the producing? When they saw the carriage or poor Katie's babe, with her mother foolishly babbling inanities, or Hunchback Johnnie shambling past, a flash of fire would dart from the carefully lowered eyes and you could feel a chill of hate pass that way.

John Joe Casey, Maureen's brother, on occasion found work helping out in the stables of the big house during the hunt season. His tales were fabulous, bearing more resemblance to the amazing stories of Irish mythology — of Cuchulainn and Queen Maeve and the great royal palaces of Rath-Cruhane and far shining Tara and red, regal Emain — than anything to do with mortal life.

'Sure, they have dresses of silk and satin with jewels on them as big as carbuncles, and the men wear silk too, and they don't leave their beds, sometimes, till noon. The halls are covered in paintings and there are great, warm rugs everywhere; and the fireplaces are bigger than Patrick's shebeen; and there's a fire in every room, an' the heat that comes from them would warm a man's soul, so Dermot Devlin says, an' isn't he a footman, and hasn't he been close and said his face was scorched, an' he standing this near.' He held his hands a span apart. 'But most it's the food ... God, even I've seen that — ducks and pigs, they eat, and beef, and they don't even finish it!' This last was hard to believe. There had never been a meal in any of their houses at which every scrap had not been consumed and room for more.

That day had seen the end of the harvest. The long, golden afternoon spilled tipsily into evening as they rumbled home, tired girls and men, women, boys and children, drowsily ready for sleep. But tonight there would be no sleep. The girls and boys knew that. Tonight they would celebrate the end of their work.

The sun had made their limbs as heavy as honey, and as liquid. There was a yearning in their bodies, made languorous by a few sips of poteen. And something more, an excitement, an expectancy in the air, which held the first snap of autumn, a peasant knowledge that death is always a breath away and life is sweet to savour.

Michael felt a vitality pulsing through his body, a hot leaping in his blood, and Maureen too, in her way, was as ripe as a plum ready to fall.

When the sun had slid to the edge of the world and drenched the fields in a crimson mantle, giving the bales of hay edges of fire, Michael had helped Maureen off the cart, and her soft round breasts had pressed against his face as she jumped to the ground. She had put the heart across him and he couldn't understand the fright she gave him, the trembling in his limbs and the powerful knocking of his heart. For a second he was pulverized with shock, and dropping her like a hot brick on the grass he had run off home to his mam.

On an ordinary night in Barra Bawn, when he returned home, Michael's mam would be sitting beside the turf fire, the sweet heathery scent of which would mingle appetizingly with the smell of the baking potatoes on the grid above the flames. She would welcome them with flushed, rose-red cheeks on her, laughing as she greeted her husband and sons back from the fields. The flickering light would shine on their strong bodies as they washed in tubs of warm water. Michael and his brothers would giggle senselessly; good-humoured banter would fly to and fro as their mam rubbed them dry before they sat down at the table to eat their main, and sometimes only, meal. They would bow their heads and say grace, crossing themselves before and after; and Danny Óg would, as often as not, be overtaken with the titters. When they had eaten their fill of the soft, floury potatoes, they would say the rosary, heads bent piously, the chanting monotone of the prayers hypnotizing them until Danny would droop down slowly to the floor, curling up and sleeping in the warm peace of the love-filled room. The other boys and Michael would drowse until Da would gently guide them to their bed in the corner where all the lads slept together, joined by any worker who happened to be helping them in the fields. His mam and da would then mount the little three-runged ladder, lift the latch and disappear to their nest above. Then the whispers and the horse-play would break out and the stories be told — scary ones in winter and romantic ones on long summer nights when there seemed no respite from the heat.

Tonight, however, was the ceilidh. So Michael washed himself in cold water and donned his black trousers and clean white shirt, and, full of a hectic, pent-up excitement, hurried out into the night.

The barn was a huge wooden structure and all the farm folk congregated there for the ceilidh that was held at harvest festival time each year. This night the barn was flooded with golden light and soft grey shadows stretched and jumped across the high rafters. The fiddles scraped merrily as the girls in their red and brown skirts jigged energetically, their breasts bobbing up and down in time to the music. Most of them were bare-legged and the men, whose pulses were set throbbing with the insistent beat of the bones on the burran and whose blood was already heated by quantities of porter, lecherously perused flashes of thigh and ankle, knee and bosom, as the dancers to'ed and fro'ed, and upped and downed, gaiety and concentration on every flushed face.

Later, Lord Jasper Lewis and his small family with Martin Bell the bailiff would pay a courtesy call, subduing the abandoned merriment and casting restraint on the gathering. And much later, the still of illegal poteen and the weed would be brought in, whereupon the children and the young people, the nursing mothers and the colleens, would be sent to bed, and only the older married women and the 'ould wans' in their black would be left with the men for the serious part of the evening.

It was hot in the barn, the air full of the sweat of animals and humans, the warm, ripe smell of people dancing. Some children slept on their mothers' laps while the more energetic jigged in imitation of their elders. A long trestle table ran the length of the barn and at one end Michael Casey lounged with the other Casey men and their friends. At the other end stood the Mulhollands — tall, dark, proud men who considered themselves a cut above the feckless Caseys, being tenant farmers while the latter were only labourers. There was a longstanding rivalry between the two families, the Caseys thinking the Mulhollands were too big for their boots (besides being foreigners an' didn't their families come from the west of Ireland with the mighty Armada, an' it scattered to the four winds casting its dregs on the shores of Mayo to scavenge off the land?); the Mulhollands, for their part, hated the fact that the Caseys got away with so much simply because they were so good-looking.

Michael Casey, in his white shirt, sipping his porter and feeling content in his skin, kept a wary eye on Rory Mulholland, who for some reason Michael couldn't fathom seemed to hate him personally, but then Rory Mulholland was like that. He seemed to be constantly in a state of subdued fury against fate, the world, the Lord of the Manor and, most of all, the gentle, easy-going Michael.

Michael Casey was a tall, strong, beautiful young man with a head of black curls and cornflower blue eyes curtained shyly by long, spiky lashes. His good looks drove the girls of Barra Bawn wild and he accepted his popularity gracefully as a matter of fact, though there was no conceit in the young man. The girls of Barra Bawn vied for a smile from his lips or a joky word or, best of all, a hoist up onto the hay cart when his hands would have to encircle a waist and a girl with her eye on the main chance would clasp her hands behind his neck and make the whole procedure of letting her go as difficult for Michael as possible.

He was hardly aware of their stratagems and tricks, but the married women were and found much to smile at in the sauce of the youngsters and the potent beauty of Michael Casey, while the ould wans tutted and spat out the tobacco they chewed and hated in their hearts this manifestation of youth and beauty, which filled them with an aching pain for all that was past and gone for ever from their ken.

Michael's foot tapped in time to the jigs and the reels as the dancers flashed by hot and flushed, backs poker-straight, knees raised like mettlesome ponies, toes pointed and ankles twirling in the intricacies of the dance. Up and down. In and out. And then he saw Maureen. Her round face was dewed with moisture in the heat of the barn. There was a streak of damp down the back of her dress. Her forehead was creased in a frown of concentration and the tip of her little pink tongue peeked from the side of her mouth. She had a nice round figure, plump and warm as a tea cosy, and there were dimples everywhere — in her elbows, her knees, the corners of her red, ripe mouth. She must have felt the concentration of his gaze for she raised her big blue eyes and looked at him a second. She blushed even redder than the exertion of the dance warranted, and she giggled and lowered her eyes, missed a few steps, stumbled and recovered almost immediately. Then she tossed her black curls and, with renewed energy, attacked the jig, her skirts whirling, her arms reaching out as she barely touched the ground, the music speeding until it ended suddenly with a whoop and a great sough of release and applause. The dancers dispersed, the men to slake their thirst with porter, the women to cool down as best they could, and Michael made his way over to Maureen.

She caught his movement from the corner of her eye and tossed her head anew in an agony of excitement, watching him closely through her lashes. Still Michael hovered as she exchanged laughter and badinage with the group of girls. The females of Barra Bawn had no animosity towards each other except the friendly 'every girl for herself' rivalry in the age-old task of catching a husband. So the Casey girls and the Mulholland girls were together, along with the Devlins, the Kennys and the rest.

Siobain Mulholland was probably the prettiest colleen in Barra Bawn. Full of life and laughter, she was in direct contrast to the dark, passionate, morose men of the Mulholland clan. She shared their colouring, though, their luxuriant, blue-black hair, milk-white skin and high Spanish cheekbones. Her mouth was wide and generous, often open in laughter that revealed her

12

strong, even, white teeth. She spent a lot of time with the Caseys, more time than she spent in the stifling company of her brothers, whose hasty tempers often erupted in quarrels that filled the atmosphere with doom and gloom and ill humour. Siobain's naturally calm and sunny disposition blossomed more in the company of the Caseys. She giggled with Maureen, loved Peader's gentle nature, and Danny Og, Michael's brother, she doted on and mothered as if he were her own. Michael himself had stolen her heart forever.

She lifted her heavy mane of hair away from her neck and, throwing back her head, shook her curls from side to side, hoping Michael would notice and see how much prettier she was than that silly Maureen Casey. Deirdre Devlin, who worked as a scullery maid up at the big house and whose brother, Dermot Devlin, was footman in Sir Jasper's service, also vied for Michael's attention and shot a bold and covetous invitation from eyes starry in the lamplight, but he was blind to all save Maureen.

As Michael advanced towards Maureen so did the taller, narrower Rory Mulholland. The colour flooded Maureen's face and drained away, rushed to her cheeks again and ebbed as the two men came to a halt opposite her. They looked at each other (like two bulls about to lock horns, Maureen thought), then Michael smiled his slow, devastating smile and Maureen moved towards him. Rory bowed to the inevitable with habitual bad grace and went to the table to douse his rage with some black porter. The fiddles tuned up, the bones on the burran started their insidious primitive beat, the music began and Michael's arm went around Maureen's waist.

They danced oblivious of anyone else, of the sniggers of the middle-aged men, the sad sighs of the married women and the venomous glances of the girls, who saw him lost to them for ever. Then their attention drifted away and was caught elsewhere. The women renewed their riveting conversation about Mother Hegarty and her methods of terminating Deirdre Devlin's pregnancy. The men attacked the porter with a great greed and the girls cast about for the next best thing to Michael Casey — all except Siobain Mulholland, who had seen Michael's sudden awareness of his cousin and Maureen's response, and who kept his every movement within the orbit of her glance.

13

Michael and Maureen held each other's eyes, drowning in the look.

'I never saw you before,' he said.

'And I never saw you,' she answered.

'You are beautiful,' he said, 'so beautiful.'

'Oh, lovely Michael, so are you, so are you!' she replied and then they were silent.

Moving to the dance, they joined the weaving pattern of the dancers. Their fingertips touched, his warm breath stirred the ringlets at the nape of Maureen's neck. He could see each hair of her eyebrows and the damp white smoothness of her milk-white shoulders, until as one, without need of a word between them, they drifted out into the night, into the drenching moonlight. The sounds of the music came to their ears and they said no words at all.

They stood a moment, out of breath, from the dancing or their feelings, neither knew. Maureen pressed her hands on her wildly beating heart, looked up at the tall height of Michael Casey, into his feverish eyes, and ran her tongue over her lips.

'Oh Michael,' she said softly, then, overcome by her emotions, she turned from him and ran into the field.

'Come and catch me!' she called to him over her shoulder.

When he caught up with her she was hiding behind a giant oak tree, one of the first that led to the density of Lewis's wood. They were panting and, as he rested the palms of his hands on the tree, one on each side of her, Maureen unbuttoned his shirt and gently ran her hands over his skin and muscle, her fingers tracing the hollow of his throat. Then quietly she took off her blouse and stood before him naked and beautiful in the moonlight. They gazed at each other for moments, then caught each other or they would have fallen. Their kisses were long and deep and content as if they found peace in each other. Michael felt the great surge as he hardened ready for her and she simply welcomed him into her body, into her centre, welcomed him home.

They never lost awareness of each other's identity as he held his Maureen, her legs curled possessively round him; and, as the music floated to them on the breeze, their passion mounted and their young bodies were flooded by wave after wave of engulfing passion until they lay spent and united in each other's arms.

Chapter

3

SIOBAIN Mulholland saw Michael Casey slip away with Maureen and she bit her lip angrily and looked at her companions to see if they had noticed, but they were too busy stuffing themselves, those of them who were not dancing. The table behind her was laden with food, courtesy of Sir Jasper. Siobain picked up a chicken wing and pulled the white meat off the bone with her strong teeth.

'Yerra jealousy doesn't suit you, Siobain Mulholland. The little green-eyed monster spoils your beauty entirely.'

Siobain whirled, her hand raised to strike, but Mother Hegarty laughed in her face.

'Oh, you're in a fine fury over Michael Casey, aren't you? It's not been lost on me and you watching him in the fields as if he were an early Christian and you a hungry lion ...'

'Shut your gob, ye ould witch!' Siobain whispered fiercely, terrified in case anyone should hear. But the ould wan would not be hushed and she leaned near the fresh young girl, her breath smelling like the sulphurous, nauseous gases of hell that Father O'Rourke was always telling them about, and her seamed old face sweaty and greasy, her eyes glittering with good humour and malice both.

Mother Hegarty was half Gypsy, and was loved and hated by the villagers. She lived up the boreen near the boundary of Sir Jasper Lewis's land, in a foul-smelling tigeen full of the herbs and other strange things she used in the making of her potions and love philtres. Small carcases of animals littered the place, frogs and toads and bats deployed in an art so old it stretched back past the High Kings of Ireland themselves to the Tuatha de Dannan, the tribe of women who had ruled the winds and the

15

seas and the peaty earth of Ireland in the ancient days.

They came to her, the villagers, when all else failed, giving in to the superstitious and pagan side of their natures, looking for a way to get their hearts' desires, for the Christian priests advocated acceptance of their lot in this 'vale of tears' where, they were told, there was 'weeping and gnashing of teeth'. Father O'Rourke talked a lot about that, 'sighing and sobbing' he said they should expect to be, and advised them to meet tribulation eagerly, for it was a sure 'open Sesame' to Heaven's pearly gates.

Many an abortion Mother Hegarty performed in her tigeen, many a gangrened leg she patched up good as new with the mushrooms, toadstools or agarics she picked in Lewis's wood of a morning in the dew of the dawn. She had the colleens chewing a buttery lard to increase the size of their breasts, and the lads a dark tarry substance to increase the size of their manhood. She gave the boys a weed to smoke that galvanized them to victory in the games and the hurling, and she was in great demand for love potions for lovelorn girls, many of whom coveted Michael Casey. Sure if all the colleens she had given the pink liquid succeeded, Michael Casey would have a harem.

Now she grabbed Siobain's arm and, pulling her round, looked into her eyes, saying fiercely, 'Ye'll get him all the same! I seen it in the cards.'

Siobain's whole body became still. She couldn't breathe. She felt as if the world had stopped for a moment. She looked around the room at the foolish, drunken stupidity of the men, the party smiles of the women. The fiddlers were mopping their faces and slaking their thirst before the next reel. There was a golden holiday glow over the whole place. Her heart near burst for joy and impulsively she threw her arms around the smelly ould wan and gave her a hug. 'Go raibh maith agut,' she said. 'Thank you.'

Suddenly there was an outbreak in the corner of the barn. Some of the big lads had been picking on Hunchback Johnnie and Danny Óg Casey was taking on all the bullies by himself, defending Hunchback Johnnie with swirling fists, dancing about on his tiny wee toes, blood pouring from his nose.

Siobain ran over to rescue him while the old men laughed drunkenly. Siobain scolded them, and Danny, roundly. But she was not really angry, she was too happy at what Ma Hegarty had just told her.

16

'Lookit all of yin sitting' there lookin' like a bunch of gombeen men — pickin' on poor Johnnie who never hurt a fly and watchin' an infant come to his aid. Aren't ye the grand men entirely. Sure Cuchulainn must be turnin' in his grave eaten up with envy at the heroic bravery of yin. An' as for you, Danny Casey, a fine red nose ye have on you an' no mistake!'

'Did ye see me, Siobain?' said the little fellow, jabbing the air with his fist. 'Aman't I a big boy now? Aman't I as good as me brother Michael any day now? Aman't I? Aman't I?'

She looked around for Michael but he and Maureen were still missing. Siobain hugged little Danny to her. 'Sure you're a desperate fellow an' no mistake!' she said, ruffling his hair tenderly. Little Danny looked up, hearing a sob in her voice, and saw she had tears in her eyes. He suddenly felt very young again, not the big lad at all. The bravado left him in a whoosh and he said, nearly in tears himself, 'Ah, don't cry Siob, don't cry . . . sure it'll be all right, I know it will.'

They had just sat down with their arms round each other when Michael's mother caught sight of Danny's nosebleed from where she had been sitting gossiping with the other women. It looked far worse from over there than it actually was and, crossing herself and muttering a prayer, she hurried over to help Siobain with the little fellow, chastising him angrily in her anxiety. The little chap, peaky faced and swollen eyed, burst into floods of tears. On top of everything else, he had eaten too much, glutting himself on goodies that were foreign to him.

'Mam, I feel sick. Me nose hurts. Oh Mam!' He yawned tremendously.

'It's time and more that ye should be abed, Danny Casey. An' haven't ye stuffed yerself like Sean O'Grady's hog? Gettin' yerself mixed up in a fight like a tinker's child.' She wrapped her shawl over her shoulders and, taking the little fellow by the hand, left the barn.

The moon shone, casting a magical silver sheen over the world. The grasses whispered and the music came faintly to them on the wind. One or two men the worse for drink staggered about outside the barn, singing out of tune. The trees were dark and full of shadows, and Hunchback Johnnie, coming out too quickly from behind one, nearly scared her out of her wits.

17

'It's only me, missus. Can I walk wid ye? I'm nervous so I am an' himself abroad in the night.'

Himself was Sir Jasper Lewis. Hunchback Johnnie kept out of his way as much as possible, especially on an occasion when Sir Jasper might have been drinking, and he always had a skinful before he paid his visit to the barn dance.

'He's a brave little fellow so he is, missus,' said Hunchback Johnnie, jerking his large head in the direction of Dannys.

'Sure I thought my last hour had come so I did. Those bloody Mulhollands, they'd pick a fight wid their own shadow. Aren't you the grand little hero?' he said and Danny Óg squirmed with pleasure, which ended abruptly as he suddenly felt his tummy reel and lurch, and he threw up in the boreen, getting rid of all the lovely food he had eaten so greedily. Then Hunchback Johnnie caught his young defender up in his arms and carried him. Mrs Casey was glad of his company and they walked in companionable silence until they reached the cottage door where he set Danny Óg on his feet and Mrs Casey wished him good evening and took Danny inside. She laid him tenderly on a mattress of straw on the floor. He lay there dozing, eyes closing, a trail of dried blood across his cheek, hiccupping and yawning prodigiously. She kissed her son and sighed. Saying a short prayer, she left him to return to the ceilidh and the rest of her men.

On the moonlit boreen as she walked along Mrs Casey thought of her menfolk with pride mixed with maternal anxiety. Danny Óg was always trying to ape his big brothers and he did not seem to realize how small he was. She smiled as she thought that in his own mind Danny Óg was at least as tall and strong as Michael, maybe as big even as Peader.

As she turned out of the boreen she thought for a moment she saw a ghost — two ghosts — and she pressed her hands to her heart. Then she realized it was Maureen Casey and Michael — her son Michael — naked as the day they were born, rising up out of the fresh green grasses like Adam and Eve at the dawn of the world.

'Jesus, Mary and Joseph!' she whispered and took a step forward with mouth open to give them the scolding of their lives. Then she stopped herself, ruefully smiling. It was a bit late for that — an' weren't they young an' hot blooded? No, she sighed, she'd wait and talk to Kathleen Casey, Maureen's mother, and between them they'd put a stop to the whole thing. Yes, that was the best plan. She watched as the two pearly shadows became one.

No one in the barn that night noticed that Michael and Maureen had left together except Mother Hegarty, Siobain Mulholland and her cousin Rory. Mother Hegarty missed nothing. She shook her head, for the mating of those two could only bring disaster. Waren't they cousins and a marriage between them taboo? No priest in the land would marry them, but they couldn't see that yet; now only the heat of the blood dictated.

Mother Hegarty watched the drama of life play itself out, enjoying every moment of it, not missing a nuance, never condemning, accepting philosophically the ups and downs, and watching, always watching. For many a year now she had seen Michael Casey grow taller and more beautiful. She watched as he went heedlessly about his work, unaware of the chaos he caused in all the colleens' hearts. She saw the girls, one and all, except Maureen, fall for him, flutter around him, advance and retreat, in the complicated mating game the young played. And always Siobain, prettier than most with her cascade of thick jetty curls and her huge brown eyes, fluttered nearest like a moth round a flame, determined to get Michael. Maureen, on the other hand, had never seemed to bother about him in that way, treating him as a brother. Quite right too an' they blood cousins, Mother Hegarty thought righteously. No good would come of it. But it was all very confusing. She had seen Siobain get her love. It was in the cards and the cards never lied. But she had seen a great disaster too. Could Michael and Maureen Casey falling in love cause such havoc? She doubted it. Then there was Rory Mulholland. She did not underestimate his propensity to evil. That he hated Michael Casey with all the dedication of his fanatic soul was quite visible to everyone, but she was pretty sure not many were aware of his passion for Maureen Casey. He would not be resting easy this night. He would never forgive Michael Casey for this, she could swear to that. But it still did not add up to the magnitude of the portents of evil she had seen in the cards.

Over and over again she had shuffled the pack and redealt, and again and again the falling down of them had been the same. She tried runes; she tried many an old spell known to her alone and the forecast was always the same — disaster on an unimaginable scale. She wanted to believe it was the love of Michael and Maureen that somehow would cause the disaster. She tried to still the little voice inside her that stirred and whispered in her ear late in the night. It always whispered one word, one terrible, tiny word — famine. She remembered 1817, but she pushed the thought away. No, no, it could not be that, never that! And the summer had been glorious no doubt, the weather making the land look like the Garden of Eden, 'that we were cast out of because we were born with Original Sin, Father O'Rourke says,' Peader Casey told her over a pint of porter. 'But the wans up in the big house were never cast out, missus. Sure aren't they in it now? An' so mustn't that mean that they waren't born with Original Sin at all? That's what I wanna know!' Yes, the summer had smiled on them all, giving the illusion of sweet content in the land, and driving poor Michael and Maureen Casey to lose their wits. Yes, Mother Hegarty told herself to calm her fears, the bad signs must be intimations of a storm brewing because the luckless Casey cousins had fallen in love and those two, Rory and Siobain Mulholland, would fight it every inch of the way. Sure, didn't she know Siobain would win in the end! It couldn't mean anything more, she reassured herself, and those cancerous spots she had seen on the potatoes she had dug up that morning meant nothing ... nothing at all.

Chapter

4

AT first the blight on the potatoes was not considered a major tragedy. Sure it was wondered at, worried about, caused a certain amount of apprehension, and the offending potatoes were thrown away, but gradually, to the consternation of the villagers, it seemed that no matter how carefully they separated the bad from the good, still every time they came to examine them they would find that somehow the rot had spread. Some of the older folk remembered with icy fear the famine of 1817, and they crossed themselves superstitiously. 'Jasus preserve us from that!'

And slowly it began to dawn on them that this was indeed what faced them. Maureen's mother selected the best potatoes she could find and tried to cook them, but the smell from the pot drove them out of the cottage, and the poisonous mess had to be burned. By October people were getting hungry and as the year dwindled the plight of the villagers became serious. Poaching or stealing seemed the only road to survival, and that a tricky one, for on Sir Jasper's land the penalty was likely to be death for anyone caught.

Michael was to look back on the night of the barn dance as a beacon in a sea of troubles; it gave him the only happiness he was to know for a long time. The families firmly separated himself and Maureen. They were going to put an end to the matter. Michael's mother had a word with Katie, Maureen's mother, and the agreement between them was complete. They were not censorious — the young were foolish and imprudent, but then you can't put a wise head on a young nubile girl and a boyo who has just discovered the joys of virility — and forbidding them to see each other would add the pinch of salt to the situation, and might precipitate God knows what sort of lunacy. The best way was to keep them apart. Michael was not an eloquent boy and there seemed no way to pierce the armour of the women. When he tried to find her, Maureen was never there; and when he found out where she was and followed her, she had left. He leaned against the half-door of the cottage and her mother said shortly that she was in the fields. When he found her friends knee-deep in the hay, laughing and teasing each other, they became silent and embarrassed and said she was not there. He only saw her at Mass on Sunday and her eyes were pools of misery and yearning as they looked into his. As the days passed and then the months, the situation did not change. Maureen was guarded, and as unreachable as the moon.

Then the world, cruel to him, became sadistic. Not only was he bewildered by the frustration of finding the person he loved most always out of reach, now the potato failure began to affect both their families seriously. Times became very hard. He could not understand the contrariness of a world that gave him the joy he had felt on the night of the barn dance — the oneness he had felt with all things, men and animals and nature — and now, vindictively, took it all and more away. Then, when he had been full of such complete physical and mental content, the beauty of the world had seemed overwhelming. Now, with a fierce, cold hand, she had struck him a blow, rejecting him and his family and abandoning them and their needs, leaving them to perish. What Michael heard and pieced together over that time filled him full of hate, warped his gentle nature and changed him from a kindly loving boy into an angry man, poisoned with fear. He assimilated the facts slowly, for he was not clever or astute, but even he asked the question, why? Why must my family starve for lack of sound potatoes when the carts rumble past each day full of food for export? When the sheep are plump but only serve Sir Jasper's needs and the English tables in far-off London? The pigs are fat and pink and only one could save my family but I'm not allowed to touch, I will die if I do. Why? Why?

The men were angry. They heard of people attacking flour mills, people hungrier than they. They were told that the English government was coming to their aid, and they wondered why ... Michael asked why? Why couldn't they just have a fair share of what the land in their own country yielded? Dermot Devlin, Sir Jasper's footman, said it all came down to prices and totally confused Michael with the explanation.

'Sir Jasper says they can't *give* us food, it would, wait now, what was that he after said, it would undermine market prices, those were his very words, "undermine market prices", then the merchants would withhold food altogether — but what he means sure I don't know and, Jasus, Katie Flanagan's bairn passed away last Wednesday and Katie went clean out of her head altogether and stuck a knife in the back of a drunken soldier on the Cork road, and was taken away screaming to the madhouse.'

Michael heard of how shipments went out of Limerick Harbour regularly, taking from Ireland Indian corn, butter, lard, hams and bacon, flour, oats and barley, taking it *from* the country when the people had begun to die of starvation in it. It takes a long time dying of starvation, Michael found. His father, watching the younger ones become skin and bone, their little hands like claws, their ribs sticking out like baskets, killed a sheep one night with some of his neighbours and friends, and the whole village had a stay of execution.

Of course word got back to Sir Jasper, who was angry and issued a reward for the names of the culprits, but as the whole village was involved one way or another there were no takers. Rory Mulholland tried to think of a way of betraying the Caseys, but reluctantly gave up as there was no way he could without implicating his own family. However, when more sheep began to disappear the matter became more serious. The reward still stood, but announcements were made stating that if the culprits were caught they would be hanged. Many a man stirred uneasily in his sleep, but the dilemma remained — to die quietly of starvation or to try to survive even at the risk of being caught and executed. It was not much of a choice, and killing the sheep at least helped the young 'uns. But it was not always possible. The sheep were well guarded. Michael had asked his da to let him help, but he was not allowed, his father feeling it would be too dangerous and he looked to Michael to try as best he might to care for the family if he were caught.

'If anything happens to me, allana, see to yer ma as best ye can,' he told his son.

Michael knew the group of poachers; the whole village knew

who was responsible. Dermot Devlin gave them the information they needed from the big house, and Michael's da, Peader, John Joe Casey, Declan Mulholland and the Casey and Mulholland tribes united for the common good. Maureen's brother and Sheebeen Brendan had the whole operation timed and worked out to a fine art.

Then the sheep stealing came to a stop. Sir Jasper had the sheep penned up, guarded so that it was impossible and foolhardy to take the risk. They had no stores, no stock to fall back on for the cottages could be, and often were, searched for incriminating evidence and so the temporary respite was terminated in Barra Bawn and the people began to starve in earnest.

And then Michael found Maureen.

It was a total accident. As things worsened Michael and some of the young and, indeed, older men of the village found jobs building roads. It was back-breaking work but at least they would get a little money with which they could buy food. The older men's pride was hurt. They were land men and to do this menial task was hurtful to their dignity, but needs must when the devil drives, and God knows the devil was driving them pretty hard. There were hungry mouths at home, and a terrible permanent gnawing hunger within. Michael and his friends did not mind the road-building at all. Anything that could help fill their bellies and contribute to the lessening of the acute hunger suffered by their mothers and younger brothers and sisters was worthwhile. But they were never paid. The Board of Works said that they had to get permission from the British Government and that took time — and they had no time!

While they were working on the road, Maureen's parents became slacker in their guardianship of her. In fact it was becoming a matter of no importance what the young people did. The priorities had changed and now food, avoiding starvation a day at a time, became their main objective, their sole preoccupation.

Michael was shocked at the change in Maureen. His plump dove had become a hungry sparrow.

He was on his way home from the road work, tired, dispirited and angry, too, at another excuse not to pay him and the other men for their work, when he saw her standing alone in the

24

boreen next to Lewis's wood. Her hands hung by her side, her head was bowed, her shoulders stooped. The sun shone brightly on her hair, and he caught her to him, holding the frail, bony body tight against him as they sobbed wordlessly in each other's arms.

'Oh Michael, I'm so tired. So tired,' she said.

'Acushla, I know. Oh God, what's amiss in this land? What did any of us do to deserve this?'

They spoke softly, helplessly, in their native tongue.

'But Maureen, it can't go on! Poor old Hunchback Johnnie is on his last legs, and there's children skin and bone that can't last much longer, and me mam is very, very ill. She won't eat a thing while the children go without. She gives them her share, when there's anything to share. We can't get at the sheep any more. Even if we could we'd lose our lives an' then what would the women and children do?'

'Ah God, Michael, I don't know. I've a wee wan comin' too . . .'

Michael looked at her, seconds, moments; astonishment, acceptance, joy, anxiety and despair chasing across his face. Then his expression changed and anger rose hard and strong in his body.

'Then that's that, Maureen, acushla. We're going away . . . we're getting out of here. You and me and the baby will find some place where a man can work and feed his family. We won't stay any longer in this devil's hole. These bastards will not take from us any more, take what's rightfully ours. They won't kill us with their indifference.'

'But Michael allana, sure it's the same all over the length and breadth of Ireland. Me da says the whole country is starving to death.'

They stood together helplessly, gazing out over the lush fields, the gently swaying green wood. It was a cold, clear day in March. The cows grazed peacefully, shading their enormous lustrous eyes with long lashes and swishing nonchalant tails against the irritation of flies. A meadowlark poured out its soul to the white clouds that drifted across the pale blue sky. The sun shed its golden light on the gentle rural scene.

Michael and Maureen clasped hands, stilled for a second within and without by the sweet serenity of the world, when at the edge of the boreen on the horizon a tiny moving object

25

appeared. At first they thought it was an animal, then they saw it was a little child. The movements were unsteady, the bairn little more than a skeleton. Its little legs, like sticks, wavered beneath the body, every bone of which you could count. The head looked large for the neck, and the great eyes were pools of misery. They saw all this as the small figure tottered down the boreen towards them. There was unspeakable horror and heart-breaking courage in the sight of his superhuman effort to reach them.

'Jesus, it's Danny Óg,' Michael cried out. 'It's Danny! I didn't recognize him. I'm only used to seeing him in the corner at home, he hasn't been away from the hearth now for weeks. I never seen, never noticed!'

'Oh God, Michael, he's a pitiful sight,' Maureen cried, running towards the tiny, stumbling creature. She held him, wrapping him in her arms, crooning softly to him. Small animal noises were coming from his tight little mouth.

'Maureen, hush! He's trying to say something.'

She held him away from her, looking into his eyes. 'What is it, allana? Take your time.'

He tried to speak but failed. His parched mouth opened and closed and his little frame shook as he desperately tried to communicate with her. Hot tears trickled unheeded down his gaunt face, an ould wan's face, Maureen thought, and he only a child. She wiped the tears away with her thumbs.

'What is it, allana?'

'Mam's dead! Our mam's dead!' He got it out at last and slid slowly to the ground.

Michael stood helplessly for a moment, his heart breaking in him. He looked at the child: tiny, balding like an old man, the bones of his body visible through the fine skin, lying like a broken toy in the dirt of the boreen. He saw that Danny Óg would soon follow their mam to the grave. His mam and his little brother, a loss too heavy to bear. He looked at Maureen, his beloved, kneeling beside the little boy, her head bowed, weeping, her shoulders stooped with the agony of the defeated, and he thought of his mam, his love, his saint, who would never again light his way. A sob broke from him and, in anger, he picked up Danny Óg and held him fiercely to his breast.

He set off towards home, sobs shaking him, and Maureen meekly followed, the weight of the world on her young shoulders. When they arrived they saw Michael's mother lying peacefully on the straw mattress. The boys sat at the table, heads bowed in silence. Peader stood looking down on his dead darling, only anger on his face. Michael sat down, Danny Óg in his arms. There was no sound in the place. There was no food in the place. There was no hope in the place.

Chapter

5

SIR Jasper was not an unkind man — that is, in his own estimation. However, he was not going to be made a fool of. His
servants guarded the sheep well; the only trouble was, could one
trust all the servants with this famine business disturbing the
peaceful running of his estate and lands? He had complete faith
in the Government. They would do the right thing. They said
that they had the situation under control and one could always
trust the British Government to act the gentleman.

Charles Trevelyan, however, Head of the Treasury, was very
careful about political economy. The state, he felt, could not
possibly give away food — what would then happen to food
prices? No, the main responsibility must rest with the Irish landlords.

'The only way to prevent the people of Ireland from
becoming habitually dependent on the British Government is
not to send them free food, or the risk is run of paralyzing all
private enterprise and having the country on you for an in-
definite number of years,' he said. But the Act of Union in 1801
stated Britain and Ireland were one, bound together for all
eternity, for better or worse. It seemed the British Government
was only interested in better. There was grain stored in Ireland,
but it was not released to the starving. The Government wanted
to wait until the new potato harvest relieved them of the
responsibility of distributing the grain and risking a fall in prices.

Men looked everywhere for work, but there were too many
men and too few jobs. Then they found the new potato crop
was blighted. The news was catastrophic. The other crops flourished, the produce destined for export was excellent, almost
every sort of food except the potato was abundant. But as the

28

people were allowed no other food than the potato the deaths increased. Some landlords evicted their tenants for nonpayment of rent and the poor starving creatures were cast out, deprived of a place to die. The women tried to save some furniture, but their strength was not enough to carry the treasured pieces. The children wailed in fear and the men were shamed because of their failure to take care of their families. If they put a few planks of wood against a wall for shelter, the bailiffs had orders to pull them down, and in the length and breadth of Ireland the foundations of cottages were being dug up to prevent people from taking shelter amid the ruins. Many of the landlords were delighted at the opportunity of ridding 'their' land of the luckless tenants and thereby acquiring more territory unencumbered by inhabitants. They burned the little cottages wantonly. The people walked away from their homes, holding their children in their arms, and died from starvation by the roadside.

And over it all was the spectre of the poorhouse, if you could reach it in time and if there was room for you, for the poorhouses were hard pressed and their allotment of money was small, and there were so many streaming through their doors.

So around the country people died, in their cottages, on the streets; on the highways pathetic groups roamed about, skeletal, begging for food: a scrap, a bite. The landlords and officials, separated and aloof, led peaceful, contented lives, daily eating their fill, while the Government in England argued the case back and forth, back and forth, and more sickened, and more suffered. England was powerful and rich, she had ships, she had gold, she had food in abundance, yet although the Queen at her Coronation swore to protect her subjects, and the Parliamentarians, honourable men all, were the first to reaffirm in no uncertain terms their 'ownership' of their emerald island neighbour, yet now they procrastinated and spoke of 'us' and 'them'. It was even said in the London *Times* that 'if food was sent free or very cheaply to the starving Irish it would probably bring out the old malady — national indolence'. And in a richly agricultural country the bewildered people died of starvation.

Maureen's baby was born prematurely and survived only a few days before it mercifully died. Michael discovered the twin deaths of his baby and Danny Óg in the same week. The discovery left him devastated and he was unable to control his tears.

Hunger had rendered him weak, and his large frame had

begun to dwindle. Gone now were the smooth muscles Maureen had loved; his skin hung loose and his eyes were wild. His brothers had cried a great deal after their mother died, then they had stopped. They had become too hungry to cry. All they could think of was the agonizing ache in their bellies. Then that stopped too.They were too numbed to notice Danny Óg's passing or to miss him. They huddled in an apathetic group, giant-eyed, exhausted. It was at this point that Michael's father and the men decided that guards or no guards they would steal another sheep.

One morning Michael, lean and hungry, steeled himself to leave the cottage and forage for food. It was difficult these days to summon up the energy to move. It was a useless task he knew, but something had to be done.

It was a crisp, cold day. The sun shone peacefully on a grey world. Michael dragged his feet slowly one after the other. His objective was the field near Lewis's wood. He thought he might find some vegetable roots there, or berries, anything, anything at all to feed the youngsters. As he neared the field he saw a figure kneeling. It could have been any age, a child, or an ould wan. As he approached he saw that someone had had the same idea as himself and was scrabbling in the clay, obviously looking for something edible. It was female, that he could tell from the skirt, and as the hands went on clawing in the ground for all the world like a cornered rat, the shawl over her head fell off and he realized it was Maureen. He had not seen her since the day Danny Óg told them his mam had died. Now she heard him dragging his feet and she turned. He was appalled by the change in her. Her hair was thin and lank, her cheeks were hollow and her teeth seemed unnaturally large in her face. Gone was the peasant beauty she had had and she now wore the mean and wolfish look of the hungry.

Still his heart throbbed with love for her and he fell on his knees beside her and drew her into his arms. Little moans shook her body like the whimpering of an animal in torment, and Michael was filled so full of hate and piercing sorrow he could barely contain the emotion within his emaciated frame. He was shaking all over when he heard the horses' hooves thundering up the road. Tired beyond belief, he did not even raise his head when they stopped near him.

'Hey you — you there! Come here! Come here at once, I say!'

He raised his head, still holding the whimpering Maureen, and looked up. There were three men on horses between him and the sun, so that he could not see their faces, but the fourth one, a little apart, was shouting at him, and pointing his whip at him, gesturing at him to follow them. He did not understand at all, but brought up to the habit of instant obedience to his superiors, he rose, and still with his arm holding Maureen's thin shoulders he slowly moved towards the men.

'You're Michael Casey, aren't you?' asked the fourth man whom he now recognized as Sir Jasper's bailiff, Martin Bell.

'Yes, mister, I am.'

'Then come on, man, Sir Jasper wants to see you. Come on.'

'Yes, mister, but listen, I'm not leavin' Maureen here.'

'Oh all right, all right. Jimmy, put her behind you, and here, Michael, up you come on Rosie. You've carried heavier burdens in your time, eh Rosie? Come on now, Sir Jasper's in a hurry and doesn't like to be kept waiting.'

His voice was not unkind, and his normal coldness seemed lacking. Martin Bell might have been moved at the spectacle of these walking skeletons. At any rate, they did as he said without question and were borne away down the road towards the manor and into the sun.

Sir Jasper was sitting in front of a huge log fire when Michael was ushered before him. He was a large, rotund, pink-cheeked man in his early fifties; sound of wind and limb; cosseted, pampered and sleek with good food and wine and healthy exercise. He had the excellent humour of a man of good digestion for whom life was an easy pursuit of happiness, a man to boot who could afford anything he wanted. Before him stood Michael, tall and gaunt, exhausted by lack of food, rendered stupid by these richly appointed surroundings and ill at ease with the affluence so abundantly displayed.

The room was sumptuously furnished. Three fluted columns at each end led the eye upward to the blue and cream Adam ceiling. The chimneypiece was of French granite mounted with bronze and gilt. On the mantle stood a French eighteenth-century clock, with tortoiseshell figures of Venus and Cupid. There was a roll-top desk, oak veneered with purple wood, pearwood, boxwood, holly and other woods. There were

31

Lancret paintings on the panelled walls.

Sir Jasper sat in a great heavy mahogany armchair. Resting on an eighteenth-century baroque table beside him was a tray containing, amongst other things, a large Georgian silver teapot, a cup and saucer of fine bone china, a small silver dish of butter curls with a tiny moist dew on them like a bloss. Beside the tray a bowl of fruit stood — enough to stave off the pangs of hunger for a week. At first Michael thought it was imitation and, when he realized it was real, he knew a moment's choking pain that removed his sight from him, causing him to totter for a second.

Sir Jasper had been watching him closely and had not missed anything. He motioned Martin Bell to sit Michael in a chair.

'Give him a drop of wine, Martin,' Sir Jasper said softly.

Martin nodded and Michael sipped the liquid which slipped down his throat, reaching out warmly to soothe his nerve ends.

'Now, my boy, you're Michael Casey, is that not so?' Sir Jasper asked, again softly, gently.

'Yes, sir, I am indeed, sir.'

Michael's head felt full of cotton wool and all feeling seemed to have left the rest of his body. The warmth of the wine within, and the fire without, the total alien comfort of the place, all combined to make him feel drugged.

'Ah yes,' Sir Jasper was saying, 'you're a good lad. I've never heard tell of a bad deed you've been up to, Michael Casey.'

'No, sir. We're honest people. But, sir, if I may be so bold, what've ye done with my Maureen?'

'She's all right and tight, Michael me lad, and by Jove she'll be righter and tighter if you can give us some help. Now do ye think ye might be able to do that?'

'What do ye mean, sir?' Michael was confused.

'Well, Michael my lad, now how can I put it? Let me see,' Sir Jasper mused. 'What would you like best in the whole, wide world? I put it to you, Michael. What? If you were asked, as indeed I'm asking you now, what would you wish for? Eh?'

'To be out of this whole mess, this cesspool of a place, sir.'

Michael had dreamed of escape often. Sometimes the strength of the impossible dream kept him going. 'Me and Maureen, sir. Without her I don't care about anything at all.'

'Well, you can have your wish, Michael,' Sir Jasper said.

Michael was nonplussed. What was the man talking about?

What did he mean? Michael decided he was having some kind of hallucination. He had often heard men babbling on about imaginings when they were in the extremities of starvation. But no . . . the man repeated it softly. 'You can have your wish, Michael Casey.'

'But how, sir? How?'

'By doing us a small favour,' he said, then went on conversationally, 'You see, Michael, we know your father is going to steal a sheep or two of mine this evening. Now, as you know, we have corralled the sheep but have had to put them in four groups. We want to know which group of sheep is going to be raided, and what men are going with your father. If you give us their names . . . Michael?'

Michael had jumped to his feet shouting, but he was restrained by Martin Bell, who gave him the glass of wine again, refilled; and Michael automatically raised it to his lips, feeling waves of mindless anger and disorientation confusing him.

'Sit down, Michael, before you fall.' Again the soft voice. 'Hear me out.'

Michael obeyed or he would have collapsed.

'We know all about it, Michael, so be sensible. We just need to know how many men, their names, and where they mean to do it. The time and the place, Michael. Don't be heroic. We'll find out anyway. This way it's time-saving and tidier, somewhat.'

Michael tried to think. How could they know? No one in the village would inform, that was for sure. The only one who could have told was the footman Dermot Devlin.

'We must stop this wanton knavery, you see, Michael.'

'It's not knavery to try to get food for your family when they are dying. It's not wrong to steal when your bairns and your mam . . . your mam . . .'

Michael, to his horror, burst into tears. He sobbed like a child, wiping his nose and his eyes on his jacket sleeve. They watched him in silence. Then once more Sir Jasper spoke.

'Michael, let me put it to you this way. We are going to catch those men no matter what you do. Now if you tell us the names we promise you that we will not arrest your father. We'll set him free. And we'll give you enough money to take yourself and your girl friend, who is even now waiting in the kitchen for the word from me to receive a bowl of gruel and mug of milk, to

33

take you and your lady friend away from this house this night, and set you on the road to Dublin, if that's where you want to go, or the road to Cork, where you'll be able to get a ticket to the New World. Well, Michael? What do you say?'

'An' if I don't? You'll never find them! I'll warn them!'

'If you don't, Michael, we'll arrest all the able-bodied men in the village anyway, *and* you, *and* your father. So, Michael, what's it to be? A meal for you and your girl now, a fistful of shillings and a promise of your father's immunity. Freedom, Michael, and a ride on Rosie's back till you reach the highway, or do I arrest the whole lot of you this very evening and send you and your girl away now with empty bellies? Your answer, Michael?'

Sir Jasper was gambling on Michael's hopeless position. There was no real threat of unlawful arrest for the villagers of Barra Bawn, but Michael did not know that. The Squire fully intended to catch the culprits, just as he determined to catch the fox on hunt day. No one was going to get the better of him, make a fool of him.

Sir Jasper smiled, and taking up the teapot he poured himself a cup. A tiny curl of steam rose from the delicate china. Michael watched fascinated as very slowly Sir Jasper added a lump of sugar. He then, with no haste, lifted the silver cover, took a fat crumpet from underneath and proceeded to smooth on two of the butter curls. At this precise moment he turned his head as he heard a groan from the chair on which his captive sat watching him.

'You answered?' he said, his voice politely inquiring.

'Yes,' Michael whispered.

'I beg your pardon? What did you say?'

'I said yes.' Michael choked on the words.

'Good. Very good. Now a piece of paper, Martin. You'll find one on the desk, there's a good fellow. The names, if you please.'

'I can't write.'

'That's perfectly all right, Martin will write down what you tell him and when you're finished you can make your mark. Then Martin will take you below for some food. What a sensible fellow you are to be sure.'

Michael looked up into the face of Martin Bell. He saw pity there mixed with contempt. He began, 'Rory Mulholland ...'

'Yes, a very sensible fellow!' Sir Jasper said and he sighed contentedly as he added some strawberry jam to the crumpet before he took a large, succulent bite.

Chapter

6

MICHAEL told Maureen all that had passed between him and Sir Jasper in the latter's well-appointed kitchen where Maureen sensibly and slowly ate her fill of gruel. Michael greedily chose to stuff himself with a mixture of bacon and eggs and kidney, only to vomit the whole mess up ten minutes later. Then Martin Bell gave Michael his fistful of shillings and told him to mount Rosie. With Maureen behind him and Martin accompanying them on Blue Boy they set out for the crossroads.

Michael never really knew why he chose Dublin as his destination. He had heard tales of the horrifying conditions that those people who had spent all they had to obtain a passage to the New World discovered when they embarked. Half the population was emigrating to escape the appalling deprivations in their own country, and Michael had heard of people packed in below decks in storage with hardly room to breathe, tiny food rations and minimal sanitary arrangements. Perhaps it was the thought of himself and Maureen crammed in a ship on the wild Atlantic, bound for the unknown, that made him choose Dublin instead of Cork. At all events, Rosie took him and Maureen as far as the main highway, where they dismounted. Then Martin Bell took Rosie's reins in his hands and, spurring Blue Boy, cantered away, leaving them alone at the crossroads to face the bleak road to Dublin and separation from all they had known and loved from the day they were born.

They were both full of shame at the manner of their leaving. They were aware of the horror of Michael's position as an informer, the very worst crime to commit in Ireland. He had betrayed his people in his extremity — for a handful of coins and a full belly.

36

Michael and Maureen were to look back on the days of peace and plenty before the barn dance until the looking back became too painful and the memories died and were buried.

Setting out on their journey they felt bewildered and yet hopeful, sad and elated alternately, and they were both fearful. If anyone pursued them from home, it would mean certain death. But who would? Who could? No one was well enough fed to follow; no one had the strength for pursuit.

Did they but know it they left behind them a nearly manless village.

Sir Jasper arrested the men named by Michael, and his father as well, and they were duly hanged. The women and children left had now no hope of survival. They died, slowly, painfully, helping each other as best they could. The living found it difficult to bury their dead decently — some of the corpses were tied up with straw. The Colleen Relief Committee devised a coffin with a slide bottom. The bottom was supported by hinges at one side and a hook-and-eye at the other. In these coffins the dead villagers were carried to the grave, or rather to a large pit which had been dug by Martin Bell and his two mates at a little distance from the road near Lewis's wood where once Michael and Maureen had stood, and there the body was discharged and the coffin returned with the pathetic little cortège, to be used by the next victim of the hunger.

The hanged men were thrown into a communal grave, and the sounds of the women wailing haunted the air for years to come. Mother Hegarty swore that a corpse rose from the grave one night and put the heart across her with fright an' she only foraging for bits and pieces to keep body and soul together, for God's sake. The corpse arose, she swore, and disappeared into Lewis's wood, and she could have taken an oath that it was Rory Mulholland himself and he runnin' like the clappers into the wood and away from this cursed place.

So Michael and Maureen slunk out of Barra Bawn near Skibbereen. They travelled the road to Dublin, and a tragic journey it turned out to be. Famine stalked the land. In the villages and towns through which they passed crowds of famished, tottering beings begged for food. Where employment was available most of the men were now far too weak to take the opportunity to earn the money and buy some food.

Cartfuls of people arrived daily at workhouses which could

not accommodate them, so full were they of dying and starving people. Sometimes they encountered groups of gaunt and ragged creatures that had once been men, angry and calling for 'bread or blood'. Their bodies could scarcely be said to be clothed and the light of madness in their eyes was replaced by despair when they realized they were far too weak to accomplish their threats.

Once they met a deranged woman wandering alone on the deserted road. She was young and seemed on the verge of collapse. Michael and Maureen tried to help her. They each took an arm and following her feeble gestures they guided her to a tiny cottage round the bend of a boreen off the road. They never forgot the sight that met their eyes. On one side of the miserable dwelling lay the bodies of two people, stiff and rigid in death, and on the other side lay a heap of dirty straw. The woman kept pointing to it in a distracted way and Michael, on pushing aside the straw, was horrified to see the mangled corpses of two grown boys, a large proportion of whose remains had been removed by rats, while the rest of their bodies had begun to fester into rottenness. The smell was appalling. Maureen gagged and had to go to the doorway of the hovel or she would have fainted from the stench.

'My family . . .' the woman cried hoarsely, shaking her head, half out of her mind and speaking with difficulty. 'Oh pity! Please!' She kept pointing to a knife on the table in the middle of the room.

'I have no strength! Please, mister, please mister.' Michael understood what she was begging for so piteously. He caught Maureen's eyes as she turned in the doorway. Maureen nodded imperceptibly and left the hovel. There was no sound as she waited patiently until Michael emerged, blinking in the cold sun as he wiped a few drops of blood from the knife. He would keep it, for it would be useful on their journey.

They never spoke of that incident again. There were a lot of things they never spoke of. As time passed, speech between them almost vanished. It was indeed a grim journey for, as they became more and more accustomed to the spectre of famine, fever began to rage through the land.

Another cottage they came to on their way appeared to be deserted, and as they crept in to take shelter for the night they discovered a pile of bodies in the corner. This was not unusual, and they had begun to settle themselves under the area of the roof that still afforded shelter when they heard a groan from the mass of dead humanity beside the wall. Maureen crawled over, and pushing aside the corpses of a woman and what had once been a man she discovered a little boy of about seven years. It was hard to tell his age, he was so emaciated; his bones stuck out and he kept up a low moaning. Maureen held him in her arms and shared their food with him. They called him Danny after the little mite they had left behind in a shallow grave in Barra Bawn.

They were very careful of their money. Maureen kept it tucked under her tattered skirt in a little pouch tied round her waist with string. They spent only enough to keep them going on their journey. They tended to avoid the towns and were slightly intimidated by crowds, nervous that someone would be looking for them. They felt constantly guilty and were happiest on the road, holding hands as they walked along, Michael carrying little Danny on his back. They had both lost their gaunt and starving look, and this in itself aroused the suspicion of their fellow countrymen, almost all of whom were dying of starvation or the fever. They became so used to passing funerals that the sight of the processions of skeletal figures carrying, with difficulty, the remains of some relative or friend ceased to register.

They wandered miles out of their way, crossing the bogs, the colour of burnt sienna in the twilight, smelling of heather, earth and bitter aloes. They passed whitewashed cottages like the homes they had left behind. They sheltered from the driving rain and the tempestuous winds under stone pile walls. They crossed the stony plateau of the Burren, alone in a landscape so ancient and strange to them that they were scared half to death and thought they had died and gone to hell; and Maureen's feet bled, but she didn't notice. Michael saw, and when they came to a waterfall spilling from a mountain pass, after they had slaked their thirst he bathed her poor feet tenderly and dried them with the moss.

They met a fiddler near that place who told them tales of the glory of Ireland, of the Island of Saints and Scholars; and through the night, passing the pot of pucheen around, to little Danny as well, he whispered to them of the legends of Cuchulainn and Queen Maeve, of Deirdre of the Sorrows, and Emer and Diramud and Grainne, and then of the march of the

English across the land and the slow decimation of the Irish heritage. They got drunk that night and pain, guilt and loneliness vanished. The dark clouds hung heavily but did not obscure the orange sun which lit the land in fire as it set. They laughed and talked meaningless drunken rubbish and were sick and vomited up the pucheen, and then drank some more and passed out on the cold, stony ground.

They bought their food in the smaller shops that they passed on the way. There was plenty to be had for those with money enough. Michael would hide what bread or cheese they felt they could afford under his now tattered shirt until they found a cottage where they could eat it undisturbed. The secrecy was not only engendered by their fear of being attacked and the food being stolen by people desperately hungry; it distressed Maureen not to share all she had with those in a worse state than she was, and this would be the worst kind of folly.

When they entered a shop it was quite usual for a row of nightmare faces to gaze at them through the window, women with little scarecrow children in their arms and eyes mutely pleading or dulled into despairing acceptance. Maureen found it hard to take the small allowance of food they had permitted themselves and watch as Michael hid it and brushed past the outstretched hands as they left the shop. But if they fed one, it would not be fair; and if they fed all, it would take all their money and they too would starve. It was, alas, the survival of the fittest and most ruthless. Maureen and Michael and little Danny gained strength although even they remained ever hungry. The shopkeepers were wary of peasants with money to spend on food, and they found the whole procedure of entering and buying an ordeal. Once when they stood at the counter of a little shop, they knew not where, a man came in and asked for money. The shopkeeper, a tidy, grim-faced woman who in the beginning had steeled herself against the harrowing sight of starving children, then slowly became used to them and finally accepted them as normal, was at first frozen in astonishment. To ask for food was usual; it was something she coped with every day, refusal becoming automatic, but to ask for money — she was nonplussed. When she vehemently refused, the man burst into tears and opening the tattered jacket he wore cast the naked dead body of a child on the counter.

'You bury him then, missus. I can't. I have no money to. For

God's sake, you bury him,' he cried and fled from the shop leaving Michael, Maureen and the shopkeeper staring aghast at each other, then at the little corpse on the counter.

'Take it away! Take it from here! I don't want it!' the woman screamed.

'Ah sure, what would we do with the poor wee mite?' Michael said, hastily snatching up the little parcel of food he had asked for. Taking advantage of the situation, he grabbed Maureen's hand, scooped little Danny up in his arms and left without paying for it. It took the woman some seconds before she realized what had happened and set up a hue and cry, but by then it was too late and Michael and Maureen were out of sight.

The trio criss-crossed Ireland, afraid to ask directions. They became quite indifferent to the horrors of the landscape they travelled through, to the scores of dead piled up in ditches, to the dogs who fed on them, to the queues waiting outside the graveyards, some carrying their corpses in baskets, some in bales of straw, some on old lids and ladders. They waited, those people, with the resignation of the hopeless, some dying beside the bodies of their loved ones as they waited, some losing heart and leaving their burdens for the beleaguered priest or clergyman to dispose of as he could. It was a nightmare they walked through, but all sense of shock was dulled by familiarity. Little Danny, though, not remembering any other life, was quietly happy to travel in the warm, loving company of the saviours he worshipped. They were careful, cautious, counting their money like misers under what meagre shelter they could find in the night. Sometimes they had to sleep in a ditch, but they kept away from fellow travellers who might be too curious about them and wonder at their apparent health, for typhus was now rampant in the land. They kept themselves to themselves and avoided the other groups they met who, similarly, were trying to escape the twin horrors of famine and fever, without realizing that there was no escape.

The situation was the responsibility of the British Government and when they finally took action it was too late and their action too inadequate to accommodate the extent of the problem. It was a piddle in the barrel, a drop in the ocean of suffering. Trevelyan said, 'If the Irish once find out there are any circumstances in which they can get free Government grants we

shall have a system of mendacity such as the world never knew.'
And again, 'There is much reason to believe that the object of
the Relief Act is greatly perverted and that it is frequently
applied solely as a means of adding to the comforts of the lower
classes.'

These 'lower classes' Trevelyan spoke of were at the time
described to him thus: 'Woe and want and misery are fearfully
depicted on the countenance of our people. Sorrow, suffering
and mute despair seem to have taken possession of their souls.
Their feelings are blunted, their ideas confused and their
energies paralyzed. Starvation has so completely prostrated
them that they have more the appearance of ghosts than human
beings.' But Trevelyan was unmoved by such terrible suffering.

The nearer they got to Dublin the more the world seemed to
Maureen and Michael like a manifestation of hell, one vast
death camp. There were dead bodies everywhere, by the sides of
the road, in the fields, in the tiny houses, anywhere, everywhere, people moaning — a great moaning throughout the
land, while down in Cork one day the fat Customs man
checked the export list of 147 bales of bacon, 120 casks and 135
barrels of pork, 5 casks of ham, 1,996 sacks and 950 barrels of
oats, 300 bags of flour, 300 head of cattle, 239 sheep, 9,398
firkins of butter and 542 boxes of eggs.

Chapter

7

MICHAEL had known sorrow, fear, hate, guilt but never despair until the day after he, Maureen and Danny arrived in Dublin. They had set the capital city as their target, the end of their troubles. Their fierce determination to reach it helped them survive on their journey. They never thought further than their arrival there, never envisaged what the future held in store for them. They reassured themselves that when they got there all their problems would cease and a fistful of money would start them on a new life.

The city frightened them. It was crowded and dirty, mean and malignant for two people who had been used only to the silence and peace and the green world of nature. People were streaming into the city, refugees who like Michael and Maureen sought Utopia in the capital, or at least a chance of work and an opportunity to earn their living. These streams of people were hard-eyed and tight-lipped, all human compassion wiped from their faces. They too had walked through wind and rain, sun and heat, past the death fires, past the corpse-ridden fields and on and on till they came to the city. They were the survivors, most of whom on their way had cheated and robbed, stolen from or killed their less hardy fellow countrymen in order to reach Dublin.

Michael and Maureen followed the stream of refugees that converged on a crowded station where people were sitting on the concrete floor wrapped in shawls. Some sat on packing cases that held their meagre belongings; some were wrapped in rugs stolen from the dead, or the living. Most of the people in the station seemed in the same state as Maureen and Michael, and this should have warned them to take extra precautions, to watch carefully this predatory mob of survivors, but they were physically exhausted, emotionally drained at the realization that this was just another beginning. They had walked, battled with the elements and the cruelty of a hostile world, and ended up here, waiting in this terminal, to go where? They knew no one; they had no contacts. Michael was very frightened when he realized the hopelessness of their situation. He couldn't think where to turn; he didn't know what work to seek, for his countryman's skills would be useless here. The station was a vast, echoing glass, wood and steel construction, for all the world like the inside of a giant whale, the like of which they had never laid eyes on before. Its sheer size terrified them. It was dreadfully overcrowded and they felt diminished as human beings as they huddled together on the cold concrete floor, and Maureen sobbed against Michael's shoulder while Danny stared with interest at the shifting scene around him. They had never heard him speak since the day Maureen had retrieved him from the pile of dead bodies and adopted him. He was docile and obedient, following them everywhere like a little puppy dog. But he never spoke.

That night Maureen, lying in Michael's arms, was seized with a trembling so bad it seemed as if her body would snap. Michael was alarmed and held her as close as he could while Danny found comfort by wrapping himself around Michael's back. There was a frightful din in the station, the noise of the occupants reverberating against the glass roof. The cacophony of sound in the giant rib cage of the terminal prevented Michael sleeping as through the long hours of the night he held Maureen's shivering body in his arms. By morning he was drenched in the sweat that had poured from her.

A woman, a new arrival, plump in comparison with most of the others, had been watching him for some time. She sat on a cardboard box, and two young wans stood one on each side of her. She had sympathetic black eyes, like little buttons, and black hair parted in the middle and drawn into a bun at the back. She looked neat and tidy and less frantic or hopeless than the others Michael could see.

'Ye must have travelled a long way — where de'ye come from?' she asked him.

'Barra Bawn, near Skibbereen,' Michael replied.

'And isn't that the South Pole, allana, or near as far as?' She looked at him with interest. 'Is yer wee wife sick?' she asked eventually. 'Poor soul. God, it's fearful times we live in.'

Michael nodded, raising himself on his elbow. Her two children stared at him and Danny's thin little face rose like a sickle moon over Michael's shoulder.

'Isn't it shockin' to see the sufferin'? Yer missus looks in extremes!'

And indeed Maureen did. Her face had become ashen and she was saturated in sweat. She was trembling and seemed in a kind of coma.

'De ye see that man over there?' The woman pointed to where, far across the crowded platform, a tall fellow with a goatee beard was bending over a sickly child in its mother's arms. 'Him's a class of doctor,' the woman said. 'You go over and ask him to look at the poor lass — mother o' God, she looks terrible.'

The woman crooned over Maureen, 'Hush, allana, hush there now. Buachaill, allana,' she said to one of the children, 'over there is the tub. Wet it, will ye.'

She gave him a piece of cloth and the little urchin ran over to the tub near the railway lines, dipped it in and wrung it out, and, as Michael and Danny stood awkwardly by, she pressed the damp linen against Maureen's face, crooning all the time. 'Acushla. There now. There.' She looked at Michael. 'Off ye go. Here, you, buachaill beag, stay with me while yer da gets the good man to have a look at yer ma.'

But Danny pulled away vehemently from the woman and, refusing to be cajoled, trotted after Michael as he obediently left Maureen to the tender ministrations of the plump woman and went to ask the bearded gentleman for help for his stricken love.

The man looked at Michael with eyes that held anger and pain. He looked at the tall, gaunt-eyed lad in front of him, tiredly shaking his head as Michael explained the symptoms.

'The shaking and the sweating, it's the fever, son. There's nothing I can do. I'm sorry. Still, I'll have a look. Where is she?'

As Michael turned around, his eyes seeking the little group he had left moments ago, he found to his horror that he could not see them. It took him seconds to realize that Maureen lay abandoned on the concrete ground and there was no sign at all of the woman and the two children. Moreover, Maureen was naked, her shawl and clothes gone, her frail body exposed to the eyes of the multitude, who, however, showed no interest at all in her pitiable state, this not being an uncommon sight in that vast place.

Michael let out a roar like a wounded animal, and taking off his jacket hurried over to her, Danny and the doctor following. He wrapped her as best he could in the tattered coat, realizing as he did so that the woman had relieved Maureen of all their money as well as stripping her naked and leaving her to die. The doctor shook his head and did not even reply to Michael's distracted queries. He was a good man, a man defeated by the enormity of his self-appointed task and the futility of it. Trying to stem, guide, offer advice to the tidal wave of refugees, helping to alleviate their sickness, was like trying to play King Canute to the ocean. All he could say, the only advice he could give, was, 'Go tomorrow to the quays. There's a boat coming in. There should be food on it, perhaps medicine. Go to the quays. Follow the mob. It's all I can advise. As for your wife, there is nothing I can do.'

Michael held Maureen all afternoon and through that night, unaware of the tears coursing down his cheeks, or of Danny's fearful whimpering. The night seemed endless and when dawn came Maureen was cold and lifeless in his arms. When Michael realized she was dead he threw back his head like a wolf and howled. Little Danny never forgot the noise — those wails tearing the atmosphere apart, raping the air with a terrible sound that caused even the others in the terminal to pause and turn for a moment from their own sufferings to look at the man yowling to the rafters like a dying beast. Over and over his cries rent the silence now blanketing the station as the people gazed at him for moments before they returned to their own concerns and his head drooped over the body of the woman who possessed his soul.

Chapter

8

LITTLE Danny didn't recollect much more of that night. Confusion clouded his memory. He did remember the kind man with the beard taking Maureen away from Michael, and he remembered being very cold and hungry, but he was used to that and he cuddled closer to Michael, drawing strength and heat from him, and in turn bringing his rescuer warmth in the closeness of his embrace.

When at last Michael rose from his crouching position on the ground, his movements were those of an old man, stiff and hesitant. Like an automaton, without premeditation and because there seemed nothing else to do, he followed the crowd of people emerging from the station and heading towards the quays, Danny trailing after him.

Sometimes the crowds arriving in Dublin remained in the station for days, stunned, confused and bewildered. Sometimes many of them made a daily journey from the station to the quays and back again, not knowing what else to do, or how to begin a new life in a strange place. The vast terminal and the promise of food at the quayside were the only two fixed points of reference in this limbo of fear and exhaustion.

When Michael and Danny arrived, the dock was crowded with people pressed together in the grey, misty day. A watery sun peered hazily through the drifting clouds, but the people below did not see it or feel the weather. They were beyond that. They stood there gaunt and immobile, with the exhaustion of death in their bodies. Hollow-cheeked, huge-eyed, sparse-haired, like living skeletons, they stood together not touching. No warmth emanated from the press of humanity; no expression changed the shadows of their eyes; no movement showed they lived and breathed. They stood gazing out at sea, all eyes focused on one spot — the ship. It lay motionless on the bay just outside the harbour, the masts tall and black against the grey sky, as still and as idle as the people on the quay. Danny never forgot the atmosphere of that hour as they waited. No feelings, not even hunger was there. The massed, expectant people gazed out at the food container, their salvation on the blurred foggy horizon, so near and yet so very far.

Then to their horror, although they stood expectantly still, the ship seemed to diminish. As they watched, it became gradually smaller and smaller and disappeared over the horizon wreathed in foggy mist. Still they stood, disbelieving the evidence of their own eyes, until a low muttering rippled through the crowd, a low rumble of anger that turned to anguish as the news spread like wildfire that the British Government had changed its mind and the boat was to return to England, its precious store of food borne away from their hunger.

The people now lost their aloofness and began to cling together, and as the crowd shifted Michael caught sight of the plump, black-haired woman from the day before. She stood at the edge of the congregation, unmistakable in her rotundity, and as the recognition dawned on Michael he let out a roar and charged towards her, Danny following close as a shadow. But she had seen him and vanished quickly round a corner just as a heavy arm was thrown across Michael's shoulders and a loud voice halted him as he stood trying to fathom where the woman had disappeared to.

'Michael me boy, sure aren't you a sight for sore eyes. God bless you, don't ye know me?'

Michael brought his eyes to rest on the large, friendly face in front of him, the face of a well-fed man, taller and broader than himself, a familiar face from what seemed to him the remote past.

'Dermot. Dermot Devlin. Dermot Devlin.'

Michael was nonplussed.

'Himself, me ould segotia, himself in person. Wasn't I sure to find you here? Aman't I the bright boyo an' no mistake.'

Pummelling Michael as if he were a bolster pillow, Dermot seemed genuinely pleased to see him and unaware of any ambiguity in their meeting. The relief of seeing a friendly face after such a long time caused Michael to forget the questions that stirred in his mind, and his arms went round the older man as his emotion overcame him and he burst into tears on Dermot's shoulder. Dermot led him away from the crowd on the quay and sat him on a bollard until Michael had sufficiently recovered his wits to wipe his face and turn his haunted eyes to the man he believed a traitor.

'But didn't you bloody split that me da was going to steal the sheep to Sir Jasper? Didn't you?'

'Ah, whist man. Didn't you too, as well as meself? An' sure what else could we have done? Wouldn't we be six feet under else? Ah sure isn't it all in the past an' over an' done with anyhow? Yerra for God's sake, now's not the time to be rakin' it all up. Will ye listen to me now? Wasn't I searchin' everywhere for ye? Didn't I guess ye'd end up here? They all do — from the length and breadth of sufferin' Ireland don't they all end up here or there in the railway? Aman't I clever with it? Tho' I nearly missed ye till I saw you chasin' Ma Kerrigan and her runnin' as if the devil himself was after her. Man, you've changed! An' where's Maureen? An' who is this little leprechaun?'

Michael drew a deep breath. His lips felt numb and stiff, and speech was difficult.

'Maureen's dead, Dermot. She died last night and this little fellow joined us on the road. I won't be parted from him. He's closer to me now than the son I lost.'

'Ah yes, I heard about that a cairde. Ah, God bless us, those were terrible times we passed through. But please God the worst is over for you. Sure there'll be plenty of time to talk over what's past. But haven't I got good news for you and a bed for yerself and the buachaill here to sleep in, and a great surprise for you that would cheer up a martyr an' him on the way to the stake! Haven't I got Siobain Mulholland here in Wicklow with me and isn't she dyin' to see you?'

Dermot had a horse and trap just a pace or two down the quay. He tucked Michael and Danny into the trap, and with a lot of clicking and a stream of chatter they set off at a steady pace through the crowded streets and out of the town to the south and Wicklow.

Michael heard that they were going to a family called Rennett, a very grand family who lived in the green hills of

Wicklow. Dermot had got himself a cushy job there as a butler, he said, and Siobain was working as a maid. They were looking for a handyman and general help around the grounds which were as wide as the whole of Donegal, according to Dermot. Siobain had worried constantly about Michael and Maureen, and had told the Rennetts she thought she knew just the person for the job and had sent Dermot hot-footing to Dublin every day for more than a week to find them, then every month.

'She never lost hope. Sure I thought it was a daft idea, and Lady Rennett began to think you'd never come. But Siobain said she knew, said some rubbish about it being in the cards. Did you ever? "Where would I find them in the crowds?" I said, an' Siobain, clever as a monkey, said, "Eejit of a man, look for where the crowds are arriving from the country. Won't you find them there if you find them at all, which I personally know you will." An' didn't I do just as she said ... an' lookit ye sittin' there large as life an' aman't I the clever boyo?' and he threw back his head and laughed. It was the first laugh Danny remembered hearing in his whole life and, though it frightened him at first, he knew he liked the sound of it; and, after a second peal, he felt safer than he had ever felt before. It was the last sound he and Michael heard before the jogging of the cart lulled them into a sound exhausted sleep.

Chapter

9

SLIEVELEA slept contentedly in her green surroundings, the house a beautiful grey stone that sometimes looked like pearl. It had a columned porch, a terrace that ran round the outside and French windows opening onto a gravelled walk. At one side of the house were the stables which housed the family's horses and at the other the rose garden which bloomed all year round, the seductive scent of the flowers wafting on the breezes around Slievelea. But when the wind blew, it was the salt-sea smell that drenched the air and sharpened the winds that roared through the chimneys. The lawns in front of the house rolled down to the sea on the right and led to the cove where the slate-grey waves crashed and sucked at sand and shingle. At the back of the house, the lawns led to the vegetable gardens, the herb garden and the bluebell wood which in spring and summer glowed sapphire like a reflection of the sky. Through the woods a little pathway under a canopy of leaves led to the lake, which shimmered violet blue like Miss Deirdre Rennett's eyes on a fair day, but turned grey and cold and mysterious when the weather was bad. A gravel drive curved gently from the portico to the iron-wrought gates, and snuggled beside them was the little gatehouse where Dermot Devlin brought Michael and Danny from Dublin in his cart.

The weary travellers were crawling with lice and the first thing Siobain did was to put them in tubs full of steaming hot water and lye and burn the tattered garments they had worn on their journey. Michael was very ill with the fever, and it was only thanks to Siobain's devotion and Lady Rennett's generosity that he made a complete recovery.

The Lady and the Lord of the house were kindness itself to Michael and Danny. Horrified at their appearance and the snatches of their history that Michael told them, or muttered about in his delirium, they did all in their power to aid his recovery and ensure his wellbeing. As though to try to make up to him for all the suffering he had endured, Lady Rennett sent down to the gatehouse, where he was lodged with Danny, calf's-foot jelly, home-made broths, fruit juice and jellies to nourish him back to health.

For Michael the comfort of the bed, its sweet-smelling sheets, the luxury of warm water and the taste of the food were bliss and, over and above all, he was aware of the radiant face of Siobain in the lamplight. From the first he confused her totally with Maureen and eventually in his mind the two merged completely to become one. The girl he had known as his cousin and part of his life, whom he had fallen in love with at the barn dance and whom he had travelled with, remained, he believed, alive and had come with him to Slievelea and grown well. The death in the station was erased from his mind. Siobain accepted her part and gracefully nodded or joined in recollections of the terrible years of the famine and the nightmare journey. In fact, sometimes she believed she *had* lived through it with him, so familiar did she quickly become with every detail of that journey.

While he was sick, Siobain sat with him of an evening, listening to his reminiscences both fevered and sane, holding his hand and gently bathing his fevered brow. She had had a qualm or two about Michael's culpability over the terrible fate of Barra Bawn, but thrust any such frightening thoughts away from her, resolutely burying them together with the memories of those awful days when people mad with hunger were driven to unspeakable deeds that could not stand the light of day. 'An' sure weren't they all marked for death anyway. The black shadow was on them wan way or another,' she told herself in mitigation, stilling her conscience. She did not have too much trouble on that score. Her feelings for Michael had always been the beginning and the end of her life, her reason for existence, the heartbeat of her universe. This darling man, lying so helpless before her, had come home to her, and whatever he had done to get there, be it, as she believed, the act of an animal caught in a trap, was fine with her.

52

Old George, the groom, a little wizened gnome of an English-
man who spoke with a strong Lancashire accent and treated
Michael with the same tenderness with which he treated his
foaling mare, spent the night's vigil with him until he recovered,
and during the day Michael was petted and cajoled into eating
and getting well by all the household, both owners and staff, in
Slievelea.

So Michael's strength returned. The light was rekindled in
his eyes and his beautiful body filled out and grew lusty once
again.

One evening he kept Siobain's hand imprisoned in his own
and drawing her towards him he softly touched his lips to hers.

'Thank you,' he said. 'I want to thank you.'

Her mouth and body had been hungry for him for a long time
and she avidly responded to his kiss. Her mouth opened and as
she darted her soft tongue into the warmth of his mouth, waves
of desire cascaded down his body. She could feel the urgency in
the valley between her legs, the tingle of her nipples hardening.
She opened her blouse and gave him the roseate tips of her
breasts to suck and bite, and as the fever of their bodies
mounted she slipped from her dirndl skirt and petticoat and slid
into the bed beside him. She felt his hard manhood immediately
and wanted it inside her at once. She guided him into her,
moving her body round and round on top of him as she gyrated
to the thunderous beating of her heart. His head was thrown
back in ecstasy and as the excitement in him grew with his
swelling body he threw her over on her back and mounted her,
riding her. 'Aha ... aha ... aha ...' he cried out as spasm after
spasm of erotic currents shot through him, 'Aha,' as the fluid
pumped from his body into hers, as every nerve end screamed
ecstasy, 'Aha ... aha ... Maureen, Maureen, Maureen, allana
... Aha ...'

And so they lay spent and damp and at peace; and Siobain
did not mind, for the girl whose name he had called out in his
coming was dead and gone and she was alive, gloriously alive,
and she had what she had wanted all her living life, with every
beat of her heart, and Mother Hegarty had been right all along.
Michael turned to her, gently holding her hips in his hands and
kissed her forehead. 'Sure I only started to thank you for bringing us here, me and Danny, and look how it turned out!'

'And wasn't it a grand way for it to turn out and no mistake?

Are you complaining, Michael allana?' she chaffed him between kisses, biting his lower lip and letting his hands travel from waist to buttocks so she could press up against him.

'No, sweet woman, never that. Sure wasn't it always a good thing between us? Remember the night of the ceilidh? Didn't your legs curl round me then as now? Didn't ye give me that much pleasure?'

'Sure well I remember my love, my big man,' she soothed him and ran her fingers lightly up from the thighs to the stomach till he felt himself grow again. This time he slid into her readiness warmly, sensuously; and, in the hot moistness, they moved languorously as golden feelings came alive in them, and slowly this time, like music swelling and growing till it reaches its crescendo, their lovemaking found newer, subtler depths of feeling and excitement, and drunk with sex and love he emptied his seed into her as tidal wave after tidal wave of passion poured through them and they came together and came again and shivered to a stop. So Conor was conceived.

'We'll marry, allana,' he said. 'I've waited so long.'

She nodded and they slept, and Old George, coming in upon them, saw them twined in each other's arms, faces rosy and beaded with moisture, her black hair tumbling over his shoulders; and he smiled and nodded and, leaving them, tiptoed away and never said a word about it to anyone, ever.

They married. Lord Rennett was pleased with Michael's work and Michael gave him unstinted value. He did much more than he was asked and he did it willingly. He never ceased to be grateful to the Rennetts, to Old George and Siobain, whom he loved with all his heart. On their wedding day, Lord Rennett said they could stay in the gatehouse and make it their home. Michael was now gatekeeper as well as assistant gamekeeper, helper for Old George in the stables, and doer of odd jobs about the place, helping the house staff on celebration days. He earned twenty shillings per week. In the fullness of time, Siobain was delivered of a baby boy whom they called Conor after the High King of Ireland; and they adored their son but were nevertheless firm with him. Danny stayed always with them. He, too, had substituted Siobain for Maureen and, though he never spoke, he seemed happy and learned to laugh and to play. Conor was, indeed, his king and Danny his king's slave. He did everything Conor told him to, trotting about after the little boy, obeying his every command. He adored Conor and the two boys had happy times fishing in the purple lakes and swimming in the icy streams, picking blackberries and catching rabbits and being Robin Hood in the copses. It was a magic life, where kindness and laughter flourished, love was constant and consideration of each other and their fellow humans made their world a warm and happy place to dwell.

Sometimes the 'little lady of the house', as Lord and Lady Rennett's daughter was called, came to join their games, which changed under her scrutiny and barrage of questions. They were quiet, soundless and peaceful together and she brought fuss, noise, giggles and other such female annoyances in her wake. Conor pretended to pay no attention to her; he let her chatter on, asking rhetorically, 'Why?' and was taciturn and shy before the autocratic little madam. He and Danny would continue what they were at: kicking the ball about, setting an animal trap, grooming the horses, sweeping the snow in winter and the leaves in autumn and making a great bonfire of them. She would tire of them and go back to the house, to her mother and Siobain. She took the indifference of the boys for granted. She thought it was their way. She did not realize how she bored them; she was too full of the importance of her existence in the world. She was born to possess all this and she was the first in the eyes of the occupants of Slievelea; Lord Rennett, Lady Rennett, her doting mamma and papa, and Siobain were her slaves.

Then Miss Deirdre went away. The boys neither knew where nor cared. They were indifferent to her presence or absence. The night before she left, Conor, coming back from Wicklow town and a great hurling match, found her wandering in the rose garden. He thought for a moment she was a ghost. Taking a short cut, he bumped into her, wraith-like in her nightgown, and he crossed himself, yelling, '*Dia is Mhuire agut!* What are ye doin' here? Oh, excuse me, miss.'

'Never mind, Conor. I'm restless, that's all. I'm going away tomorrow, did you know?'

Conor nodded. 'Yea. Me mam said. Said she'd miss you too, Miss Deirdre.'

'Oh, and I'll miss her, Conor, indeed I will. I don't want to go, really I don't.'

'Then why do you, miss?'

'Oh, I *have* to, Conor. It's a duty. I have to be educated.' She tilted her chin in the moonlight and stood on her tiptoes, stretching up as tall as she could. 'I have to see the world and broaden my mind, my father says.' She twirled around in the moonlight, the diaphanous material of her nightgown making her look more and more like a faerie child, he thought.

'I couldn't go, miss, no matter how much it was my duty.'

He sounded very sure, very firm. She was surprised; he wasn't usually so vehement.

'But if you *had* to, Conor. Like me. I *have* to.'

'I wouldn't go.'

'Suppose there was a war? Suppose you had to fight for your country all in a scarlet uniform? Suppose England was threatened by, by Mongolian hordes and suppose you had to fight for her?'

'England is not my country, miss. Ireland is.'

'Oh, stuff and nonsense, Conor. It's the same. They are the same and you know it.'

'No matter what, miss, I'd never leave Slievelea. I'd die away from her.'

'Will you miss me, Conor?' she asked a little wistfully.

He looked up, surprised.

'Em ... yes.'

'Will you be longing for me to return?'

'Em ... yes, miss.'

'Oh, it's so exciting, Conor. Don't you think so?'

'What miss?'

'Life!'

'I dunno about that. I know me mam will kill me if I'm not in soon.'

He ran down the drive, shaking his head over the incomprehensibility of women. He told Siobain of the conversation. She too was surprised at the vehemence of his determination never to leave Slievelea.

'I never thought about it before, Mam,' he said in the glowing amber light cast by the lamp that floodlit the little front room of the gatehouse. 'I feel a part of this land, this place; the woods, the fields, the mountains. Oh, Mam, even the big house itself. I can't explain.'

'I understand, Conor allana. All Irishmen and women love the land, and sure the bit you're on would be hard to beat.'

56

Siobain missed Miss Deirdre sorely when she was gone. She had been assigned to the only child of the Rennetts when Deirdre was born in the same year as Conor and she had been nurse and confidante to her enchanting little charge until Deirdre's departure for Europe.

It never crossed Conor's mind to question the devotion Miss Deirdre roused in his mother, but he sometimes wondered at his mother's worried preoccupation with Michael who, after all, was his father, a god, a king, a big strong one at that. What Conor did not realize was that Siobain's constant anxiety, the shadow on her mind, was the fear that Michael would have a shock some day that would send him over the edge, and she would lose her precious man. Mother Hegarty had not told her further than that she would get Michael, and Siobain, loving Michael as she did, was only too aware of the effect the horrors he had been through had had on him, and how precarious was the balance that kept his mind sound and still.

But apart from Siobain's secret fear only one shadow darkened the sky for them through the years, and just as quickly it vanished, leaving them puzzled as to whether it had ever really happened or not.

Michael and Siobain had not seen much of Dermot Devlin since their arrival in Slievelea. He was house staff and their paths seldom crossed. During Michael's recovery he sometimes popped down to the gatehouse dressed in butler's livery and had them all in fits of laughter until he left. Michael tried many times to talk to him about all that had happened in Barra Bawn, but Dermot slithered out of it with a joke and couldn't or wouldn't be pinned down. When he was getting married, Michael asked Dermot to be his best man and he had been the life and soul of the wedding party, getting a little too drunk for Siobain's taste and eventually passing out. Rumours filtered through Old George that the Rennetts found him far from satisfactory; and there seemed, according to Siobain, always to be trouble with the young tweeny and parlour maids.

Then one day Michael was called in to the library to see Lord Rennett. It was a beautiful room covered from floor to ceiling in books, with ormolu lamps, a Japanese screen and big leather chairs. A log fire was blazing in the hearth. Lord Rennett was gentle with Michael. He was a shrewd man and a good judge of character and he was pretty sure that this was not the guilty man. Michael's wide blue eyes gazed unperturbed and serene into his own. He looked at the young man, noting the sweet good nature on the handsome face and the twin wings of premature white on the sides of his head, a certificate of his suffering.

'Now, Michael, I'm asking you because I've got to ask everyone. Lady Rennett is missing some silver and we are trying to find it. If you know aught of it please tell me now and we will not say another word on the subject.' Michael blushed a deep red; another man might have deemed him very guilty indeed.

'Oh sir, I hope ye don't think that I ... well, sir, I have no need of money. Sure ye give me plenty as it is. That is, Mrs Casey and meself have all that we need, sir, and more.'

'No, you mistake me, Michael. I mean pieces of silver — knives and forks and cruets.'

Michael's face looked blank and Lord Rennett realized the young man did not know what he meant and was genuinely confused. He was pretty certain the culprit was the butler Devlin. Lord Rennett did not like Devlin. Oh, the man had a glib charm on first encounter, but he was an accomplished liar and had such a gift of the gab that it was impossible to pin him down. He had thought that, as Dermot had been instrumental in Michael being in Slievelea, the two were probably friends and Michael's honesty might not be able to conceal a thief if approached fairly. It was obvious, however, that Michael was completely ignorant of the situation and could be no help to him.

A few days later Michael was passing the kitchen window on his way from the woods and, looking in to see if, perhaps, Siobain had a moment's break in her duties and hoping they could wet a pot of tay and have a gossip, he was shaken out of his usual calm by the unbelievable sight of the plump, black-haired woman from the station in Dublin sitting at the table drinking tea and chatting animatedly with Dermot Devlin. Images flew through his head; the vast, echoing station, someone, a woman, lying on the ground dead, naked; a money belt gone; himself howling and howling like a wolf; and he quickly rounded the corner of the house, out of breath and shaking, bumping into Lord Rennett as he did so.

'What on earth's the matter, Michael Casey? You look as if you've seen a ghost.'

'Oh God, sir, I have, sir. It's the woman in the kitchen with Dermot. She's bad, sir, bad. She's wicked, she's a thief.'

As he spoke Michael was pulling at his hair in a demented way quite foreign to him. Lord Rennett, used to the calm slow ways of his servant, was surprised into attention and pricked up his ears at the word 'thief'.

'Oh, sir, she's an evil wan. Evil, I tell you. Don't ask me how I know. I just do!' and Michael turned and ran down to his cottage as if chased by the hounds of hell.

The rest he heard later. Apparently Lord Rennett and Old George had gone into the kitchen; and so unexpected was a visit from the master of the house that Dermot lost all his self-possession and ran out of the door, through the stables, into the woods and eventually vanished into the backstreets of Dublin.

The master, restraining the woman, Ma Kerrigan, found on her person and in her voluminous pockets one silver salver, six knives and forks, a milk jug and sugar bowl set, and quite a dozen spoons, all of the most exquisite Georgian design.

Ma Kerrigan had taken the master by surprise — and surprised he was already by the extent and quality of their haul — and had suddenly belted him one round the ears. Not having received such a blow in his life, especially from a woman, Lord Rennett staggered back, more astonished than hurt, while the large woman bounced Old George against the kitchen table with her hip and, suddenly galvanized, fled the place with amazing speed for her size, leaving the two men gawking where they stood.

Michael had had a fever for a few days after the incident, reliving some of the memories he had buried, but with Siobain's tender care he soon recovered. Their peaceful existence continued as if there had been no interruption in the tranquil harmony of their lives.

Chapter

10

IT was winter and the snow lay thick on the ground; the trees swayed gently in the cold breeze, occasionally dropping their burden of snow with a soft plop. Great fluffy white feathers fell steadily from the blanched sky, cocooning the world in cotton wool. On either side of the drive a hard white crust was banked where Michael had cleared the way for the carriages arriving for the party at Slievelea. All the lights of the house shone a twinkling welcome out over the snow-blanketed lawns. The sounds of the orchestra tuning up wafted into the little cottage where Siobain sat, plump and sleek in the lamplight, sewing a button on Danny's shirt. The turf fire burned brightly in the small, cosy room, casting dancing shadows on the intent faces of Conor and Danny as they sat patiently waiting to receive their shirts.

A peaceful calm lay in the little room, and Siobain's face and sturdy peasant body radiated the contented air of the fulfilled woman. She smelled mildly of baking and soda bread, of the heather-honey of the Wicklow mountains, and the harsher smell of the carbolic soap she used liberally on her menfolk to keep them clean; she had been overzealous about this since Michael and Danny's arrival in Slievelea all those years ago.

As Siobain sewed the shirts that her men would wear that night, memories of the years since she had found Michael again passed through her mind. She looked at the men fondly. Danny would never quite lose the fearful, anxious look he had worn since the day Maureen had found him. He gazed now through the little window at the gentle snowdrifts with a far-away look in his eyes. Siobain never knew what he was thinking or what went on behind those wide, grey eyes. He had a gentle face and an awkward body, his feet and hands disproportionately large for his short frame. Opposite him Conor sat looking into the flickering fire, watching the turf sods drop in a flurry of ash, reading stories in the glowing caverns and gold-red mirages created by the voracious greed of the flames. She could read every expression that flitted across his mobile face, so like Michael's that they seemed two sides of the same person; the same face, in youth and middle age. The boy was tall and lean-limbed with the beautiful body and the slow animal grace of his father. The dark hair grew close on his head in the soft curls she loved so much to caress, and they had exactly the same eyes, startling, cornflower blue fringed by thick, inch-long lashes, eyes put in with sooty fingers, Old George said. The only difference was the expression deep in the depths, the father's tranquil and sometimes puzzled as if he had lost or forgotten something, the son's eager and trustful — a trust his mother hoped would never be betrayed.

As Siobain put the last stitches in the boy's shirts she exhorted them to hurry. With Michael, they were to open the carriage doors as the guests arrived at the portico and give an arm to the ladies to help them over the ice in case they slipped, and to hold umbrellas over their heads to shield them from the powdery snow which might disturb their coiffure.

Later they were to help Malcolm, the English butler, to serve the guests refreshments when the banquet was over and the dancing began. They would not be allowed into the dining room as they were not *au fait* with the mysteries of the art of serving, the intricacies of which, Malcolm assured them, were quite beyond two such clumsy peasant lads. It required finesse, Malcolm solemnly informed them, to transfer slices of roast lamb or duck, beef or capon from salver to plate without slurping juice on the ladies' pastel dresses.

In the meantime, Siobain must hurry up to the house to help her young mistress into her finery for her first official dance. The Christmas party was a coming-out ball for the beautiful daughter of the house, and Siobain smiled to herself when she thought of Miss Deirdre. She had been with her mistress every day of the young lady's life except for the two years when Miss Deirdre had completed her education by spending time in Italy, France, Germany and Austria, and all the interesting and educational places recommended for the finishing and polishing of

61

young ladies to prepare them for society. Siobain loved and cared for her almost as much as her own family.

Admonishing the boys and her Michael to hurry, she wrapped her shawl over her head and around her shoulders, pulled on her boots and set out into the swirling, snow-filled world. The soft flakes flurried around her, stinging her parted lips as she made her way up the drive. She could hear the musicians practising the waltzes they would play, and remembered the different sound of the bones on the burran and the scraping fiddles of that barn dance so long ago, when Michael seemed certain sure someone else's; and she hugged her shawl closer round her and gave a little squirm of joy at the thought of how things had turned out.

The myriad flickering candles sent a glow through each window that turned the snow to gold and sent welcoming messages to the travellers who would soon be arriving from all points of the compass. When she arrived, her cheeks were red from the icy winds. Shaking off the clinging white flakes, she ran up the back stairs to her young mistress's room.

Deirdre's bedroom was a scene of total femininity. Multi-coloured ribbons and bibbons, laces and knick-knacks, silk posies and swan's-down puffs, gewgaws and beads and strands of seed pearls, lockets of gold and silver-backed brushes, crystal phials of perfume and rabbit's-foot applicators, dusting powder, frills and flounces, petticoats and corsets were littered everywhere, and in the middle, in her stays and pantalets, the gorgeous, adored and adorable, Miss Deirdre Rennett.

Masses of white-gold curls tumbled everywhere. Siobain was to coax them into a pile on her head, strategically arranging a stray frond on her forehead and a strand of gold on each side of the little heart-shaped face, studding the rest with flowers. The soft coral cheeks needed no pinching, no rabbit's-foot help; the ruby lips, dented in the middle of the full lower one, needed no biting to keep their colour; and the twin sapphires that were her eyes sparkled with such life and gaiety and excitement that Siobain remonstrated, 'Remember, miss, you are a young lady. It's not seemly to be so up in the air. Sure you'll take off and fly out the window if you don't calm down.'

'Oh, Siobain, I'm so excited I can't bear it. I think I'm going to burst. I feel as if my heart,' she pressed two little pink hands over her bosom, 'as if my heart is going to fly away. Oh, you're

62

right, Siobain, you're right. I will sail out through the window up into the silver snow and off to the Snow Queen's palace in the sky if I'm not careful. Oh! See! You can see my heart bumping through my skin! Look!'

She pointed to her chest just above the mother-of-pearl curves of her breasts.

'Now, Miss Deirdre, sit down at once or I shall be so cross with you. Calm down, pull yourself together and behave. You are eighteen, not eight.'

'Oh, Siobain, I know, I know. I'm sorry. Dear, darling Siobain, don't be cross with me, there's a dear. I'm just so excited. And so would you be if this was your first really, truly, grown-up party.' She threw her arms around Siobain as her mother's voice floated down the corridor.

'Deirdre, Deirdre, my love, are you nearly ready?'

Opening the door, her mother stopped and, quickly putting her gloved hands to her mouth, said in a semi-severe way, 'Darling! What's this I see? In your underwear? Oh, I shall have to put you to bed early like a naughty child and forbid you to come downstairs at all tonight.'

'Oh no, Mamma, no,' Deirdre pleaded, raising her hands and arms over her head while Siobain slipped first her petticoats, then her dress of pure Brussel's lace over her head. The lace was thick and a magnolia white with tiny silver threads through it, almost invisible but catching the candleglow when she turned, as she did while Siobain fluffed out the frill around her pale shoulders.

'The pearls, Siobain, the pearls. Keep quite still, Deirdre my love. Oh don't jig about so!' Her mother fastened the clasp of the necklace.

'Mamma, Mamma, I can't help it at all. Weren't you excited too — your first ball? Oh see how pretty I look, Mamma.'

Her mother chuckled softly, proud of her daughter's beauty, but clucking at the suggestion of vanity.

'My darling, of course I was; but how many times have I told you to keep your feelings under control? A lady never shows how she really feels but ...'

Deirdre's voice joined her mother's and they finished together, '... always looks calm and serene.'

'Oh Mamma, how can I when the world is fairyland and I am a princess?'

Lady Rennett laughed, joining in her daughter's joy. She was a tall, graceful, disciplined woman, immaculately groomed, twenty-five years happily married to her loving and kindly blond giant of a husband, a man who had the appearance of a big bear and the disposition of a gentle and contented man. It had been an arranged marriage that had worked extremely well. It had helped that they were both very attractive people, kindly, with a sense of humour; and they had made up their minds to make a go of a marriage they were stuck with willy-nilly. They had surprised everyone by falling in love with each other and no one had been more amazed than they themselves. Now Lady Rennett stood in her green velvet gown, her emerald necklace glittering on her white skin, as cool and lovely as an orchid, smiling at the beautiful, vivid face before her.

'Come on, my pretty one,' she said, 'your fan,' slipping a little fan made of lace and seed pearls with ivory bones over her daughter's wrist, 'and handkerchief,' as she tucked the fine cambric bordered with gossamer lace into the gentle crevice in the low bosom of the gown. She smiled into her daughter's eyes, her glance full of love and encouragement. 'Now we will go down. Head up, shoulders back, slowly, remember, slowly.'

Deirdre took a deep breath, trying to subdue the excitement that lit up her eyes like stars and heightened the colour of her cheeks to deep rose. She nodded, and her mother's sweet smile reassured her, told her that she was lovely.

Lady Rennett took her daughter by the hand and led her from her room down the gallery to the top of the curving staircase that sloped to the wide and welcoming hall which was filled with guests. Boys and girls and their parents from as far north as Dublin and as far south as Wexford had come to celebrate Christmas and Deirdre Rennett's coming-out ball. All the County, of course, were there. They were mostly Anglo-Irish landowners whose sons were suitable riding and dancing partners for the beautiful daughter of the house. They stood about now in little groups in the great hall at the bottom of the stairway, tall handsome youths and posies of giggling girls in their sugar-almond dresses. Deirdre's mother held her hand and they stood a moment at the top of the curving stairs. Then she gently detached her daughter's fingers from her own, and Deirdre turned her face to the crowd below. She saw her dear papa, who stood smiling and dignified at the bottom, and heard the soft sigh of admiration ripple through the guests. She placed her fingers gracefully on the banister, narrow wrist raised, fingertips barely touching the cool marble, and made her slow descent — a hesitant vision in silvery white leaning imperceptibly forward as if reaching out eagerly towards life and the music and the colours and the gaiety below her. Her mother watched the straight, youthful back moving away from her, pride and love filling her heart, and as Deirdre reached the bottom stair she saw the little hand, so recently clasped in hers, grasped firmly by young Anthony Tandy-Cullaine, the very person Lady Rennett hoped with all her heart would one day claim Deirdre for his bride. Then her father took her hand gently from Anthony and, placing it on his arm, nodded to Conor and Danny who in their footmen's livery flanked the dining room doors. At his signal the would-be flunkies, awkward in their unaccustomed tight clothes, opened the doors, and the guests, the ladies with palms lightly on the men's sleeves, walked two-by-two into dinner.

As Deirdre went through the doorway, leaning on her father's arm and followed closely by Anthony Tandy-Cullaine with her mother, she twisted her ankle a little in her tiny, satin, high-heeled shoes. With a slight skid she regained her balance and her remarkable dignity, but not before she had driven the little heel hard into Conor's foot. He let out a high snort of pain, a kind of whistle through his nose, trying very hard to control an almost ungovernable urge to yell aloud at the wave of agony that shot up his leg. Deirdre blushed, grimacing for him, as she realized how awfully the jab she had inflicted must hurt; and, looking up at him, she was stunned by the beauty of his eyes, wide now and full of tears of pain. Her heart stopped for a split second. Then she tossed her curls and looked beneath her lashes at Anthony behind her. He leaned towards her as they entered the dining room, much to Lady Rennett's amusement, and said, 'My, you look lovely, Dee.'

Deirdre frowned at the 'Dee'. She hated being called that. She never felt at all like a Dee but very like a Deirdre.

For Lord and Lady Rennett the evening was a triumph. The soups were excellent; the salmon from their own streams a delicious success; the duckling succulent; the sauces piquant; the lamb pink and perfectly cooked. The French champagne, Château Mouton Rothschild, was superb. When the *vacherin* and *bavarois*, then the fruit and cheeses, had all disappeared and the ladies had retired to the blue salon upstairs, the men went to the library, where Conor and Danny had been instructed to help Malcolm distribute cigars and fill the gentlemen's glasses with fine French brandy. Conor was very successful in his role as footman and won approving looks from Malcolm. Danny, however, was permitted only to stand at the door and open and close it as the men went to relieve themselves. His clumsiness hampered him and the more Malcolm noticed it the worse he became.

Conor, working deftly, caught the drift of the conversation, the first such dialogue he had been privy to in his life. He was aghast and amazed at the totally different viewpoint cast on events he had heard of many times at his mother's knee. Conor had been brought up speaking Gaelic. The history of his country had been ingrained in him, especially the events of 1845 to 1847 and, most particularly, the story of his father's suffering; and now, in this quiet, masculine room, as the scented smoke from the cigars hung in grey clouds at the edge of the ceiling and the fiery brandy heightened the colour of the men's faces, scraps of the conversation brought a flush to his own cheeks.

'... bring back all that Famine unpleasantness. No. We can't have it,' a portly squire with a bulldog face glowing redly in the lamplight said. 'These people will have to be kept in control. The peasants here are a lot of lazy good-for-nothings who would sit on their arses all day and do sweet damn all if you don't show them firmly who is boss.'

'Yes, Rowley ... quite agree. Let them see who holds the whip hand,' a giant, bucolic, red-haired man called Vestry said.

'Oh, gentlemen, be reasonable!' Lord Rennett's voice was placatory. 'The famine was hardly the fault of the peasants. More like God's mistake, I should have said.'

As a ripple of laughter spread through the room Malcolm wordlessly handed Conor an empty crystal decanter, and Conor knew he had to leave and have it refilled in the kitchen where the brandy had been brought up from the wine cellar to warm before serving. He was glad to have an opportunity to still the turmoil in his breast. He felt a sickening anger churning inside him, the violence of which frightened him.

In the hall as he passed through he saw that the younger people had started to dance. The musicians sitting in the gallery above were playing a Viennese waltz and, as he skirted the hall to reach the door to the kitchens and the servants' quarters, he glanced idly at the swirling throng of bright laughing youths his own age, a careless, moneyed, pampered lot — and an un-accustomed resentment added poison to his rage. As his curious gaze travelled around the dancers it was caught by the violet-blue eyes of the young lady of the house, who held his look with her own, refusing to relinquish his gaze as she gracefully waltzed in the arms of Anthony Tandy-Cullaine. Her eyes sent a message he did not understand and he pulled his gaze away and went on his errand.

Moments later, back in the library, his anger was rekindled. The conversation had continued and Darcy Blackwater was say-ing, 'The Irish are a lovely people but quite incapable of carry-ing anything off. Governing themselves? Why, it's madness! Like allowing the children in the nursery to run the house.'

'The Fenians proved it, Goddamn it, last year. Look at that débâcle!'

A murmur of assent rippled through the now smoke-filled room.

'That fellow Stephens. Wretched fellow, hid out right beside Usher Castle — my home!' a gentleman, who had been appar-ently comatose except for holding out his glass for refilling, now roused himself sufficiently to say. 'My house, Goddamn it. Zounds in hell. Fellow's a traitor. Hang 'em, I say!'

A tall jovial man standing beside Lord Rennett at the fire-place snorted, 'Oh Jeffries, old fellow, stop being so personal. The whole thing is nothing but a storm in a teacup. They haven't got the talent for intrigue, poor bastards, and there's always a Judas in their midst.'

'It's the bloody Americans. Those fellows over there are uncivilized devils and they're joining up with the Irish and teaching them all sorts of treason and sedition.'

'The Americans *are* all bloody Irish.'

'They don't know what they're talking about. They're like children. My doctor told me their brains are different, Irish are smaller, and the fellow's half-Irish himself! Father married the cook or some such, poor devil.'

'Quite so!'

'Full of sentimental nonsense about the "Faith of our Fathers" and "Kathleen Mavoorneen" and the "Bold Fenian Men". It's a treasonous dream.'

'And the men who carry on such talk and behave so treacherously to Queen and country should be executed, like Larkin, Allen and O'Brien.'

The library door had opened and one of Deirdre's young friends stood there listening. He was a stocky youngster with abundant reddish hair and fiery eyes, which now glittered dangerously in the lamp's glow. Conor, his head lowered as he poured brandy into a glass, looked up as the young man spoke.

'Traitors to whom? To whom may I ask? What Queen? Whose country do we talk about? I'm sorry, sir,' he said to Lord Rennett, 'I opened this door by mistake. It's rude, I know, to interrupt your conversation, but really, gentlemen, we should try to remember we are guests in this land and these men are the rightful tenants of this island.'

Lord Jeffries interrupted this flow. 'Enough, sir! You young whelp! How dare you speak to your elders in such a way! What is your name, sir? I will inform your parents of your behaviour.'

'Now, now Jeffries, calm down, the boy is a little overexcited and perhaps has had a mite too much champagne.' Lord Rennett tried to smooth the matter over.

But the young man was not one whit put out and answered angrily, 'Charles Parnell, sir, is my name, and it's of no consequence if you tell my father or my mother, for they are both of the same mind as I. Your servant, sir,' and with a bow the young man left the room.

'Young whelp, Goddamn. The manners of the young today ... scandalous,' Jeffries spluttered, purple with rage, while Lord Rennett tried to calm him.

The man called Rowley spoke. 'The Irish insurgents will have to be stopped. It's imperative that we put an end to all such treasonable speech and nonsensical ideology.'

'Quite so, quite so,' Vestry interpolated. 'Must be put an end to. Bad for the locals, bad for the natives. Puts ideas into their heads.'

Jeffries said, 'There has, I believe, though I find it hard to credit, there has been drilling, with guns, would you believe, in the mountains here.'

Lord Rennett smiled. 'Silly boys with fever in their heads.'

Conor suddenly became aware that Lord Rennett was looking at him, and he bent again solicitously to refill Vestry's glass. That gentleman was muttering, 'Some of our own servants —

thank you, me boy — some of our servants found creeping out at night . . .'

Lord Rennett interrupted. 'That will be all, Conor, Danny, you may go. Please remain, Malcolm.'

Conor and Danny left the room and took up their duties in the main hall. The girls and boys were now seated round the sides near the long windows that were framed in snow on the outside. They overflowed into the dining room, which had been cleared, and Conor and Danny helped to push the piano from the music room, which was too small to hold the crowd, to the hall so that it was clearly visible to everyone. There was a rustle of fans, murmured whispering and a flurry of noise as the men emerged from the smoke of the library, and frills and flounces were smoothed as they took their places beside their wives and daughters. Smiles were exchanged, hands touched hands and cheeks were patted, and Lady Rennett sat gracefully at the piano to play and accompany Deirdre. She sang the songs sweetly to her father, whose kind eyes reassured her of his love, to her mother, whose gaze was on the notes she played, and to the assembled company of her girl friends, admiring young men, gently nodding papas, slightly dozing after the brandy, and sentimentally tearful mammas.

Oh sweet vale of Avoca how calm could I rest,
In thy bosom of love with the friends I love best . . .

And she sang, involuntarily, to Conor, without even realizing fully that she was, just looking towards him as he stood stiffly at the foot of the stairs, her eyes diamond bright.

If I were a blackbird I'd whistle and sing,
And I'd follow the ship that my true love sails in,
And there in the rigging I'd build me my nest,
And I'd pillow my head on his lily-white breast.

At the last sweet note, she dropped her eyes and shyly accepted the enthusiastic applause. Deirdre's mamma sighed, remembering the romantic days of youth, and looked towards her husband, who in her eyes was still the dashing young blade she had married.

Anthony Tandy-Cullaine had put a peremptory hand on

Deirdre's arm, for the two-handed reel was about to commence. Soon whoops and cries reverberated through the hall as dance followed dance. The girls became sensuously relaxed in the arms of their swains as the waltz set their bodies swaying. Gentlemen sipped champagne, and ladies fluttered their fans to cool their hot cheeks until the last voluptuous slow waltz when Anthony Tandy-Cullaine heard himself propose as the violins sobbed and the lights were being put out one by one. Deirdre felt unaccountably angry and tapped him quite cruelly on his cheek with her fan, saying, 'No, of course I won't marry you, Anthony. I don't want to marry *anyone* yet. And don't call me Dee.'

Conor yawned surreptitiously at the door and thanked God Miss Deirdre's coming-out party was at last over. The ladies were wrapped in their fur cloaks, the carriages brought to the door. The horses trotted carefully through the snow; the last candle was snuffed; the last lamp was extinguished; and Conor and Danny trudged down the drive, snow falling in soft flakes on their shoulders and eyelashes. The windows of the gatehouse shone a golden welcome, and the tired young men, hastening their walk, broke into a run and at last reached their home.

Chapter

11

WHEN Deirdre opened her windows on the snow-white world next morning the air was clear and the snow had a dusting of silver crystals that sparkled in the bright sun. She hugged herself, drinking in the pure fresh air, and giggled and twirled as if to invisible music. When Siobain knocked at her door and entered carrying a silver tray with a cup of steaming chocolate on it, Deirdre gave a little hoot of joy and called to her maid to bring her riding habit.

'But Miss Deirdre, you can't ride out today,' Siobain started to remonstrate, but her young mistress stamped her foot impatiently and interrupted.

'Siobain, I want my riding habit. That's an order!' Then, relenting, she coaxed her maid. 'Ah, Siobain, don't ask me. No, no, you can't guess. I'm sorry. I didn't mean to be rude. Please, it's a secret. My riding habit, quick, quick, quick!'

She gulped down the steaming drink as she was dressed and as soon as she was ready she fled, fleet of foot, from her room along the gallery and down the staircase to where she had stood the previous night gazing at Conor while the music played. She opened the front door to hurry towards the stables, barely noticing that Michael, Conor and Danny had cleared most of the snow from the driveway and from the circular gravel patch that led to the stables around the side of the house.

When Old George saw her he cried, 'Oh no, miss, ye can't ride today. 'Tain't suitable, miss, at all. The weather ...' and Deirdre paid him no heed for she had caught sight of Conor, her main reason for dressing and coming down.

Conor was in the square in front of the horse boxes clearing

71

the snow there. On seeing him she faltered, uncertain moment-arily as to what to do next. She called him but he paid no heed, so she called him again. Again there was no reply, for Conor could not hear her over the scraping of his shovel. Running over to him, cheeks aflame, she deliberately pushed him into the five-foot pile of snow. She didn't know what made her do it. She was only aware of an irresistible urge to provoke him. As he fell, she threw back her golden head and laughed while Conor struggled to rise. Then her little teeth snapped together and she held out her gloved hand to help him up.

'Why were you so angry last night?' she asked him.

'Beg pardon, miss, angry? Me? I don't understand.'

'Oh yes you do, Conor Casey. Don't you dare lie to me. Why, you were angry enough, I declare, to do murder!'

'I promise you, miss, I dunno what yer talkin' about, truly I don't!'

'Liar, liar, liar!' and Deirdre laughed and pushed him once more into the deep drift.

'For God's sake, Miss Deirdre, will ye stop now or I'll be drowned in it,' he spluttered. As he rose from the powdery cavity she tried to brush away the snow with her little gloved hands, but he pulled off his coat and shook it, paying her no heed, and got on with his work, calling over his shoulder, 'Off with you now, miss, and leave me be.'

Deirdre gave a shout of rage and putting out her foot tripped him up, and this time he fell on his face. He did not struggle to get up. The shock of cold on his face had winded him and he had cut his forehead on a stone. The sudden jar of pain in his temple stunned him momentarily.

'Oh Conor, Conor, I'm sorry. Oh, I am a beast, please forgive me.'

She pulled him up and, as he rose unsteadily, she saw the scarlet blood on the snow.

'Oh my God, Conor, what have I done? Oh please be all right! Say you're all right.'

'I'm all right, Miss Deirdre, truly I am. I'll go down to me mam. She'll fix it.'

She put her hands up to his face, trying to see the extent of the damage she had inflicted, tenderly touching his forehead, pushing the soft, snow-covered hair back from the cut.

'Please let me help you. After all, it was my fault.' She was nearly in tears.

72

'No, miss, thank you. I'll go to me mam. She'll do it,' he said very firmly. Removing her hands, he left her standing in the stable yard, frustrated and angry, tears of disappointment in her eyes.

Siobain was surprised to see her son home at this time of the day. After she had dressed Deirdre that morning she had hurried to the gatehouse for a cup of tea and a quick rest before she commenced her other duties. It was a custom she really enjoyed, the rest of the family being out at work by then. It was also the only time she was alone. She usually spent her free moments in solitude, contentedly thinking of her beloved menfolk and her happiness in this place, so at the sound of Conor's voice a frown of irritation crossed her brow.

It quickly changed when she saw the blood on his forehead, and she crossed herself in fear, her heart beating hard within her, until the fact that her son was walking and obviously in an unaccustomed rage reassured her that he was not, as she feared, on his last legs.

'*Conus ta tú, allana?*' she asked her son, slipping into Gaelic as she invariably did when she was frightened. 'How are ye, darlin'? What happened?'

'Miss Deirdre kept pushin' me in the snow, Mam, an' I hit my head on a stone. Sure it's nothin', nothin' at all. But maybe you could stop the flow.'

'Sure, Conor, surely.' Siobain's face was full of motherly sympathy, but underneath she was in turmoil and an icy hand gripped her heart. Miss Deirdre she knew inside out and she knew her little mistress's passionate, ardent temperament; she also knew her son was blessed with much more than his fair share of good looks and for a moment an awful possibility crossed her mind, but she quickly brushed the shocking thought away.

'What nonsense to think such a thing,' she muttered to herself. Then she caught the drift of what her son was saying and a new and equally serious anxiety took hold, '. . . asked me why I was in such a state, a rage she called it. An' I don't know, Mam, but she was right. I was in a rage, an awful rage at those old fools talkin' about us as if we were scum or something. I never thought about it before, Mam, but when that young fellow said that they were *guests* in our country, sure . . .'

'Son, son, that's dangerous talk. Very dangerous. Listen to

73

me. Don't go gettin' ideas in your head that will lead you astray and maybe destroy you entirely. Tonight when you come in you must have a chat with your da. It's about time that you did, an' he'll put you straight, that's for sure.'

She realized as she spoke that her words were as much to reassure herself as her son.

'There now, the witch hazel has done its work. Off you go, Conor, allana. Don't dwell on those thoughts. They have poison in them and many a good man's been destroyed by such ideas. Now off you go, a buachaill, and peace be in your day.'

As Conor left the gatehouse, he heard Old George calling him, 'Art all right, boy? Miss Deirdre wants sleigh fixed oop and we're doin' it now, so 'urry along wi' you and we'll do't now.'

As he walked along moodily brooding on his thoughts, he looked up and saw Deirdre swathed in furs sitting in the comical old sleigh George had put together from the bits and pieces of worn-out carriages. Two ponies were harnessed and she was calling to him.

'Come here, Conor Casey. Come and drive my sleigh for me. Come on!'

He walked towards her, angry and ungracious, feeling awkward and clumsy.

'No, I can't, Miss Deirdre. What do ye' think I am, yer slave? I've better things to do than to go joy-riding wi' you.'

'Oh, you are angry, aren't you? You're raging, Conor Casey. Won't you tell me why? Come on here and tell me why you're in a permanent thunder.'

'No, I will not, Miss Deirdre. Yer da asked me to muck out the stables and that's just what I'm going to do.'

'Can't it wait, Conor? We don't get *that* much snow and I do want to ride, and I *do* want to talk to you.'

'I said no, Miss Deirdre, and I mean no. I'm going to do what your father asked me. He employs me to . . .'

As he spoke his voice became high and he felt ashamed and loutish. There seemed something uncouth about his voice and stance and refusal that he could not understand.

'Well, I had to get Kitty to change me. Where was your mother? She should have been there to look after me. Kitty is so clumsy and Father employs your *mother* to take care of *me*!' Deirdre felt a blush rise to her cheeks as she said this and she

74

could have bitten off her tongue.

'My ma was fixin' my cut, and I only got *that* because you pushed me, so it was your own fault!' he shouted triumphantly and tramped away, leaving her at sixes and sevens with herself.

She was angry with him but also felt like crying because she had wanted so much to have him drive her out in the snow on this magical day. And not only would he not do so, but he was angry with her and obviously did not even like her at the moment. No one had ever not liked her before! She couldn't understand it! She looked around and the magic of the white-breasted world enchanted her again so she shook off the black thoughts and called Danny to drive her through the snow, but somehow she felt very deflated. She hugged her furs round her shoulders and looked with a hollow feeling of loneliness at the vistas of virgin white stretching to the high dark mountains.

Chapter

12

A few weeks later Lord Rennett asked Conor to clear out the gazebo on the island in the lake. Miss Deirdre, he said, wanted to have a party there in the summer. Really, he said, she was becoming quite a little socialite and he personally would be relieved when she stopped all this gadding about and settled down and married young Anthony Tandy-Cullaine. He often spoke to Conor in this way, ruminating aloud and not expecting an answer.

It was true, though; Deirdre had hardly been at home during the past weeks, except to change her clothes. Siobain never knew when she would be summoned to her young mistress's room and there find her amid clouds of muslin and silks, satins and brocades, trying to decide what to wear to this ball or that. Afternoons might find her taking a dish of tea with the Countess of Wicklow, or riding with the Gormans or the Parnells. Often mornings were spent drinking chocolate with her female friends, the Vestry girls or the Jeffries, *en déshabillé* in their bedrooms, giggling and shrieking, full of gossip and speculation. She seemed caught up in a whirl of gaiety, and Conor had not set eyes on her since the morning she had tripped him up.

The lake, which lay less than a quarter of a mile through the woods from the house, was beautiful; it was a mysterious purple, a reflection of the sky which often looked like a huge bruise. The gazebo, on the island in the middle of the lake, was a stone building, its ceiling decorated with white stucco acanthus leaves, supported by three Greek columns of the Corinthian type. Conor bent over the dead leaves and debris accumulated

76

there during the winter, felt his back ache, straightened up, and massaged the dull pain at the base of his spine with his hand. His anger was forgotten; he had never bothered to have the talk with his father and the whole episode of the library had vanished from his mind. Life had settled down to its even, peaceful tenor once more.

This afternoon there was a mist on the lake. It swirled in gentle drifts of pearl grey, like gossamer scarves draping the trees at the edge and rising from the surface like ghosts. All the world was silent except for the gentle lake water lapping against the shore and the occasional raucous cry of a seagull.

Conor was not scared of ghosts, but he got quite a shock when he saw the tall, black-cloaked figure gliding towards him over the water. He thought at first it was Lord Rennett, but this was a far taller and thinner man, wrapped from head to foot in a black cloak with a broad-brimmed hat on his head. The mist floated around him eerily and the skin on Conor's neck prickled and rose in goose bumps. Conor realized the strange figure was poling a punt towards the gazebo, and he knew a moment of terror at the appearance of the stranger wreathed in mists coming towards him. However, the man leaped off the punt and secured it humanly enough. He came slowly to the gazebo and, leaning against one of the pillars, lit a cigar and looked at Conor speculatively. Conor gazed speechlessly back at the stranger.

'You're Conor Casey.' It was a statement, the man speaking in Gaelic.

'Sure I am.' Conor answered him in his mother tongue.

'Well now. You're the very one I came to see. Well, almost.' Conor was more and more confused. How did this tall, cloaked stranger know his name? How did he know who he was, where to find him? Most of all, what did he want?

'I know all about ye, Conor Casey, and more,' he said. 'The thing is, I, we, need your help.'

'How so?'

'Ah well, that's it, isn't it? We need information. Information about the Rennetts that you could supply us with.'

Conor felt himself growing hot. He was beginning to get some inkling of what this was all about.

'Ye mean spy? Like spy on the master beyond? Well, I'm not doin' it. You've got the wrong boyo, so ye have. He's been kindness itself to me, to my father, my folks.'

'Ah yes, kindness itself, your master!' The mysterious stranger did not raise his voice but it was full of venom. 'And why wouldn't he be? He's English. His family came and took our land. We're going to get it back. I promise you that, Conor Casey. Soon no Irishman in this land will call anyone master.'

'Well, I won't help you, you can be sure of that. I won't betray Lord Rennett!'

'No? I'm afraid, Conor, you'll have to! Ye see, I don't think ye have any choice.'

'What are ye sayin'? I don't understand.'

'Oh come now, don't play the fool with me. There's many a relation of the people of Barra Bawn would like to know the whereabouts of Michael Casey, indeed'n they would. Informers are a hated breed and vengeance is the only honourable retaliation.'

'I don't know what you're talking about. My da came from Barra Bawn over twenty years ago, well nineteen anyway, and what this has to do with him . . .'

'Don't play the amadán with me.' The tall man's voice was cold and hard. Then a thought struck him. 'Or maybe your precious da never told you about his thirty pieces of silver?'

He leaned forward and for the first time Conor caught a glimpse of his face under the brim of his hat, like a skull, he thought, gaunt and saturnine with brilliant black eyes, but younger than he had supposed.

'Ye don't know, do ye?' the man asked, amazed.

'Who are you?' Conor whispered, shaken against his will, frightened of a sudden about he knew not what. There was something evil about the man, an uncomfortable sneering in his intimate speech to Conor that caused his flesh to creep. The man answered him, and the mist obscured him again, swirling about the two men where they stood. His voice changed, became stronger, less unpleasant.

'I am a patriot and an Irishman who believes in freedom. These bastards have kicked us around too long and now the gloves are off and by fair means or foul we'll get our liberty. And you'll help us, Conor Casey, willingly or no, you'll help us. Go home and ask your da how he got out of Barra Bawn. Go ask him about that. I'll be here one week today. Here on this spot at midnight. I expect you to be here too.'

He turned to go, then paused and looked back at Conor. 'I

78

wouldn't say anything to his high and mighty Lord Rennett if I were you. If you did we'd find out and your chances of living out the year would be *nil*, your family too. So take my advice and don't. Remember, Conor, and ask your da to remember too.'

He made his way to the punt, his cloak billowing out bat-like behind him in a sudden gust of wind that raised Conor's black hair from his damp brow. The stranger untied the punt and, picking up the pole, turned before he stepped into the little boat.

'My name is Declan Mulholland. Me da is Rory. Me cousin is a woman called Siobain. Do ye know anyone by that name, Conor? Do ye?' He laughed, a cold mocking staccato sound. 'Tell your da that,' he said.

Conor watched as the tall dark figure disappeared, slowly swallowed up in the veils of mist. He was gazing after him, lost to all but the stranger's parting words, when another sound caught his attention and he realized someone else was calling him, in a high frightened voice, over and over; and he became conscious that behind him on the bank Miss Deirdre was sobbing, 'Conor, please Conor, oh, Conor, I'm frightened. It is you, isn't it? Please come here, Conor, please.'

He withdrew his eyes from the ghostly black figure gliding away from him over the lake through the fog and turned to the calling voice. Galvanized into action, he ran to where he'd left his rowing boat and, getting into it, rowed himself as fast as he could to the bank.

When he had secured the boat he followed the sound of the sobbing and found Deirdre Rennett in a little pool of misery on the muddy bank, weeping noisily like a child. He raised her up and she clung to him, sobbing and hiccupping.

'Oh Conor, Conor, you don't know how glad I am to see you. I was riding. Oh don't scold, I know I shouldn't have in this weather, but the mist is not at all bad above, and anyhow I was feeling restless and I thought a ride would calm me, and then something or someone frightened Bonnie and she reared and I fell and oh, it's so horrid, but I saw something distinctly odd, Conor, and I don't know what it was. A tall, tall ghost, a devil maybe, some evil spirit, and Bonnie does not imagine things, so don't you dare say so, and she shied and oh I'm so scared.'

79

'There, there now, miss, sure 'twas nothing, nothing at all,' he soothed her, stroking her hair gently as he would have done a frightened pony. 'The light here plays tricks, so it does, on horses and men. Now you never fret, I'll take you to the house and to me mam, and you'll feel much better after a warm bath. You're all wet and muddy, have ye hurt yerself?'

Deirdre raised her tear-filled eyes and shook her head. Her little face was streaked with her crying and mud from her gloves where she had rubbed her cheeks to brush away the tears. Her lips trembled.

'Oh, Conor, I'm so glad it was you who found me. I knew I was safe when I saw you.' A frown creased her brow. 'I was sure I saw a dark-cloaked spectre move away from you out there over the water,' her eyes examined his face earnestly, 'but I expect I was wrong. I was only imagining it. Oh, I feel so silly. I'm not usually such a vapourish female, but oh, Conor, I'm so glad you're here.'

'Well now, Miss Deirdre, so am I. Me mam will be glad to see you too, so let's go back now.'

Deirdre, however, stood quite still like a wide-eyed child, intently scrutinizing his face until Conor became embarrassed and turned to go, but she pulled him back to face her and went on looking at him. Her eyes caressed his every feature, every plane and hollow of his face. Her gaze lingered on his broad white brow, the thick black fringe of lashes, the long slender nose and flaring nostrils like Bonnie, and the outline of his mouth. She seemed in a trance he was afraid to break, then just as he was about to speak she leaned forward on tiptoe and very gently kissed him on the lips. The touch was as light as a butterfly's wings, but he felt as if he had been pierced by an arrow. He jumped back as if shot and, roughly grabbing Deirdre's hand, almost ran to the house, dragging her behind him, so that her feet hardly touched the ground.

They found Lady Rennett and Siobain on the gravel driveway in a state, on their way to look for Deirdre. Bonnie had galloped back to the stables and Old George had rushed to the house to inform them of Miss Deirdre not being on her mare.

Lady Rennett clasped her daughter in her arms, thanking God and Conor profusely, and Siobain clucked over the dishevelled girl like a mother hen. Her sharp senses had detected an indefinable something in the atmosphere and once again she felt a surge of pure panic as she thought of the consequences if either of them dared to think of the other in any way but that of little lady of the house and servant.

Her charge did nothing to allay her fears. As she rubbed the soft white skin to warm pink with scented soap and rinsed the golden hair, Deirdre's customary chatter was strangely lacking. Siobain wrapped her mistress in her silk peignoir and as she dried and brushed the shimmering tresses the silence lengthened and became so unusually long as to be embarrassing.

'What is it, Miss Deirdre?' Siobain could not keep the trepidation out of her voice. 'Did you hurt yourself? What has happened to make ye lose your tongue?'

Deirdre gave her maid a swift, sharp glance. 'Oh nothing, Siobain. Well, you see, I can't understand. Bonnie saw something that made her rear up and throw me and that's not like her. She's so safe! Then after I fell I saw something so strange, Siobain, it makes me shiver now to remember.'

'What was it, miss?' Siobain asked.

'An apparition. No, don't laugh. A tall black figure like death itself crossing the lake from the gazebo where Conor was. Oh, Siobain, I was so frightened I called Conor and he came over to me ...' She paused and after a moment Siobain prompted her.

'And then?'

'Oh, and then nothing, nothing at all. He brought me back here.'

Deirdre had not managed to conceal from Siobain that something else had happened down by the lakeside and she determined to get the truth from her son that evening. In the meantime, she briskly chided her young lady.

'Now, Miss Deirdre, that was all imagining. A ghost? An apparition? Yerra, miss, that's not at all like you! It was all a trick of the light.'

'I expect you are right, Siobain.' Deirdre stretched her arms voluptuously above her head and yawned. 'I expect you are right. Now I will rest and then have some tea with Mamma. Oh, Siobain, you're so good to me. And all your family. I don't know what I should have done today if Conor had not been there.'

'Ach, miss, anyone would have done the same.'

Because of the untoward happenings of the day, Siobain was

home to the gatehouse later than usual. Michael was already there, cleaned and tidied up ready for supper. He sat in his chair by the turf fire peacefully sucking on his pipe. A wave of love for him so engulfed Siobain that she rushed over to him and, to his surprise, threw her arms around him and pressed his head against her breast, kissing his hair.

'What is it at all, a gradh, that has you cuddlin' me like this, tho' I'm not complainin'?'

'Oh Michael, I'm afraid for Conor,' she said as she stroked the greying curls, and she told him all she knew.

'Ach, I'm sure it's all in your head, acushla.'

'No, Michael, no. Miss Deirdre had a look, a certain something. Oh Michael, pray Conor always remembers his place. We're so lucky here, his Lordship and my Lady are so good to us and when I remember what we came from . . .'

'Yes, what did we come from? That's what I want to know!'

They had not heard Conor come in. He stood now tall and dark with his back to the door and once more Siobain felt a surge of love, but this time she restrained herself from expressing it. She loved her menfolk so. Dear God, she prayed, let nothing spoil it.

'Sure ye know all about that, Conor. Many's the time we've gone over the story in detail. Ye've heard it so many times sure ye must know it by heart as well as I do myself!' Michael said in his quiet, good-humoured way.

'Oh I know all that, yes I do, an' that's not the question. The question is how did you get out of Barra Bawn in the first place? Where did ye get the money to make the start?'

There was a sudden, death-like silence in the room, an absence of sound that was almost audible. Michael and Siobain turned their faces towards him and Conor knew his worst fears were justified. He felt a chill of terror shiver through him. What a frightening day this had been! He had never felt this way before and he did not like it at all.

'You better tell me,' he said.

The story Michael told was confused. He kept talking about Maureen Casey, a name unfamiliar to Conor, who thought he knew every name from his father's past. He described the scene in Sir Jasper's great salon and, slowly, as his pa relived the scene, Conor felt that he, too, was there. His eyes filled with tears as he thought of his starving father watching this man

have his elegant tea. For the first time the stories of his childhood became events that had really happened, were really felt
and suffered. This gentle, kind man had been pushed to his
limit by an intolerable and unjust situation, but to betray? To
condemn to certain death most of the male population of Barra
Bawn? This was a terrible thing.

'Ye must understand, they would have died of starvation anyway,' Michael said, exhausted by his confession to his son, trying to excuse himself, to make this boy understand.

'God, Da, 'twas a terrible thing to do.'

'An' he'd do it again, and so would I, to live, to survive.'
Siobain laid her arm across Michael's shoulder. "'Tis not up to
you or anyone to condemn. That's the good God's job and his
alone. But what I want to know is why did you ask this
question, Conor?'

Conor shook his head sadly. Michael had been supreme, an
ideal, beloved and perfect person Conor had looked up to all his
life. Now in one moment he had crashed from his pedestal. He
had proved no different from most men, weak, frightened and
not in the least bit heroic or noble. Well, so be it. He felt a sob
rise in his throat. 'Ah, Da ... Da ...' he cried, then ashamed he
brushed the tears from his eyes with the back of his hand and
told them all that had happened in the gazebo that afternoon.
They were thunderstruck. Michael's face lost its healthy glow
and turned a snail-belly colour from pure fear. All his peace of
mind, gently accumulated year by year, had been blasted away
in one moment. All Siobain's tranquillity had vanished and from
now on the element of fear would always be there among them.
The peace of their little home was gone.

'Declan Mulholland! Rory must have escaped. Jasus, Mary
and Joseph. So there was a survivor after all! He must have sent
his son to get us.' She shivered in fear.

At that moment the door opened and Danny came in. He
sensed at once the atmosphere of crisis and looked from one to
the other questioningly like an alert animal. They told him all as
supper was prepared and eaten. They discussed what they would
do, Michael insisting that he should keep the rendezvous with
the tall dark stranger, Rory's son, and Conor refusing his help,
saying it was a matter between himself and Declan Mulholland
and that he would send him away with a flea in his ear if he
thought he could intimidate the Casey family. Siobain, for her

part, said she would go and plead family ties, and that, anyhow, you could catch more flies with honey. Danny listened and, as usual, said nothing.

Chapter

13

THE following week, on the day of the meeting, Michael and Conor still had no plan of campaign. They had argued and discussed plans and counter-plans endlessly, coming to no definite conclusion. They were both of a mind to refuse to do Mulholland's bidding and risk the consequences. Siobain was racked with anxiety but agreed it seemed the only thing to do; then she changed her mind and said that someone had to keep the rendezvous otherwise they would have no peace of mind. Still Danny held his peace.

Both Michael and Conor knew about the Fenians and their fight for Irish independence, but they neither of them felt strongly enough to become involved — Michael perhaps because his experiences in '45 seemed to have drained him of anger and resentment rather than the opposite, and Conor because he had not truly come to grips with the idea of a free Ireland, and because he had been treated so well by the Rennetts.

At supper that night they were uncommonly quiet. Afterwards they said the rosary on their knees before the picture of the Virgin Mary dressed in vivid sky blue, holding an outsize plump blond baby in her arms, which hung on the whitewashed wall. The wind howled, caught in the chimney, blowing gusts of smoke into the room, and moaned through the trees like a banshee. At the end of their prayers, Siobain added a prayer for a 'special intention', and they all knew what it was. They bent their heads reverently in the flickering light and Siobain prayed fervently for the security of this beloved family. She looked at Michael, the grey in his hair taking over from the black, his dearly loved face creased now with tension and bowed over his workman's knotty hands — hands that had held her, giving her such pleasure and confidence, such reassurance and comfort over the years. She looked at Conor — the young handsome face troubled, perplexed, unsure of what to do but filled with a desire to show his manhood by somehow saving the day for them all and miraculously extracting them from the trouble they were in. And Danny! What was Danny thinking, his face buried in his hands and not revealed at all? she wondered.

When they were finished, Michael rose wearily to his feet saying, 'Well, I suppose it's time.'

'No, Da, no. Yer not coming. I told you and told you.'

Both of them were so busy arguing the point that they did not notice what Danny was doing. He had pulled on his oilskin coat and boots and, lifting the latch on the door, he took the big iron key off the hook. He closed the door firmly behind him and locked them in. Danny had made them prisoners.

It was pitch dark as Danny crossed the drive and made his way over the lawns and around the back of the stables through the bluebell wood and down to the lake. The clouds were thunder black and raced across the sky as if being blown by an angry god. The moon was a silver sliver when she made her infrequent appearances and a cold skittish wind blew in from the sea. Danny's thoughts were as clear as the others' had been muddled. Michael was his god, his father, his idol, Siobain his loved mother, and Conor his blood brother, his other self, his beloved companion. They were being threatened, so it must be stopped. It was that simple. *They* could not do it, but he could and would. *They* would not let him, so he would lock them in the house and take their burden on his own shoulders. They had given him all the love he had ever had in a hostile world; he would do this little thing to help them now in their hour of need.

He walked quite calmly to the edge of the lake. Tonight there was no mist but the darkness was intense and the place ghostly. He untied the rowing boat and, getting in, rowed himself to the gazebo which he could see intermittently, etched sharply in the sudden moonlight against the turbulent sky like a pagan temple of long ago. Danny tied up the boat and went and stood leaning against one of the columns.

He had not long to wait. As he gazed searchingly into the distance for a sign of his adversary, he saw the punt emerging out of the darkness with a tall, black-cloaked figure poling his way towards the island. Danny's breath whistled through his teeth as the tension left his body. Here at last was the enemy, the one who threatened the people he loved. He straightened. He had never thought that this man would know he was not Conor, and he was right. The man glided towards him like a shadow.

'Conor,' he whispered, 'Conor.' Then, seeing Danny detach himself from the column, 'You're here before me, boyo. Good! Did yer da tell ye, Conor, the terrible thing he did? But yer not Conor ...'

An amazed expression crossed his face as he felt the vice-like grip on his throat. He struggled like a landed fish, thrashing about in an agony of realization, desperate to explain, to threaten, to make the fool realize this would avail him nothing. He felt his brain cloud over as if one of the racing clouds had wrapped itself inside his head and then it was as if his head burst open. Choking, his neck broken, he fell like a limp marionette to the ground.

Danny smiled and flexed his fingers, which felt strained from their gory job and the violence of the act they had just committed. Declan Mulholland lay lifeless at the foot of the gazebo like a sacrifice to some ancient god. Danny effortlessly lifted him up and, carrying him to the punt, put him in carefully, draping the cloak around him. There was an old rusty anchor beside the boat and taking the rope that fastened it to its moorings he slowly, deliberately and calmly tied the anchor around the dead man's waist and, poling to the deepest part of the lake, he tipped the body in. It sank, the cloak holding against the water for some time. Danny sat in the punt, motionless, watching until it disappeared and the bubbles and stirring of the waters subsided and a glassy calm settled over the black surface of the lake. Danny smiled into the sickle moon's face as it peeped from behind the racing clouds and touched the water with a silver sheen. His smile was triumphant, cold and satisfied.

Then he returned home. He unlocked the door and went in. The three faces turned towards him — anxious, strained. He smiled his strange new smile at them, made a gesture with his hands crossed to signify the end, that it was finished, and went wearily to his bed to sleep dreamlessly until morning.

There was once more a secret in the gatehouse, something that could not be spoken of, something no one dared examine; and with it came an unease that marred the serenity they should have felt that spring in Slievelea.

Chapter

14

IN the dark, dank basement of a tenement in Dublin in Foley Place off Gardiner Street, Number 13, sat Maggoty Murphy and Ma Kerrigan silently sipping black porter while the third member of the group stared out through the small barred window at the legs of the passers-by on this dark afternoon. It was raining outside, had been raining monotonously for days. The feet that passed the window were ill shod and the children were barefoot in spite of the cold. The scene in the basement looked cosy enough, although the only light was from the fire and an oil lamp which left most of the room in shadow.

Maggoty was of indeterminate years, a small man, thin as a hound, very scrawny indeed, Ma Kerrigan said. His nose was long and permanently red in the parchment yellow of his face, with an expectant drop permanently pendent from his violet nostrils. His teeth were discoloured and crooked and his small eyes hidden in the soft folds around his eyes. He cleared his throat often and irritably as if impatient with the bronchitis of which he was a chronic sufferer.

Ma Kerrigan was fatter than she had been when she had stripped Maureen Casey of her money belt and clothes, leaving her on the station floor naked as the day she was born. Her black hair was greying now but dressed exactly the same, parted in the middle and knotted in a neat bun behind. The blackcurrant eyes looked out ironically and humorously at life. There was nothing sacred in this world to Ma Kerrigan; there was no opportunity she missed and she was very philosophical about defeat and success alike. Not that she knew much about the latter, the area of her enterprises being, perforce, limited by the huge gulf between wealthy and poor, allowing her no leeway to work in the monied environments that would bring in a rich harvest. The struggle for existence was a challenge she met with energy and determination and a complete lack of scruples.

The house in Foley Street was rented, as Ma Kerrigan said, 'from the dissolute second son of an English peer whose inheritance is this street, Foley Place. A poor inheritance an' no mistake. Sure who'd want it? It's as poor a street as you'd come across in a month of Sundays.'

She herself lived on the first floor, and sublet the rooms to the likes of Dermot Devlin, who lived with his family in one large room at the top of the house, and the room under to Rory and Declan Mulholland. Maggoty Murphy lived in the basement and Ma Kerrigan enjoyed paying him a daily visit when they would gossip an hour or two away over a pint of porter and discuss schemes and stratagems.

Ma sat now in the shadow, a speculative eye on the third occupant of the room, a man as tall and as gaunt as the Angel of Death, sombre of face and dress, tight as a coiled spring, repressed anger in his every move.

There was no sound in the room for a long time. Then the tall man cursed loudly, a string of obscenities tumbling out of his mouth, shaken by a rage so great that he trembled. The other two remained silent and still. Maggoty Murphy slurped some porter and Ma Kerrigan sighed and eventually broke the silence.

'Will ye come and sit down now and stop standin' there like a long streak of misery, Rory Mulholland?'

Maggoty Murphy said, 'Sure maybe he's been delayed on the road from Wick-el-eh.'

Rory Mulholland turned furiously on the speaker, imitating him, mimicking his pronunciation, 'Delayed on the road from Wick-el-eh, he says. Listen to him, missus woman, the fool. Delayed on the road from Wicklow? Hasn't he been doing it for years? An' why should this be any different? Hasn't he been goin' up in the mountains drillin' and doesn't he know them like the back of his hand? I ask ye! Maybe, I say, maybe the Casey bastards have done something to him. Maybe.'

'Yerra sure didn't he ask for it?' Ma Kerrigan was tired of the man and his fury. 'Didn't I say to you that he shouldn't go alone into the lion's den, didn't I? If the Casey son is as big and strong as the father sure they'd take some whacking.'

'Shut yer gob, ould wan. Shut it, do ye hear me.'

'Oh, I hear ye all right but I'm not take a blind bit o' notice of ye, ye loud-mouthed hulk of a repressed windbag. There's not an ounce of humour in ye. For God's sake, all this happened nearly twenty years ago. Isn't it about time ...'

'Listen to me, ould wan. This is a war we're in an' I helpin' the Brotherhood and they are interested in Lord Rennett and it just so happens that an ould enemy of mine is living offa him, livin' off the fat of the land while I waste here in this rat-infested ...'

Maggoty tutted and shook his head and the pendent drop on his nose wobbled but did not fall. 'You've no call to that kind of talk. When have ye ever seen a rat here? No, tell me. I'm a civilized man, when have ye ever seen a rat here?'

Ma Kerrigan interrupted. 'God help us now, isn't it yer own bloody fault ye're here? Ye spend all day, every day, thinkin' of Michael Casey an' what he did to you back in Barra Bawn. What did he do anyhow? Ye've never told us. Ye've never said.'

Maggoty Murphy poured him some porter. Rory took a long gulp. Then he looked up. His wild eyes were full of tears.

'I'm that worried,' he said and shivered. 'Where is Declan, me son?'

No one answered. The light flickered on the intent faces of Maggoty and Ma Kerrigan watching him, waiting. A sod of turf collapsed in the grate. Ma Kerrigan said, 'What happened in Barra Bawn? Why don't ye tell us? It'll ease your anxiety.'

Rory took another swig of his drink and nodded. He had to talk, he was that restless. He wiped his eyes and nose on his sleeve and began.

'Back in Barra Bawn ...' You could almost hear the excitement in the room. The faces had an eager look, an expectancy that was feverish. They had waited so long to hear the facts but always before they had been disappointed, for Rory had never confided in them.

'Back in Barra Bawn we never did like the Caseys. They were feckless folk, proud and clannish, thought themselves a cut above the others. Descended from the High Kings of Ireland, no less. They never took life seriously and were always too good-looking for decency.'

Ma Kerrigan remembered appreciatively the beautiful young man in the vast terminal and nodded her head in agreement,

'Aye, he was a tasty morsel an' no mistake.'

'Well, when the Great Famine was abroad we used to kill a sheep when we could in Barra Bawn to keep alive, most of us men in the village.'

Again Ma Kerrigan nodded in agreement. Not to act thus would have been a crime in her opinion.

'It was a tricky, bloody business. The work had to be silent. Sir Jasper Lewis, the landowner, offered a reward for the names of the sheep-stealers. He intended to hang them, he said, and who was there to stop him? Strictly speakin' he shouldn't have terminated a man's life for such an offence, but who could stop him in the back of beyond, I ask ye? Well now, none of us thought anyone would be bastard enough to betray us, but didn't Michael Casey take up the offer, scurvy scum that he is, and get the reward and off he goes to Dublin, lands a cushy job in Wicklow and takes to bed that bitch of a cousin of mine, who ups and marries him. A thing like that ruins a man's stomach, betraying the family name. The two of them, traitors to their country and their families alike. Bad cess to them, they deserve each other.'

Ma Kerrigan nodded a third time. The story satisfied her completely. Plain common sense and sharp wits had won out over honour and duty and all the other high-class attributes she knew did not work in the jungle world of poverty.

'An' you lot? How did you get out yerself?' Maggoty asked.

Rory Mulholland's eyes turned feverish and a fanatic light of hatred burned in their depths. The other two hardly dared to breathe in case they disturbed him. They hung on his every word and he became calmer — his anxiety at the delay in his son's return from Wicklow, and the restlessness generated by it, forgotten in his memory of hell. He spoke softly and somehow seemed more threatening thus.

'We were rounded up, twenty-four of us men and boys. I was eighteen. We had to queue up and wait our turn to be hanged. There were three gibbets and they cut the bodies down when they stopped jerkin' and twitchin'. It takes a while to die hanging. The sun shone all the time, like the colleens might come out any minute with a picnic; but I was cold, cold as death and wet all over. I watched Peader and John Joe Casey die and I cursed them, I wished them in hell. It was their scum relation that caused this hellish thing. Then me mam said little Dec and

Owen, me brothers, should go with Da, but little Dec was only fifteen and he'd messed his pants waiting. I'll never forget his eyes. I never sleep nights. His eyes haunt me, staring at me over the years. I'd break my heart if it wasn't so full of hate. It keeps me going, this hate. Me mam's heart broke after Dec died, just split in two, and she was in the grave in a week.

'Then it was my turn. I messed my pants too, I can tell you. Hearing the birds sing was the worst. Knowing you'd not hear the end of the chorus. Martin Bell's cheeks were wet with tears, an' him our bailiff! He was Sir Jasper's man but his cheeks were wet with tears of pity at the horror of it all. I remember thinkin' I never knew he had a soft bone in his body. Then he put the rope round my neck. I felt it tighten and I said a Hail Mary. But that was all that happened. The rope must have stuck. I remember thinkin' that dying was not so bad, but there I was just swinging there with the rope round my neck but not tight. Martin Bell saw and cut me down. I knew by the look in his eyes he wanted me to escape. He didn't *say* anything, he couldn't, just cut me down and left me with the others. I lay as still as a stone, it seemed for hours. I heard the others die. Some screamed, some prayed, some begged. Sir Jasper Lewis sat all the time on his great stallion, outlined against the sky. You couldn't see his face, what he was thinkin'. He sat on his horse against the light. He looked like the devil himself to me. Then we were all thrown into a big open grave.

'That was the worst. I was sure I was going to be smothered or buried alive in corpses. I kept crawling over the bodies of my friends and family as they fell on me. Kept tryin' to see the light. I knew I was all right if I could see the light. Then I heard Martin Bell ask Sir Jasper if we couldn't be left till morning. We'll cover them in the morning, he said, and Sir Jasper must have agreed. They would wait till morning to cover the bodies with the clay of Barra Bawn. I felt sure he did it for me. That night, sick and my soul in despair, I escaped that pit of death. I made a promise that night. I swore on my brother's dead eyes that I would get the man who had betrayed us if it took me till the end of my days. I swore I would stay alive and get the Caseys for what they had done to me and my folk. I haven't slept a full night since then, the nightmares haunt me. When I close my eyes I'm always in that pit of corpses struggling to get out. I will always be there until the debt is settled, until the score is paid. It was Declan who decided to come here to look for the Caseys. It was Declan who said that time had come. Declan is a true Mulholland. He follows his quarry over the highways and byways until he catches him.'

There was a great silence after he had finished. The others were impressed in spite of themselves. As Dubliners they were committed to an ironic acceptance of the most bizarre events, but this story had rendered them speechless. Ma Kerrigan was the first to speak.

'Isn't that the most amazing thing. Did ye ever hear the like, Maggoty, did ye? How the devil did ye survive after? And where did Dermot Devlin from Barra Bawn upstairs fit into all this? Don't tell me he crawled outa' the pit with ye?'

Mulholland snorted. 'Him! Him you say, sure didn't he do what he always does, take the easy cushy way out.'

'And isn't it well for him that he can?' Maggoty muttered enviously.

'He stayed in the big house, where he was a servant until after the hanging. But even though he had nothin' to do with the sheep-stealin' he knew he couldn't stay in Barra Bawn. The women would have had his guts for garters. They never would have accepted anyone of their own being on Sir Jasper's side, in with him, so to speak, under his protection. All the women, that is, except me cousin Siobain Mulholland.'

'Was that the wan who died?' Ma Kerrigan asked.

'No, that was *his* cousin, Maureen Casey. But Siobain was always crazy for Michael, and the ould witch woman down in Barra Bawn swore she would end up with him, that she had seen it in the cards, so when she heard that he had gone to Dublin, and that Dermot Devlin was going too, she begged him to take her with him. He stole a horse and trap, food, articles of value from the big house, and didn't they travel in style to Dublin town. Jasus, the luck of some people.'

'The devil a bit luck comes into it. Yerra ye make yer own luck, me boyo,' Ma Kerrigan said, sipping her porter and nodding sagely at Maggoty.

'Aye, 'tis true for ye, woman,' Maggoty replied. He was very content. He loved this kind of an evening, and the gossip and the warmth of the communication of dark secrets gave the evening spice and flavour. 'Go on, go on,' he said.

''Twas in Dublin he heard about Lord Rennett having been

away abroad and coming back to Slievelea and lookin' for servants, and bold as brass takes himself and Siobain off there and gets the job of butler and maid. But she made him hang around the depot until Michael Casey turned up. The ould witch woman proved right with Maureen dead, an' waren't you there that day yerself, Ma?'

Ma Kerrigan nodded her head. 'The pickin's those days waren't so good, but I got a fistful of coins from that pair. But Dermot Devlin's a fool. Look where he's ended up. Here! He always gets caught. I thought we were onto a good thing at Slievelea.'

At this moment Rory let out a howl.

'What's happened to Dec? Oh God, what's happened to Dec?' The man seemed as if he would collapse under the weight of his anxiety.

'Go on up to bed now,' Ma Kerrigan said soothingly. 'Sure maybe he's stopped off to see a girl on his way.'

'Don't blaspheme, woman.' Ma Kerrigan flinched back at the ferocity of Rory's snarl and for a moment she thought he would hit her, but he let his hand fall and turned and left the room. Seconds later they saw his feet splash past the window.

Ma Kerrigan and Maggoty Murphy, relieved of the tension his presence created, sighed contentedly, settled back in their chairs and gave their full attention to the porter and the marvellous things he had given them to think about.

95

Chapter

15

SPRING came to Slievelea. Down by the lake the crocuses carpeted the grass, violet, yellow and white, thrusting upwards. The daffodils nodded their yellow heads in golden profusion. Leaves and buds burst forth everywhere and the mares foaled. In the orchard clouds of blossom clothed apple and cherry trees in a delicate, lacy abundance of pink and white, and the hawthorn and forsythia put forth their delicate blooms. The bare, black branches of the trees became clothed in luxuriant green and the lanes and boreens of Wicklow turned from lonely barren muddy tracks into verdant passages of foliage, hedges and trees, cloaking the byways in magical mysterious green. A million delicate flowers, tiny and fragile, lurked in the woods and the verges of the lanes, around trees and in the mountains and hummocks and hills. Violets, snowdrops, pansies, primroses and wild iris; felestrom, yellow and mauve; the gorgeous broom and gorse, crocus, buttercups and devil's pokers.

It got lighter in the mornings, and Deirdre Rennett loved an early before-breakfast ride with her father. They rarely spoke but rode side-by-side in companionable silence, feeling the great bond of love flowing between them without the necessity of words.

This morning was particularly lovely. A soft breeze fluttered the newly clothed trees and the sun had an extra sparkle that picked up the glitter of the dewdrops shimmering in the grass and the cobwebs in the hedges. They cantered along totally in tune with each other and nature.

Deirdre was grateful for the silence and the balm of her father's company. He was her anchor, her reassurance that nothing bad could happen to her. In his presence she felt safe and secure and she needed that now. Her feelings and emotions had been in turmoil since that misty day by the lake when she thought she saw a ghost and had surprised and frightened herself by kissing Conor. She had thought through the scene in her head over and over again and still she couldn't make sense of it. That she could have dreamed up that fearful dark-cloaked figure of Death on the water, she who was a practical down-to-earth female to the point of unfashionability, seemed improbable in the extreme. But that she could have, without invitation or encouragement, kissed the gatekeeper's son stunned her to the very core of her being and shook her faith in her self-knowledge. She felt confused and amazed at her own behaviour.

The most peculiar thing was her continued obsessive interest in Conor. She could not get him out of her mind. Awake or asleep she was always thinking of him or trying not to think of him. She daydreamed about his soft black curls against the whiteness of his forehead, about the long lashes that swept against his cheek the instant he saw her, and of how very blue his eyes were, like pieces of the spring morning sky. She thought about how long and lean he was and how his hands were reassuring and strong, tanned and brown, his nails broken from manual work.

She hated herself for her thoughts. She was embarrassed by them, confused by her daydreams, and she tried with all her considerable self-discipline to put him out of her mind and substitute Anthony Tandy-Cullaine. Anthony was just as handsome in his way as Conor. There was no high-water mark on his forehead where the working man's cap separated the tanned lower half of his face from the protected white forehead. His nails were not jagged and unkempt, and, most important to Deirdre, he was just what Mamma and Papa wanted for her. Eminently suitable. But no, the wretched images of Conor would drift into her thoughts the moment they were unguarded, and refuse to be banished.

If she could have confided in her mother, that lady would most likely have sent her away from Slievelea for a season in London, and Deirdre's biggest problem with herself was understanding why she did not talk to her mother. She told her everything, and she could have told her how she felt about

Conor, yet she did not. Her mother would have been sensible about it. Deirdre knew she would not have been angry, only concerned for her daughter's welfare. Deirdre could only think that she did not want her obsession with Conor to end.

Now, with the sun playing hide and seek at them through the quivering leaves, she and Lord Rennett stopped simultaneously as they rounded the little boreen to the cove. The sea spread out before them. The sun was casting golden rays on silver breakers topped with crests of foam.

'I can hear the sea laughing, Papa,' Deirdre said.

Her father listened and nodded. 'Yes, it sounds like that, my dear.'

The breakers roared their way to the beach and broke, chuckling on the sand. Deirdre looked at the sky. She thought of Conor's eyes, 'his eyes are bits of the sky', then she pushed the thought angrily away.

'Papa, did you love Mamma terribly when you married her?'

They dismounted and walked their horses along the beach. Her father, always completely honest with her, considered his reply, then shook his head.

'No. It took time. Ours, as you know, my dear, was an arranged marriage. But your mother came from the same background. We were familiar with each other's manners, expectations, and the milieu in which we would live. All this helped. We were comfortable with each other's social and intellectual upbringing. Then, we both worked hard at giving and taking, and understanding; and it became easier and easier. In time we grew to love each other. The best kind of love, my dear, the love of kindred spirits. It has been very good for both of us, your mamma and me. Then you came along and made it perfect.'

He gave her the special smile he had for her, a smile brimming over with his love for her. For all Deirdre's life that smile had been her beacon, her security; and now her heart flooded with love for this big man and she slid her arms round his waist and hugged him. He kissed the top of her head, gleaming golden in the early sunshine.

'Papa, did you love anyone before you married Mamma?'

Lord Rennett looked at his daughter's troubled face, again paused and chose his words carefully, honestly.

'Yes, my dear, I *thought* so. There was a love affair with one

98

of my mamma's maids when I was about eighteen. It was a passion rather than a love affair, and really rather jolly. It could have become nasty, though, if Father had not nipped it in the bud and sent me away for a rather long holiday. He explained it was not the thing at all.'

'Oh, Papa, I do love you so.'

She remounted Bonnie and spurred her forward suddenly, urging the canter into a gallop, feeling the wind whipping her cheeks and the sun dazzling her eyes. Her father was surprised but not alarmed at his daughter's energetic burst. Deirdre was as mettlesome as her horse and he was not afraid for either.

He caught up with them on the small road from the seashore to the stables. As they cantered together, Deirdre suddenly reigned in her horse and called to him.

'Papa, stop a moment.' She pointed her riding crop. 'Look over there, do you see?' He followed her gaze, wondering at her excitement, but he could see nothing.

'What? What, my darling? There is nothing there!'

She shook her head, very puzzled now and not a little scared, for she thought she had once more glimpsed the dark ghost creature of the lake; and when her father did not share her vision, she knew a moment's panic at the realization that perhaps she *was* seeing things.

As they approached the stables, Conor came up the drive behind them, calling out that he would rub down the horses; and, as they dismounted, once more Deirdre saw the spectre slipping between the trees.

'Look, Papa, look!'

This time her father saw as well. 'Stop! Stop, I say! You there, stop!' He started to run after the man; but to her surprise Deirdre saw Conor stick out his boot and, she could have sworn, trip her father up so that he fell on the gravel. This was so unbelievable an occurrence that she doubted the evidence of her own eyes. Conor then ran after the shadow as fast as he could and Deirdre helped her father to his feet.

'Papa, are you all right?'

'Yes, my dear,' he brushed his riding breeches, 'no bones broken. Don't know how I managed to fall, damn me I don't! Got away, did he?' he shouted as Conor came running into view.

'He had a horse near the wood, my Lord. He took off like the

99

devil himself. I nearly caught him tho', would have if it waren't for the horse.' Conor was out of breath. 'Are you all right, my Lord?'

'Yes, Conor, quite all right. I'll just go and change. Any idea who the fellow was, Conor?'

Conor's face was red from his sprint across the lawn, but Deirdre felt sure he turned a deeper crimson as he shook his head.

'No, my Lord.'

'Probably some damned Gypsy or beggar. No poacher would come this close to the house. Never mind, we've scared him off.' Lord Rennett sprinted up the steps and disappeared into the house.

Conor turned to go but Deirdre placed herself in his way.

'You do know that man, Conor, don't you?' Her heart was beating so fast she could hardly speak.

'No, Miss Deirdre, I don't!' Conor said very firmly.

'Then you know who he is, I know you do. He was down by the lake with you that day, that day . . .' Her violet eyes faltered and she looked away from his troubled gaze. She caught her breath in her throat and, putting her little hands against her cheeks, she cried, 'Oh Conor Casey, I hate you!' and ran up the steps, following her father into the house.

She went directly to her mother, who was playing the piano in the music room.

'Deirdre, my love, you musn't charge into the room like this. It's not seemly.'

'Oh Mamma, I do apologize. I don't mean to, it's just . . .'

Her mother rose with a fond smile, gently rebuking her daughter. 'And you mustn't ride so wildly. It's not ladylike. Look at you.' She shook her head, tut-tutting. 'You are all hot and bothered.' She took her daughter's hand in hers, and sat her down on the chaise.

'Oh, Mamma, I'm terrible I know. But I won't do it again. I promise.'

They both knew the promise was empty. Deirdre could no more control her wild galloping on Bonnie than she could change the colour of her eyes.

'I need to ask you, Mamma. What is it like to be married?'

Lady Rennett burst out laughing. 'Oh Deirdre, you are too direct. Heavens, what a question. You take me unprepared, but, well ...' Her mother's face became serious. 'I think it depends very much on the man you choose. Some men are brutes. They have no consideration, and consideration is, I feel, essential to a woman's happiness. A lot of men treat their wives like possessions. They don't take any notice of how their wives think or feel. In fact some of them cannot acknowledge that their wives *have* any serious thoughts. Your father has always taken me into his confidence. He has never patronized me. I have loved being married to him. Does that answer your question, miss?'

'Yes, Mamma. You love Papa very much, don't you?'

'With all my heart, my love. I don't think I could live without him.'

'But you didn't love him when you first met?'

'No. I grew to love him, though, very quickly. Now he's my whole life. Your father, my love, has given me everything and made me a very happy woman.' There was a pause in the room. The call of the seagulls came over the wind from the cove, and Deirdre thought she heard Conor's and Old George's voices from the stables.

'It's Anthony, Mamma. I don't love him, I don't think. But I don't know. I'm not sure. Oh Mamma, I'm so confused.'

Lady Rennett gathered her daughter into her arms. She smoothed the tumbled curls and smiled at the impetuosity of youth.

'There now, my dear. Don't agitate yourself so. You agonize too much over your feelings. Learn how to flow with life, not to battle upstream against it on some course of your own. Anthony is a fine and honourable young man. In my opinion he will make you a considerate and caring husband. Now off with you to Siobain. She'll help you change and bathe, and compose yourself as befits a lady.' She rose and gave her daughter a gentle kiss on her cheek. 'Off with you now, and leave me in peace to play Mr Schumann to the best of my poor ability.'

Conor had watched Deirdre vanish into the house, then shrugged his shoulders and turned to walk the horses into the stables. He was shocked at the discovery that an older version of Declan, who could only be Rory, lurked around Slievelea, and he knew of a certainty that this man came searching for his lost son.

Old George had chided him for leaving the horses to cool down and Conor had to explain what had happened. He used

Lord Rennett's deduction and said there'd been a Gypsy or a beggar lurking near the house and he'd given chase until the man had ridden away. Old George cocked an eye at Conor.

'A beggar on horseback? Not bloody likely!' he guffawed. 'Ah think we'd better warn his Lordship and the staff to keep an extra eye out and make sure no one prowls around here again. The whole thing sounds decidedly fishy to me.'

So it was arranged that the men would keep watch, and the doors and windows would be securely barred at night, a thing never necessary before. Lord Rennett considered the whole business a storm in a teacup and tended to dismiss what had happened as trivial. Lady Rennett had no thoughts at all on the subject. Poor Deirdre was thrown into fearful confusion. She was sure Conor knew the sinister stranger, but she could not fathom who he was or what he could want. The servants' lives were an open book to the family and a secret seemed an incredible, impossible conjecture, so she wondered at and doubted her own instincts. Conor and Michael knew the stranger to be Declan's father and they were frightened both by the fact of his presence near Slievelea and the knowledge that they were completely ignorant of the fate of his son.

Chapter

16

THE days passed and inevitably the episode faded from their minds. Spring hurried along into summer in luxuriant profusions of flowers. The countryside, dappled in sunlight, threw off shyness and revealed the glory of its colours — so many shades of green, from emerald to lime. Soft breezes cooled the forehead and fanned the hills, carrying on them the scent of roses. Down in the boreens and lanes of Wicklow quietude reigned and a drowsy stillness drenched the motionless air, no leaf astir, the droning of insects filling the air with a hypnotic buzzing. Crumbling grey stone walls covered in ivy, banks of wild herbs, and the sweet smell of honeysuckle and thyme on the wind filled the soul with lassitude. Rhododendrons burst into passionate bloom, and geraniums swanked gaudily in their brilliance of red, purple and cerise.

The Rennetts had tea on the lawn and reclined, hardly speaking, on little wicker chairs under the chestnut tree. Lady Rennett used a fan, old-fashioned but so cooling. Lord Rennett fingered his collar irritably in the heat. They drank tea from wafer-thin Spode, and ate tiny cakes as they chatted in a lethargic, meandering way. Deirdre joined them when she was there, which was seldom. She had continued her round of hectic socializing and now spent a lot of time, much to her parents' delight, with young Lord Anthony Tandy-Cullaine and a group of friends. They went riding and dancing, to parties and balls, and Lord and Lady Rennett worried about what Lady Rennett called Deirdre's 'feverish gaiety'.

'It's not like Deirdre at all to be so excitable. I fear she's become very nervy of late,' she said to her husband, tapping her forehead gently with a handkerchief drenched in eau de Cologne. Her husband waved a wasp away from the home-made jam in its little silver dish.

'I expect it's her age, my love. Dare say it's the weather too. Wouldn't be surprised.'

'There's something else there, something feverish. I worry, my love, about her.'

Lady Rennett sighed and gazed upward through the lacy patterns made by the gently swaying leaves about her. She saw a swallow glide across the sun and wondered if all the air had been sucked from the world.

'Well, I have great hopes she'll decide this summer to settle down with young Anthony. If only he'd stop calling her Dee. She hates it so, it sets her teeth on edge and puts her in a pet. Have you noticed?'

'Yes, my dear. Perhaps you could have a word in his ear. It would be more suitable coming from you.'

For the summer party planned at Slievelea, Deirdre had announced that she wanted an orchestra down in the gazebo on the lake, with fairy lights in the trees, and lamps hung every-where.

'Oh Mamma, Papa, I want the most romantic party. Can you have them make a platform for dancing down by the lake, and the little boats all decorated?'

Lord and Lady Rennett were only too delighted to comply with her whim. They engaged labourers to help Michael and Conor with the preparations. A platform was duly erected and it seemed the gods favoured the young people for the weather became more and more beautiful and nature clothed herself in her most dazzling garb.

Deirdre grew more excited as the days passed. She nearly drove poor Siobain mad with her changes of mood, one moment in fits of giggles over nothing at all, the next in floods of tears for no apparent reason. She changed her clothes so many times each day that Siobain seemed to have no time for anything else than to look after Miss Deirdre's wardrobe. As for what she would wear at the ball, it seemed quite beyond her to come to any decision.

None of this went unnoticed by Lady Rennett, who became increasingly concerned about her daughter's irrational moods.

'The sooner she gets married to young Anthony the better,'

she said to her husband with an edge to her voice he had never heard before.

'Oh, there's no rush, m'dear. She's only a child.' Lord Rennett wanted his daughter to settle down with Anthony, but not yet, not yet. He visualized a long betrothal period, and was mildly alarmed whenever he thought of his beloved Deirdre actually getting married and leaving Slievelea. Ah, there was the rub! Leaving Slievelea . . . it was a thought he was not at all anxious to dwell on.

'Nonsense, my love!' his wife tartly replied, her tone causing him to frown, 'it's high time she settled down, and they will deal very well together. They are perfect for each other. They've known each other all their lives, they come from the same backgrounds and they are young and healthy. I think I am right, my dear, and our high-spirited daughter has a bad case of summer fever. Settle her in an engagement and she'll soon calm down.'

Deirdre decided on a white silk organza dress embroidered with hundreds of tiny stars and sprinkled with sequins and seed pearls so as to give the impression that she was moving in a cloud of shimmering cobwebs. Siobain spent many hours stitching tiny alterations, preparing the gown so that the gossamer fabric moved diaphanously about Deirdre, making her seem ethereally clothed in moonbeams.

The workmen came from the village, helping Michael and Conor, erecting the lights, decorating the lakeside, and turning the wood into a fairy place. The kitchen staff also had help. The cook was lost in the creation of unheard of delicacies: her duck would be enfolded in fat crumbling pastry and *foie gras*; her lamb would be drenched in cherry sauce; her meringue would be a creation of such airy fragility that it would hardly bear the weight of the raspberry sauce, pipless and thick, to be poured over it with whipped cream. The chestnut purée, the *bavarois* of chocolate mousse and the chicken in its pale green watercress sauce were all guaranteed to please the palate and receive the congratulations her hard work deserved and which she knew she would receive, along with a bonus from her appreciative employers.

At last the day dawned, greeted anxiously by the family, for the climate at Slievelea was not renowned for its predictability. The weather, however, was perfect; a faint morning mist rolled away to reveal a glorious sun, smiling serenely. Lady Rennett spent the day supervising and Lord Rennett took himself off to do some business in Wicklow town. Conor and Michael were on their feet checking and overseeing the final touches to the dance platform and the decorations down by the lake, and Siobain was hard put to keep Deirdre in any sort of calm frame of mind.

The orchestra arrived and struck up waltzes from Vienna. They seemed none too happy at first about having to play on an island in the middle of a lake. However, they were offered a few extra shillings and a jug of wine and soon settled down to their music and the evening ahead.

As the guests arrived, the butler and footmen moved about amongst them offering refreshments. The grand buffet supper was in the great hall in Slievelea, and afterwards, like a flock of birds set free from gilded cages, the bright young girls tumbled out onto the lawns. Some of the guests played blindman's buff and an anxious mamma, Lady Vestry, called out to her giggling young daughter to be careful she did not stain her pretty dress on the grass. Clarissa Vestry tossed her curls and put an arm round Deirdre's waist.

'Oh, Mamma is so stuffy! Your mamma never scolds like that in front of everyone, Deirdre, does she?'

Deirdre laughed. 'My mamma is far too busy seeing everyone has a good time to think about me,' she said.

When Lord and Lady Rennett arrived at the lakeside the ball was officially opened and the dancing could start. It all looked like a fairy tale. The lights were strung over the water and each boat, softly padded for the occasion with velvet, had lights fixed at either end. In the dazzling long twilight on the shimmering waters the young girls sat on the velvet cushions while tall, handsome young men poled or rowed them along, dodging the swans and lingering under the weeping willows' massy shade. The lake shimmered in the moonlight, black as night, like a silver mirror dotted with the boats, twinkling with their myriad coloured lamps, glow-worms moving through the velvet dark. Lord Rennett turned to where his daughter stood, the soft white clouds of her dress billowing out about her. The music swelled voluptuously. The strains of the waltz fell seductively on their ears across the water from the gazebo; the musicians in their black and white, encircled by the Corinthian columns, seemed suspended between sky and water.

'May I have the pleasure of dancing with the most beautiful woman in the world, except of course your mamma?' Lord Rennett asked, looking into the flushed, excited face of his daughter. Deirdre felt like a featherweight in his arms. Her eyes sparkled up at him like stars as they turned and turned, around and around.

'Oh, Papa, you're the dearest, handsomest man in the world. If only I could find someone like you to marry me!'

'You will, my dear, and better I'll warrant. I was quite a young blade at your age and not at all "dear" when your mamma took me on!'

They laughed together, and Deirdre laid her hot cheek on her papa's sleeve, breathing in the odour peculiar to him that she liked, a heathery sort of smell, the aroma of cigars and brandy, of clean soap and Macassar oil. The night and the music filled her with an ache and a longing she did not understand and she felt she would die if something, she knew not what, did not happen.

'Oh I wish, I wish,' she whispered, then threw back her head and smiled up at her father, a dazzling smile of moonlight and tears, 'Oh Papa, I love you so.'

'I know, my angel, and I love you.'

The music sobbed to a stop. The chattering crowd shifted and regrouped. Anthony Tandy-Cullaine came over to her as the music commenced once more.

'Will you dance with me?' he asked.

'Oh, I don't know, Anthony, I really don't. I'm quite worn out, dancing with Papa.'

'Oh come on, Dee. You've been avoiding me all evening. I took a dish of the nicest strawberries to you in the hall. I chose them myself, and, before I could give them to you, you had disappeared with that silly Clarissa Vestry.'

'Don't call me Dee. I've asked you, Anthony, again and again. It's very boring. You never pay the least attention to my pleas.'

Tears had filled her eyes and he saw to his horror that they were just about to spill down her flushed cheeks when she turned and ran away from him into the bluebell wood. There was a little path through the wood and Deirdre ran up it, almost colliding with Conor.

'Excuse me, Miss Deirdre. I'm taking some cigars down to

your father. He says the smoke will drive away the gnats rising from the lake.'

'Oh Conor, stop a moment and talk to me.' There was a desperate plea in her voice that Conor was deaf to.

'I can't, miss, I can't. Your father said to hurry,' and he brushed past her. Deirdre stamped her foot, and stood a moment perplexed, at cross-purposes with herself, full of an enormous longing. She thought a moment about continuing on up to the house. But no one would be there now except the servants and the old men. She stood for a moment, irresolute, then turned and went back towards the lake, following Conor.

Conor had come from the library, the French windows of which were open on this warm night. Within, the men were in almost exactly the same positions they had been at Christmas, once again discussing the 'Irish Question'. Their talk was almost word for word the same as the conversation they had had then, Squire Rowley, Lord Vestry, Darcy Blackwater, Lord Jeffries and the Gorman brothers mouthing platitudes. Conor had felt the colour flood his face as he excused his interruption and fetched the large wooden box of cigars. But they paid him no heed; it was as if he were invisible.

'The Fenians are all disbanded at any rate,' Lord Vestry said.

'The Brotherhood, they called it. Pack of traitors would suit better, don't ye think?' Barth Gorman said.

'Full of sentimental rubbish about Home Rule ... faugh!'

'They're children. Children couldn't govern Ireland.'

'Let them try. That's what I would do. Let them try. See the mess they would make.'

Conor had left the room quickly with the cigars, full of conflicting feelings. On the one hand he was angry at the talk he had just heard, the more so because of their attitude to him, their total indifference to his presence. On the other hand he knew that, if Lord Rennett had been there, he would have been aware of his servant's presence; and his loyalty to Lord Rennett was, once more, at war with his pride. So when he met Deirdre he was not thinking of her or even conscious of her presence, and he forgot her instantly when he had hurried past her.

Deirdre wished with all her heart she could be seventeen again — before Christmas and the ball, when everything had started to become complicated and she could not trust her own feelings any more. If only she could once more be Papa's pet —

108

irresponsible, looked after, without a care in the world and no Anthony Tandy-Cullaine or Conor; always Conor, muddling her so.

She came to the clearing by the lake and looked at the two men who caused her such internal strife: Anthony, his face turned to the wood, worried, searching for her, his lighting up, like a puppy dog — such a doggy look, she thought — as he saw her standing there; Conor holding out the box of cigars on the silver salver to her father — his face angry again. She wondered why he so often looked angry these days, and her heart lurched, as it always did, when she looked at him. And her darling papa. She sighed as she looked at him putting out his hand to take the cigars from Conor. Then, to her horror, she saw the tall, gaunt figure at the other side of the lake.

The tall spectre, black-cloaked with the broad-brimmed hat, was outlined against the moon and looked incongruous amidst the lights and the pretty pastel dresses. It took a split second for Deirdre to see the metal object in his hand. The gun was pointing at her papa; fingers of death, she thought. Panic rose in her and she screamed, 'Papa, Papa,' and ran towards him as fast as she could, 'Papa, Papa,' and she threw her arms around him as she saw Conor's white face, horror-stricken, looking at the place where the cloaked stranger stood. Simultaneously, she heard the two blasts as the shots were fired and felt the strength leave her father's body. He fell heavily on top of her and she staggered to the ground. She sat with his head on her lap, her white dress bright red with blood. He was dead and lifeless. She looked at her blood-stained hands and she heard the enormous silence. It seemed as if nature held its breath in horror and everyone was frozen where they stood. Then suddenly everyone and everything became mobilized again.

Deirdre sobbed out, 'Papa, Papa, oh my darling Papa,' again and again, over and over, cradling his head in her lap, holding on to him with all her strength. Her mother tried to separate them, pleading with her daughter, her own face pale with shock, but she could not unclench Deirdre's arms. She nodded to the frozen Conor, and as he leaned over to lift Lord Rennett Deirdre's head snapped back and she looked at him with blazing tear-filled eyes.

'Don't you dare touch him,' she whispered, 'don't you dare. I never want to see you again, Conor Casey. Never. You helped to kill my father. I don't know how, but I know you did.'

He looked into the small, grief-stricken face and moved back from the accusation in her eyes. But a lot of her hysteria had gone with her speech and now she whimpered like a lost child. Her mother held out her hands to her stricken daughter.

'Mamma?' She looked up at her mother piteously, took her hands and stood up. Siobain, running down from the house, put her arms around the devastated girl and led her back through the wood. Lady Rennett ordered the servants to carry Lord Rennett's body to the house. The guests did not know how to behave. A woman giggled loudly, hysterically, and someone else shushed her. Some offered to help, some slunk to their carriages and made a quick getaway. The orchestra played on and on. No one thought to tell them that the party was over, so the violins throbbed through the night and the fairy lights twinkled on in the dark.

Chapter

17

IT had slowly dawned on Rory Mulholland that his son was not coming home. The realization had tipped his fanaticism over the edge into madness.

Ma Kerrigan had been the first to realize this. The wild look in Rory's eyes had become fixed and distant, as if he were gazing into space at some unimaginable horror.

'Yerra he'll do something outlandish so he will,' she said to Maggoty Murphy, 'I know he will. It fair makes my blood run cold to think of what he could do. He's capable, that he is, of murder.'

'Oh for God's sake don't say that,' Maggoty had said, crossing himself as he spoke. 'Yerra woman, never even whisper it.'

On the midsummer evening of the shooting at Slievelea, Ma Kerrigan and Maggoty Murphy sat as usual in the basement in Foley Street. The shadows lay heavy in the corners as the evening turned into night, but the occupants were too hot and tired to sleep. The room looked cosy to the passers-by, its window open to the mild night air as Maggoty and Ma drank their stout. One of their favourite topics was the Devlin family at the top. They deplored the careless, hand-to-mouth existence of the feckless tribe, relishing their moral superiority and smacking their lips as they sipped their favourite brew.

'What are they going to do about the babby now, I ask you?' Ma Kerrigan threw her eyes to heaven. 'Jasus, if it's true and Declan has disappeared. Not that it's too much of a loss, God help us, but who's to look after the babby?'

'Is that lassie sure he's the father?' Maggoty squeezed up his eyes as he gave her a knowing look.

111

'Oh yes! There's no question of that. Sure everyone in the house knew about it, an' isn't the babby the spittin' image of the ould fellow, God help it. Colleen Devlin is callin' him Liam an' you'd think it'd be some consolation to Rory, but it doesn't seem to make a blind bit o' difference to the old geezer.'

'Well now, listen to me, didn't I hear ould Rory saying he wasn't at all sure the child *was* a Mulholland. That one, he said, would drop her knickers for a cherry brandy, he said.'

Ma Kerrigan hooted. 'Yerra she'd drop them for a half of porter, for Jasus' sake, but the fact remains that the night the babby was conceived, yes I'll say it again Maggoty, it's no use you squintin' up your eyes in that prissy way an' why ye never got married yerself is not so much of a mystery as ye might think. Now, as I was sayin', the night the babby was conceived sure the whole house heard the music that pair made together, an' then wasn't Colleen beaten up next morning by Dermot, the ould bastard, an' he shoved her down the stairs after whippin' her wi' his belt, the wan with the Claddagh buckle, an' she broke her arm an' was constricted in her movements, in other words wasn't she there stuck in her bed under her mammy's nose for a whole month after, so renderin' her opportunities of whorin' null and void for the relevant dates.'

Ma Kerrigan stabbed the table with her forefinger during this last speech and, when she had finished, she took a deep slug of porter and nodded her head at Maggoty, winking one eye to finalize the argument.

'Well, glory be to God, a child more or less in the Devlin household isn't going to make much difference. But I wonder what became of young Declan, and what's going to become of his da above?' Maggoty ruminated.

'I'm gettin' tired of Mister high and mighty Mulholland and that's a fact,' Ma Kerrigan said irritably. Maggoty nodded his head and sniffed.

'He's as daft now as a headless chicken,' Ma continued. 'If I'da' known them pair were goin' to carry on this way I'da' never let them cross the threshold, but it's a weird ould world. Who'd'a' thought that lovely boy would sell his friends? Who'd'a' thought that?'

The front door slammed and the speakers started from their meandering chat, startled by the vehemence of the bang.

'Someone lost their reason,' Ma Kerrigan shrugged. 'Closin'

the front door. Did ye ever hear the like?'

The front door of Number 13 was never closed, winter or summer.

'Whoever it is is in a whale of a temper. Lookin' for ructions,' Maggoty added with relish.

'An' I'll give ye three guesses who it ...'

They heard footsteps and both turned to the door, which was thrown open unceremoniously. Rory Mulholland stood there looking like an 'escapee from hell' as Maggoty put it later. The eyes were wild in his parchment-coloured face and filmed over with madness. He wore his cloak although the night was humid and hot. He carried his hat in one hand and they saw, to their consternation, that he had a gun in the other. His face was beaded with sweat, giving the skin a marble sheen, and there was a crescent of foam where the saliva had congealed on his bottom lip. His mouth was open and he was muttering over and over again, 'Did it. Did it. Showed the ... Showed 'im. Did it. Did it. Showed ...'

The other two sat, pinned to their chairs, immobilized, watching, not daring to breathe. Then Rory threw back his head, laughed insanely and left the room as precipitously as he had entered. They heard his footsteps reverberate up the stairs, and the door to his room slam. Then the house was enveloped in silence once more.

Chapter

18

THEY put Deirdre to bed and she grieved. Siobain stayed with her night and day, leaving her own family to fend for themselves. At first Deirdre was shocked, stunned, and she seemed in a coma; then it turned to fever and delirium. She tossed and turned on her bed and talked and rambled incessantly, while Siobain bathed her brow with lavender water and soothed her young mistress as best she could. The doctor came and prescribed laudanum and rest, and said that only time would heal. He was far more concerned about Lady Rennett, he said, who refused to grieve and wandered about the household, behaving as if nothing had happened. She constantly referred to her husband as if he were there, and her physician became increasingly worried about her.

Siobain was profoundly grateful that Lady Rennett was not looking after her daughter, as Deirdre's ramblings were frighteningly lucid. They centred on her father's death, her love for her father and the sinister-looking stranger, which was all to be expected, but at other times her whole soul seemed to be concentrated on Conor. All Siobain's secret fears were realized, and she listened, shocked to the core at the passion of Miss Deirdre's lament, broken and muttered, in stops and starts, but pieced together in Siobain's mind like this:

'Oh Conor, Conor my beautiful man, why don't you see that I love you? Why don't you look at me, kiss me, love me? You are my heart and soul, Conor, yet you don't even notice me. I'd die for you, Conor my love, for one kiss, one look from your sky-blue eyes I'd consider the world well lost. Oh Conor, Conor, hold me in your arms. Let me melt into your arms and be one with you. Conor, I'll wither away and die without your

114

kiss, without knowing your arms about me . . .'

Siobain could not bear to listen. She was appalled at the ardour of her young mistress's words and was shamed and embarrassed to hear them and she felt very frightened at what was to be the result of the knowledge she now possessed. Deirdre loved Conor. That much was horrendously obvious. But the whole thing was an impossibility, a pathway to tragedy, and would have to be stopped at once.

Siobain was profoundly grateful that Conor seemed ignorant of the situation; and, listening carefully to Miss Deirdre's sentences, she could find no evidence of his having taken advantage of the young mistress of the house in any way. It seemed thankfully plain that Conor had not overstepped the bounds of his position. What to do about the situation became Siobain's whole preoccupation during Miss Deirdre's illness.

The fever finally broke and the little face became pale. As health gradually returned, Deirdre became very quiet. She lay hour after hour motionless, her arms over the sheet on either side of her body, her golden hair spread over the lace pillows and her violet eyes searching the pale pink canopy over her bed as if she would find an answer to the dilemma that plagued her in the roses and carnations embroidered there.

The problem was taken out of Siobain's hands quite unexpectedly. As Deirdre lay there, on the third day after her father's death, her face framed in the spun-gold of her hair and the lace trim of her nightgown, she spoke directly to Siobain for the first time. The room was unusually tidy, the disorder caused by Miss Deirdre's social round missing. The pale pink and cream Samarkand silk carpet caught the rays of the afternoon sun which poured in through the tall open windows. The scent of roses was wafted on the gentle summer breeze and drifted opulently towards the bed from the Chinese vase on the delicate marble-topped table. There was a vase of full-blown salmon-coloured blooms, and every time a petal fell it seemed to release a little explosion of perfume. The breeze caught the transparent curtains and, as they billowed out, the smell of the roses intermingled with the sweet smell of new-mown grass.

Siobain sat beside the bed stitching a fine cambric handkerchief. Her bent head was greying and there was a frown between her brows, and lines at the corners of her eyes, even when her face was in repose. At first she did not hear Miss Deirdre speak.

115

'Siobain, may I have some tea?' Deirdre repeated her request, and Siobain jumped to her feet.

'Oh Miss Deirdre, angel, of course. I'll ring right away. Oh God bless us, don't you look better. Sure I'm that glad, miss. I ... I ...' and to her horror tears began to splash down Siobain's cheeks. The exhaustion of the days and nights of nursing had taken its toll.

'Oh Siobain, Siobain, I'm sorry. Oh dear, darling Siobain ...' Deirdre stretched out her arms, and maid and mistress cried and sobbed wearily in each other's arms and ended up laughing through their tears.

'Oh I'm sorry, Miss Deirdre. It's a relief, you see, to see you well again. You don't know how I've worried about you, allana.'

Kitty, the maid, brought the tea in with bobs and smiles to see the young mistress propped up on her pillow. Siobain poured the tea into the china cup, added a slice of lemon and, having plumped up the pillows for the umpteenth time, gave Deirdre her cup and saucer.

'Siobain, I want to say something to you and I pray you'll understand.' Siobain's heart skipped a beat. 'Oh yes, miss?'

'It's this, Siobain. One day down by the lake I saw Conor with the man who shot Papa. I am not accusing your son of any-thing, Siobain. And I have no intention of mentioning anything about this to the authorities. It would not bring my darling papa back, or help me, and it could only do untold damage to you and your family. You have always been so very good to me, darling Siobain, but, well, I feel it would be best for all of us if Conor leaves Slievelea and does not come back. I'm sorry if that sounds unfair, even brutal, but that is the way it must be.'

'Yes, miss. I understand,' was all that Siobain said.

'Do you, Siobain? Do you?' Deirdre asked, looking plead-ingly at her maid.

Siobain raised her eyes to her mistress and looking directly into the violet pools said very firmly, 'Oh yes, miss, I do. I do.'

They held each other's gaze for several heartbeats, then Deirdre blushed and lowered her eyes; and no more was said on the matter.

That evening Siobain went home for the first time since the accident. Michael had kept the house beautifully in order and had prepared their supper. They sat around the scrubbed wooden table that night, and the candle glowed on their faces as they said grace and broke bread. Siobain's heart was full to breaking point. This would be the first split in the family. However, she had no intention of allowing her emotions to rule her head. Whatever the cost, it was better those two young people were kept apart.

She looked at Michael. His shoulders were stooped now and his hair was grey. She smiled, thinking how she loved him, how good and fine and passionate he was; but how the terrible years of the famine had robbed him of any ambition but the will to survive. He ducked opportunity, slid away from confrontation and opted for peace at all costs. Well, he had got what he wanted. No life could have been more tranquil than the life they led here in Slievelea — that is, until this moment. She sighed. She had been happier than any human could expect in this 'veil of tears'. The priest in the little church warned the congregation not to expect happiness. Life was a stony bridge to Heaven, he said, and full of pain and woe. Well, for her, life with Michael here in Slievelea brought the joys only expected in the life hereafter. So Heaven would be an anticlimax, she thought. Yet here on earth she had not asked for much; not even for Michael to forget Maureen Casey. Just to love her, Siobain, to the best of his ability for as long as the good Lord decreed. And he had. Perhaps she had so much precisely because she asked for so little.

She looked at Danny and she smiled at him and the smile he returned was as warming as a fur coat on a cold day. She wondered what he had done that day down by the lake when he had locked them all in and taken their burden on his shoulders. Well, doubtless, they would never find out; but doubtless, too, whatever he had done had precipitated the present tragedy. Ah well! There was no use in idle speculation.

Lastly she looked at her son, and she spoke before she lost courage.

'Conor. You'll have to leave Slievelea,' she said. Everyone stopped eating. Their faces turned to her anxiously.

'Oh no, Mam, not that. Anything but that.'

'I'm afraid so, son. Don't make it difficult for yourself. You know you can't stay here. Not with Miss Deirdre thinkin' as she does. Not after what's happened. She says she saw you with that man, my ...' She tried to get out the word 'cousin' but couldn't.

Conor sat still as stone looking at her with despair in his eyes. He said simply, 'I'll die, Ma. I'll wither and die away from Slievelea.'

Michael was aghast. 'No, no, Siobain allana, he'll not go. I will.'

'Yerra hold your whist, amadán. You leave? An' what about me? Ah, don't be a fool, Michael. Sure no one knows your involvement and Conor is young, is, is,' she faltered, the brave words tangling with the lump in her throat but, blinking fiercely, she continued, 'is young and he'll fare well in Dublin City.' She knew in her heart her words were just wishful thinking.

'But it's all wrong, Conor, a buachaill. We had nothing to do with Lord Rennett's death.'

'Not in fact, Michael, but there's some truth in Miss Deirdre's thoughts an' Conor could have warned his Lordship, been honest with him, as he was with us. No, it's better he goes. He wouldn't be happy here now anyway.'

At that moment, Danny stood up and went to Conor and put his hand on his shoulder. He pointed to himself and then at Conor, then at the door.

Michael said, 'You'll go with Conor, Danny? Is that what yer sayin'?'

Danny nodded. Michael and Siobain looked at each other and Michael said, 'Aye. It's better so. Who knows what ye did that night, Danny? Go with him and guard him for us, allana.'

Siobain smiled, a sad little smile. 'Sure it's goin' to be very quiet here without you, an' lonely. Just me an' yer da.' A sob broke from her and Conor threw his arms round her and held her fiercely to him. Tears splashed down his cheeks. He felt so young, so vulnerable, so lost. All his security was being taken away from him, all the dear familiar things that had woven the fabric of his life up to now. He was being cast out among strangers, into a cold other world, and he was going to have to leave everyone and everything he loved. He was desolate.

'Ye'll be all right, Conor. Ye've got Danny and you'll come an' see us, eh, Danny?' She opened one arm to include Danny who awkwardly joined the circle. Siobain sobbed in the arms of the two tall young men she loved so much, whom she was sending so far away.

Chapter

19

UNLIKE most of the Anglo–Irish aristocracy, the Rennetts were Roman Catholic. The family had escaped to Ireland during the reign of Henry VIII and remained there, quietly practising the faith of Rome ever since. On their lands, where the fields met the hills, nestled the small family church, cruciform in shape, its grey walls covered in ivy and lichens. Adjoining the church was the ancient graveyard, its tombstones uneven and higgledy-piggledly, the ground above its dead occupants covered in wild flowers.

Lord Rennett was buried there next morning. Siobain would never forget the funeral, although the exact details and sequence of events she could never piece together.

The mourners were many. From far and wide they had come: the Gormans; the Jeffries; the red-haired Vestrys, Clarissa giggling and crying and hiccupping in the silliest way imaginable, making Siobain think, viciously, *if I could I'd slap her face hard.* Then she tried to push such thoughts out of her head. The Blackwaters and the Rowleys stood by the graveside, and young Lord Anthony Tandy-Cullaine held Miss Deirdre's arm with one hand, and supported Lady Rennett with the other. Lady Rennett seemed half unconscious. She had the air of a sleep-walker. She greeted people in a high, clear, unemotional voice.

'My dear Lord Jeffries how delightful to see you. How glad, Barth, I am to have you here. Lord Rennett and myself are so pleased to see you, Anthony,' and the latter tenderly put his free arm about her and held her firmly in his embrace. He looked very comforting, very strong, Siobain thought, supporting the two women. Miss Deirdre's little back was poker stiff, and, though her upper lip trembled, and once, when the first sod of earth fell on the coffin, a sob escaped from her chest, she held with great dignity a brave and courageous stance. Siobain was proud of her, for she knew the effort it took. The child is a marvel, she thought, all the strength and breeding showing in the straight little figure and the lift of the head.

The Governor General of all Ireland was there and many more dignitaries. For this was thought a political act, the verdict having been reached that the murder of Lord Rennett was committed by the ragged army that the powers that be knew to be drilling in the Wicklow hills. There was anger at the graveside as well as fear, and Siobain sighed, wondering what they would have said, these great men in their elaborate uniforms, if they had known it was a matter begun among starving men in little Barra Bawn two decades ago.

When the service was over and the people drifted towards the house, relieved to shrug off the pall of death, glad to escape from the heat of the sun, looking forward to a drink and some of the renowned Slievelea cooking, Siobain stood irresolute for the first time since her arrival in Slievelea and tried to catch Miss Deirdre's eye. When Deirdre turned round and saw her, she gently shook her head in a negative gesture, put her hands, so pale against the unrelieved black she was wearing, to her veil and lifted it back from her face. The golden hair had escaped its chignon and her forehead was damp. She looked, eyes narrowed against the fierce sunlight, at Siobain and the three men around her. Her eyes were full of tears. She shook her head again and turned, leaning on Anthony Tandy-Cullaine, and walked towards Slievelea, leaving Michael, Conor, Danny and Siobain to make their way back to the gatehouse.

Michael put his arm round Siobain's shoulders and they moved away towards home, Danny following a few paces behind them. Conor, left alone, gazed at the mountains and the sky and breathed the salt sea air in a great gulp to stop himself from crying. He stooped and picked a lone buttercup and examined it intently, his vision blurred. The velvet yellow petals seemed to him a wondrous miracle. He stood looking at it for a long time, feeling an overwhelming tide of loneliness engulf him. He did not know what it was, this feeling, for he had never been lonely before.

The following morning Siobain was in a state of uncertainty about whether to go up to the house or wait until sent for. Eventually, she decided to follow routine and when she arrived she found Deirdre up and sitting at her dressing table in a delightful pale pink satin peignoir trimmed with ecru lace. Her hair was like a cloud about her shoulders, in the untidy state it reverted to if it had not been brushed its two hundred times by Siobain the night before. She seemed fully restored, her natural vitality glowing in the sparkle of her eyes and the energy of her movements.

'Good morning, Siobain, how good to see you. Please will you do my hair? It's quite untamed and I cannot do a thing with it.'

Siobain picked up the silver-backed brush and commenced a rhythmic stroke as Deirdre continued, 'Mamma, I'm afraid, is quite undone by all that's happened. I'm dreadfully worried about her. I sat up with her most of last night, just as you, dear Siobain, have had to do with me. I thought a lot in the night and I came to many decisions. I have made up my mind to marry Lord Anthony Tandy-Cullaine. I know it will come as a shock to you, Siobain, and deciding at this particular moment may seem strange, but I don't want you to say anything. It was Papa's last wish and with no man around to take up the running of the house and poor Mamma in the state she's in ... I'm afraid, Siobain, it will take her a very long time to get over this, if she ever really does. Well, it seems a very mature thing to do. So I'm doing it.'

Siobain started to say something but Deirdre hurried on, 'No, no, Siobain, it may not be the most romantic affair in the world, but dear Papa, dear Papa assured me,' she faltered and Siobain caught the glitter of tears in Deirdre's eyes, 'assured me that love comes with time in marriage, and it's the best kind of love there is. He said so. Oh, Siobain, he was such an honourable and fair man, loving to his family and servants, upright in every way, courageous and kind. How could anyone shoot him down like a dog, Siobain, how?'

Siobain shook her head dumbly, feeling the pain of the loss of Lord Rennett for her mistress as well as for herself. Then Deirdre, as if reminded, said, 'Siobain, I want to see Conor before he goes.'

Siobain made as if to protest, but Deirdre continued, 'I insist.

121

I promise it will be a brief interview.'

'Danny is going with him, miss. It's better that way,' Siobain said.

Deirdre's bright eyes met Siobain's in a sudden searching inquiry, but Siobain's eyes were neutral and revealed nothing, so Deirdre merely murmured, 'Perhaps so.' Then she sighed, shaking her hair. 'So we both lose the men in our lives, Siobain. It's a very sad day for us both, a very sad day. Only, Siobain, you at least have Michael.' She gazed out of the window, her eyes wide open, a look of such grown-up pain in their depths that Siobain shivered. The loss of her father had taken Miss Deirdre's childhood away for ever, Siobain thought. Yes, indeed, it was a sad day.

Anthony Tandy-Cullaine arrived later in the morning and spoke with Deirdre in the library. He emerged some time later looking flushed and excited, and, calling for his horse, galloped away. Siobain was then summoned and sent to find Conor.

He was touched at Deirdre's appearance. She looked so tragic and frail in the black mourning clothes she now wore. But there was nothing tragic or frail in her manner. She had authority and dignity, unusual in one so young, he thought. She turned from the window where she had been standing when he entered and looked at him a moment while her heart stood still, then beat fiercely in her breast. When, oh when, would Conor Casey cease to have this effect on her? Then she said, calmly enough, 'Conor, before you go I want you to know that I do not blame you for my father's death. What I said, down by the lake, was in the heat of the moment. You understand that, don't you?'

Conor lowered his head and nodded.

'You see, Conor, my father was an honourable man. He had such high principles, and if I allowed myself to condemn on flimsy evidence I would be degrading his memory, all he stood for.' She paused, then continued, 'I do not imagine you will tell me, but Conor, you do see how important it is to me, and how much more tranquil I could be if I knew something of the facts.' She faltered a little and her voice caught in a stifled sob. 'Oh Conor, I miss him so much.'

'I'll tell you all I know, miss.' Deirdre froze, her hand over her mouth. 'If it'll help.' She nodded, afraid to speak.

He told her the story. She stood with her back to him looking out of the window into the trees. The grass beneath the trees was carpeted with the last bluebells, giving a hazy mauve glow to the ground. The leaves of the trees scarcely stirred in the somnolent sunny day and, as she looked, she focused on the path, the path up which they had carried the dead body of her papa that night. She listened, still as a statue, as Conor told her of Barra Bawn, of Sir Jasper Lewis, of the famine, of the terrible bargain made by a starving man for a handful of silver and of his flight to Dublin, of the grim penalty paid by all in the southern village, save one who had escaped, Conor knew not how, and who had killed her father. He told her of the first visit of Declan Mulholland and his request that Conor spy on Lord Rennett, which he had refused. Of the rendezvous kept by Danny, the result of which they remained ignorant of, and of how Declan's father had cast his evil shadow on Slievelea and eventually shot her father by the lake that fateful night.

She listened attentively, quietly, and when he had finished was silent a long moment. He heard a linnet sing and a black-bird whistle in the trees, and he remembered her sweet young untroubled face the night of her coming-out party and her song,

If I were a blackbird I'd whistle and sing,
And I'd follow the ship that my true love sails in

and he was filled with a melancholy that the carefree young girl had been so prematurely changed into a grief-stricken woman. He heard the dogs bark out in the stable and he thought he should get them some bones from the kitchen, then pulled him-self up, as he remembered he would never do those duties again. Slievelea would henceforth function without him.

Deirdre turned eventually and walked towards him. She took both his hands in hers.

'Conor, Conor, how I wish you had trusted me enough to tell me this before. But you never understood, did you? Listen to me. I loved my papa so much and I feel easier now that you have confided in me. It's a terrible story, terrible! I never knew such things could happen. I cannot apportion blame. That you should have told Papa about this man is obvious, but we cannot undo things, so it's best forgotten, and life must continue. I remember Papa saying recriminations were wasted thoughts and words, damaging only to the injured one, not the guilty, the perpetrator. So. It is finished. Except,' Deirdre paused, her hands clenching his fiercely, 'except, Conor, if you ever meet this man, or find out where he is, I want you to deal with him for me and my papa. I charge you to ... Do you understand?'

Conor nodded. 'Oh, yes, miss, I do understand exactly.'

'Good. And, if you are ever in trouble because of it, I want you to let me know at once. I can look after that, never fear. Your mother and father will have my address. I'm leaving Slievelea, Conor. It's too painful for me now, and Mamma is very distressed so a change will do her good, please God. I expect your mother has told you I shall marry Lord Anthony Tandy-Cullaine. We have a house in London, in Park Lane, where I shall live until I get married. I shall be glad to leave Slievelea. I have been too happy here to remain now, after this tragedy. All my childhood is here, Conor. Now I must put away childish things. Do you understand?'

Conor smiled at her, his eyes full of tender concern and she thought her heart would leap out of her body — yet this was the man instrumental in her father's death. She took the hand she was holding, his rough workman's hand, and laid it on her cheek.

'Well, that's all, Conor. Farewell, my beautiful lad.'

'Goodbye, miss. God be with you.'

He gently disengaged his hand and, bending, kissed her forehead. He heard her gasp, then turned and left the room.

When he had gone, the stiff little back crumbled and with a piteous sob she sank to her knees and buried her face in the cushions of the chair her father had called his and cried as if her heart would break.

PART TWO

Chapter

20

BIG Dan watched the twilight fall over Slievelea. All afternoon he had sat at the French windows thinking. He remembered the blue days of summer when he had been at his zenith as a man, full of his love for his wife and children. Why, then, had there never been time to tell them? he wondered. Life had gone at such speed.

He remembered a day in high summer. Why he should recall that particular day he did not know, but it was a day full of the scent of Slievelea roses, a day when Livia sat across the table from him, a cup and saucer in her long fingers, the shining cap of her hair damp at the forehead from the heat. He remembered the debris of the tea things on the table beneath the hot sun, the bees buzzing around the jam, the scones curling at the edges, and Livia, cool and beautiful in white linen, except for that pearling dampness about her forehead. Aisling, her face alive and full of glee, whispering to David. David, his legs dangling, his thin little face laughing, but not able to let go, not able to lose himself properly in his merriment as Aisling had always done.

But the area of memory he wanted to dwell on was Livia. Livia, every line of her beautifully boned face, every plane of that aristocratically chiselled countenance, the exquisite nose, the wide, sapphire eyes, the long sweep of the lashes, but mostly the features, proportionately perfect but strangely tense, taut, contained behind that smiling mouth. Was it his imagination, he wondered, that now in retrospect he saw an amazing resemblance to their son David? Why had he never noticed it before? What was the secret of Alain his wife had carried to her grave?

127

He stirred uneasily. This was not what he had wanted to remember. He thrust the recollection away and selected the third corner of the mental picture. Aisling. The face lit up from within, that beautiful face shining with inner light, the radiance illuminating the features then, that day, that perfect summer day, the dazzling untrammelled love emanating from her eyes that took his breath away. And as they exchanged looks she had jumped up and, running round to behind his chair, had thrown her arms about him, hugging him fiercely, ardently, to her thin, childish chest. Love, love, love. How had he abused this gift? he wondered. Deirdre, Jessica, Livia, Aisling. Perhaps only his love for Deirdre had been perfect, equally balanced between them, that grand old lady and himself, as love should be to be complete. With Livia there had been something missing and he didn't know what. Aisling he had poisoned, yet he still could not think what else he could have done, how else he could have avoided their split — the changing of that great outpouring of her love to a malignant hatred. She did not know the truth about Alexander. It was his tragedy that he could not tell her. Yet, as he thought, he wondered why not. Why not, now that the end was near, unburden himself of the great secret that lay so heavily on his soul?

He watched the Wicklow mountains in the distance turn heavy purple and marvelled at the mystery of Irish colours for the first time. Deirdre had taught him to appreciate the mellow tones of Tuscany, the magnificent brilliance of the south of France, the pastel shades of Switzerland and the edelweiss delicacy of Austria, but now he wondered if the dreaming Celtic twilight did not put all those other memories to shame — the mossy greens and peaty browns, and most of all the plum-coloured mist that drowned the senses and weakened the will, drying up energy and inspiring great poems and loves and songs full of sorrow. He had never had time to think before of such things and now there was so little left. He tried to remember further back, before that sundrenched teatime, back, back further than he normally allowed himself to remember. What had he himself been like as a boy, as a little lad?

He smiled softly at the memory. What a right little Dublin gurrier he had been — barefooted, tattered, trousers short, and he a lad of twelve, hair chopped and shaved close to his head and the wide hungry eyes in him, sharp as a bird's and sly and greedy. He could see himself that day in Easter week in Gardiner Street. It had been the first rung on his personal ladder to success. It had not been an easy climb, but that day had begun it all. It was the first time success had smiled at him and so seductive was that smile that he had laboured for it for the rest of his life. And at what cost? If he had relaxed his efforts, could he have held more completely the love of his family? Would Aisling now be winging her way to him full of the love she had felt for him that day in Slievelea when she had hugged him with a heart so full it could not be contained? Would Livia have died with another man's name on her lips? Well, he would never know, and he realized ruefully he could not have done it any other way. To change the tragedy he would have had to eliminate Jessica from his life and, worst of all, give up Slievelea. The thought of Jessica still had the power to arouse him, give him the illusion of virility, even now. No, he reckoned, if he had to live his life over he would probably have followed the same path exactly.

He closed his eyes wearily. The terrible pain attacked again. He fought it as he had fought his weaknesses all his life. He was a fighter, a survivor. Who would ever have believed that little gurrier would have ended up here? In Slievelea. He chuckled again aloud, but the sound changed to a hideous moan of agony. The old man in the chair bit his lip till it bled and all was silent again.

Chapter

21

CONOR had never envisaged life away from Slievelea. To leave there was expulsion from the Garden of Eden. Spring, summer, autumn and winter, the weeks, months, years, the slow passage of time in nature, was a daily miracle for Conor. His heart fair burst within him every spring at the rejuvenation of the land. He knew where every tiny clump of forget-me-nots hid, where the wild cherries cast their blossoms on the clover, where the linnet built its nest, and where the salmon leaped. There was not a living thing, plant or animal, on Slievelea lands that held secrets for Conor. Autumn's golden glory and winter's fires, the everlasting summer days, were Conor's diary, an extension of himself, as much a part of him as his skin. Going to Dublin was his undoing, his spiritual death. Like a parched tree or plant he shrivelled from lack of nourishment. Dublin changed him, squeezed him dry.

When Conor and Danny left Slievelea with their knapsacks on their backs, the first place they stopped was at Riley's forge. They asked for a drink of water, for the road was hot and dusty and their throats were dry. Riley the blacksmith, a giant of a man, six foot six inches and nearly as broad, with eyes as innocent as a child, for once in his life was short with strangers.

'Yerra sure can't ye see I'm up to me neck in emergencies? Will ye lookit? Wife? Where are ye? What the devil is the woman doin'?'

Mrs Riley emerged from behind the forge. 'Will ye listen to the man, will ye? Aman't I here? Where else would I be in the name of God? Have I been outa' yer sight in twenty years? Have I, man?'

She was a round little dumpling of a woman with cheeks as firm and rosy as a side of ham and eyes as merry and sparkling as the waves on a sunny day.

The boys saw the problem; there were two horses to be shod and an axle to be fixed on a cart.

'Sure we'll help ye, sir. Just tell us what to do.'

'What in the name of God do ye know about it? It's a skill. Not every Tom, Dick or Harry can manage ...'

'We only said we'd help. You just tell us what to do but for the good God's sake and his blessed mother give us a drink of water before we start, we're parched.'

'Ach, ye poor fellows, why didn't ye tell me? Here first then come in and have a cup of tay and a doorstep of fresh brown bread an' then ye can help, couldn't ye do with it an' no mistake.'

The pair of them tucked in and then set to and helped the blacksmith. Danny fell in love with the forge at first sight. The dark interior with its glowing fire belching crimson flames, the sparks flying about like fireworks, the thick clouds of smoke as he worked the bellows, the warm smell of horseflesh and dung and the sound of the hammer on the anvil appealed to Danny as nothing ever had before. They stayed a week but Conor was restless and wanted to move on. He saw that the silent Danny was the Rileys' favourite. He saw also that Danny loved being there, that the work suited him, and so he urged Danny to stay. The Rileys were delighted. Their own children, a boy and a girl, had scarpered off to England in the hopes of instant riches and nary a word from them since. Danny was a godsend. So Danny allowed himself to be persuaded.

Malcolm, the butler at Slievelea, had given Conor Dermot Devlin's last known address, and Conor felt that Dermot was the only man who might know the whereabouts of Rory Mulholland. He had not forgotten his pledge to Deirdre. He told Danny that he himself would not be alone, that Dermot would help, and that he would come often to the forge on the Wicklow Road to see them. With many prayers and blessings the Rileys sent him on his way.

Dublin astonished and scared him. The houses, the noise and the bustle bewildered him. It had been a long and weary day. Asking people for directions to the Devlin address was a strain as the speed of their replies confused him. As evening came and he travelled north of the city, the streets became meaner and dirtier. The houses, some half fallen down, were dark and foul-smelling. He had never seen their like before, a far cry from the Wicklow cottages, the gatehouse and the houses around Slievelea. Here ragged loungers hung about in front of doorless buildings and answered his questions with ill humour and often curses. When he reached Number 13 Foley Place he could not believe it was the correct address. How could people live in such a place? He marvelled that it could be possible and made up his mind to do his business there as quickly as could be and escape to a better class of neighbourhood.

He entered the dark cavern of a hall. It smelled of stale sweat and was full of the fumes of yesterday's alcohol and vegetables. Shadows cast a miasma of menace over the place, and to Conor it seemed incredibly sinister. There was a door to his right and a broad flight of rickety stairs in front of him, at the top of which was a window. The glass was thick with dust and broken. Some-one had been using it as a blackboard and had scribbled on the opaque panes. As his eyes became accustomed to the dark, he saw a girl sitting on the stairs. He could not tell what age she was. Her face was delicately moulded, the bones nearly showing through under the pearl-like skin. She had flat, straight hair and her eyes, which were fixed on him, unblinking, were a curious greeny-white like the waves at the edge of the lake at Slievelea. She seemed about seventeen and she wore an apron over her printed cotton dress. She was spotlessly clean and seemed some-how starched and laundered and strangely at odds with her environment. She sat on the top of the stairs under the window staring at him for a long time. He opened his mouth eventually to ask about Dermot Devlin when the door on his right opened and Ma Kerrigan appeared. He turned to look at her and she said, 'God blessus, I know you. Yer a Casey, aren't you? Yer the spittin' image of Michael Casey.'

'He's my da, missus.' Conor wondered how this ould woman knew the Caseys.

'An' what brings ye here, may I ask?'

'I'm looking for Dermot Devlin if ye please, missus.'

'Up there. Top floor. No noise, mind, there's a sick man below.' Then noticing the girl on the top step, she cried, 'Aideen, come down outa' there an' inside wi' ye.'

The girl ran quickly down the stairs. She stopped and looked at Conor for a second as she passed him, and then vanished into the room the woman had come out of.

Conor mounted the stairs and turned round the curve to the next flight up. At the top was a closed door and from within came the curious sound of someone muttering, as if talking to themselves, Conor thought, as he followed the stairs up another flight to the top.

Dermot was delighted to see him. 'Yer the spit image of yer da,' Conor heard for the second time that day. Dermot said he had fallen on hard times and he certainly looked it. He had aged in the service of petty larceny and the company of drink. The flesh on his face was putty-coloured and puffy, his eyes were bloodshot and his hands shook. Two of his teeth were missing, which detracted somewhat from the charm of his smile.

Sure he and the missus would let Conor sleep with the chislers on the floor. They had three, God bless them, and another on the way. The skinny, hollow-eyed woman did not look to Conor as if she could be pregnant; she stared sullenly at him and he could see no welcome in her eyes.

An' what had he come for? Dermot asked. Did he know where Rory Mulholland was? Sure, Jasus man, wasn't he right below them. Yes, in the room underneath! Sure all the Barra Bawn people had stuck together, although the Mulhollands were queer ones indeed, and sure they hardly ever spoke to each other, they were so bloody bad-tempered and morose; never bid the time of day like any decent Christian. Rory Mulholland and his Declan came to Dublin from Galway where he had gone after the famine, though how he had escaped was a mystery to one and all! It had crossed Dermot's mind that maybe he had done some deal with Sir Jasper (he gave Conor a smirk as he said this), just like Michael Casey did — an' who could blame them? Anyhow, in Galway he had married a widder woman, who, it was said, had a few pennies, and was a comfortable enough body. She had given him Declan but it looked as if he had given her precious little — a bad bargain he was, and she had eventually thrown them out for his violent, ill-humoured, lazy ways and took up with a travelling man, who recognized a good thing when he saw it, and had settled in snug as a bug, grateful for his good fortune, not like the Mulhollands, bad cess to them, who if they owned Switzerland wouldn't give you a slide! At any rate they had turned up here in Dublin, bent on

133

God knows what disaster course, said Dermot, an' one thing was clear, he didn't want hand, act or part in it, that was for sure.

Dermot gabbled on, the woman a disinterested audience, staring at him with distant eyes, filling his cup with hot, strong, black tea when it was empty. The taste of the tea was harsh and the tannin in it sharpened Conor's nerve ends.

'Rory's son Declan went out one night an' never came back,' Dermot was saying, 'an' since then the ould man has been like a lunatic. God bless us, not that he was ever exactly ordinary! Can you imagine it tho', a growed man Declan is, and his da carryin' on like that! Jasus, it takes all sorts! He went outa' here one night, Rory I mean, an' he comes back — wild he looked and talkin' to himself he was, an' he took to his bed, been there ever since, roars like a madman if you bid him the time o' day. An' what would you be wantin' with him?'

'Ah, just a message I have to deliver. Nothin' much,' Conor replied, drinking up the last of the tea. He gave Dermot the price of a few drinks and left the overcrowded room. He went down the flight of steps to the room below. He knocked on the door, his heart pounding in his chest. He had no idea at all what he was going to do, or what to expect. There was a shout that could have meant anything and Conor opened the door and went inside.

The room, which was very bare and cold, was lit by the flickering light of one candle. Rory Mulholland lay in bed in his dirty underwear. He was unshaven and his face looked like a skull, his white hair stuck out as if he had been tugging at it. His black eyes burned in his head like coals; Conor, scared, could see the red lights there, feverish and full of hate. For the third time that evening Conor was greeted with shock.

'Jesus, Mary and Joseph!' the man in the bed cried, looking as if he had seen an apparition. In his deranged head, when he saw Conor, it was Michael Casey at the barn dance. Sitting up, he heard the music of the fiddles and the bones on the burran, and he was back in another place, another time. He saw Maureen and Siobain smiling up at Michael, vying for his affection, not wanting to give him, Rory, even a glance, and he was filled with hatred.

He leaped out of bed, quick and jerky as an animal, and ran across the room to the table. Conor saw him pick up a gun. Is this the gun he killed Lord Rennett with? he thought. The old man hesitated a split second and in that moment of indecision Conor streaked across, grabbing the old man's hand. They struggled, Rory gasping and cursing with an unholy strength, the sounds of their grunting and their dancing shadows on the walls scaring Conor, frightening him more than the gun. He gripped the old man's skinny wrist, the chickenish skin slipping loosely between his fingers, and at last Conor wrenched the gun away from him, his fingers wrapped round the barrel.

He was going to put it in his pocket when he saw the old man spring at him, his two claw-like hands going round Conor's neck with a strength that astonished him. He tried to elude the talons that held him. He felt the roughness of the old man's nails beneath his ear as the fingers tried to secure their grip. Conor felt his feet slipping on the mat and the dark light in the room became a red glow. He could see the picture of Christ on the wall through a crimson haze, a crown of thorns encircling an agonized face, scarlet drops dewing the forehead, and his head was full of cries, 'Oh Jesus, Jesus, Jesus', in a wine-red world. But it was the old man's voice, jubilant, ecstatic behind him. 'Oh Jesus, Jesus, Jesus,' he was chanting and Conor felt the blood rush to his head. For a moment the room darkened as Rory's vice-like grip tightened and he tasted bile.

Conor gathered all his strength, raised his arm and brought the pistol butt down as heavily as he could. He could not see, but he felt the weapon make contact. The old man's fingers loosened and fell away and there was a sudden, ghostly silence. Then, choking and coughing, Conor staggered to the bed and sat down, gasping for air.

'Mother of God, ye've killed him!' Ma Kerrigan stood in the doorway. 'Jasus, we've got to get him outa' here.'

'Oh my God, missus, I didn't mean to! It wasn't my fault, he went at me with the gun.' Conor began to shake all over.

Ma Kerrigan slid down next to him on the bed. 'Don't fret yourself at all,' she said. 'It's going to be all right, never fear. I'll deal with it. Me and Maggoty'll cope. Just sit there while I get Maggoty. Don't let anyone in, y'hear? No one. Especially the Devlins,' and she was gone, closing the door behind her.

Conor shook his head and looked at the man on the floor. He lay on his back, his eyes open and staring, still full of hate. Conor saw he must have hit him on the head because the side

135

of his face was bloody and there was a dark stain on the floor-boards under his white hair. Conor gazed into the eyes of the man he had killed and felt nothing. He couldn't understand how it had all happened. It was only moments ago he had entered the room. Only minutes ago this awful deed had not been done and he, Conor, had not killed a man. Full of self-pity, he wept over the fact that it had occurred at all. Yet deep within him he knew that since the conversation in the library with Miss Deirdre this event had been inevitable.

He would have kept the corpse company all night, weeping for himself, if Ma Kerrigan and Maggoty Murphy had not hustled into the room. Conor wept on, unaware of the little man standing in front of him saying, 'Oh dear, dear, dear, dear! Oh dear, dear, dear!' and clicking his teeth with his tongue.

'Pull yerself together an' don't carry on like a puling baby amadán,' Ma Kerrigan shook Conor as she spoke.

'Jasus, he's a right babby an' him a growed man,' Maggoty said.

Ma Kerrigan gave Conor a smart slap on his cheek which caused him to hiccup and look up at her helplessly, his eyes full of tears.

Maggoty Murphy carried a sheet which he laid out on the floor. Ma Kerrigan, groaning under her weight, knelt down beside him, and with Conor sitting on the rumpled bed watching, the two of them pushed and pulled Rory Mulholland onto the sheet. The candlelight flickered on the grisly scene and caused their shadows to leap darkly about the peeling walls like demons in hell.

Suddenly the place was torn apart by piercing screams which rent the air like stab wounds, tearing the silence to shreds. The three turned to the doorway, and Conor saw the girl from the hall standing there, her mouth wide open, her eyes filled with fear. Ma Kerrigan got quickly to her feet and was across the room like an arrow from a bow and she once more raised her hand, this time administering two smart slaps.

'Not now, Aideen,' she said, and the girl shut up immediately and stared at her in astonishment.

'Ma,' she said. 'Oh Ma.'

'Get below, Aideen, an' not a word outa' you, de'ye hear? Not a word to anyone! Thanks be to Jasus, Dermot Devlin is gone out for a jar an' that wife of his wouldn't rise to an earthquake.'

Aideen nodded and scuttled away, but returned almost immediately. Her mother opened her mouth to remonstrate but Aideen breathlessly said, 'It's Da McCabe, Ma, below. He wants you. He says he's come to sip porter with you an' Maggoty.'

Ma Kerrigan nodded and smiled. 'Sure I'd forgotten we asked him for a sup or two. God be praised, that's just what we need — isn't that the helping hand of God, to be sure?'

Maggoty nodded. 'Isn't that grand? The cart at the very door.' Then seeing Conor's bewilderment he added, 'Da McCabe has a barrow. 'Twill make a great hearse.'

They had Rory Mulholland wrapped up smartly in the sheet and Ma Kerrigan told Conor to take the shoulders while she and Maggoty took the end. 'Sure he's a ton weight. He was always a large man, and Maggoty and me are jiggered, we're not up to it, so you take the top and we'll get at the legs and down we go.'

They carried him down the two flights to the hallway where a fat little man stood with his barrow, seeming the worse for liquor.

'How are ye, Ma?' he cried in jovial greeting, then he pointed at the white-sheeted parcel. 'Jasus, what's that? It looks like . . .'

'Never you mind what it looks like, Da McCabe. It's better for you if you remain in total ignorance.'

'But I can see that it's a . . .'

'Total ignorance,' Ma repeated.

As they were putting the corpse of Rory Mulholland on the barrow and decorating him with fruit and vegetables to disguise their true burden, the white little face of Aideen slowly emerged round the door.

'Get in, Aideen Kerrigan, or I'll take the hide offa' you.' Tension made Ma Kerrigan's voice shrill.

'But Mammy . . .'

'Don't "but Mammy" me, get in there an' close the door, d'ye hear?'

Conor was dropping with fatigue when they returned to Number 13 Foley Place in the early hours of the morning. They had wheeled the barrow through the streets of Dublin until they reached the swollen grey waters of the Liffey, which welcomed the body of Rory Mulholland more avidly than the lake had received his son.

Ma Kerrigan tucked Conor up into Rory Mulholland's bed. He was beyond knowing what she did. It was only when he awakened at high noon that he realized where he was, but he was too emotionally exhausted to complain. He felt will-less, dispirited and revolted by the smell of the covers he had slept under and the atmosphere of the place he was in, so unlike his mother's home. The aromas of the country, he thought now, were so very different to here, and he squeezed his eyes shut as he remembered the smell of verbena, of lavender, of flowers and herbs, of cooking bread, and the very air itself so pure and sweet while here everything smelled foul and stale. If he was appalled by his surroundings he was even more dismayed at the situation he found himself in when Ma Kerrigan, bringing him up a pint of porter and a wedge of bread and butter, put her proposition to him. She called it a proposition but to him it seemed much more like an ultimatum. What it amounted to was that either he marry Aideen, her daughter, or she would give him up for the murder of Rory Mulholland.

He had been surprised by her willingness to help him the night before, but now he understood her alacrity in assisting him. He still did not understand why she was so anxious to marry off Aideen, whom he saw she loved as much as she was capable of love; and he was not to find out until after the wedding three weeks later.

Chapter

22

AIDEEN had never found it easy to communicate. Shy and help-lessly inarticulate in a land of verbal acrobats, she had felt trapped in her girlhood, acutely embarrassed for no apparent reason. Her mother had smothered her with engulfing love but some quirk in her character made her construct a barrier between herself and the loving, sharing, caring world of Foley Place. Her mother had kept her apart from the others, deeming her above them, somehow better, and Aideen drew further into herself. As a child she rarely left her mother's apartment and when she did she slipped about like a shadow, insubstantial, intangible.

When she had been sixteen, slipping through the hall one day to Maggoty Murphy's with a message from her mother, there had been a big strange man in the hall. She never forgot how he looked. His face was puffy and grey, like a slug's belly, and his eyes were bloodshot. He was unshaven and his teeth were bad. He had stood there breathing heavily, smelling of stale beer. She had stopped, frightened, unable to move, para-lyzed by fear, when he had suddenly opened his tattered coat and she saw his big red thing sticking out. His fingers fondled it and he laughed in a low excited breathless way. She screamed and screamed and the big thing seemed to droop and the man ran away. The next thing she knew she was lying on the ground and her mam had put a spoon between her teeth and she knew she had been jerking and that there was foam on her mouth. She looked up at the circle of faces staring down at her and she saw the Devlins and the face of Maggoty and she wanted to die. She felt guilty and shamed yet she did not think she had done anything wrong. She went to church and was consoled. Repent, she was told, you are a sinful creature, your body is an instrument of the devil, but say you're sorry and pray and above all be pure and you'll bathe in the love of God. No one told her where she had erred, but she knew she had, and somehow had been punished. She became even more inarticulate. Suppose she let slip the truth about herself? Suppose one day people found out about the man? Then they would despise her. When the priests spoke of wanton women she thought they referred to herself. And her sickness was always a fearful shadow in the back of her mind.

When she saw Conor the night he first arrived in Foley Place, sitting on the stairs gazing at him, she had not been able to believe her eyes. He was so beautiful it almost hurt her to look at him. Then moments later she was sitting with her ma in their room when the noise of a scuffle shook the ceiling. It came from the Mulhollands' apartment and her ma had jumped to her feet saying, 'You are not going to start any trouble here, me fine Casey bucco. Out you'll go if there's any trouble in my house.'

'Oh no, Ma, don't say that. He's the most beautiful thing I ever saw.'

She could not believe her own ears at the sound of her voice and her mother had turned and looked at her in astonishment. Then a crafty look had come into her eyes and she smiled at her daughter and patted her head. Just then they heard a terrible thud and Ma Kerrigan ran out of the room as fast as her fat legs could carry her.

Aideen remembered her own feelings that night — the horror of seeing Rory Mulholland dead on the floor all covered in blood. At first she thought he had the same sickness she had. She believed when she had her attacks that God was punishing her and that she died then, and if she had been very good he would resurrect her and she could live for another span, until the next attack. If she was bad, then she would not come out of the next one and she would live for ever in darkness. She had felt the sickness start and then her mother had slapped her. Her mother had never done that before and Aideen was shocked out of her senses and the attack never happened. Then she saw them in the hall and her mother sent her away again. But later she told her she could marry Conor Casey if she wanted. And she did. Oh dear Lord, how she did. And then the thing happened again.

It never occurred to Conor, brought up in the country, to be discreet and perhaps be in bed before he took his virgin bride in his arms. Conor threw off his clothes, unconscious of his fine body, but very conscious of his sexual excitement, his arousal and readiness for his wife. Aideen, unprepared, to her horror saw again the man in the hall and slid into her nightmare world. When she came to, her beautiful husband had his back to her and her mother was holding her in her arms, calling him an animal.

Then Conor realized that he would pay for his guilt for the rest of his days.

Chapter
23

SIOBAIN and Michael used to take the pony and trap and come in through the blackberry hedges of the Wicklow lanes to the blacksmith, Malachy Riley, on the Dublin Road to see Conor, once a month, regular as clockwork, the last Sunday.

On the Sundays when he was meeting his mother and father Conor loved the walk to Riley's forge. He caught the train to Bray and walked from there, away from Slievelea which lay to the south. His feet often led him towards the beloved home of his childhood, but always he forced himself to change direction, travelling northwards until he reached the forge. The country lanes soothed the simmering resentment that poisoned his soul and mind like a fungus, always spreading. He could pretend he was a boy again, kicking his boots through the hummocks of leaves on the road. Even in the driving rain when the wind beat mercilessly into his bones and the landscape was a grey desert, Conor rejoiced in his journey. He felt released from the prison of his life, from his total inability to adapt or adjust to the ludicrous situation he had found himself in. He was a married man who had never had a woman, a frustrated, repressed prisoner in a world of slum streets and hovels whose soul craved the larks in the sunshine, the mystery of the broom-starred bog, the shimmer of amber light on the high road to Wicklow town and the purple crown of mountains lifting their heads to the sky. Sometimes, when he walked to the rendezvous with his mother and father in Riley's forge, he ached all over with forlorn regret for the past, and on many a winter's day he would lift up his face to the drifting white snowflakes as they stung his cheeks and remember Miss Deirdre's face framed in fur, laughing.

Danny made their meetings easy for them. He radiated a peace and security that was soothing and kindly. He was so genuinely glad to see them, so satisfied with his occupation — blacksmithing contented him completely — that Siobain and Michael and Conor unbent in his presence and they ended up chatting together as if they had never left the gatehouse, with Danny silent as ever, beaming at each of them in turn as they spoke. At the forge they drank the tea that Mrs Riley made by the gallon and ate her hot soda bread and barm brack with lashings of yellow butter. Michael would apply the butter liberally to the sweet black bread filled with raisins and sultanas, remembering another world and starvation on an open road.

Michael came to the twilight of his life wonderfully grateful for many things. Most of all for Siobain: her strength and her deep unswerving love for him; her trust in him and her quiet beauty and tender ways. He never forgot the terrible journey he thought they had made together, and so each day made him more grateful for the food he ate and the warmth of their home, the hospitality of the Rileys and the magnificent lavishness of their table. He never took it all for granted. He was still grateful to the Rennetts, and never took advantage of their absence to cut down his unstinting labour on their behalf. He had totally forgotten or buried all memories of Maureen's death and the murder of Lord Rennett, and Siobain kept him shielded from these realities. He had no conception of the place his son lived in now.

Conor sat and listened as they talked of Slievelea, and the seasons unfolding there became visible to him through their speech. They chatted of tree-pruning and leaf-clearing, of the mare's foaling, and the poaching never lessening, the mountainy men being the scourge of their life; Old George dying peacefully in his sleep, a smile on his face; and his heart would swell with the longing that seized him to be back in that sweet natural world. Yet, even as he yearned, he steeled himself against the softness towards them, as he knew it could never be. That dark murder in the tenement house and a sexless cold marriage stood between him and the heedless boy he had once been. Readmittance to that Eden would find him ill at ease there as everywhere, for he was not at peace with himself.

Siobain knew that Conor never really recovered from the shock of exile from Slievelea. The warmth and closeness of their life together had ill prepared him for the cut and thrust of tenement life in Dublin. She had some small idea of what it must be like for him in Foley Place, and she grieved for her son. Although the Rennetts lived in London, Miss Deirdre married to Lord Anthony Tandy-Cullaine with a child of her own now, it never even crossed Siobain's mind to have Conor at Slievelea. He had been asked to leave and that meant he could not return no matter if it were never found out. Siobain and Michael were simply too honest and honourable to break their word to the Rennetts. She watched Conor change, helplessly seeing all the joy squeezed out of him, knowing there was nothing she could do.

So through thick and thin, fair days and foul, Conor went monthly to the Rileys and sat down to tea with his mam and da and Danny in the pretty living room of the thatched cottage that leaned against the forge as warm and cosy as two brown hens.

Then Michael, now in his seventies, became ill. Siobain had written to Lady Tandy-Cullaine to tell her of Michael's sickness and to warn her that he was now totally curtailed in his work. She was very worried, she said, for she could not arrange the work force needed to keep Slievelea in good and sound condition, as over the years Michael had dealt with that. She knew that the agents that Miss Deirdre had sent to Slievelea, once every year, had been satisfied with his work, but Siobain fretted that should the estate deteriorate poor Michael might be blamed. Oh, not by Miss Deirdre, she felt confident of that, but the agents could take exception. So she was hoping Miss Deirdre could see her way to pay Slievelea a visit, and to tell the truth she longed for the reassurance of her presence in the hour of her terrible sorrow. Deirdre's reply was quick and generous. She would come at once.

Siobain sent for Conor, knowing that the seriousness of Michael's condition warranted breaking the promise. Things were extreme, she said, or she would not have asked for him there. So Conor came to the gatehouse, seeing Slievelea for the first time in thirty years. Michael could not move and lay in the bed where he and Siobain had found such joy together. He lay there fighting for every breath. Conor sat in the old familiar room, listening to the clock ticking and feeling the slow peace of the place enter his soul. The ghosts of yesteryear slipped in and out of his mind and once or twice he thought he heard Miss Deirdre laugh.

Slievelea was closed, its windows shuttered, its elegant furniture covered in dustsheets. Everything had been scrupulously cared for by Siobain over the years, the dusting, the polishing, the cleaning, but the human life necessary to a house to give it warmth was missing. The house was soulless.

Conor's heart went out to his mother, white-haired now, her soft skin finely lined, her eyes filled with anxiety. She could not contemplate life without Michael. She had loved him in fulfilled contentment since she was twenty. What was there for her without him now?

He hardly recognized his father. He seemed suddenly to have collapsed as totally as if his mainspring had burst. The flesh had melted from his body, the muscles seemed to have dissolved. He was all bones and pallid skin stretched taut. His eyes followed Siobain everywhere, brimming over with the great love he bore her. Their attitude to each other made Conor wince.

There was no name for Michael's illness, at least not specifically. Old age and all its accessories had been waiting to claim him for a long time, and it did so now viciously. It was as if everything crumpled, gave out, and packed up at the same time. He had arthritis, bronchitis and a very tired old heart. He wandered a lot in his mind and talked incessantly in his wanderings about Maureen and a barn dance. His mam had told Conor it was another name he had for her and Conor left it at that. He did not really care.

If Conor was shocked at his father's decline, Siobain was dismayed at her son. She had watched him over the years change from the beautiful young boy that Miss Deirdre had loved so much into a bitter, surly man, humourless, monosyllabic and angry. She knew that Foley Place had been a shock to him. To move from rural peace and beauty to a filthy slum would upset and confuse anyone, but that did not account wholly for his disagreeable temperament, so different from the happy contented child she had reared. The warmth Mrs Riley spread over their teas in the blacksmith's house had disguised, somewhat, the full change in Conor, or, at least, it had not been so apparent there as it was here in the home of his youth. She could only blame 'that woman', as she called his wife. She often thought and pondered over the mystery, but now there was no

145

time. Her darling man was dying and she was more frightened than she had ever been in her life before.

Conor spent a week at the gatehouse while Michael wheezed and gasped for breath and wandered in his mind, until Siobain admitted to herself that she wished Conor would go. She was horrified at her feelings, appalled that she could think so disloyally of her own kith and kin, and wondered with dismay at her lack of maternal love for this one and only son, but his perpetual ill humour and the gloom he cast over all their activities were getting on her nerves.

So when Lady Tandy-Cullaine wrote to say she was coming home, Siobain was very relieved. Conor would have to leave, and she could once more be at peace with Michael.

In the event, Deirdre arrived in Slievelea much sooner than planned. Anthony had to visit his mother unexpectedly in Bath, and Deirdre seized on the opportunity to set out at once for Ireland.

As her carriage bowled along the golden Wicklow roads, memories flooded back, melancholy as the season itself. Autumn cast a golden glow over the land. The leaves had begun their slow separation of leaf from tree and evidence of a bounteous harvest greeted her on every side. The sun was a huge orange disc hanging low over the mountains. The apple trees dropped crimson fruit on the orchard floor and the lanes were heavy with ripe, coal-black berries. Haystacks stood in dreaming fields, burnt sienna in the afternoon light. Thirty years. It was a very long time.

Deirdre sighed for a lost happy past, when responsibilities were few, and day folded over day full of careless pleasure. She was a beautiful woman still, though age had marked her, and life had written its story on her face. In truth, it showed more than she realized. The years of submitting to Anthony's perfunctory lovemaking were there, the fact that her ardent nature was unfulfilled, that gaiety had dried up and become irony, that cynicism lurked behind every response to the beautiful and unexpected.

Her life in Park Lane seemed perfect on the surface. Visitors and friends envied her her way with servants, her perfect management, her housewifery. The parties she and Anthony gave were always a success. While they greeted their guests she could see people envying her her beauty, the stylishness of her gown and the handsomeness of her charming husband. They could not know of her dread of the last guest leaving and his eventual onslaught on her body, an invasion that never, for her, became easier. She could not understand her revulsion as he thrust himself into her dry, tight, unwelcoming body and the awful yearning ache that engulfed her after he had satisfied himself and fallen asleep.

Eventually Edward had been born and for the first time since her kiss at the lakeside in Slievelea and the few moments she had touched or merely looked at Conor all those years ago, she discovered the delights of sensuality. The birth of her son had been the most satisfying experience of her life. Her healthy animal body, made for lovemaking, rejoiced in the pain, the pushing, punishing effort, the sheer sweaty drive of childbirth, and afterwards she could not be prevented from breastfeeding Edward for far longer than necessary, such was the pleasure she derived from it. She felt the long slow darts of sensation slide down her loins as his rosy mouth sucked at her breast and she knew somehow there were pleasures she was missing. She could have taken a lover but her father's teaching ran deep and she was a naturally honourable woman, incapable of living in peace with intrigue and deception. Besides, she blamed herself entirely for the whole thing. She knew she had not loved Anthony when she married him, and had not grown to love him as her father and mother seemed to think she would. Perhaps, she told herself, it was different for men. She found Anthony shallow, stupid and mundane. He was incapable of understanding her bright, witty, mercurial temperament. She never let him know how she felt about him and this in itself put a strain on her. He lived his life believing his wife loved and admired him above all men, and he respected her for her modesty and reticence in bed.

She never let him know either that not a day went by that she did not think of Conor Casey, remembering the way his eyes shone blue as the sky, the way his black hair curled and the back of his strong neck was brown from the sun. The smell of him, the taste of him she never forgot. She often thought of the first time she had seen him as a man — her young childhood companion changed for ever into the only person in the world who could make her heart beat so very hard, and the shock of awareness that had shot through her in that moment. It seemed

147

to her now that the waltz that night summed up her whole life: dancing in Anthony's arms and gazing over his shoulder at an unaware Conor. That strain too showed on her face, giving her an air of severity. She frowned a lot these days.

But she adored her son, could find no fault with him, was the over-indulgent mamma to a ridiculous degree. The result was that Edward was a plump, spoilt fellow, who took himself very seriously, and tended to be a little pompous. He was with his father in Bath, and his fond mamma sighed as she thought of him, making up her mind for the millionth time that he really must be married soon. And as on every other occasion that the thought had entered her head, her heart said, but not yet, not yet. Not just yet.

When the carriage reached the gatehouse, the coachman rang the bell and she was surprised that the gates were not immediately opened. She instructed the coachman to ring again. Only when the gates opened and the carriage entered did she realize that Siobain had opened them. She stopped the carriage, jumped out and ran over to the white-haired woman standing there weeping. They stared at each other, then fell into each other's arms.

'Oh Siobain, dear, dear Siobain. How I missed you.'

She gently drew back and took her maid's face between her gloved hands. Siobain's cheeks were wet with tears and the two embraced again, holding on to each other for dear life. The great hard lump in Deirdre's chest melted and a storm of sobs shook her body as she clung to her dearest friend and servant. All the golden days of the past came surging back and they stood there together, weeping, as the leaves fell and the sun set behind the mountains.

'Oh Siobain, we must talk. I miss you so. I had forgotten how much. No, dear Siobain, that is quite untrue, I had not forgotten. I simply could not bear to dwell on it too much or I should have lost my reason. Oh dear, dear friend, how good it is to see you. But how is Michael?'

'He is ill, Miss Deirdre, very ill. You see he's, he's ...' A sob choked her voice; she could not bring herself to say that he was dying. Deirdre held her close again, breathing the comforting clean smell of starch and lavender and the faint aroma of carbolic she had known as a girl, when Siobain had listened to her grievances and gently guided her and loved her. Her father was not the only one who influenced Deirdre Rennett. Now she realized the roles were reversed, and her maid needed to be comforted, helped, and she made up her mind that they would not be separated again. Deirdre wiped the tears from her maid's face and Siobain added anxiously, 'Conor is here. I had to send for him. I wouldn't have done it if it wasn't that his father was so ill. He's never set foot in the place since, since ... as you asked. I give you my word.'

'Oh hush, dear Siobain, all that doesn't matter now. Of course he had to come. But where is he? I want to see him.'

'He's gone for a walk, down by the lake, Miss Deirdre. But come in, do, and I'll wet the tea, then you can sit a moment while I prepare your room for you, and heat the bed, for we weren't expecting you until next week, as you told us. You must be wore out from your journey.'

'Yes, Siobain. You go in and get me some tea. I'm parched and would love it. I'll follow Conor down to the lake. I want to talk to him a moment.'

Conor was by the lake when he saw her coming towards him through the woods. He caught his breath and, for a moment, thought he would faint. The shimmering twilight played tricks, and she looked the same Deirdre she had looked thirty years ago. They stared at each other across time, until moving towards each other they saw, sadly, the passing years on each other's faces. Deirdre was still very beautiful and her movements were youthful, but she had become a trifle severe, he thought, and autocratic. There was a firmness of mouth and jaw that revealed strength of character and the habit of command. It intimidated him.

Now she said, 'Conor. I'm glad to see you.'

He nodded, unable yet to say anything.

'Is the boat still there, Conor?' she asked.

He nodded again.

'Row me over to the gazebo. I wish to speak with you awhile.'

'It will be dark soon, Miss Deirdre. We must be careful.'

She laughed. 'Still the same Conor. Being cautious. "Better not, Miss Deirdre, take care, Miss Deirdre." Well, tonight we'll take a risk. Besides, there is a moon.'

Conor obediently untied the boat and gave her his hand. She jumped softly as a cat into the boat beside him, and he rowed them across the silvered water towards the gazebo, a ghostly

149

temple in the hazy air. The prow of the boat cleft the waters of the lake with the strength of Conor's pull on the oars, sending trails of crystal droplets over the side, splashing Deirdre's crimson cloak. But she did not notice. She felt flooded with memories and was amazed at the intensity of her feelings. She had been away from Slievelea so long and had played the part of the calm, self-contained wife and mother in Park Lane to such perfection that she had quite forgotten how emotional she could feel. The soft magic of the Irish twilight on this familiar lake, the man rowing her across it, the questions she knew she must ask him, the memory of her childhood here, the face of the tall, cloaked stranger she would never forget, and the last terrible night when she held her father as he died, all crowded together to heighten her melancholy.

When they reached the island she went up the few steps to the gazebo, now silver in the moonlight, and, taking out a handkerchief, she laid it on the stone bench and sat on it. Conor tied up the boat and went and stood beside her. They watched two white swans cross the jade waters like waxen creatures in a fairy tale. The water lapped against the pebbles at their feet and sucked them as the waves fell back, and the moon, full and platinum, draped her silver light over everything in sight. Deirdre sighed.

'I had forgotten how magical Slievelea is, Conor. One can believe in enchantment here. Perhaps that is what you once did to me, Conor. Do you remember?'

He shook his head. 'No, miss,' he said, and she searched his face for the boy she had once loved. Sadly, she realized he had vanished without a trace. She felt a moment's bitter regret for all the wasted years during which she had fought his memory like a mortal enemy. She had prayed that her obsession would be removed and no one had answered her prayer. She had imitated love for her husband, Anthony, because she had loved this man in her heart. What had she loved but the memory of her own youth? A passion not reciprocated, a love felt by her alone, which if she had stayed here, if she had not run away and exiled herself from the home she loved, would have died a natural death and she would have been free. Perhaps that was why her prayer had not been answered. She had not met the challenge. She had run away.

'Oh, the pity of it all,' she said.

'What, miss?'

She pushed the thoughts away, cleared her head and asked him, 'Do you remember the pledge I asked of you, Conor? That day in the library?'

'Yes, miss.'

'Is it done?'

'Yes, miss. By me own hand.'

'Good. That's good.'

She wondered on this very melancholy evening why the news gave her no joy. She felt no elation, she simply felt an overwhelming sadness.

'We will go back now, Conor.'

'Don't you want me to tell you about it, miss?'

She must want to know. She had to ask him about it. Perhaps that way, he thought, he could divest himself of some of the guilt.

'No, Conor. I don't wish to talk about it.'

Her hair was silver under the moon, but her eyes smiled up at him, suddenly very young again.

'Did you know how I loved you, Conor? Did you ever realize? No, I suppose not. Well, Conor, I would have followed you to the gates of hell. I would have lost my immortal soul for you.' She looked at him quizzically and he stared back aghast.

'Oh Conor, you never guessed!' She shook her head in disbelief at her own folly. 'Conor, you weren't worth a minute of my time, were you? No, no, I don't mean to hurt you. Dear, darling Papa was so right. What did he say to me? Oh, I remember. Never imagine other people feel the way you think they do.' She laughed again but he saw there were tears on her cheeks.

'Come on, Conor, take me back. I must see your father, see what I can do now to help. Your poor mother needs us now, Conor. She needs us very badly.'

151

Chapter

24

CONOR could not grasp the full impact of Deirdre's confession to him. He did not want to have to think about it at all. His one desire was to leave Slievelea and get back to Dublin. Slievelea had let him down; the home of his childhood had not brought the expected peace of mind and he had been horribly disillusioned. There was no escape. Despite not truly understanding Deirdre, her words and the evening's events had filled him with a storm he had no control over. He knew he could not face his mother and father feeling as he did, no matter how much his mam needed him.

He walked down the Wicklow Road, kicking the leaves, at odds with himself and the whole world. He passed Malachy Riley's forge. The interior looked like the pit of hell, the great fire burning in the dark, sparks flying, and the two male figures hammering and bellowing the fire, silhouetted against the dark orange glow. One was Danny, and Conor felt his chest squeeze with pain for the old days and a lost companion. He could hear Malachy talking and joking, his deep laughter blending with the ring of the hammer on the anvil, and though he could not see Danny's face he could sense the calm content that radiated from the man's every movement. Then Danny turned, and for a moment his face was visible in the ochre light. There were deep lines running from his nostrils to his mouth, lines so etched that even with his face in repose they were visible. There were laugh lines around his eyes, white against the tan of his skin. His eyes were peaceful, humour lurking in their depths. He had walked to the arched entrance of the forge, and there he stretched his arms above his head, pushing outward as if against something,

152

and yawned widely. He was very near Conor, who drew back into the shadows on the road, under the shelter of the trees. Danny shook himself like an animal, peered into the roadway, then turned and went into the forge and back to his work.

Conor walked on in a tumult of frustration. It seemed to him his whole life was a sham, a bitter, barren, lonely twisted existence. Miss Deirdre had said tonight that she would have gone to the gates of hell with him. Well, he had gone to hell itself for her, if only she knew! But she had not heard, she did not listen. His head was full of questions he could not answer. Always the women, he thought, they all seemed to know something he did not; they were all in on a secret from which he was excluded. His mam smiling at his da, her eyes overbrimming with love, the way her fingers seemed reluctant to leave off contact with some part of Michael for even a second if she could help it. Miss Deirdre smiling secretly, her woman's smile, assuming he understood what she was saying, and it all Greek to him! Ma Kerrigan, ould and decrepit as she was, gave him the look too out of her prune-like eyes, sneering at him, at his manhood — or lack of it. And Aideen, his beloved wife! Sometimes he thought he hated her and it was the strongest emotion he had ever felt. Church every day, prayers, prayers, prayers and her lips pursed up as if she had bitten into a lemon. The screams of her if he laid a finger on her, and the frightening foam on her lips, the body jerking and out of control and Ma Kerrigan marching into the room without a by-your-leave and berating him, threatening him, holding Aideen in her fat arms like an old toad, her eyes dripping contempt as she looked at him, saying 'Animal! Animal!' as she tenderly bathed her daughter's face.

Conor let out an exasperated high-pitched snort and scuffed the leaves viciously as he walked along the road. The only female who, he thought, seemed nice and natural with him, who smiled at him as if he were of some importance, some value, was Sinead Devlin, Dermot Devlin's youngest daughter. She seemed to Conor like a ray of sunshine in a very grey world. But he felt uncomfortable when he thought of her and he didn't know why.

A cart stopped and the driver offered him a lift which he moodily accepted. The occupants were a merry band returning from the harvesting, passing the jug of porter round while singing bawdy songs. They soon regretted their generosity when he refused to join in their laughter and song, maintaining a taciturn silence which had the disastrous effect of reducing the air of conviviality that had reigned in the cart and dissipating the jollity. They were glad to be shot of him at the city limits as they turned into a welcoming shebeen and he trudged on home.

When he reached Foley Place in the early hours of the morning it was very dark and the contrast with Slievelea hit Conor as never before. A week in Slievelea had accustomed his senses to the beauty and aroma of the country. Now the sour, animal smell of human sweat and rotten vegetables, of spilled beer and stale smoke, the inimitable smell of poverty pulverized him as he entered the hall. He stood for a moment, his eyes adjusting to the darkness. A shaft of moonlight crept through the window at the top of the stairs and little motes of dust slid gently down the silver beam.

He realized someone was sitting on the stairs just out of the moonlight, and he thought suddenly that he was back at the moment of his arrival in this house, that somehow he had been transported back in time to his first meeting with Aideen. Then he realized that the girl sitting there in that same position was Sinead. He felt his throat dry up and his knees became weak.

'Is that you, Mister Casey?' He heard the sibilant whisper. She slid directly into the beam. The light caught her hair and it looked as silver as Deirdre's had done on the lake. He stood frozen to the spot, fascinated, mesmerized.

He saw she was smiling, biting her lower lip between her little white teeth. Like babies' teeth they were, he thought, and he gazed at her as she rubbed her fingers up and down her shin bone, her cotton skirt riding up with every movement and down again over her knees, up and down. It seemed to Conor as if all his pent-up rage against his wife, all his frustration, broke its bounds and something in him exploded. The girl's smiling expectant eyes had a feverish excited quality, the biting teeth, the rhythmic movement of her hand caused a dam to burst in him. He felt his body become strong for her and he knew there was no stopping him now.

'Oh God help me,' he cried and he fell on her in the shaft of moonlight on the stairs, ripping open his trousers, pushing up her skirt, taking her by force and in anger and loathing. Very quickly he reached his first climax inside a woman with a roar of

154

delirious excitement. It was the only sound that had broken the stillness of the hall. He did not see Aideen leaning over the banisters, hand to mouth; he did not see her withdraw as he lay for a moment spent in a cocoon of bodily peace, before he jumped up, pulling his trousers together, and fled to the second floor. He did not see Sinead Devlin carefully rearrange her tousled clothing and shrug. 'Jasus, he coulda' waited for me to get my bit of pleasure. Like a bloody bull him. Still ...' and smiling slowly she climbed to the Devlin flat above.

Aideen was in bed when he entered the room. He threw himself without undressing onto the mattress he had been given to sleep on when he married, a narrow oblong under the window. He slept dreamlessly until late next morning and, when he awoke, he felt young and virile and alive. He felt peaceful and potent and ashamed. He did not know what to do with himself.

Later that day Dermot brought him a message that Michael had died in the night and would he go to Slievelea as soon as he could. He felt relief at the news; he could postpone facing his confused emotions and the events of the previous night in this more immediate crisis, but he felt little sense of loss. For so long now he had resented his father, been jealous of his obvious physical delight in his mother compared to his own sterile relationship with Aideen, that it was not in his heart to grieve as he ought. And his father had been old, and ill, and he had had little interest in Conor's life for many years now. Conor was glad to go, get out of Foley Place, glad to set off for the country.

His mother was stunned with grief, cold and remote. Miss Deirdre seemed the only one able to reach her.

On a glorious golden autumn day Michael was buried. Half of Foley Place came to the funeral, greedy for a free jar, and happy in the knowledge that there would be food enough and more and, who knows, maybe some choice of illicit pickings to be had. Dermot Devlin, old and infirm, feeble and drink-sodden, wept copiously. Siobain stood implacable as stone, the depth of sorrow and loss in her eyes unfathomable. Her face, looking like a tragic mask, had lost its mobility, was frozen. She gave no heed to Aideen, about whom she had been so curious for so many years; but Deirdre Tandy-Cullaine gave free range to her interest. She saw a tall, cold woman with a handsome, spiritual face and marvelled at the oddness of the pair. She was also intensely interested in Dermot Devlin's youngest daughter, who

155

was there with her mam and her sisters and their bairns. She was pretty in a fluffy, baby-duckling way, and wanton by the looks of it; and she aroused Lady Tandy-Cullaine's curiosity by the sly amorous glances she cast in Conor's direction, seemingly totally unaware of the solemnity of the occasion. In fact, when the first sod of earth fell with a dull thud on Michael's coffin and Deirdre felt a shudder tear through Siobain, who would have fallen to the ground if she had not held the widow tightly around the shoulders, the saucy young lady was smiling languidly at Conor, who, however, paid her no attention at all.

After the funeral, they repaired to the gatehouse to eat ham and pickles, bread and currant cake, and to drink porter and tea. Truly a feast. Deirdre told Conor that she would be taking Siobain to England with her.

'She cannot stay here alone,' she said. 'I doubt if she would be happy with you and your wife, Conor. What do you think?' She glanced at that lady, who was clearly uncomfortable in her surroundings, unlike the Devlins, who made themselves quite at home, and Ma Kerrigan, who went for a little walk. Conor said, 'She'd hate it, Miss Deirdre. Anyhow, there's no room.'

'And she would break her heart alone here. I'll keep her busy in Park Lane. I think it's the best thing for her, Conor, don't you?'

He agreed, and she assured him kindly, 'I'll look after her, never fear.'

Her heart stopped a moment as she looked at Conor. He was different somehow this morning, she thought, he seemed more like the boy she had loved; there was a curious defenceless look in his eyes. Then she shrugged and her common sense flooded back and she patted his hand with her gloved fingers.

'I will take good care of your mother, Conor, rest assured. I'm going to keep Slievelea closed for the time being. It's funny. I came here hoping to open it up, perhaps live here again. Now I've lost heart, and your mother cannot remain; it wouldn't suit. We'll leave Slievelea until my son marries and wishes to live here, and then we'll see what's to do.'

Conor had had a wild hope that he might be able to come back here and live with his mother, perhaps do the work his father had done, but his hopes were dashed by this speech.

They went soon after. Ma Kerrigan had found the house barred and shuttered against her and empty of pickings, but she

156

had managed to get to Lady Tandy-Cullaine's room and steal some trinkets from that lady's escritoire. She was wise enough not to take anything obvious; she just took a few souvenirs, to assuage her grief, she said to herself.

Deirdre took Siobain to London the next day, determined to care for her and keep her occupied so that she would not have time to be overwhelmed by the loss of Michael.

Back in Foley Place Conor sank into his usual depressed gloom. The burdens of guilt and resentment were doubled now. And he could not bear to be in the presence of Sinead. He avoided her like the plague, scuttling past her when they met on the stairs. That young lady was disgusted with his lack of interest, philosophical about his rejection of her, and was confined to the Devlin apartment a few days later when Aideen Casey had a word with her mother. Conor also stayed more and more in his room, terrified of what he had done. This was the second time in his life that he had committed an unplanned crime, impulsively, instinctively, and he was petrified at his potential.

Dermot Devlin's news that Sinead was pregnant by Conor came as no real shock to anyone, but, as was the custom in Foley Place, once the facts were established the subject was never discussed. No one talked about it, not Ma Kerrigan, Conor or Aideen, and certainly not the Devlins.

Sinead died in childbirth, and Dermot Devlin died soon after. A slow decrescendo seemed to fall over Number 13 Foley Place. No one missed Sinead; her death slipped into the darkness of time as so many deaths in the slums did. Life was very cheap. Dermot was remembered. All the energy had gone out of him after Michael's funeral and he ended his days mouldy drunk, falling down the stairs at Number 13. His youngest son was the only Devlin who stayed, the others fleeing to the richer potential of Liverpool or America.

Little Dan was handed over to Conor on the day of his birth and his mother's death, and Conor looked at the small baby without interest. Aideen, too, was indifferent to the baby. In fact, she seemed almost repelled by it. It was a wonder, Ma Kerrigan said, that the poor little boy survived at all. But he did. From his first moments on, he clung tenaciously to life. He managed to survive the indifference of his parents, the crowded tenement, the lack of love in his home, the scarcity of nourishing food, the dirt, the unhealthy atmosphere and the contagious illnesses, and to struggle to the very top of the world to become Big Dan Casey, a man to be reckoned with.

Chapter

25

THE house in Park Lane was an attractive family dwelling. It over-looked Hyde Park and it was delightful to watch life pass by from the wide bay windows. Coaches and horses trotted by; gentlemen and ladies in the pink of fashion took a turn beneath the chestnut trees; soldiers in their gaudy uniforms, scarlet and black, passed through on their way to Buckingham Palace; children bowled hoops and called to their uniformed nannies; and, on Sundays, a brass band could be heard joyfully playing in the distance. It was a very far cry, in Deirdre's estimation, from Slievelea. It was safe here, the house seemed to emanate security, and it was comfortable and easy to run.

Deirdre had sent orders ahead for a small but prettily arranged room annexed to her own dressing room on the third floor to be prepared for Siobain. The other servants slept on the top floor, but Deirdre would assuage any ruffled feelings by announcing that Siobain had been her nanny and she needed her close. This arrangement would give Siobain a deal more comfort than was afforded the rest of the staff. The room had been Edward's nursery as a child, and, before that, the room Lady Rennett had closeted herself in after her husband's death and her departure from Slievelea. Unable to let go of her grief, to shout, to scream, to cry out against the horror of Lord Rennett's murder, she had held it all inside her till it festered in her mind and the brain recoiled and fragmented into thousands of pieces, and Lady Rennett shot herself. She had left no ghosts. No phantoms haunted that neat little room, Deirdre thought, as they would have done in Slievelea. For that she was grateful. Oh yes, in Slievelea her mother's shade would wander restlessly

159

through her beloved rose garden as assuredly as the ghost of her husband must haunt the lake there.

Edward was at the house to greet them. He was a plump, roly-poly person with an anxious face. He seemed to bear only the most fleeting resemblance to his fond mamma, but looked uncommonly like his papa, as far as Siobain could recall. The carriage had barely stopped when the front door burst open and Edward flung himself upon his mother, more in the manner of a six-year-old than a mature man. As Deirdre hugged him she noticed over his shoulder a pretty, fair young woman standing in the doorway, who seemed to be in a state of acute anxiety. She was about to ask casually who this stranger was when her son blurted out, there on the pavement, with Siobain half in and half out of the carriage, the butler Bates at the door, the footman and the coachman standing in the street, 'Mamma, meet my wife, Letticia. Letticia, this is my dearest Mamma.'

Deirdre stopped, stunned. Siobain wished she had never left Ireland and Bates looked pained and apologetic as he quietly but quickly said, 'Master Edward, please! There is some tea ready for you, m'Lady, in the withdrawing room. You must be tired after your journey. Please, Master Edward, let us go inside.'

'Oh yes, of course. Oh, Mamma, I'm so excessively happy. You cannot imagine! Letticia is an angel. You two will get along famously, I'll be bound.' Edward did not sound as certain as his words indicated.

'Bates is right, dear boy, please let us go in.' Deirdre could not keep the irritation out of her voice.

This staggering news took the edge off Siobain's arrival and helped her to slip into the household unobtrusively. The servants wanted to tell her all about the events leading up to her arrival and were delighted to have an audience. Nothing quite so dramatic had happened in Park Lane since Lady Rennett had shot herself, they said.

They explained Master Edward's character to her at length, how immature he was, how spoiled, but, they said, he was really a nice fellow who had never grown up.

Lady Tandy-Cullaine, they confided, doted on him and that had been the whole trouble. She was unable to resist his smallest request. She indulged him in everything, but she had constantly interfered with any love affairs that had seemed to become serious. As Edward was a great lover of women and was easily led by them into all sorts of follies, she had encouraged him to take a mistress, hand-picked by herself, one Dolly Sears, a pretty fluffy blonde who, they said, looked uncommonly like his brand new wife.

Miss Letticia Handsford-Smythe and he had eloped to Gretna Green and married there even though there was really no necessity, Bates said. Lady Tandy-Cullaine was in Ireland and Lord Anthony and the dowager lady, his mother, in Bath, and in any event Master Edward was of age!

Siobain sat in the comfortable kitchen which ran the whole length of the house in the basement, sipping a refreshing cup of tea. She looked at the polished copper cooking utensils over the range, winking in the lamplight, and smelt the sweet, warm smell of fresh-baked pastry and apples. A simmering stockpot was on the stove and she heard the soothing tick-tocking of the grandfather clock and the gently complaining voices of the staff, all of whom were behaving so kindly to her.

Mrs Bundy, the cook, a motherly soul, was particularly sensitive to Siobain's bewilderment and shock at the change of environment and told her so.

'I remember when I left Wales. A little town I came from, you wouldn't see it on the map, so small, isn't it, and me coming to this big city. Oh Lord, how I was at sea. For days I didn't know whether I was coming or going. Now you drink your tea and take off your boots. John will put your things in your room, so this evening you can rest. My Lady's nanny, she said you were, God save us. And what was she like and you'll tell us.'

Bates came down the steps to the kitchen. 'All hell's broken loose up there,' he said. 'Lady Deirdre's in one of her states.'

Siobain suddenly felt extremely tired and suppressed an overwhelming urge to burst into tears.

Upstairs the family were gathered in the withdrawing room. It was a pretty room overlooking Hyde Park. The trees outside reflected the leaf green in the Aubusson carpet. There were Chippendale chairs, covered in pale grey brocade with a mossy design tinged with pink. There were paintings by Watteau and Fragonard on the walls and a magnificent ceiling and fireplace by Adam.

Deirdre sat on one of the upright chairs and her son and his

161

new wife sat facing her. Letticia's large green eyes stared fearfully into Deirdre's and she batted her eyelashes nervously, the corners of her mouth quivering pitifully. Her head was a halo of white-gold ringlets which looked silky-soft and baby-fine. Edward had his arm protectively around her and they both jumped nervously when Deirdre spoke, which irritated the latter excessively.

She was saying, 'What is this bizarre story? Gretna Green? I have never heard such foolishness. Edward, have you lost your reason? What have you got in your head for brains? I shudder to think! No member of my family has ever behaved in this way. Nor your father's family, Edward. One wonders about yours, miss.'

'Oh, her family have disowned her, Mamma. Quite cut her off!' Edward said wildly, heaping coals on his own head.

'How dare they! The trumped-up, second-rate Handford-Smythes cut off their daughter for marrying a Tandy-Cullaine, a Rennett! Letticia — what an excessively silly name, to be sure. Good God, Letticia, have your family taken leave of their senses?'

'I'm not sorry, Mamma. I love Letticia and I've never been so happy in my life.'

'*You're* not sorry. *You've* never been so happy. What on earth has it got to do with you?'

Deirdre's voice rose angrily, causing Letticia's eyelashes to flutter like bees' wings out of control and large tears to veil her eyes. She cried, 'Oh please stop!'

She had a lisp, Deirdre noted with satisfaction. A silly little empty-headed female with a lisp, she thought. Oh why hadn't Edward asked her advice? It was too vexing!

'Please stop!' The silly little chit was speaking to *her*. 'I love Edward and he loves me and the only reason we went to Gretna Green ...'

'Gretna Green at *your* age,' Deirdre interrupted. 'I could understand it for star-crossed lovers, for Romeo and Juliet, but for a ...'

'We are star-crossed lovers, don't you see?' Letticia's voice rose to a wail. 'We *couldn't* tell you. We *knew* you'd say no. We were afraid to.' The tears burst and a storm of crying shook the small, fragile body of the new member of the family.

'Stuff and nonsense,' Deirdre said. She was taken aback at

162

this statement. Afraid, were they? She had never thought any-one in the world afraid of her, and she was not too happy at the idea that these two were to the extent that they had planned such an important event behind her back. She was even more surprised by her son's reaction to his wife's tears. He rose like a lioness defending her young and she saw him through new eyes.

'Yes, Mamma, we were afraid to ask, afraid you would sep-arate us. And see what you've done now? You've made poor darling Letticia cry. Oh Mamma, how unkind of you!' Edward was now nearly in tears himself.

Deirdre was relieved when Bates rapped on the door and interrupted to ask at what time they wanted to dine. Deirdre told him, making up her mind to confide the whole thing to Siobain. She badly wanted to talk about it to clarify her feelings to herself.

'I feel a rest would be beneficial to us all. We will talk about all this nonsense later.'

She rose as Letticia squealed, 'Nonsense!'

They all left the withdrawing room and retired, Edward to pacify and console his weeping bride in their room and Deirdre to lie on her chaise longue talking to Siobain without inter-ruption until the whole situation became clear to her. Siobain's eyes were closing as she listened to her mistress, but it didn't matter. Deirdre's monologue needed no comment, no outside opinion. She said at last to Siobain, 'I'm a selfish woman, Siobain, and I've brought it all on my own head. I've cosseted that boy. I don't love him at all as deeply as I thought. I *needed* him, as a pet, someone I could indulge, grant wishes to pamper and play with. Real love demands discipline. Oh Siobain, I'm such a fool! I seem to spend my life finding out too late that I was wrong, wasting so much time. If only Papa had lived. Edward has married this silly little miss because of me. He will be happy with her, no doubt, but me? How can I endure such a daughter-in-law?'

She looked at Siobain for the first time and saw the fatigue on her maid's face. She realized suddenly the other's weariness, from the death of her beloved husband, the long journey to a foreign land, and the arrival here, so full of drama and hysterics in a milieu foreign to her — the people, except for herself, strangers. She felt a pang of shame at her selfishness and thoughtlessness.

'Come along, Siobain,' she said softly, and she put her arm round the older woman and guided her into her room. She gently helped her exhausted servant to undress, and tucked her up in bed, remembering with a wry smile how in this room she had done the same thing first for her poor mother and then her son when he was a child. Well, the child had grown up and belonged to someone else now. She looked at Siobain lying fast asleep on the bed. She smiled tenderly as she thought of the many times the maid had put her to bed in those far-off days in Slievelea. She sighed. She kissed Siobain's forehead and tiptoed out of the room, closing the door gently behind her.

Chapter

26

DURING the following years Siobain found herself more and more the person that Deirdre confided in and trusted with her most intimate thoughts and feelings. She talked to Siobain about Conor, of her unrequited love for him. Siobain simply listened and held her peace. Deirdre poured her daily troubles into Siobain's ear, told her of her problems with Edward and Letticia, and of the latter's amazingly ineffectual attempts to become wife and mother. Deirdre, Siobain saw, was competent, artistic and inspired in all she did. She was a casually graceful hostess, quick to anticipate people's needs, with a wonderful ability to pair people suitable to each other and to match her guests to bring out the best in all. This she hid under a calm poise that gave the impression she was not doing a thing. She was a skilled conversationalist, an above-average musician, and ran her house extremely efficiently. She seemed to do it all effortlessly. Poor little Letticia couldn't seem to manage anything. Anthony Tandy-Cullaine bought them a house in Chelsea and Deirdre found them servants, but from the outset, according to Deirdre, things went wrong. Siobain reserved her judgement.

Letticia, Deirdre said, couldn't manage the servants and they took advantage of her. As a hostess she was tentative and fussed too much so that her parties were not a success. She lost her first two babies in childbirth (an experience that frightened her and drove Edward to distraction), and when at last she produced a whole, healthy, living child it was a girl, and she was told she could not have any more children. It really was, in Deirdre's view, a sorry record of failure.

Yet in Siobain's opinion, despite all this, Edward and Letticia were a very happy couple. They referred to each other constantly in company, liked always to be together and presented an air of shared intimacy that only the happiest couples have, that Siobain had shared with Michael, and was certainly absent when Deirdre sat beside her own husband.

Deirdre said that Edward had broken her heart by marrying such a silly female. She was an empty-headed creature, in Deirdre's opinion, and not fit to do up the button on dear Edward's boot. Siobain thought that if his dear mamma had bothered to examine the situation with eyes unclouded by prejudice, or to try even remotely to put her son into perspective, she would have realized it was the best thing that could have happened to him. He adored his flighty little wife exactly because she was so dazzlingly incompetent and a direct contrast to his dearest mamma of whom he was terrified and who threw his nervous system into total confusion every time they met. He found his little wife adorable and absorbing, and except for his gambling at White's, Tattersall's, Boodle's or Crockford's, spent every minute with her, waiting on her hand and foot, jumping to fulfil her every need and anticipating her every want.

Siobain saw a new side to Deirdre that she realized had always been there, but was not apparent at Slievelea. Perhaps, Siobain thought, at Slievelea Deirdre had been too happy to show the hard edge of her nature. During those enchanted years until her father's death, the family had bent to each other, like trees to the wind, with grace and consideration, and no tussle of wills was necessary in that loving atmosphere.

In Park Lane it became evident that Deirdre was at odds with everyone except Siobain, and her main aim in life seemed to be to get her own way. This amazing determination was met with acquiescence. Her husband, his family and her servants and friends all bowed to her will, until Edward married Letticia. For this reason Deirdre, Siobain understood, could never approve of the girl. On the arrival of Livia, their daughter, Deirdre had alienated herself too much to have any say in the little girl's upbringing, and pride refused to allow her to re-think the situation and admit, even for the sake of her relationship with her grand-daughter, that she could have been wrong. She visited the house in Chelsea often, but her visits were not a success;

166

and there was a formality about the proceedings that forbade intimacy.

Anthony Tandy-Cullaine had a heart attack in 1903 and died soon after. Deirdre was sad but in all honesty hardly noticed his absence in her life, so little part had he played there. She felt relieved, too, that the sexual demands were over. There had been a gradual decline but Deirdre had still felt that Anthony had asked too much of her; once, in desperation, feeling exhausted, she had suggested to Anthony that he take a mistress, 'For I am becoming too old for you, my dear.' He had been horrified at the idea, and very embarrassed. 'Nonsense, Dee, you know I've only ever loved you, ever wanted you, as much today as all those years ago when we married,' and Deirdre sighed and wished he wouldn't call her Dee!

Siobain tried hard to enjoy life in London, but to no avail. It was not that she did not like the capital city, she wished that she and Michael could have come years ago, then what fun they would have had. No. It was just that she could not adapt to life without Michael. She carried within her a deep enfeebling grief that could not be assuaged. Yet comparing herself with her mistress, she was heartily glad that she had loved so much to feel so bereft, for Deirdre accepted her husband's death when it came with equanimity. If Deirdre felt daily relief at the peace her body felt in its freedom from Anthony's demands, Siobain's ageing body yearned for Michael's arms with as much fever and passion as it had at eighteen.

So the years ticked slowly by, and gradually Siobain lost her hold on life. She felt sometimes like a shadow. She dreamed of Slievelea constantly. She visualized the thick, raspberry-coloured blossoms bunched together on the sooty branches of the cherry trees, and the scattered rose-and-cream flowers hanging from the gnarled, twisted boughs of the apple trees in the spring; of the carpets of buttercups and daisies under the trees in the bluebell wood in the summer, and the long, dream-like days when the butterflies and bees played among the perfumed roses and the sound of the sea sang a constant harmony in the background. She dreamed of the golden autumn when the whole of Slievelea was carpeted with amber and gold, fiery red and orange leaves that she ploughed through on her way up to the house; and, most of all, her heart yearned for the winter mornings when the whole land was drowned in a mysterious purple mist and the mountains hid their tops in pearl-grey clouds and every leaf on every tree and shrub and bush was studded with diamond drops of moisture trembling in the imperceptible movements of the world.

She dreamed of soothing Irish voices; she hated the sound of the Oi-Oi-Oi of English spoken by Cockneys and she clove to the Welsh voice of Mrs Bundy, finding it more soothing to her ear. She found the reticence of the English irksome and longed for the spontaneity of the Irish who allowed you to laugh and cry immoderately when you felt like it, not realizing that it was not a lack of emotion that caused the reticence but stalwart English discipline. She assumed English restraint like a shield and withdrew further into her own world of memories where Slievelea became Utopia and the past more real than the present.

She watched Livia grow, marvelling at her, but with a curious detachment that had become habitual. Her eyes became bigger in her face and held the far-away look of a dreamer which surprised Deirdre when she eventually noticed it. Siobain had always been so practical, so down-to-earth, so full of life and laughter, that to catch her still as a statue, her eyes far away in some distant place, surprised and irritated her. She wanted to bully her maid into rejoining the human race but Siobain paid no attention. She was always solicitous of Deirdre's needs and, indeed, enjoyed her confidences, listening gravely and keeping her own counsel, but she never felt part of the family she lived with or involved in its affairs as she had at Slievelea. This made her the perfect confidante. All the servants confided in her. She would listen until they had talked themselves into a solution or into accepting a situation, whatever it was. Siobain rarely spoke but she listened so closely and her manner was so sympathetic yet detached that they derived infinite consolation from her presence.

As Siobain looked back, Deirdre lived very much in the present and she was not at all sure she liked it. She saw her youth slip away, her beauty lose its gentle curves and take on a harder, sharper, diamond-like brilliance, and all the time she felt unfulfilled and wasted. She realized as time passed that even her son had never really cared for her, for all her doting; indeed he was intimidated by her and preferred the wishy-washy company of the little dithery creature he had married to her bright wit and

168

stimulating mind. When the spring of her life had gone and the long summer days of her loveliness passed into regretful autumn, Deirdre accepted the inevitability of it with her usual grace and courage, but she did not like it and she wondered what it had all been about. To have loved Conor for one brief summer with all her heart and soul and then to find out he had not even been conscious of it (or if he had been, then it was unimportant enough in his life for him to have long forgotten it), was this to be the sum total of her experience of adult love? Or had she to pay the price of a childhood so filled with love that perhaps she had had more than her fair share? After all, was it not her own fault? Hadn't she chosen to follow this path of her own free will? To settle for a marriage with Anthony Tandy-Cullaine, and to produce a child like Edward? That was not facing the challenge life held out, that was running away?

She thought, as she often did, how differently Siobain had faced fate, how courageously she had gone after life and wrested so much happiness from it. She watched Siobain gently losing her hold on life and sighed, envying her maid her Michael. She thought about how it could be to love and possess a man so much that life was not worth living without him, and was angry with herself at her inability to envisage it at all. Life to her was very important indeed. Survival was essential no matter how beaten or brokenhearted you were. Siobain's acquiescence to her feelings, her giving in to her desire not to live in a world without her love angered and appalled Deirdre.

Yet she clung to Siobain, spending long hours talking with her maid. She told her how lonely she felt despite an active social life. There was no spice in her life, no excitement, she said, and sighed, supposing this to be the normal turn of events when one reached her age, albeit exceedingly tedious. She talked to her about her mother and her mother's madness and those years when Deirdre had cared for her, looking after the poor deranged woman with Anthony's help and support. It had not been easy for him, she realized, a young married man with his bride and the frail madwoman constantly there, but he had never complained, he had looked upon it as his duty. He was that sort of man, Deirdre thought, and dull, dull, dull! She hated herself for feeling thus but was honest enough with herself not to deny it.

One glorious autumn afternoon Siobain sat in her chair in

169

Deirdre's drawing room waiting for her to arrive for afternoon tea. She felt very peaceful sitting quietly, sewing as usual, and musing on the strange occurrence of the previous night.

It had been very windy and the rattling of the window had awakened her. She liked to leave the window open while she slept, and now with the wind so high it was as if a hand were rattling the panes against each other. She got out of bed slowly. She did everything slowly these days, and, slipping into her cosy slippers, a thing she never did without gratitude and a fleeting thought to the past, she wrapped a woollen shawl about her shoulders and went to close the window. She pulled back the curtains and saw Michael. Or thought she saw him. He was sitting in his chair near the fireplace in the gatehouse. It seemed to Siobain as if the dear familiar room were on the other side of the window. Michael looked at her and smiled. He looked much younger than when he had died, younger and tranquil and his eyes had lost the anxiety that had dwelt within their depths since the famine; now they were clearly full of love and peace. Her heart rose within her and she felt flooded with joy. This only lasted a moment then all was darkness and the casement rattled again. Siobain secured it and went back to bed feeling foolishly happy.

She thought about it now in the golden afternoon. She wondered what it meant. She thought about how he had looked. Not as he had been at the barn dance. She smiled as she remembered the fierce jealousy of Maureen and heard again the throbbing ceilidh music and the laughter of the people. Her wild, handsome boy going out into the fields with Maureen! How she had hated her then. She shuddered as she remembered the famine and her meeting with Michael at Slievelea with Dermot Devlin, and how he looked. A walking skeleton. How hungry his eyes were then. Her mind slid over the days of his recovery and dwelt on the wild passion of their meeting and the years of their love. Only the death of Lord Rennett had interfered with their constant joy in each other, and now ... now? She felt a hand on her arm, so light, as light as the brush of a swallow's wings. She looked up and saw him there, dear, beloved Michael. She was not afraid. His jacket needed brushing, she thought, but then didn't it always. She smiled at him and he smiled back and her heart seemed to burst with joy. He said gently, 'Come, my own darling love,' and she nodded.

When Deirdre entered the room for her afternoon tea and chat with Siobain she knew immediately that her maid was dead. Siobain was seated in the blue Genoese chair beside the chaise longue, her back to the door. Her silver head rested on the back of the chair and there was no difference in the scene from the thousand other occasions Deirdre had come into this room to have tea with her, yet she could feel the presence of death, an alien intruder in the sanctuary of her drawing room. She felt overwhelming sadness engulf her and steadied herself against the door. She waited a moment, catching her breath, then went to her maid.

When she saw Siobain's face she was amazed at the joy she saw there. The maid's face was positively radiant, her eyes looking out as if she was greeting someone, and suddenly Deirdre knew. She had seen, or thought she saw, Michael just before she died. Deirdre was filled unexpectedly with an overwhelming rage. She wanted to shake the dead woman, hit her face, slap her. How dared she die? How dared she have a love like Michael, when she, she, Deirdre Rennett Tandy-Cullaine, had always had to do with second best? She tried to control herself. She was shaking all over. After a few seconds the spasm passed and, disgusted with herself, she went to the bedroom and picked up the eau de Cologne from her dressing table. She drenched her handkerchief from the crystal bottle and pressed the wet cambric to her throbbing temples.

Deirdre paid a brief visit to Slievelea and Siobain was laid to rest beside Michael in the family cemetery after a Requiem Mass in the little church. It was a rain-washed day and everything seemed to be weeping. The mist was silver-grey and hung like a veil over the countryside. The leaves slipped from the trees in slow motion and lay on the ground. Deirdre stood in the small graveyard, unheeded tears coursing down her cheeks, filled with a loneliness such as she had never felt before. She looked at the dove-grey headstones and examined the names, spelling them out to herself: Michael Casey; Siobain Casey; Lord Alfred Rennett; Lady Amanda Rennett. And she thought of Anthony too, and the memories flooded back unbidden. She allowed sorrow to flood through her unchecked, and when the storm was over, she straightened her back and left the graveyard.

171

Chapter

27

DEIRDRE hadn't known where to find Conor and couldn't summon the energy to start looking. She felt profoundly guilty about it but a curious lethargy sapped her and she lost her usual efficiency and sank into apathy. Besides, the idea of seeing Conor again was repugnant to her and so she simply gave up and saw Siobain laid to rest by herself. She did not stay in Slievelea. The look of the closed house depressed her and, for the moment, the house itself seemed in mourning for its servants. It seemed a very strange place without Siobain and Michael Casey. She stayed with the Jeffries for the few days she was in Ireland and then, with relief, returned to Park Lane.

But Park Lane missed Siobain too. She had only been with them a relatively short time, yet her quiet, unobtrusive presence left a much bigger gap than anyone could have believed possible. The constant sympathetic ear she willingly gave to all their problems was sorely missed.

Deirdre made up her mind to go away. A change would help to throw off the apathy and the boredom that oppressed her. She thought it time to take up the invitation the de Beauvillande family were constantly issuing and spend some time in the company of the delightful Sophie de Beauvillande, an erudite and amusing woman; and the Paris scene, which she adored, would be bound to lighten her spirits. And after Paris, perhaps Biarritz or Baden-Baden? She felt relieved as soon as she had made up her mind.

She received an ecstatic, exuberant Gallic reply from Sophie. Her friend assured her of every comfort, and excitement, the French capital could offer, 'which unfortunately, my darling,

172

means mainly delights of the mind at our age'. She wrote that she would adore to have her dear friend Deirdre for as long as she chose to stay and hoped to entertain her in the style in which she herself had been entertained so charmingly in Park Lane and, 'Please, please come as soon as you can and try to shake off your ennui here, for I feel so dismayed at the thought of my darling Deirdre being out of sorts.'

Deirdre decided to leave immediately for Paris. First, however, it was necessary to see her son and his wife in Chelsea. She wished there was some way out of it but there was not. So one miserable October day she ordered her carriage to be ready for her at 4 p.m. and set off for Chelsea through the rain-washed streets and muddy ways, feeling as dismal as the day.

Letticia and Edward lived in attractive disorder in their little house overlooking the river. Though Deirdre did not see it, the house was an extremely happy one and the atmosphere infinitely more full of life and laughter than Park Lane. It certainly was untidy and Deirdre loathed chaos, and was worried by it, her fingers itching to impose her will and have the place straightened up and everything put in order. She had once tried to organize this, but in the ensuing pandemonium of maids, Livia's nanny and Letticia fluttering about, all that had happened was that things were moved from one place to another and no real order was achieved. Now she sighed and accepted the untidiness but was uncomfortable in it.

Her arrival threw the small household into minor panic. Deirdre tried to ignore the fact that Alice, the maid, let her wrap slip to the floor, then tied her feet up in it before she retrieved it and took it to the cloakroom. What would happen to her things there she did not dare to imagine; probably thrown in a heap on the chair to become creased beyond belief, or to be used as a cushion by a dog. She hated the King Charles spaniels that were given free rein throughout the house; their over-friendly dispositions led them to excesses of welcoming attacks which played havoc with one's toilet and poise.

Ah well! It was only for a short time, she thought, stepping over a headless doll in the hall. She tried to find a chair free of toys, sewing, bonbons, spaniels or cats. She could not, and so stood by the fireplace, noting with growing irritation that the mantlepiece was dusty and some of the flowers in the vase were decidedly past their prime. She took a deep breath to calm her-

173

self and fixed a smile on her face as the door opened and her son came forward to greet her.

She had always loved handsome men and for the millionth time she wondered what she had done to deserve Edward. His small, plump body was balanced on short, plump legs and miniature feet, and his pudgy good-humoured face could by no stretch of the imagination be called good-looking. He did, however, have an air of jollity and bonhomie about him and he exuded well-being and exuberance, like a small Bacchus, Deirdre thought wryly.

'Dear Mamma, we did not expect you. You must forgive, bit untidy. Still suits us, y'know. Don't worry me. Still, you may find it . . .'

'Oh for heaven's sake, Edward, stop rabbiting on! Can't you string a sentence together yet? I would like a place to sit, however, if you can manage that?'

'Of course, Mamma, how remiss of me. Spot, Mabel, off, off, off, down, down, that's it, now off you go. There, Mamma,' he said triumphantly, brushing his hand over the seat of the chair the dogs had been curled up on and pointing to it victoriously.

'Do sit down, Mamma. It's quite the most comfortable chair.'

'You don't expect me to sit there?' Deirdre looked in astonishment at her son and smoothed the skirt of her pale lilac taffeta while the dogs, resenting their upheaval, yapped frantically at her feet and scrabbled excitedly at the hem of her dress. 'Get them off me. Do you wish to have me naked? Get them down!'

Edward looked bewildered and the dogs began to run wildly round Deirdre in circles so she sat down involuntarily or she would have fallen.

'I don't know how Siobain will remove the dogs' hairs from . . .' then she shuddered for she remembered that Siobain was dead.

Edward, seeing her shiver, pulled a light shawl from under the cat, sending that animal screaming to the door, and before she realized what he was going to do, draped it about her shoulders.

'There, Mamma. Although I would have thought this room was warm enough with,' he pointed to the fire. 'Still, can't have you catching . . . Ah, Letticia, my own! Mamma, see, it's Letticia.'

174

'I have not lost my sight yet, Edward, and will you please take this, this, thing off me?' She pulled the offending shawl off her shoulders and as she did so she smelt a strong whiff of cat and cat fur which made her sneeze.

Edward looked triumphant. 'See, I knew it. Insist you wear ... Filthy weather. Can't have you ill, Mamma.'

Deirdre nearly asked him tartly when he had ever seen her ill but decided against it and offered her cool cheek to her daughter-in-law for a kiss, wondering, as she always did, what on earth had made Edward marry her. True, her finespun hair was like a gossamer halo about her head and her emerald eyes unusual, but she was too thin and characterless ever to please Deirdre.

Letticia called Livia, and the seven-year-old went over to her grandmother gracefully and smiled fearlessly with eyes so similar to her own that Deirdre was always astonished when she saw them. In fact, Livia was a fair copy of the portrait of the ten-year-old Deirdre that hung in Slievelea. Her grandmother had to admit that the child was delightful. She was obedient without being fearful, full of vitality and energy without being forward or ungainly. She was charming and pretty, and Deirdre found it hard to swallow the fact that Letticia, with all her faults, had been spectacularly successful as a mother, while she, Deirdre, had so dismally failed.

Having kissed her grandmother Livia was packed off to the nursery and Letticia rang for tea, which Alice brought in. As usual the tea was not hot enough. The maid had slopped some in the saucer. Although she was dying for a drink, Deirdre gave up after one sip. She put the cup down and announced. 'I have come to inform you of the fact that I am going to France for a visit. I shall be gone for some time, some considerable time.'

She caught a look of mingled joy and relief cross Letticia's face before her son said, 'Are you sure it's wise, Mamma? Rumours in White's ... unrest ... In Crockford fellow said murmurs of ... Could be dangerous.'

'Stuff and nonsense, Edward. How silly you are! In any event I shall stay with Sophie and enjoy myself. Hanson's will look after my finances. Get in touch with them at Lincoln's Inn if you need anything.'

'Yes, Mamma. Sorry to trouble you, dearest Mamma, but I was going to speak of it to you. Well, fudge, Mamma, I am a bit behindhand. White's are dunning me and it's a trifle awkward.'

'You mean gambling debts, Edward! Really, my boy, you'll have to watch yourself. There is only so much. Do try to be more moderate. However, I expect Hanson will give you a hard enough time. Do take your troubles to him, dear boy. Now I must go.' She rose, giving a relieved sigh. 'Goodbye, my dear. Letticia, bid Livia goodbye from me. How prettily she is growing to be sure. Goodbye.'

When the door had closed behind her, Letticia wound her arms round her husband's neck in the girlish way he loved and sighed theatrically, 'Oh Edward, do you think your mamma will ever become reconciled to our marriage?'

He kissed her delicious little nose. 'Heart of my heart, don't trouble your pretty little head about that now. She's off to Europe and bound to stay there for simply ages. Oh joy! Oh bliss! Dear little treasure, let us relax and enjoy ourselves while she is away.'

'Divine, divine, dear precious dumpling,' Letticia cried, clapping her hands, and they jumped up and down and danced around the room like two children told of a treat.

'Still, dear dumpling,' Letticia said when the excitement had abated, 'still, I do so pine to be a better wifey to you.'

Suddenly serious, Edward pulled her clumsily into his arms and held her tightly.

'You are absolutely everything in life that I want,' he said fiercely. 'I love you to distraction exactly as you are. Never let Mamma change you. Never, never, please.'

And happily snuggling up to him she promised not to.

Deirdre spent the next two years in Europe. She rediscovered her favourite places, or some of them, which she had visited on her grand tour, when she had been an expectant young girl, and later on her honeymoon with Anthony, a bride, still full of hope that passion would eventually awaken and love blossom. Sophie was a delightful companion and maturity had given Deirdre a deeper awareness of beauty, of works of art, of other cultures and music, until as Edward had predicted the rumbles of war sounded too loudly to be ignored.

She returned home to find the Chelsea house in turmoil. Not, she reflected, that that was so unusual, but this time Letticia was in hysterics and when Edward arrived it was to announce that he was going to the defence of his country against the Kaiser. Nothing Letticia or his mamma could say would budge him an inch from his patriotic fever, so, perforce, they had to let him go. His eventual departure threw the two women together and they tried, without too much success, to lay down their differences and call a truce.

The period that followed was difficult for Deirdre. She had to cope with Letticia's daily hysterics which drove her mad. Letticia, too, had to tolerate Deirdre's perfectionism, which went against the grain. Letticia was in a constant state of anxiety no matter whether the news was good or bad. Edward, in any event, had not been accepted in any of the active armed forces as he was too old. They put him to use, however, in Brigade Headquarters as the oldest lieutenant with a general service commission, doing dogsbody jobs for the brigade major, which he enjoyed hugely, although Deirdre thought acidly it made no difference to Letticia whether he was in Colchester or Flander's Field. The woman could not seem to pull herself together or function at all in her husband's absence. So to Deirdre fell the task of looking after Livia.

The child had her nanny, her school, the Catholic School for Young Ladies run by nuns, the formidable *Sacre-Coeur*. She was being brought up impeccably but at this important moment in the girl's life Deirdre brought wit and a knowledge of art and music and introduced her to the finer, more sophisticated things in life. Livia was a very pretty, precocious child except when worried about something. Then, as her nanny said, Miss Livia made herself ill. She had a quick intelligence, and she and her grandmother became close. They spent their time peacefully together and would exchange understanding glances when Letticia came fluttering into the room in one of her states. Livia was wonderful with her mother, gently soothing her, for all the world, Deirdre thought, as if she were the mother and Letticia the child.

Edward was often home from Colchester and Deirdre's restlessness returned. The war ended and, though it had meant little to her, she now felt her life lacked purpose again. To her surprise she yearned for Anthony, whose presence she had hardly taken account of before he died. She was angry that Siobain was no longer alive to console her and give her companionship in her autumn years; though her energy appalled her

177

daughter-in-law and wore out her many friends, a quiet old age was not really what she sought.

At last she decided to return to Slievelea. As soon as she reached that decision, she felt a great peace descend on her troubled spirit. To go home, she thought. Home! Then she realized she had always thought of Slievelea as home. She had not really lived there since the tragic night of her father's shooting — that and her foolish passion for the Conor of her imagination had alienated her, had separated her from the land she loved. The land of her childhood — Ireland. The only place she had been truly happy. The green lanes of Wicklow beckoned, the purple hills called, the sound of the great sea whispered to her to come home. But most of all that sleeping house stirred in its dreams and yearned for occupation again. It was time, she decided, that Slievelea came out of mourning.

PART THREE

Chapter

28

DAN Casey and Spotty Devlin had been lurking behind the Pro-Cathedral in Marlborough Street one Sunday morning in spring, having a great time screaming insults at Da McCabe, who was languorous in charge of his barrow. He sold apples, plums, chestnuts and pears to the crowds coming out of Mass of a Sunday. So there he was this Sunday and not able to keep his balance, staggering about with apples and plums skedaddling over the side of the cart and the nimble and quick among the crowd pocketing the unexpected windfall. As the boys looked on, the Archbishop's car rounded the corner of Cathedral Street into Marlborough Street, a great black thing, unique in Dublin City it was.

Dan gazed at it covetously while Spotty Devlin's attention was concentrated on the antics of Da McCabe, who was lurching about the street as if he was playing blindman's buff, as indeed he was in a class of a way, him not being in total charge of his limbs. The two boys watched, shouting insults at the unfortunate inebriate, then suddenly they were silenced, gripped and immobilized by the inexorable journey of the car down one street and the weaving Da down the other until they converged at the corner and Da was thrown, as if in slow motion, into the air, where he did a somersault and ended up spread-eagled on the bonnet of the Archbishop's car, fixing His Lordship with a drunken glassy stare that interfered with the prelate's sleep for many a long night, before gliding grotesquely onto the road, to be pronounced dead on arrival in the gutter, which end surprised those who knew him not one bit.

But Dan's attention was on the unattended barrow. His nostrils quivered and quick as a flash he pulled Spotty's sleeve and,

181

in perfect unison, they crossed the street, grabbed one handle of the barrow each, whisked the cart across the road, and wheeled it nonchalantly up Marlborough Street and on into Gardiner Street, looking for all the world as if this had been their route for ever.

They took their acquisition to Foley Place and the tenement street welcomed them and swallowed them up. Here barefoot children skipped or played 'one potato, two potato', or queued up to jump rope singly or in pairs, chanting, 'I met Molly Tansey an' she told me this!' They could safely play in the middle of the street for no carriages and certainly no automobiles came this way. The noise was cacophonic. Everyone spoke as if the hearer was deaf; women shouted across the street to each other; some leaned out of windows and yelled at children playing below; babies screamed in makeshift prams; men idled singly and in groups, caps over eyes, lounging the day away with a Woodbine between their teeth, quiet-bodied compared with the nervous mobility of the females.

The men had the air of acceptance of defeat. There was no more effort left in them and sometimes they seemed too dispirited even to engage in conversation. Twelve-year-old Dan Casey was determined not to become like these men, not to join the lounging group of layabouts when he grew up. The women, however, were well aware that there was no idling for them. They somehow had to continue, day after day after day, tending their husbands and children, feeding, cooking, keeping house as well as they could under the circumstances, and working at whatever work came along from the rich houses in Fitzwilliam and Merrion Squares, Rathmines or Rathgar.

The street was a lively, rowdy place in spite of, or perhaps because of, its inherent despair, the daily life-and-death struggle of its inhabitants. There was no privacy here; tenement apartments sometimes had no doors, coal sacks hung in place of a door which had been used for firewood. Furniture was scarce, it, too, often going the same route to keep the family warm during the cruel winters when the wind from the sea blew morning, noon and night, splitting a body in two and invading every nook and cranny of the rickety, neglected Georgian houses.

When Spotty and Dan entered the street they were swallowed up and camouflaged. It was difficult, almost impossible, for the authorities ever to catch a criminal who dis-

182

appeared into this rabbit warren, this tightly-knit self-protective community.

Spotty and Dan were greeted with inquiries and congratulatory remarks on their acquisition.

'Is it after stealin' from yer own, Dan, me boyo, ye are?'

'Where'd ye get it Dan-O?'

'Are ye after robbin' Da McCabe then?'

'God, yer a smart young 'un, ye'd nick the tanner owa' a prossie's suspender.'

'Where's Da McCabe? Ye never took it from him? Ye never left a man without his meal ticket?'

'Da McCabe's dead and I'm only takin' what's up for grabs,' Dan shouted in reply to their catechism. Spotty pulled Dan's coat.

'Me and Spotty that is,' he added reluctantly.

He had sworn a vow to become rich, by fair means or foul, he didn't care, and Spotty was not part of the plan at all, at least not as an equal. However, for the moment, he would have to be tolerated. There was a strict code of ethics in the street. The laws were severe here, more binding than the laws of the land and woe betide anyone who transgressed. You did not take from your own and you cared for the weaker ones in the community.

'I'll take care of it, Spotty,' Dan said as they reached Number 13 where they both lived, one floor above the other, Spotty in the topmost flat with the rest of the Devlins, under the eaves, freezing and damp in the winter with the rain coming through an unkempt roof, and stuffy and hot in the summer.

Spotty nodded goodnaturedly. 'Yes. If ye gave it to me, me mam would mend the roof with it. She wouldn't see its intrinsic worth, Dan, so she wouldn't.'

Dan shivered at the thought, and nodded vehemently. Spotty's mam was an enormous woman with a tongue like a whiplash, a heart of gold and pendulous breasts that both embarrassed and fascinated Dan. She had ten children, and her husband, Dermot Devlin's son, was a carbon copy of his da in looks and character. He lounged all day on the steps to the house, dispensing advice and merry quips to all and sundry, dragging on a Woodbine, until his wife would call to him from the top window, when he would obey her command, whatever it was, instantly.

183

'God blessus, ye hit the jackpot there, Danny me boy. Is it yours and Spotty's then? God, yer on the pig's back now! There'll be no stoppin' you. An' what happened to poor ould Da?'

'Da McCabe fell on the Archbishop's car. He was kilt all right, there and then. He was intoxicated, Mister Devlin, he was plastered, maggoty with booze he was, and never felt a thing.'

'Yerra sure how could ye know that?'

'Ah well, it was the way he looked, sorta' peaceful, like he wanted me to take care of the barrow for him.'

Spotty's mouth fell open. 'But ye never went near the man, Dan, ye were in too much of hurry to get the cart ...'

Dan's face flamed but Mr Devlin was poking around the barrow, his thoughts on another track.

'There's nothin' on it though. Ye might have saved us a bit of fruit.'

Spotty hooted. 'Janey Mac, yer a bloody amazement, Da! If ye went to live in Dublin Castle itself you'd be complainin' of the fixtures! We had to scarper quick before anyone caught on what we were doin'.'

Dan stood silently listening, furious. The way Spotty told the story made them partners, which in the strict code of the neighbourhood would start them on a course of behaviour which could not be changed without a lot of trouble. Dan thought quickly. He wanted to assert his proprietary claim on the barrow, and to this end his mind raced about, looking for an answer. Mr Devlin gave him an unexpected opportunity. He fingered the side of the barrow saying, 'Well, yer ma can use that wood to seal up the spot over the bed. It's gettin' like a bloody geyser spoutin' water over us every time it rains and that's every day in this benighted land.'

'Ah, Mister Devlin, that's not really what it's for at all.' Dan's voice was louder than he intended, but it gave him courage, and winking broadly at Spotty to form a secret bond between them he continued. 'No. It was my idea, ye see. I have the major claim on the barrow. Spotty just, like, helped me like, came along for the ride. Ah no! I'm going into business I am, and Spotty here will have his share of it, never fear. He'll have his half-pound, don't you worry.' Dan was sweating as Mister Devlin and Spotty stared at him open-mouthed. No one in

Foley Place ever talked about 'going into business' and the mere sound of the sentence coming from juvenile lips deprived them of speech.

At that moment the huge form of Mrs Devlin appeared through the top window, hanging out over the sill, and over the noises of the street her voice sounded like a foghorn.

'There ye are, me fine bucco! Entertaining the troops I see and me lookin' for you left and right and centre. Get up here will ye or I'll knock yer block off. Aman't I waitin' here like an eejit fer you to fix the tap? The bloody thing can't be turned off and Mrs Casey will have a deluge like Niagara Falls on her head if the sink overflows! Come on up here now. An' you too, Spotty, or I'll crack yer heads together, so I will.'

They scuttled obediently through the gaping doorless entrance, leaving Dan in sole charge of the barrow; and that was the way he intended to keep it.

Dan had no trouble after that making ends meet. There was bacon in the pot for the Casey family along with the vegetables, and a pat of butter along with the bread. Dan dragged his barrow early and late through the streets of Dublin collecting what the rich thought rubbish and selling it to the poorer folk who considered it essential. Nothing was too tatty to be patched up or mended. Worn sheets could be end-to-ended, (split in the middle where the threadbare patch was, the sides stitched together), blankets similarly. Chipped china, burned pots and pans, broken furniture patched up and mended, laundered and re-sold. The pennies rolled in.

Spotty helped and Dan gave him a small percentage of the takings. He did it grudgingly. He was covetous of every penny he made. His thin little frame burned with the intensity of his purpose: to become rich. Not just make a living, not just crawl out from under the heavy burden of poverty that bowed their backs in Foley Place, but become as rich as it was possible to become. He dreamed of marble palaces and treasure chests of Spanish gold gleaming in the sun. His mother had taught him to read and write, and he had learned with an aptitude that surprised her. He did everything with the urgency of someone who is in a great hurry and has no time to spare. He worked morning, noon and night. The men in Foley Place were amazed at his energy and purpose.

'Jasus, he'll kill himself afore he's growed!'

185

'The lad will have a heart attack so he will. It's not natural.'

Spotty's mam had at first made an issue over the cart and its joint ownership, but soon even she was willing to relinquish her son's entitlement to more than Dan offered.

'Jasus, Mam, I couldn't keep up wid him,' Spotty had told her between the haphazard blows she rained on his head as automatically as she rubbed her hands on her apron after washing the bowls (the only eating utensils they possessed), or poked behind the little grey bun at the back of her head with the handle of the spoon.

A realistic look at her son was all Mrs Devlin needed to convince her he could never, never keep up with the 'human dynamo' downstairs, as she mentally called Dan. Spotty, who had inherited her largeness and tendency to fat, sat in the chair, pooped. His face was red and he was panting. The guileless grey eyes, innocent as the dawn, looked at her with anxiety.

'God! He's as useless as his father,' she sighed to herself, her heart full of love for him. She was as large of heart as she was of body and she often felt sorry for Dan and his cold, thin-lipped mother and soured, aged father.

'Things were terrible for them to be sure,' she would whisper to Mr Devlin as they lay in the big bed of a night, 'but we've got to go on. Jasus, ye can't just let the light go out of yiz, otherwise what's the point? C'mon, give us a cuddle ...'

Mrs Devlin loved her ten children and her husband. Their large room over the Casey's apartment, with whom they shared the lavatory at the bottom of the passage, was furnished with a table in the middle, a big bed under the window, and five little mattresses on the floor opposite. The children slept there, two a bed. When Dan Casey brought some wooden bedsteads (to help out, he said, but really to assuage his conscience for the amount of lying he had been doing with regard to the weekly take) the Devlins preferred to use them as firewood, for waren't the little ones snug as bugs in their pallets on the floor?

A sink and an iron stove, a range, were the other essentials in the room, a prototype for all the rooms in the house. Mrs Devlin went from day to day rarely giving a thought to the conditions in which she lived. Her preoccupation, like her neighbours', was daily survival. Heat and food. Enough warmth to stave off the cold and illness; enough food to keep them going till the next day.

Below them in a similar room lived the joyless Casey couple and Dan. Their room was vastly different since Dan had had the cart. The bric-a-brac and miscellaneous goods Dan procured from the houses in the wealthy streets and squares of Dublin were littered everywhere. Not people but things predominated. On one side of the range his father sat, his tall body stooped, his once beautiful eyes narrowed and puffy and full of resentment. All the softness was gone from the mouth, which turned down in a permanently sour line. Irritation lay behind his expression, and frustration and self-loathing. Over the years, Conor Casey had changed from a beautiful young man into a humourless, bad-tempered and frustrated being, mean of soul and spirit. His wife sat opposite, her black dress hanging limply on her gaunt frame. She stitched and mended wordlessly, a shadow, completely lacking the vitality so abundantly present in her son. Conor smoked a pipe. He had sucked a pipe as empty as a barren woman until Dan got the cart. Now Dan provided his father with the money for a pouch of tobacco and a few pints, but his father never thanked him. He seemed to derive no joy from them either. He simply sat slumped, the pipe in his mouth, and the only flicker lighting his eyes was the occasional spark of anger.

Like a pair of bloody crows, Dan thought as he sat glueing a leg back into the socket of a chair he could sell to Mrs Mahony, the pub-keeper's wife. He had spent all his young life vainly trying to coax a smile to his mother's lips or win a word of approval or encouragement from them. Even the day he had returned with the barrow his mother had not changed her expression when he had pushed it into their room. She hadn't even asked what it was!

'Mam, Mam, lookit what I've got.' He had peered anxiously, hoping for a reaction, a cry of joy, even a smile. A barrow, after all, was a passport to security. But nary a move she made.

'What's that then?' she had asked disinterestedly.

'A barrow, Mam. Now I can start goin' up in the world, an' you too. I have it all worked out. I can go to the big houses in Fitzwilliam and Merrion Squares and get anything they want shot of an' . . .'

'Where'll we put it?' she had asked mildly.

'For God's sake, Mam, what does it matter where we put it? Don't ye see? We can be sure of surviving now.'

187

'Is that so important, son?' she had asked.

He had felt empty, and a wave of hopelessness had flooded over him as if he were carrying too big a burden. The street was full of the sounds of caterwauling children and a barrel organ grinding out a sentimental song. The barrel-organ man lived in Foley Place, otherwise he would not be playing in the street. There were no spare pennies here.

> I'll be your sweetheart,
> If you will be mine;
> All my life,
> I'll be your Valentine;
> Bluebells we'll gather,
> Keep them and be true;
> When I'm a man my plan
> Will be to marry you.

He had looked at his mother and wondered if she could ever be anyone's sweetheart. His father's? He could not imagine it. He had said, 'Ah Mam, don't be like that! I'll work hard with it. I'll be out morning, noon and night. Sure I'll only be here when we're in bed. An' I'll get you things, honest I will.' He couldn't think what. 'Clothes and things,' he had ended lamely.

He was as good as his word and the Casey family had fires in the winter, oxtails to stew and even sometimes a saddle of lamb — a thing almost unheard of in Foley Place. They had warm blankets to cover them in their beds. It should have been a happy home, mealtimes should have been happy, but the dark figures of his father and mother and the sombreness of their emotions cast a pall of gloom over the proceedings. They listened in silence to Dan's nervous, high-pitched gaiety. They chewed away in methodic unison and never uttered a word. If Conor Casey ever remembered the warm evenings in the gate-house, full of loving conversation, shared troubles, gossip about the big house, and the fund of laughter always at the edge of the talk, he gave no sign. He and Aideen sat at opposite ends of the table as isolated from each other as if the one were at the North Pole and the other at the South.

Dan never forgot those meals eaten silently; sitting there he could feel no contact between them at all, and looking from one to the other he wondered how they got together long enough to produce him.

188

Chapter

29

DAN'S work with the barrow did not bring him the dreamed-of riches. True, the Caseys were better off now than anyone in Foley Place, but Dan's dreams were grandiose and unfulfilled. He was far from giving up hope, however, and he listened, watched and learned. He listened to the pulse of the city, to the gossip and temper of the town. He listened to the rich — that separate body of people in their elegant white Georgian houses in Fitzwilliam and Merrion Squares. They were a whole different breed of person, Dan saw. Their bodies were more beautifully proportioned, straighter, more upright, used to space for movement, which gave them a grace absent in their brothers in the slums. Their skin was clear, their teeth were strong and white, and their hair shone. He eavesdropped too, on the poor, on the men and women in the pubs and the newsboys in the street. He heard the grumblings of the Irish working class and all about the founding of the Irish Transport Union by James Larkin and James Connolly, and he saw, himself, what happened when the workers went on strike and families starved. Some of the families in Foley Place were involved and Dan did not make himself popular when he refused requests for charity from people who took neighbourly assistance as a right.

Larkin and Connolly had formed an Irish Citizen Army, he heard, as he slipped about Dublin, a thin little shadow, sly and energetic, sorting and storing information; and he heard about Home Rule. If Ireland could be run by the Irish for the Irish then he would make damn sure there was a place for himself in it where he would realize his potential and become rich.

It was in Ignatius Shaughnessy's pub on the corner of

Gardiner Street that the political chat flew to and fro and sur-
mises were made over pints of porter, defeats whispered about
and victories celebrated. It was in Shaugnessy's that Dan heard
about the Home Rule Bill being passed through Parliament and
joined in the singing of 'A Nation Once Again', but in his head
he had nothing but contempt for these fools celebrating a
pyrrhic victory. Sir Edward Carson would protect the militant
Orange north and the south would not accept division. Blood
would stain the streets and the last word would be
Westminster's. He liked what John Redmond of the Irish
Nationalist Party said: 'Irish nationalists can never be assenting
parties to the mutilation of the Irish Nation.' He liked the
sound of it, but in his heart he was indifferent to all but his own
interests. He wanted a free Ireland but he wanted others to free
it for him. In the ensuing chaos of an emerging Republic, there
would be rich pickings for the boy from Foley Place, but he was
not going to risk life and limb for anyone. He could not see the
point of dying for his country with a brave smile on his lips.
He heard a great deal of talk about the Irish Citizen Army and
many times they had tried to seduce him into becoming one of
them, but he held back, played a waiting game, and watched for
his opportunity, never doubting for a moment that it would
arrive, determined not to be asleep like the foolish virgins
Aideen had told him about — although his mother would have
had a heart attack had she known the context in which he used
the parable.

His ma was a religious fanatic. She was also, which was very
unusual in that place at that time, a puritan. She went to Mass
daily and attended the Sodality, Benediction, the Legion of
Mary and the Temperance League. She attended religious
ceremonies by the score, sometimes three a day, whilst her husband sat silent by the fire. She got no pleasure out of life and
rarely smiled.

It was in 1915, when Dan was seventeen, that the break in
the awful monotony of their lives occurred.

One evening Aideen Casey came home from church later
than usual. Dan was mending some pots with twine, binding the
rickety handles and painting them with glue for resale. Conor
sat in his chair as usual, sucking his pipe. He looked older than
his sixty-six years and although his back was turned to Dan the
anger emanating from him filled the room so that his son could

190

feel his resentment and fury saturating the atmosphere. The room was silent except for the erratic ticking of a clock Dan had rescued from the scrap heap and an occasional crackle from the fire the Caseys now always had to warm their bones and keep the damp at bay. Not that they ever expressed gratitude to their son who provided it, and who now had given up hope of ever winning their approval. Dan sat there in the silence he had become so used to that he took it for normal. He could hear Molly Devlin singing, in her nasal Dublin accent. The song sounded wistful but full of hope.

> Over the rainbow, far away,
> We'll take the kids on a holiday,
> Say goodbye backstreet morning, bye-bye.
> Goodbye backstreet morning in the pouring rain,
> Goodbye coldwater tower, goodbye crowded train.

The door opened and Aideen came in carrying her missal, and Conor spoke to her, actually addressed a question to her: 'Well, did ye enjoy yerself then?'

Dan and Aideen were so stupefied they both stared at him open-mouthed. Conor turned and looked at his wife, his face a twisted mask of fury. 'I said, did ye? Did ye have fun down there with Father O'Connor? Did ye go to confession to him and tell him how ye deny yer husband his rights? Well, did ye?'

Aideen stepped back from the unexpected onslaught of Conor's pent-up rage. He had never spoken of this subject before. No conversation had occurred between them about anything at all and least of all about this; and now, to her horror and in front of his son, Conor was shouting at her about this.

'Well, woman, I'm asking you. Well? Did you tell him you're still a virgin and you an ould hag now? No man ever had any pleasure from your body. Sure probably they think that's grand. Guaranteed first-class ticket through the pearly gates.'

'Hush, Conor, for God's sake hush.'

Aideen lifted a shaking hand as if to ward off a blow. Her naturally pale face was chalk white.

'I will not hush. Don't you tell me to, either. Jasus, every Saturday night the Devlins up there,' he pointed with his pipe at the ceiling, 'up there, overhead, hump about in the bed and groans of pleasure coming from them. Jasus, *every* Saturday

191

night, and once, only once in my whole bloody life, in my pathetic bloody life,' his voice broke, 'an' not with you. No, never, never with you. You'd never let me, would you? No.'

It suddenly seemed as if he might cry, but he pulled himself up and continued on at her in a cry of fury. 'An' you, you down with those eunuchs in the church who pontificate about sex and them knowing Sweet Fanny Adams about it, sure what would they know about it, in the name of God? Oh, the shame of it all, the stupidity of it, the waste, the waste,' and grabbing his jacket he left the room, slamming the door behind him.

Silence fell once again. Aideen removed her coat and hung it on the back of the door and busied herself cutting thick slices of bread and buttering them and arranging them on a plate for supper. She looked dazed and shattered. Dan went back to his pot-mending. He was elated and excited by his father's outburst, but it took some time to assimilate all the information. Like the fact that he was a bastard. It all made his father more human and therefore more likeable. He did not care about who his real mother was. He was supremely indifferent to the facts of his parentage. He treated the whole episode lightly and was glad he understood Conor's anger and resentment at last, relieved to realize it had nothing to do with him.

Aideen on the other hand was devastated. She adored Conor and moved around inside the prison of her inability to communicate with him, desperately trying to break out. She had been locked in the cage of her inarticulacy ever since their wedding night, praying, hoping that some day, one day, she could break out and reach Conor. But it was not to be. She did not desire him, her mind had never reached full understanding of physical love, she had been too warped by her childhood experience and her own ignorant reaction to Conor, and until this night she had truly never realized the strain under which she had put her husband. She was appalled and frightened and bewildered at her own ignorance.

Conor went to the pub, to Mooney's, in a red-hot temper. Deeply shaken by his abandoned outburst, he was frightened by the fact that once again he had lost control of himself, and acted irrationally and, without thinking, caused untold damage. His memory of the killing of Rory Mulholland had undergone a metamorphosis over the years and had in his mind become the brutal slaying of an old man; his rape of Sinead, a willing and eager partner in reality, had become an attack on a frightened, unwilling little girl; and now he had put the cat among the pigeons in his own home. How could he trust himself? What was it in his nature that seemed so hell-bent on destruction? He remembered his gentle mother and father and was filled with self-loathing.

That night he downed a whiskey with his porter. The fact that all this and everything else he had was paid for by his son, and before that by Ma Kerrigan, did nothing to help his tattered pride. He never got drunk and wouldn't now, but he fully intended to get a buzz on and ease the tension a little, or, he felt, he might do some other stupid bloody thing.

'There's a man in a right state to be sure,' a cheerful voice said beside him, and he turned to look into the smiling brown eyes of the man beside him. He was small and wiry of stature, with a weatherbeaten look and greying hair, a little button nose and the face of a clown, melancholy with dancing eyes.

'Isn't the hostility emerging from yourself in waves?' he said and took Conor's elbow. 'Come on an' we'll set here at the table and you'll do me the honour of raisin' a glass with me.'

Conor started to protest but the little man wouldn't hear him.

'No, no. I'll get us a jar an' we'll sit here nice an' snug and we'll have a bit of a palaver.'

He sat Conor down at the table, which was stained with wet rings and liberal sprinklings of ash. The pub had a warm, womb-like atmosphere, smoky and dark; the windows were opaque glass with engravings on them. The little man put a pint in front of Conor and looked at him with mischief-filled eyes. He sat down opposite Conor and took a long pull at the stout, then licked the foam off his lips with appreciative smacking noises.

'When I saw you I said to meself, I said, there's a man in a rage. Now I wonder, I said to meself, I wonder if it's anger about his poor oppressed country that's eatin' him up? I wonder if the tears of Kathleen Ni Houlihan are drivin' him crazy, I said, an' I also said, if it is then Lefty Leary has the answer to the man's problems.' He looked at Conor. 'That's me name, Lefty Leary, because of this.' He suddenly thrust the stump of his left arm under Conor's nose. His eyes had become steely and the twinkle had gone, but only for a moment, then he shrugged.

'I lost it for my country, Erin go bragh. Lovely Ireland has it for a favour, an' welcome. An' I'd lose the other one if I were asked. An' what's your appendage?' He saw Conor's frown. 'Yer name?'

'Conor Casey.'

'Conor Casey! A grand Irish name begob, with a ring to it. A heroic ring. Wasn't Conor the High King of all Ireland, for God's sake! And tell me, Conor Casey, are you a patriot?'

The question took Conor aback for a moment. 'Sure I am,' he said uncertainly.

'Well then, let's you an' me toddle down to the meetin' in Liberty Hall and yerra sure ye never know, ye might hear something of interest.'

Conor leapt at the chance. More than anything he wanted to avoid Dan and Aideen that night and with them the consequence of his rash outburst, and this seemed as good a way as any.

When he returned home late that night the Irish Citizen Army had an ardent supporter. What he had heard in that smoke-filled hall set him on fire and reawakened his patriotism, dormant since that long ago time in Slievelea when he had silently handed round the cigars. It was also a handy way of deflecting his anger to a justifiable cause. It shifted his resentment away from his wife and son and, most of all, from himself, and onto a more satisfactory target — British oppression. He had a righteous cause for his indignation.

From then on Conor was a changed man. He completely forgot, or conveniently buried, his outburst and was rarely seen at home. He spent his time and energy involving himself in the heady business of rebellion. A united Ireland was the aim. They were not prepared to accept a divided Ireland and Home Rule to them was a sell-out. The words on the Statute Books were, after all 'Home Rule for all Ireland under the Crown'. The north would never agree and the south refuted 'under the Crown'. They wanted complete independence.

Conor's age mattered no longer. The Irish Cause needed every able-bodied, and even not so able — witness Lefty Leary — man or boy it could get, as now half the male population of youthful Irish men were off dying in Flanders for the British flag. He even tried to entice his son into the movement, but Dan was noncommittal.

'Ah, Da, I've got my own way of proceeding,' was all he said.

Lefty and Conor went everywhere together. Sometimes

Aideen did not see him for weeks on end. When he did come home it was in the wee small hours and it was only to collapse on his mattress and slip into a dreamless sleep until he awakened to rush out, sometimes without even the benefit of a mug of tea. He heard about and agreed with the decision of his idol James Connolly and his co-leaders to rise against the British before the war in Europe was over for 'England's difficulty was Ireland's opportunity'. He felt, like Padrig Pearse, that Ireland needed a blood sacrifice to show the British Crown that the rebels meant business and were set upon an Irish Republic completely independent of Britain. When the great old Fenian O'Donovan Rossa died, having served a term in British jails for his part in the Fenian conspiracy, Conor Casey was at the funeral which to his pride and joy turned into a dramatic affirmation of Irish nationalist feelings. Thousands of people filed past the coffin to pay their respects. An armed guard of honour of Irish Volunteers were there and a volley was fired over the grave. When Padrig Pearse spoke of the glorious Fenian dead and said, 'Ireland unfree shall never be at peace,' Conor openly wept. He took part in the great march through the Dublin streets on Saint Patrick's Day, which the British Army in Ireland allowed, for they felt, as did many of Conor's acquaintances, that this was the work of a lunatic fringe. The Rising, due to take place on Easter Day 1916, and postponed to Easter Monday because of muddled communication and misunderstood commands and counter-commands, failed. Indeed it was a débâcle, but it changed the course of Irish history and the lives of the Casey family for ever.

Dan strolled about the Dublin streets on Easter Sunday. He had gone with Aideen to Mass, not because he wanted to, but because he could not see how to get out of it. It was packed in the Pro-Cathedral, and he could not but remember his acquiring Da McCabe's cart outside the imposing monstrosity of a building all those years ago, and the turn their fortunes had taken with its acquisition. He thought, as the priest intoned in Latin and his mam (he still thought of her as that) mindlessly murmured the responses, of the growing pile of silver under his mattress, and he prayed to God quite sincerely to hurry up and help him to find a way of making more and faster. He found a way the very next day.

Chapter

30

DAN'S father had not come home the previous night and Spotty Devlin called out to Dan from the street below that great things were afoot. He did not see so much of Spotty Devlin these days, not because their friendship had cooled (Dan was scrupulous in always asking Spotty to accompany him) but for the simple reason that, as Dan very well knew, Spotty could not possibly keep up with him, nor indeed did he want to. He was a lazy buachaill. All the Devlins were the same. Dermot had been the most energetic of the clan, but all the energy seemed to have dried up with him. His son, Molly's husband, was usually at a standstill unless there was money for porter and then you couldn't see him for dust getting to the pub. Spotty was a chip off the old block. Dan still kept them happy with small percentages of his earnings but, more than ever, he bitterly begrudged whatever he felt was necessary to pay them. Although Spotty was slow and lazy he was a good-natured dogsbody. He loved Dan, hero-worshipped him, and was his slave. Dan was surprised at Spotty being up so early on Easter Monday and it a holiday and all, and shouting out at him from the street. It was usually the other way round, Dan thought, as he went to the window and called back, 'What is it has you wakin' the neighbourhood, Spotty?'

'Oh, there's great things happenin' in Dublin City this day. C'mon, c'mon, will ye come an' see, c'mon.'

Something in the excitement Spotty felt aroused Dan and he pulled on his trousers. He slept in his shirt so that was on already. He put on a pair of socks and his boots, which came to his ankles and rubbed his bone till it bled, so he did not tie them up. Pulling on his cap, he left the room without exchanging one word with his mam. Aideen stood at the ancient stove, peeling

196

potatoes for the evening meal against the hope that there would be someone in the room to eat it. She sighed hopelessly when Dan left and rubbed her forehead with the back of her hand.

Dan and Spotty set out for Sackville Street together. Spotty told of rumours he had heard of people breaking into shops and taking anything they wanted.

'It's like Aladdin's cave, they say,' Spotty said enthusiastically, 'I didn't want you to miss it.' He lookd at Dan, hoping to please, like a little mongrel dog, Dan thought. 'I heard it from Rosie Moore.'

Dan halted suddenly, disappointment written all over his face.

'Ye heard it from Rosie Moore! Sure she's an eejit, Spotty Devlin, an' is incapable of tellin' the truth. Jasus, ye have me on a wild goose chase. I'm going home.'

'No, Dan, let's give it a try. Sean O'Toole and Mary said so too, so let's go on and verify the truth of it for ourselves.'

It was a typical spring day, sunny and bright with a fresh nip in the air. They walked into the town together. There was the holiday atmosphere of the Easter break, but there was something more, Dan felt, an excitement that was alien to this dreaming city. As they passed Findlater's Church and entered Sackville Street, Dan's jaw dropped in delighted astonishment. People were rushing in and out of the shops. Fat little women owed their sudden weight to the bundles tucked under their shawls. Everyone was running. Some carried lamps and bedclothing; others pushed beds along or dragged chairs; still others were eating great boxes of chocolates as if this were their last meal and someone would take it away from them any second. Others were ripping open fancy tins of biscuits. Dan's eye fell on two women dragging sacks. The sacks seemed to contain crockery and bounced along the pavement, the sound of breaking china apparently not deflecting the women from their purpose. Eejits, Dan thought, and his brain clicked into place. He knew it would take too long to go back for the cart, but he was not prepared to make do with only as much as he and Spotty could carry. He looked around him.

The mob was running riot; people were looting and fighting each other over things like golf clubs and dress suits which could be of no possible use to them and might also be traced. Eejits, he thought again. His eye fell on Patsy Prosser's pony and cart outside Mooney's pub and he quite coldly decided to commandeer it for his own purposes. Patsy Prosser gathered the horse dung from the city streets and sold it to the small market gardeners and anyone who needed fertilizer, so the cart did not smell like Rosie Moore after a bath in her Purple Passion Jasmine Bath Essence, but that could not be helped. He crossed the street and asked a woman on the way why there were no British soldiers about. His heart beat hard under his shirt, his excitement almost choking him, but he did not want to end up in jail. He would make the most of this opportunity, please God, but not if prison was at the end of the road.

'Sure *they've* all gone to the races at Fairyhouse,' she said. 'An' Connolly an' Pearse were all over at Liberty Hall at the crack of dawn and they're sayin' that they'll take over the whole of Dublin City by the afternoon.'

At that moment a youngster about fifteen years old came haring past her. He was wearing the uniform of the I.R.A.

'Seamus! Is that yourself?' She grabbed him by the shoulder. 'Will ye lookit yerself an' you only a chissler not long outa' wet pants. Does yer mammy know?'

The young fellow blushed, his hairless face turning rosy pink. The woman gave another shriek. 'Gawney, he's got a gun! What de yiz think yiz are doin', Seamus Riley? Will ye go home now or do I have to beat you?' She removed her hand and raised the bag she was carrying to give him a belt over the head, but he was too quick for her, and taking advantage of his opportunity he fled down Sackville Street, leaving the woman shouting shrilly after him. Then she looked at Dan and Spotty again.

'An' I've got seven pairs of false teeth outa' that window there,' she said with relish, and let out a cackle of laughter, showing her bare gums.

Dan jumped into the cart, Spotty obediently following, and pulled the reins and clicked the horse. Dan had never driven a horse and cart before, but he was full of feverish excitement and nothing mattered now. He knew exactly what he was going to do. He got the trap down to Cleary's, Dublin's most elegant and expensive store and, parking it in front, told Spotty to wait and hold the reins and not on any account to stir. Spotty heard the crash of breaking glass. Dan must have smashed a window or a door, Spotty thought, covering his ears in an agony of fearful suspense. He did not see Dan vanish into the store and

198

emerge with his arms full. Dan commenced loading the trap and he did it methodically and without haste, coolly, as if it was work he did every day. He left the cumbersome objects, concentrating on the most saleable, valuable things, and he worked like the wind. Watches and clocks, rings, jewellery, lamps of buhl, lamps of copper, cut-glass goblets, silver cutlery, cruets, punch bowls, ladles, frames of leather tooled in Italy, leather-bound diaries, writing folders, little Italian writing desks, small and dainty, made of rosewood and inlaid with ivory. Ivory letter openers, watered-silk bookmarks and gold-rimmed monocles were all neatly packed in the cart.

Opposite Cleary's Spotty could see the Irish Volunteers and the Irish Citizen Army still arriving at the General Post Office. Spotty called to Dan who was piling some jade ornaments into the cart, 'Lookit, Dan. There's Connolly and Pearse after coming, and yer da. Janey Mac, Dan, yer da's there and a whole lot more. They're goin' in the Post Office. Lookit, Dan, there's yer da. What's happening?'

Dan said, 'Shut up about me da, just concentrate on the horse. How should I know what's happening?'

People in the street didn't know either. Some had heard via the grapevine that the Rising that had been cancelled yesterday would take place today. They said there would be ructions in Dublin City that day. But the majority were holiday-makers out for a stroll, and people passing through on their way to visit friends or relatives, so they were bewildered when they heard the Proclamation read out by Padrig Pearse, looking every inch the poet soldier he was, but speaking to a confused and uncomprehending crowd. Spotty looked about for Dan but he was paying no heed, moving calmly and efficiently between the store and the cart. Spotty could, therefore, give his attention to the speech and the words made his heart swell. He tied the horse to a lamp post and drifted over to the G.P.O. across the street from Cleary's, the better to hear the words. He waved at Mr Conor Casey, who was standing bolt upright to attention, but Conor did not see him. His eyes were fixed far away, looking at some distant dream.

'In the name of God and of the dead generations from which she receives her old traditions of nationhood, Ireland through us summons her children to her flag and strikes for her freedom.'

There was a roar of approval from the crowd, but as Spotty shouted out, 'Hello, Mister Casey. Good on yourself!' he felt a heavy hand on his shoulder and turned round to see the angry face of Dan, who looked remarkably like his father at that moment.

'You little shit,' Dan hissed furiously, and yanked Spotty back across the street to the cart where he pinned him against the lamp post. He was trembling with rage.

'But yer da's there. It's great to see him, Dan. Yer da!'

'You little shit,' Dan said again, his face contorted with anger. 'Don't leave this cart again or I'll have yer guts for garters. Anyone ... anyone could have taken it in this confusion, in this crowd. Ye think I care about me da? Anyone could have ...' The enormity of this appalling thought rendered Dan speechless and he gave Spotty another shake. At that moment shots rang out. A party of Lancers who were not at the races were fired on by some Volunteers as they came down the street. The killing had begun.

Dan was instantly galvanized into action. He wanted to get his goods out of there before the trouble became acute and he might be stopped. Spotty got on the dray and they were driving up past Mooney's when Patsy Prosser, a little itty-bitty gombeen man, emerged flushed with the drink and wanting to see what all the fuss was about. He arrived in time to see his cart and horse disappearing past Findlater's Church, and with a roar that was out of proportion to one so small, he started running unsteadily after it. Seeing it vanish down Frederick Street he shrugged, blinked several times then swung round on his toes and trotted back to Mooney's and the warmth of the booze.

Dan missed the violence of the rest of the day and the following days. He unloaded his loot, thankful that the house and the neighbourhood were quiet as very few places in the city were. Everyone able to walk flocked into the city to join the excitement and see what was in it for them. Some of them never returned.

Conor was in the thick of it and did not get home at all after that fateful week. He lived in an enclosed little world at the centre of the fight, and he had never been so alive in his life. He knew he was fighting for Ireland's freedom and he was exhilarated by the battle. He stuck close to Connolly, and he and Lefty were busy all week, run off their feet. He was inordinately proud that he had helped to raise the tricolour at the G.P.O. That was the first thing. Triumph surged through his veins as that green, white and gold flag rose high above them. But it was when the shooting began that he was most surprised at himself. He felt important, he felt virile, he felt like a man who could hold his head up high like the flag. He executed his orders efficiently, and his orders were mainly to shoot British soldiers. His aim was deadly, his accuracy lethal, for he had been trained well over the last few months. There were breaks between the flurries of shooting. Then he didn't know whether it was night or day. He felt the same release from tension he had felt only once before, when he had raped Sinead on the staircase of Number 13 Foley Place. In moments of rest he slept the same dreamless sleep he had slept that night.

All his life since he had left Slievelea there had been a coiled spring of tension within him and now it was released, gone. He wondered why he felt sad. The anger had gone, but it had been replaced by an enormous melancholy. He knew that the rebels had done well and, now that the general public were aware of what was happening, they were helped in many ways. They had the Post Office and Jacob's Biscuit Factory and a garrison in St Stephen's Green, but there had been no English soldiers to stop them. By afternoon, however, the Third Cavalry Brigade had arrived from the Curragh and after a wireless message to London the 176th and the 178th Infantry Brigades of the 56th North Midland Division were dispatched to Dublin and arrived on Tuesday at Kingstown. Conor heard of the shooting of Sheehy Skeffington, the pacifist writer who was arrested in Dublin and taken to Portobello Barracks by some British officers where he was shot without trial. Two firing parties had to make an end of him, the first did the job so badly. Conor was outraged. He had taken Ireland's cause to his very soul.

The British troops marched into Dublin. The gallant and pathetic little bands of patriots fought on, but it was a losing battle.

'Jasus, the whole fuckin' British Army is marchin' up the streets of Dublin,' Spotty told Dan after creeping back to Foley Place from one of his sorties to the city. Dan shrugged, his decision not to go out until the whole bloody mess was over hardening. He had made up his mind to stay with his treasure in Foley Street until all was quiet again. He was sure it would not last long and he was right.

The British cordon tightened around the rebels in the city and, as they moved closer to the Post Office, they used their artillery, and Dublin began to burn. Much of the damage was done by two eighteen pounders firing at close range in the streets. By Friday the Post Office was on fire and the whole sky was a mass of flames, and from this burning holocaust Conor looked out and wept.

Aideen remained on her knees for most of the week, and seeing the fire crimsoning the sky, begged Dan to go and see what was happening, to try and find his father. Dan was so surprised at her request that he finally went, much against his will.

At first he couldn't believe his eyes. The city was devastated, and many people, citizens as well as rebels, had been killed. Afterwards he found out that 300 citizens had been killed with 60 rebels and 130 British troops.

He did not find his father, however, and it was days later that Aideen heard he was in a British jail. He had been captured with his companions, and they were marched down the quays and shipped to England. Lefty Leary went with them. Aideen wept. Dan had never seen his mother cry before. She wept silently for weeks, and she wondered yet again what terrible thing she had done to be so severely punished.

She was told that Conor was lucky. Tom Clarke, Thomas MacDonagh and Padrig Pearse had been shot. Willie Pearse, who had nothing to do with the rebels, had been shot, too, simply because he was Padrig's brother. John MacBride, Cornelius Colbert, Eamon Ceannt, Michael Mallin, Sean Heuston, Thomas Kent ... They told her the roll call of the executed, and then they told her Sean MacDermott, who had been with her husband, had been shot. Last, her husband's hero, James Connolly, was shot in a chair — because he could not stand on his wounded ankle. And the Irish people who had been lukewarm about the Rising were now angry. Their determination to have a Free State was hardening. Things would never be the same again. The old tolerance of the English boot on Ireland's neck was gone, drowned in the blood of martyrs. Now the Irish wanted the foreigner out.

Chapter

31

PHYSICALLY, Dan had remained a small, wiry little fellow until that Easter week when, along with his loot, he suddenly acquired inches on his height and width, shooting up and out and becoming all of a sudden the Big Dan Casey he was to be known as for the rest of his life.

The nickname started in Foley Place where people started saying, 'Janey, you've suddenly got big, Dan,' and it stuck. His face, too, filled out. Perhaps the treasure he had plundered from Cleary's helped to remove the anxious tension that had screwed up his eyes and mouth. At all events, Big Dan Casey was a remarkably handsome man, and the girls suddenly began to notice him.

They liked the Casey eyes, so blue with sooty lashes sometimes concealing the steel that always lurked behind the twinkle, but not always managing to disguise it. They liked that, it made him look dangerous. They did not realize he *was* dangerous. There were no lengths to which Dan Casey was not prepared to go to achieve his aims. They liked the thick black hair and rakish grin, the white teeth and determined chin. They liked the six-foot-two size of him and the broadness of his shoulders and above all they adored his cavalier treatment of them. Dan was not really interested in them. He had bigger fish to fry. He was chasing a dream relentlessly. This only increased their interest — the more unattainable he seemed, the more determined to capture him they became.

He found, down the quays beside the River Liffey, a little jewellery and hock shop a cut above the one in Gardiner Street frequented by the inhabitants of Foley Place. The customary three balls swung and creaked in the foggy mist from the grey Liffey waters outside the shop, and within Dan found a kindred spirit and an accommodating friend in Hymie Klein. He was an orthodox Jew in a city where there were few of his kind. The Dubliners, needing all their energy for battle with the British, treated the small Jewish population with tolerant kindness and allowed them to conduct their affairs in peace.

Hymie called himself a jeweller, but the shop bore the title 'pawnbroker' in gold letters outside. It was dark and warm inside, musty with second-hand goods, dusty and exotic, damp from the proximity of the river. It was overcrowded with items of every description, except for the jewellery counter, where everything was orderly. The shop was partitioned by a glass panel engraved with flowers, effectively shielding the jewellery customers from the unfortunates putting their goods in hock. These clients were not always the poor, who took their paltry possessions to more modest establishments, except, perhaps, the odd valuable — the engagement ring bought in a moment of high hope from a life's savings, a pair of grandmother's ear-rings handed down carefully from generation to generation and now the passport to a moment's financial freedom. No, Hymie's customers were more likely the gamblers from the aristocracy, and many a fine lady or gentleman caught up in the party round had had to leave family heirlooms in Hymie's care. Also families selling up and leaving Ireland deposited the articles they wished to be rid of with Hymie Klein. He resold at bargain prices many a treasure, and so was very popular with antiquarians and antique dealers both in Dublin and London.

Hymie himself dressed in the manner of a bygone age in red or blue velvet smoking jacket, a cravat, black trousers, and black pumps on his little feet. His hair hung in greasy ringlets and his prayer cap was struck firmly on the back of his head. He wore half-glasses, gold rimmed, and he had shrewd knowing eyes that saw all and comprehended all. He viewed the world tolerantly and he got Dan's measure right away and liked him. 'This fellow will get where he wants to go,' he told his wife, noting, too, the eager interest on his daughter's face whenever Dan Casey was mentioned.

Jessica Klein was a voluptuous seventeen, and Hymie and his wife in total unspoken understanding contrived to keep her out of the shop when Dan Casey came to call. Hymie, looking over

204

his glasses, would see Dan's tall figure coming down the cobbled road, past the second-hand bookshops and McCarthy's pub and would clear his throat. Martha would instantly call Jessica, their apartment being behind and above the shop, and the way would be clear. Dan trickled the looted goods little by little to Hymie's shop and Hymie never let on he knew exactly where they came from and how. Dan and Hymie understood each other. Business was conducted amicably, a satisfactory bargain was struck and both were pleased with each other. Dan realized that Hymie was probably making a profit out of the goods he sold him, that is, a bigger profit than was strictly ethical, but he did not worry about that. He considered it only fair and acknowledged that if he were Hymie he would do the same.

Within a few months Dan was in a position to move from Foley Place, the first move, he felt, on the ladder to success. He was sick with excitement. He had found himself a small first-floor apartment in Mount Street, a fashionable enough address and alien to the desires of most of the Foley Street dwellers whose dreams were of a small house somewhere in the suburbs.

Dan had no desire for simple security. His ambition embraced power and, above all, social position, although how exactly he was to proceed was obscure to him. He only knew Mount Street was a turning point, a step in the right direction, as he said to Spotty. He begged Aideen to come with him but was relieved when she bluntly refused. She did not confide to Dan her daily hope that one day the door would open and Conor would be home. It was the only thing that sustained her, but she was incapable of sharing her suffering with her son, of telling him the depth of her pain. She hated even to go to the local huckster shop in case Conor might return at that precise moment and, finding her absent, would leave, perhaps for ever. She lived caught up in a tension so great that Dan could hear her grind her teeth at night when the both of them tried to sleep.

At first Dan had been disgusted that his father was in jail but, ever interested in turning events to his own advantage, soon came to the conclusion that eventually and inevitably Ireland would gain her independence and to have a father who had fought and had been jailed for the Cause could only be an advantage.

He kept Spotty in tow by offering him a job as his assistant. He told him he needed someone to help him and to run errands, be 'general factotum', he said, and Spotty thought that sounded very important, as long as he was not asked to do more than his fair share, he said to Dan anxiously. Dan said he would be paid well and, no, he would not have to work too hard. He wanted Spotty for the things that might not stand up to the light of day. Because of Spotty's loyal and blind faith in him he knew things would be 'done an' no questions asked'. The money he paid Spotty was astronomical in the eyes of Foley Place dwellers, but in fact peanuts compared to the sums Dan was now making. At all events, Spotty was satisfied. He was quite happy in the position Dan put him in for he was some-times frightened at the changes in his boss and alarmed that he would be expected to keep up with him.

So Dan left Foley Place for good and heaved a great sigh of relief, standing up straight, squaring his shoulders and exulting in his heart. He bought Aideen a beaver fur coat he saw in Hymie's shop and gave it to her on one of his rare visits to Foley Place. She accepted it with indifference, murmuring a 'thank you, Dan, but sure I never go out'. He was disappointed but not too downcast. The sick, rejected feelings he had had over her reception of the barrow had changed. He no longer worried about her for he was too busy with his own affairs. He was not at all sure why he had given her the coat, but was aware deep down that all his folks should reflect his prosperity; for them not to do so would be a slur on his character. It would be a bad thing if the father or mother of Big Dan Casey went in poverty.

He now went about his business with a lighter heart, but the urgency was still there. Then in 1917 the Sinn Fein put up an Irish candidate at a by-election in Roscommon, and another, who was still in jail in Britain, in Longford and both delighted the Irish by winning by a landslide. The extent of the victory astonished the British, who always treated the Irish like way-ward children and were constantly amazed that they minded being totally constricted, and would insist in breaking out of their prison. The government, horrified, made the conciliatory gesture of releasing some of the prisoners involved in the Rising. Among the prisoners who came home to a hero's welcome were Eamon de Valera and Conor Casey.

Dan wanted to be very much in evidence at this political event, he wanted to be noticed, and he waited with a group on the steps of the G.P.O. The building was in the process of being

206

rebuilt, but the state it was in reminded people of the events of the Easter Rising, of the young and old who had given their lives for Irish freedom.

The returning heroes marched down the street to the tumultuous cheers of crowds flanking both sides. The crowd was enormous, shouting its lungs out, screaming and waving the tricolour. There was a reception committee and Dan made sure he was prominent among them though he had no right to be there at all. Having pushed and insinuated himself, he waited with the others, who were too intent on the events to query his presence there.

His heart twisted within him when he caught sight of his white-haired da, holding himself as straight as a ramrod, chin up, eyes full of tears, marching down the street, face putty-coloured from months without the sun. He seemed frail and weakened from his year in jail, but proud none the less. Dan came down the steps as he saw his father approach, and in the same instant Conor saw his tall son. He broke away from the group and greeted Dan. Dan's heart swelled and for the first time in his life he held his father in his arms, feeling the thin body and the sharp bones through the cheap suit he was wearing, courtesy of His Majesty.

'You'll be proud of me, Dan,' Conor sobbed as he hugged his son. 'See,' he turned to the deliriously cheering crowd, 'you'll be pleased I was your da.'

'I am, Da, I am.' Dan sniffed back his emotion. 'I am. You're the hero of the hour. You've earned a place in Irish history.'

Conor drew himself up and took a deep breath. 'You think so, son?'

'In the history books, Da. In the history books.'

He took Conor back to Foley Place. Aideen awaited them. She sat in front of the fire in the beaver coat and when they came into the room she remained seated, her back to them. For a long moment there was silence and then she turned. Tears ran down her face and she seemed to Dan old and defenceless. His parents both seemed at that moment very old. They looked at each other, Aideen and Conor, and it was as if all the tension left them and they reached some understanding, as if they were on a plateau above the world, calm and at ease with each other for the first time. No word was spoken and Dan did not try to understand what happened, he just felt a warmth in the atmos-

207

phere that had never been there before.

He had a cup of tea with them, in silence as usual, but this silence seemed more comfortable, more companionable somehow. Then he bid them goodbye and went back to Mount Street and to bed.

Chapter

32

IRELAND the next year was torn by two groups of men, the Irish Republican Army and the Black and Tans, a vicious group of men sent over by the British government to subdue the I.R.A. and impose peace by force and terror. They became known by the name Black and Tans because of the khaki additions to their uniforms. They were the British Government's only response to the demand for an Irish Republic and had the effect of hardening the Irish people's determination to fight for their freedom. The Black and Tans were recruited from the British Army, returned from the European war, and from jails and the criminal community in England. They were a ruthless, aggressive force moving about Ireland in their big Crossley tenders, killing individuals, bringing in people for interrogation. They did not conduct themselves according to the law and followed a policy whereby for every member of the Crown forces shot, two Sinn Feiners would be executed.

Burning houses became the standard practice and guerrilla warfare broke out all over the country, not least in Dublin, where the streets became a dangerous place to be after dark. Men lurked in doorways and were shot down in dark alleys, dying alone and unaided. There was deception and intrigue as fugitives were hidden, and the sound of solitary footsteps echoed on deserted streets as doctors, Republican sympathizers, were called out to remove bullets and tend gunshot wounds, or priests hurried to administer the Last Sacrament. Whole areas of the city were cordoned off, people were rounded up and searched, any time, any place. Shootings were everyday occurrences and prisoners went without trial to the gallows. The land was awash in the blood of its sons, and family was divided against family as brother fought brother. Those who had returned from their services to the British flag in the Great War were suddenly faced with the choice of either killing former comrades in arms or betraying the motherland and shooting their brothers.

For Conor there was no conflict. He joined in the fight with renewed energy and dedication. Because of his term in prison he had become one of the grand old men of the struggle for freedom, a hero, a god. Revered, looked up to, he had achieved a kind of sainthood in his own lifetime, and was sung about in rebel songs. But he was also known as the 'Silent Man', a taciturn man, a monosyllabic man, a loner, icy calm, withdrawn, a man of stone. He listened, he nodded, he executed the deed without emotion. His head was full of impossible dreams for Ireland.

Aideen lived on a knife-edge of fear every time Conor left Foley Place. He was often away for days at a time and she tried to possess her soul in patience and pray. She was very frightened for herself too, because she had stopped going to Mass or to the church at all and this meant she was in mortal sin and would go straight to hell if she died. But her fear of Conor returning, perhaps hurt and in need of help, and finding her not there was much greater than her dread of hellfire and damnation. She sat all day in front of the fire, her stomach churning and gripping with anxiety. Sometimes Molly Devlin came down to bide with her a wee while. The woman did not speak much but since Conor had become the great hero, the attitude of the Foley Place folk had changed towards them and they were looked on as 'The Caseys', a different class of people and, therefore, not to be categorized with the rest of the mortals in the slum. Besides, the son, Big Dan Casey, was out of their world and, in their imagination, up there with the British in luxury and comfort and the more cushy things in life. An' more power to him, they said, for if he could do it, who knows? Who knows? Little Sean or Padrig? Who knows, and hope springs eternal, an' ye never know in this life, do ye?

So Molly did not pay much attention to Aideen's inability to communicate and, truth to tell, found peace sitting there in the calm comfort of the Casey apartment. She was glad to escape from the hurly-burly of children and husband to the relative

210

peace of Aideen's home. It was nice to have a fire and chairs and a carpet, and in the kindness and good humour of Molly's presence, Aideen unbent as never before and sometimes confided in the large, warm-hearted woman her fears and worries over Conor's safety, and was consoled by her cheerful reassurance that, 'Sure, wouldn't everything turn out for the best.'

Molly, herself worried about her two sons who were heavily involved with the I.R.A. and Michael Collins, was very relieved that Spotty was under Dan's wing and kept out of all the trouble in the land. 'Isn't it a miracle now,' she said to Aideen, 'that those two are involved with a very different business, an' wouldn't it be grand if the rest of Ireland and the bloody British followed their example!'

Conor walked down Gardiner Street in the dark, drizzling rain. He was on his way to a rendezvous in Merchants Quay beside the Liffey to a safe house where they were to plan their next manoeuvre. The rebels changed their meeting places constantly so as not to be predictable, in case they were betrayed and trapped. Secrecy was everything. There were always informers. Conor spat. Informers; scum, he thought. For him this was routine, this slipping through the dark streets, these secret meetings. This was his life. He limped slightly as he walked along the street for he had suffered terribly with arthritis in his right shoulder and knee ever since his sojourn as the guest of His Majesty in England. Those days had left their mark on him an' no mistake, but he did not begrudge one twinge, one ache. He was fired by the Cause, the fever was in his blood, and he knew that the price he would eventually have to pay was death. Ireland demanded no less of her lover, for she was a ruthless mistress. He knew how his countrymen loved their land and for him that love manifested itself in Slievelea, the home of his childhood, the place where he had dreamed contented dreams and known joy.

Now as he walked along, the damp on his shoulders, the street slippery, its cobbles shiny under the pale moon and the steady driving mist, his thoughts returned there and dwelt in the dark places of the wood and the coolness of the lake. He thought of the smooth grey stone, and the gnarled branches of the apple trees. And thinking of that reminded him of Danny

211

and the burning glow in the forge, and he wondered about his childhood friend and what had become of him.

'Ah! That was in another time entirely,' he thought, when suddenly all his senses were alert and he felt the hair stand up on the back of his neck. His fingers closed over the gun in his pocket and his eyes sought the cause of the trouble long after his instincts had warned him of danger.

At the corner of the street two Black and Tans were beating someone up. Their shadows in the moonlight leaped about on the wall as their arms rose and fell with each pummel, like figures in some ghastly dance. Conor did not hesitate. He saw beneath the men the red hair of the O'Brien boy, all of seventeen but an I.R.A. man like himself, and he cocked his revolver. With a calm and steady hand he aimed. This was when he was at his peak, and he knew it. He fired once, then again, deadly accurate. The two figures seemed to rise as if on tiptoe, raise their arms pleading to the drowning sky and drop like stones to the pavement.

All sound in the street stopped and for a moment the place was still, then O'Brien staggered to his feet, his face bruised, his nose bloody.

'Jasus, I thought they'd got me, I thought I was done for for sure,' he breathed as Conor helped him to his feet. 'God, it's you, sir. Oh, Janey Mac, thank you, sir.'

The boy had pulled away from Conor and stood awkwardly and stiffly to attention. Conor was tense and alert. The Tans rarely travelled in pairs. They cruised around in groups.

'Never mind that now. Let's get out of here.'

He knew better than to proceed. He knew not what lay before him. Safer to return the way he had come.

'Are you all right?' he said brusquely to O'Brien.

The lad shook himself and grinned at Conor. 'Sure aman't I grand, Mister Casey. Sure they were only a couple of eejits I could polish off any day. Gentlemen Jim Corbett look out.'

Conor was moving along briskly, pushing O'Brien a little ahead of him. He could not understand why he had not heard the pounding of boots until it was too late. His instinct had never failed him before. 'Bastards! Bastards! Ah'll do for you! Ah'll git you you mother-fuckin' bastards!'

Conor heard the voice yell out in the Lancashire accent he recognized because it sounded so like the voice of Old George.

A voice from the past. A voice from Slievelea. He heard shots. He felt nothing, just a wonderful sensation of flying. Then he saw the pavement rise to meet him.

O'Brien's teeth were chattering. He had slipped down the steps to the basement of one of the houses, and he crouched there listening. He heard the Tan cry, 'Bastard!' again, then shots from afar. He heard feet running away and the Lancashire voice calling as it receded, ''Ere, ah'm 'ere.' Then all was silent.

Suddenly O'Brien felt a hand on his shoulder and as a scream started in his throat a firm hand went over his mouth.

'Shut up,' a Dublin voice said, to O'Brien's infinite relief, and the hand was taken away. The voice whispered, 'It's me, O'Malley. Will ye hold yer whist now?'

'Oh Jasus man, ye scared me outa' me skin.'

'Never mind that now. Who is that? Do ye know?'

He pointed to where Conor Casey lay spread-eagled on his face on the dark street.

The rain had become heavier. It streaked O'Brien's freckled face, washing away the blood, cooling the pain of his bruises and plastering the red hair down on his forehead. It fell in rivulets down the lined and battered face of the veteran O'Malley.

'It's the hero himself. That there is Conor Casey himself,' O'Brien whispered reverently, shivering and turning up his jacket collar.

The older man saw the youngster was close to breaking down. 'We'll have to get him back to Foley Place,' he said firmly. 'We must. I know where he lives. We've gotta do that. We can't leave him there like a dog.' He looked at O'Brien's frightened young face. 'Do ye think ye have the stomach for it?' he asked. The boy nodded vigorously.

They looked cautiously to right and left and when they were sure the coast was clear they left the basement and started to move swiftly and silently into the rain-washed street. As they did so they heard Conor groan, and the body twitched and moved imperceptibly.

O'Brien jumped again and grabbed O'Malley's arm. 'God, he's alive.'

O'Malley pushed the youngster ahead.

'Here, you help me an' we'll get him home.' They raised Conor's body and each of them took an arm which they draped over their shoulders. Holding onto his hands, they dragged

Conor between them slowly down Gardiner Street, into Foley Place and to the hero's home.

Aideen and Molly Devlin were sitting on either side of the fire sipping tea, when they looked at each other with startled eyes, for the noise coming from below was the pounding of boots, furtive yet loud in the silent house. They stood up in unison, Aideen dropping the rosary she held and pressing her hand to her mouth to stop herself screaming. Then the door burst open and two men staggered in carrying Conor's limp body between them.

'Where'll we put him, missus?' the young red-haired lad whispered.

Aideen rushed over and helped them deposit Conor gently on the bed. The two men were respectful and white-faced, tension in their every move. They whispered to Aideen that Conor was not dead but badly wounded. She was quite calm now that the crisis was actually here, and asked O'Brien to fetch Dr O'Grady from Gardiner Street. But the lad coloured and said he was sorry but he had to get on, and Aideen realized he had probably risked his life to bring Conor home. Her heart filled with gratitude and she took the boy by the shoulders. 'If ever you or any of your friends are in need of a hiding place, yer very welcome here.' She looked at the older man, including him in her message. 'I mean it,' she said.

Molly said, 'Janey, Mrs Casey, don't get involved. Isn't it enough that Mister Casey is lying bleedin' there for his country? Why should you ...'

'Quiet, Molly. I mean what I say. Do you hear? It's a safe house for ye here.'

'Jasus, Mrs Casey, I'm telling ye, ye'll be in all kinds o' trouble.'

'Aman't I in all kinds of trouble anyway? Sure what would ye call this!'

'I'll go for Dr O'Grady,' Molly said and pulled her shawl over her head.

'Let us go first, missus,' O'Malley said and, pushing O'Brien ahead of him, he touched his cap and they left the apartment, glad they were leaving the evening's troubles behind them.

Aideen and Molly listened as their feet clattered down the stairs. Molly was about to follow when they heard the rat-a-tat-

tat of gunfire. Both women crossed to the window, quickly putting out the lamp on the way. Aideen opened it a sliver. She saw O'Malley running down the street, silent as a cat, disappearing into the shadows, and the great nightmare outline of a Crossley tender at the other end. They must have shot randomly, killing the youngster with the red hair, for he lay there in the street, spread-eagled, his mouth open, gazing at the stars. The Black and Tans disappeared as they watched. Molly Devlin left the apartment, and Aideen was left alone with Conor.

He died before Dr O'Grady reached him, and Aideen was quite calm and cold when Molly returned. She had smiled at him and said, 'I'll keep up the work, Conor. I'll help the Cause now for you. Do you understand?'

And Conor had smiled at her and pushed forward his lips before his face relaxed and life slipped away. He had been going to say, 'Good.' She decided he had said 'love', and a great contentment settled on her.

By his death Conor released Aideen from bondage, and gave her a purpose in life far more satisfactory than the church. She became a strong, formidable freedom fighter; her home became a refuge for men on the run. Number 13 Foley Place became a safe house and Aideen was so busy she never noticed that nearly two years passed without her laying eyes on her son.

Chapter

33

DAN was also too busy to think of his mother and father during those turbulent years. He had never been happier in his life and the only unpleasant occurrence was Conor's death. But the funeral suited him down to the ground. In the forefront of the large crowd, holding his mother's arm in a firm supportive grasp, he basked in the notoriety and attention his position received. In true Irish fashion, the funeral was turned into a mass demonstration for the Cause and Michael Collins, leader of the I.R.A. and himself the most wanted man in Ireland, came in spite of this to lay a wreath. A volley was fired at the graveside and the Last Post played, and Dan felt his mother straighten her back and stand up tall, her head flung back; and when he looked at her, surprised because he had been sure she would collapse, he was amazed to see an exultant smile on her lips, and he realized he did not know her at all. He shrugged, for he had neither the desire nor the time to work out the complexities of Aideen's personality, but he wallowed in the limelight his father's funeral had thrust upon him. After that he turned from Foley Place and all its associations and proceeded with his business deals and Hymie Klein and his illicit relationship with Hymie's lovely wanton daughter Jessica.

He had known that Jessica was more than casually interested in him, and he realized that Hymie had known it too; and he saw through Hymie's ruse to keep them apart. He liked Hymie, and had not intended to avail himself of Jessica's obvious inclinations towards him even though he found her disturbingly provocative, with her wild, tangled glossy masses of blue-black hair and her enormous, slanted, coal-black eyes set in a milk-white face like jet in snow. But Jessica Klein was a determined and wilful young lady and was used to having her way, so when she realized that Dan was not going to initiate a romance, in spite of her amorous glances, she decided to take matters into her own hands.

One day on reaching Mount Street he opened the packet of home-made apple strudel Mrs Klein always gave him and found a note. *I will come to you in Mount Street on Sunday morning*, he read. It was signed 'J.K'.

Dan was not quite sure how to behave, so he did what he normally did in such circumstances. He waited to see what would happen. He was not at all prepared for what did.

Dan had had his fair share of physical encounters with the opposite sex but always with 'girls no better than they should be', as he called them, and his sexual experience was limited to furtive, heated and extremely quick coupling followed by relief and no feeling of emotional involvement at all. Things with Jessica were very different. Dan's room in Mount Street had been furnished in a dark exotic style he thought in the pink of fashion. It actually looked like a cross between a courtesan's boudoir and a sheik's tent. There was deep crimson velvet on the walls, a four-poster bed with red velvet drapes, a wine-coloured carpet on the floor and a chaise longue covered in patterned Chinese silk. Scattered about were Chinese vases, cushions, a hookah in brass and a large brass table. A lot of paraphernalia purchased in Hymie Klein's and originating somewhere in the Orient cluttered up the already crowded room.

Into this apartment Jessica came, as promised, in a neat little black coat and cloche hat. She stood with her back to the door, looking first around the room, recognizing quite a lot of the *objets d'art*, and then at Dan. She laughed, a deep chuckle pulled off her hat, and shook out her luxuriant hair. She undid her coat, took it off and laid it on the chaise longue. She then slipped out of her dress, kicked off her shoes, and slowly peeled off her sheer silk stockings. Dan was nonplussed, fascinated but not overwhelmed. He savoured the tones of her flesh, the black of the silk against the white of her leg, the shadows of pearl on her shoulders and breasts as she removed every stitch of clothing and walked over to the bed, sat on it and pulled the

217

crimson velvet cover up to her chin.

'I've imagined doing that for months,' she said, giving a deep sigh of contentment and pointing a finger at him. 'Now you,' she said.

He laughed and obeyed her and when she saw his large, beautifully made body naked before her she gave another deep sigh of contentment and opened her arms to him.

Every Sunday morning they wallowed in his big four-poster bed exploring every avenue of eroticism, plunging into realms of sensation and delighting in each other's bodies, the pleasure they gave and received. Jessica had been a virgin and Dan her first lover, but it seemed not to hinder her at all, and she threw herself into lovemaking with the greed of a child in a sweet shop. In his dark, voluptuous room Dan plumbed the depths and heights of physical experience and love with a partner who matched him in passion and sensuality.

Dan spent those years joyfully making money and making love with equal success. They talked endlessly too, shared secrets, hopes, dreams and experiences, or at least Dan did. Jessica mainly listened, her head resting on the palm of her hand, propped on her elbow, looking down on him tenderly, occasionally tracing his lips or eyebrows with her finger. They would lie in the rosy glow from the lamps, their bodies the colour of rich cream, intertwined, gossiping and giggling. He told her what he knew of the family history, about Barra Bawn and the famine.

'How they got from Skibbereen to Dublin is beyond me, but they did, and survived and went to Slievelea. That was because of the Devlins. Spotty Devlin's grandpa . . .'

'God, Dan, aren't you curious about Slievelea? I'd be dying with curiosity.'

She shook the blue-black tresses away from her pale forehead. 'I'd go there if it was me, so I would. Oh, I'm that romantic and curious.'

'You are that, my milk-white maid,' he laughed, rich in the warmth of her love, and, nuzzling her generous breasts, he forgot about Slievelea for the moment. But not for long. Her suggestion nagged at him. He had never thought of going to the big house in Wicklow before. Conversation about it had been kept to the minimum in Foley Place, but now he was curious, and pondered over the house and wondered what it was like.

218

Eventually, of course, he had to go, he had to find out.

All he knew of the place were the bare facts: that Michael Casey, his grandfather, had come there from Barra Bawn in 1848, and that he and Conor had lived there and worked there. The house, the name, the grandeur of its reputation were a siren's call to Dan, irresistible, and one day he set off on his bicycle to investigate.

The day was magic, the air alive with birdsong, the hedgerows verdant, full of butterflies and bees, honeysuckle and buttercups, and green leaves trembling in the sweet-scented breeze from the sea. He passed fields of golden grain stained scarlet by clumps of poppies, woodland foliage, green, waist-high grasses, meadows swept by sea winds. He peddled on till he came to the entrance where the pale mother-of-pearl stone gatehouse nestled, its dark-grey roof missing slates here and there and studded with velvet mosses. A chestnut tree shielded it from the sun. This then was where his da had lived. He rested his bike against the low stone wall. All was silence, a silence so profound he could hear his heart beat, hear the sound of the grasses moving, hear the wash of the sea in the distance. He suddenly felt small and insignificant as he stood there. The iron gates were closed but not locked, so Dan opened them and began to walk up the drive. The rhododendrons were running wild and the drive was overgrown with weeds and moss. There was a mysterious hush, and Dan, for a moment, felt a chill of fear. It passed and he stared up to the shafts of light which filtered through the lacework of the leaves where the trees' branches met over his head — so tall, so strong, he thought, reaching to the sky.

When Dan turned a corner and saw the house he was stunned by its beauty. Warm grey stone, elegant terrace, finely proportioned windows, the mountains rising behind it, and the sea at its feet, crowned by the hills in a saucer of green land. He stared with his mouth open till his eyes watered in the sun. The house looked neglected and had an air of dusty disuse about it, but the simplicity of style and outline delighted his eye. Suddenly his little apartment in Mount Street appeared to him common and vulgar.

Then he noticed a French window on the right-hand side of the house ajar. There was a beautiful magnolia tree beside it, and Dan went to investigate, his shoes scrunching on the

219

gravel. When he rounded the corner he jumped as he came face to face with someone standing framed in the French windows. The sun shone full on the face of a beautiful old lady. It showed up pitilessly the network of lines on her soft skin. It dazzled her enormous violet eyes so that she had to raise her pink-nailed hand to shield them from the fierce illumination. The skin on her hand was fine as parchment, blue-veined, and the sapphire and diamond ring she wore seemed too large for the delicate bones.

'Who is that?' she said in a firm voice, but Dan could tell she was startled so he quickly reassured her.

'It's all right. Don't be worried, ma'am. I'm Dan Casey. Me father used to live in the gatehouse and sure I had a yen to see the place.'

'Aha ... aha.' Her voice sounded full of relief. 'So that's why. I thought for a moment you were a ghost. But it seems my ghosts are always flesh and blood. I couldn't understand. Now I do. I'm Deirdre Tandy-Cullaine. I knew your father well. But come in, come in. The sun is in my eyes and I cannot see you properly. That's why I thought for a moment ...' her voice faltered.

'That I was a burglar or a Black and Tan?'

'Oh, don't be absurd. Of course not! I'm too old to be afraid of burglars and Tans. No, I thought you were a ghost and now that I can see you properly you look even more like one.'

'I hope not, ma'am.'

They had walked inside. It was the library, Dan saw, and he was impressed by the rich discretion of the room, the understated elegance where everything blended and no discordant notes were struck. He winced as he once more thought of his Mount Street room.

The mahogany shone and the backs of the leather-bound books with their gold tooling gleamed with a luminosity that reeked of good taste. The big sedate leather chairs and the rosewood humidor entranced him and opened his eyes to a style he had never seen before, had never known was there to appreciate.

Lady Tandy-Cullaine motioned him to a chair, and he waited until she sat across from him, then perched himself on the edge of it. It made him feel large and ungainly, awkward as he had never felt before in his life.

220

'I swear you have aged me ten years with the shock I've just received, young man,' she said, and as he started to protest she held up a hand to stop him, 'but I forgive you. I would forgive such a handsome creature even if you *were* a burglar or a Tan. No one has any right being so beautiful, my boy, and I can say that to you at my age.' She laughed. He found her enchanting and responded to the flirtatious gleam in her eyes.

'An' I would die if such a gracious lady as yourself was angry with me even for a second. Sure a frown would mar the perfection of your beauty and that would never do.'

'Well! Well! Well! The gift of the gab and no mistake, young Dan! It's amazing how like your father you are in looks and how unlike him you are in personality. Do you have a girlfriend, young man?' and the memory of his Sunday mornings flashed across Dan's mind as she continued, 'Ah ... I see you do.'

'Not serious, ma'am.' Dan stumbled over the thoughts and the words.

'She is a lucky girl, but then, perhaps, not so lucky! Such a one as you won't be tamed, I bet.' She shrugged. 'Tell me about yourself. What do you do?'

'I'm in business. I moved to an apartment in Mount Street and I'm working to be rich,' he said. 'Very rich!' he added, smiling his rakish, most charming smile at her. She smiled back a moment in silence.

'I believe you,' she said, 'and you'll do it. To Mount Street from Foley Place? That was it, wasn't it? It's quite a journey. Oh, I didn't mean ...'

'I know what you meant, ma'am.'

She gave him a shrewd look. 'Yes,' she said, 'of course. Please don't call me ma'am. How is your father?'

'He died,' Dan said bluntly. He did not notice her hands clasp the chair arms and the knuckles turn white.

'He was shot by the Tans. Oh, he asked for it, it was bound to happen sooner or later. He died a hero's death, and he's gone into ballad and song, and history too. At the heel of the hunt he had a grand funeral. Half Dublin was there.'

'When you are rich what will you do?' she asked after a pause.

'I'll be a gentleman and live in a house like this,' he said, and she saw the fire in his eyes and nodded.

'I'm here for the summer, young man. Why don't you come

221

and see me? Often! Leave the patriots to fight battles in Dublin's fair city and you and I will talk in peace here. I'm bored to death at the moment and I enjoy your company excessively. I haven't felt so in a long time. Heaven knows I have little enough to amuse me these days.' She sighed and looked at him, smiling slowly, her great eyes sparkling like jewels. 'Perhaps I can turn you into a gentleman,' she said lightly.

'I'm willing. Oh, I'm willing. I'm quick at learning,' Dan said eagerly, taking the offer very seriously.

'You've got a lot to learn. You'll have to change your mode of dress, young man.'

'Yes, ma'am!' he said, saluting in mock imitation of a soldier.

An amazingly beautiful young man, she thought, interested in only one thing, self-advancement. Well, that was not such a bad thing, she mused, ambition was something his father had sadly lacked. Or had he? Dan had said he died a hero, a patriot. It was another kind of success, another kind of achievement. It was not an achievement this one was interested in. Young Dan here before her was chasing a different prize. She eyed him speculatively. He had charm but few scruples, she thought; there was very little he would draw the line at in his pursuit of fame and fortune. But he would be good to those he loved. Yes, he would be a wonderful person to have on your side.

She rose, terminating the meeting. 'Does the weekend suit you?' For a moment her mind went blank, his resemblance to his father swamping her again. 'I forgot your name. I nearly called you Conor.'

'Dan, ma'am. Sunday I visit me mam,' he lied easily.

'My mother.'

'What? Oh yes, my mother. Perhaps . . .'

'Let us say Tuesdays and Thursdays. On Tuesdays come for lunch and Thursdays come for dinner.'

'What . . . what . . . what do you mean, ma'am?'

She realized he did not know the difference. 'Lunch is midday. Dinner is evening. Your first lesson. My mother and lunch and dinner.' She laughed again. 'I'll expect you on Tuesday at twelve thirty sharp. Now leave me. I'm tired.' She held out her hand and was surprised when he raised it to his lips. He turned and left the room in a graceful movement and she stared after him for a long time without realizing her cheeks were wet with tears.

222

'Oh Conor, Conor, if only you had been like this one,' she thought. Then she pulled herself together briskly, and began to plan, feeling an excitement she had not felt for a very long time.

Chapter

34

THEY became very close that summer. Every Tuesday Dan came to lunch and learned to eat from fine porcelain and china and to use the Georgian silver cutlery correctly. He learned to shake open his damask napkin and place it on his knee in one elegant gesture, and how to balance strawberries on a small spoon, to sip soup without spilling or slurping it. Before he returned to Mount Street they had tea on the terrace, the tinkle of the spoons on the delicate Limoges saucers mingling with the twittering of the birds and the distant sighing of the sea. He learned about food and wine, and Deirdre corrected his speech and introduced him to the delights of light conversation. He learned how to concede lightly to her opinions, how to express himself without sermonizing or being boringly dogmatic.

Every Thursday they had dinner by candlelight in the formal dining room. The dinner table, laid with the best silver and gold, the crystal dazzling in the light, at first intimidated Dan but, loving the challenge, he quickly became accustomed to its splendour. Afterwards she encouraged him to express his views about more serious subjects and was often amused by his insularity and his blindness to anything but his own ambition. Sometimes they played cards, or backgammon, or chess. He proved himself an adept pupil. She taught him to dance. In the flickering light of the candles, he held the slim frail body in his arms and one-two-threed her round and round the hall to the music from the creaky recording of Johann Strauss on the gramophone she had asked him to purchase in Dublin in Cleary's, the shop he had looted that Easter Monday of the Rising.

She asked him where he had learned to kiss ladies' hands. He told her he had seen it outside a house in Merrion Square, a gentleman bidding farewell to a lady, and he had promised himself he would do the same one day. She was the first person he had met who would not have laughed at him.

One July day they lunched in the music room on iced cucumber soup, poached salmon with watercress sauce and little bowls of raspberries and cream. Outside the drifts of soft rain swept across the green countryside.

She said, 'Dublin is running red in rivers of blood and I suppose I should care. But I can't seem to get excited or outraged about it. I don't feel Irish and I certainly don't feel like an oppressor.'

'Why don't you feel Irish?' he asked her. 'You were born here, you love it here, and you are called after the great Irish heroine. The only one who loves this place as much as you is me!'

'Perhaps it's because of my father's death. I think I always felt part of my family more than part of any country. We lived here, but we went to Park Lane too. I loved here best but I didn't think of it as Ireland, a country apart from England; it was just a different place. Then when my father was shot I felt very English indeed,' and she told him about it. She remembered herself then, a pretty young girl, so heedless, so in love with this man's father. She remembered the emotional confusion she had felt that party evening and she saw herself once again sitting on the grass, her white gown floating out about her, the crimson stain spreading from her father's wounds. She told him of the sinister dark-haired man, heavily cloaked, who lurked around Slievelea and that his father had known him. She did not tell him how she had felt about Conor in those days. 'I'll never forget that man's face. Like a skull covered lightly with parchment skin. So, so if what you tell me of Conor, of your father, is true, Dan, then it seems I never really knew him, I just thought I did. I don't know what to think sometimes, but the suspicion is there.'

'You mean that even then he was a freedom fighter, that he was involved with the Cause?'

She nodded. 'He must have always been part of the Irish cause and he must have known they were planning to kill my father. If only I had known. How stupid I was. I thought I

225

realized the extent of my stupidity the last time I saw your father, Dan, but that was not the half of it! The present is distorted when the past shadows it. Perhaps I can forget I know. Perhaps facing the truth is better. Who can say?'

'I'm sorry my father should have harmed you in any way. He was a cold man. There was no love in him, at least not that I saw.'

The rain stopped. Deirdre opened the French windows and the room was flooded with the fresh smell of wet grass. They stood outside on the terrace under the magnolia tree whose long, slender, waxen petals shot with rose gently shook in the breeze, and cast off little drops of rain which splattered on the ground and on their faces. The birds sang loudly and they could hear the gulls calling out at sea.

Dan went inside without being asked and returned in a moment with Deirdre's woollen shawl. It was crocheted in the finest cream wool and looked like a pearly cobweb about her shoulders.

'Thank you, Dan. And how do you feel about your father's politics?' she asked as they walked up and down the terrace.

'Me? Oh, I can't get worked up about it, Aunt Deirdre.' She had decided he should call her that. To have him simply call her Deirdre would have been too intimate and lacking in respect, and her full title too formal and subservient for the role she decided he would play. For she had a very clear plan in mind for him.

'I can't see the point of dying for Ireland with a brave smile on my lips.'

She laughed, delighted with his honesty. 'You're a rascal, Dan Casey, and what's more you're a hedonist.'

'What's that?'

She told him.

'It's not *just* that,' Dan said, 'I'm not in favour of killing. I don't think anything — God, your country — is worth a human life.'

'Yours, you mean! How about someone else's? Suppose, Dan, you saw someone take all your money and possessions from you, and the only way to stop them would be to shoot. Would you? Would *that* life be so very valuable then?'

He knew the answer and he looked quickly at her and recognized her accurate assessment of him in her eyes, and throwing back his head he laughed aloud.

A sunray peeped from behind a dove-grey cloud to flood the lawns and mountains and turn them gold and rose. They stopped a moment, both stunned by the play of the sombre black rain clouds and the transparent blue sky, and the magical shifting of light and shadow on the gently curving countryside.

Deirdre sighed. 'Politics are deceit. Power leads to corruption. So my father used to say. The trouble with God, with religion, is it tries to force humanity to be perfect and punishes us when we are not, and we all know quite well we cannot be, otherwise we would be gods ourselves. Surely striving for perfection should be enough?'

Dan shrugged. 'I have no time for it. Religion brought no light into my mother's life. It condemned her to fear. Power on the other hand is something I like the feel of.'

'Ah yes, you would! But be careful, Dan, the price is high.'

That evening, after Dan's departure, Deirdre came to a decision she had long been toying with.

The following Thursday in the candlelit dining room they ate roundly of smoked salmon, saddle of lamb with mint, little potatoes and peas, some fine Stilton, and a vacherin of meringue and strawberries and Chantilly cream. As they were finishing their fine French wine, Deirdre asked him quite bluntly, 'How would you like to come away with me for a time?'

She watched him closely for his reaction. The bright open look of excitement and pleasure that illuminated his face stilled any doubts she harboured.

'You see, I have to leave Slievelea soon. We intend to open the house again and live here and it has to be prepared for us. So an army of workmen will arrive next month and after them come the servants, then Letticia and Edward.' She sighed. 'These lovely days are numbered for us, my dear.'

'Yes, yes. Where would we go? To London? That would be grand!'

'Oh, not just London. London is too dreadful at this time of year. No, I thought of Monte Carlo, Italy, Florence, Menton and Venice, and, oh, Baden-Baden. If you felt you could take a year off to educate yourself, we could go to Vienna and London, too, if you really want, in the Season, the correct Season.'

Dan could hardly contain himself. This was an opportunity beyond his wildest dreams. And she had said, if he could take

227

the time. If! He had been shrewd enough to recognize the difficulty of stepping from one world into another, to move from one class, the working class, into the upper. It imposed more obstacles than the mere making of money. He had been confident that by fair means or foul he could do it, but, although he had been optimistic about it, the way to open those society doors had remained an insoluble problem. And now here was the 'open Sesame' he could never have dreamed of in a million years.

These things were foremost in his mind, but at the same time he did not discount the importance of this old lady in his life. Dan had a great fund of love within him, frustrated and untapped all his childhood by Conor's and Aideen's lack of it and their inability to feel and express any affection at all for him. In his relationship with Jessica the physical was predominant and although their lovemaking incorporated laughter and shared feelings, it was concentrated on the erotic and the sensuous. He had come to love Deirdre Tandy-Cullaine deeply and sincerely, to take pleasure in her company and enjoy the sharp stimulation of her mind. She caused him to ask questions and debate subjects he had previously never troubled to think about at all. He was entranced by her magical beauty, her delicacy, her innate poise and breeding, and loved her as most sons loved their mothers, but without feeling the irksomeness of commands, or the discipline mothers have to impose.

Deirdre knew this and it afforded her great pleasure. In the twilight of her life, she had at last found a totally satisfactory love and this time she did not intend to waste a moment. They made their plans accordingly. They would spend August in Monte Carlo, and in September they would go to Italy. They planned to visit Vienna and Salzburg after that and hoped to be in Switzerland for Christmas.

Lady Tandy-Cullaine sent Dan to Mr Hawkins, Dublin's best tailor, who fitted him for clothes suitable for his travels. He ordered the minimum. Aunt Deirdre told him there were much more beautiful garments available in France and Italy, so he must not splurge in Dublin. Dublin, she said, was best for linens and tweeds and crystal, but sadly behindhand in leather, silk, cashmere and cotton. The few basic items Dan had had made for himself — a white linen suit, evening dress, white tie and tails, a cloak, black, lined with damson-coloured satin — the

228

brogues he purchased, the alligator luggage obtained in Cleary's, all cost such an astronomical sum that he frightened himself. If these few things cost so much, what a vast amount of money it must take to own and run a place like Slievelea, to entertain and keep horses, to maintain the standard of living he aspired to.

However, he put such bleak thoughts out of his head. He told no one that he was leaving Dublin. Nothing would spoil his trip, not even Jessica. He knew he was being craven and cowardly but he was secretly afraid of what she might do if he told her. Her passionate nature extended beyond the bed and he felt that keeping her in ignorance in this case was the best policy. They made love every Sunday except once a month when she 'wasn't well', and fate smiled on Dan, for the trip was planned for the last week in July when Jessica should be fretting in her little room over the shop, cross and frustrated, as she always was at such times, partly due to the aching pains and partly to missing Dan Casey.

However, Jessica's period had not arrived that July weekend and she was scared. She was as regular as clockwork and couldn't understand why there was no sign of it, for it was due on Friday and it was now Sunday. An awful possibility crossed her mind, but she quickly pushed it away, determined to take herself and her worry to Dan. He would know what to do. She found the Mount Street apartment shut and Spotty Devlin on the stairs outside reading a note in Dan's handwriting.

'Where's Dan Casey?' she asked fearfully.

Spotty looked up at this exotic apparition, not in the least surprised at her appearance there. Spotty put nothing past Dan at all, including the possession of mysterious and beautiful women.

'Sure he's gone away,' he said, tapping the letter with his finger. 'He says here ... Let me see ...'

Jessica snatched the letter from him. Spotty made no move to stop her.

I am going away and don't know when I'll be back ... carry on the business ... money in the wardrobe ... trust you ..., she read. 'Nothing ... nothing about me! The bastard!'

'Oh, miss!' Spotty was shocked rigid. It was all right for his ma or his sisters to use such a word, but not this beautiful lady. 'Oh, miss!'

'Don't you "oh miss" me. He *is* a bastard,' and she threw the letter at him. 'What's that?' She noticed an unopened envelope in Spotty's hand.

'Oh, this? It's for Jessica Klein. Is that you?'

'Yes, dolt! Give it to me!'

She grabbed the envelope from him and tore it open. Inside there was a single page. It said:

Dearest Jessica,

I am called away on business for a year. I look forward to seeing you when I come back. I hope you keep in good health.

Dan.

Jessica was shaken by wave upon wave of fury. She was rendered speechless. She crumpled the letter in her fist.

Spotty said, 'Is anything wrong, miss?' and she hit him savagely with her other fist. Luckily she only caught his shoulder, but he skidded down two steps, hitting his head on the wall.

'Oh gawney, miss, what did I do?'

'Dolt,' she cried, 'idiot,' and ran down the stairs. She turned at the door.

'What's your name?' she asked Spotty. He told her.

'Well, he says in that,' she pointed to the letter in his hand, 'you are to continue with the business. Will you?'

'Oh yes, miss, but in a modest way. You know, like not on the scale he does things, but well, miss, he always said if he went away I was to keep things ticking over. That's what I'll do, keep them ticking over.'

'Good! Then I'll see you again.'

'Yes, miss. Very good, miss.' Spotty was not at all sure he wanted to see this fiery creature again.

'I'm sorry I hit you,' she said. 'It's just that he's a lousy bastard.'

'You said that before, miss, and you mustn't. He's a darlin' man, yes he is, miss, a darlin' man.'

He watched her leave the house, then he shrugged philosophically, scratching his stubble. He took out the key Dan had left and opened the door to his flat. It was gorgeous. He marvelled once again. What style! What magnificence! He wondered if Dan would mind if he slept in the big crimson bed just once. Just once to sleep alone! Just once to sleep in a real bed! And what a bed! He decided he'd sleep there on Saturday nights to keep the apartment safe from burglars. Yes, that was a good right and tight reason begob, yes, and he hugged himself gleefully at the treat in store.

Jessica left Mount Street shaking with fury and very near to tears. How could he? How could anyone treat her like that? Leaving a paltry little note, without even a loving message? It was unbelievable. She knew he was not a man one could cage, but she had hoped to bind him to her at least so that he would tell her, himself, face to face, if he was going to disappear for a while. A whole year! Why? Why hadn't he told her? But she knew, she knew Dan Casey would always avoid awkward and uncomfortable confrontations.

Jessica walked the distance home automatically, not noticing where she was going until she reached the quays and found herself on the middle of the metal footbridge, or Halfpenny Bridge as it was sometimes called, from Noonan's Shirt Factory. There she stopped and looked down at the peaty water of the Liffey making its turgid way to the docks below. She felt betrayed and fearful. Her fingers played with the metal knobs on the lace-like balustrades of iron-wrought metal, and at last, looking down at the water, she drew in a sobbing breath and tears splashed down her face.

Hymie was coming across the bridge to his shop on the other side when he saw her. He was well aware of his daughter's affair with Dan, but he was far too *au fait* with human nature to have tried to stop it once it was fully under way. He loved his daughter with all his heart. She was the apple of his eye and all he could hope for was that she would grow out of her infatuation before any harm was done. He hoped they would not marry. He was not anti-Christian, but he hoped for a nice Jewish union for his daughter. Unfortunately, attractive Jews, or in fact any Jews at all, were thin on the ground in Dublin, and poor Jessica's choice was sadly limited. He nevertheless had hopes of Stanley Rosenthal, the furrier's son, a nice upstanding boy and moderately wealthy. Hymie, however, was realistic and few men in the whole of Dublin, Christian or Jewish, could match Big Dan Casey for good looks and charm. How poor Stanley could hope to compete didn't bear thinking about. All

231

Hymie could do was summon his considerable patience and wait. And now, on this glorious August day, here she was standing in the middle of the bridge, crying her heart out. He put his arm round her and gently guided her home. He put his fingers to his lips and smiled, and she choked down her tears so that her mother would not hear. He led her into the shop, which was cool and dark, and sat her down. He went to a cupboard and took out a decanter full of warm Spanish sherry and two small glasses. He carefully filled the glasses with the amber liquid, and, sitting opposite her, gave her one and said, 'Is it Dan Casey?'

Jessica looked up, surprised. She nodded.

'Well, tell me.'

'He's gone. Gone away on business. On business he says.'

She still had the ball of paper in her hand. She sipped her sherry and put it down and smoothed out the crumpled sheet of paper, wordlessly handing it to her father. He read it in silence and passed it back. He hid his great relief.

'Well, then. There's no more to be said. There is nothing to be done. Let him go. You'll have to get on with the business of life, daughter. We none of us have that much time that we can afford to waste it.'

But Jessica was crying again. 'It's not that, Papa. I think I may be pregnant!'

'Oh my God!' The words were out before Hymie could stop them. 'I'll kill Dan Casey. How dare he! My daughter!'

'No, no. Papa, you mustn't be angry. It was my fault. I went to him, you see. He never would have made advances to me because of you, he told me, unless I had started the whole thing. I love him so, Papa. I ... I ...' She gave a weak smile through her tears. 'I enticed him!'

Hymie threw up his hands and shook his head.

'What kind of a daughter do I have?' he asked rhetorically. 'What kind of a daughter that will throw herself at a man? What kind of a ...'

'Oh Papa, hush! As you said yourself, life must go on.'

'I didn't mean ...'

'I know, Papa. I'll have his baby. I've quite decided. It will be something of his. If only I can stay here, please, Papa ... you won't throw me out?'

He opened his arms to her and held her tightly. 'As if I

232

would. What a terrible thing to think I would do. Of course you may stay here. I'll speak to your mother. But Jessica, he will be back in a year. He will, perhaps, want you back. What then?'

She shook her head. 'No, Papa. Dan Casey wants much more out of life than I can ever give him, and as he has charm, looks and ambition he'll get it. You see, Papa, much and all as I'd like to be able to blame him I really cannot. He made me no promises; he gave me no vows. All this is my own fault. But he had a love for me and I don't want to spoil that. Best accept the situation as it is.'

Hymie nodded, appalled at his daughter's culpability, surprised at her adult sense. He wasn't too distressed, for deep in his heart his greatest dread was losing Jessica. He had long subdued in his breast the desire to postpone her adulthood, her inevitable growing up and going away, marrying and leaving him and Martha alone and ageing. Her beauty and gaiety kept them young. She was the spice of their lives, the sun on a dark day, the star that lifted their hearts, and now she was going to stay and bring new life into theirs.

Hymie thanked the Lord silently and hugged his daughter, then went and poured another sherry.

Chapter

35

DEIRDRE enjoyed every moment of their year together in Europe as much as Dan did. He made sure of that. She took up most of his attention and he was glad, but she did not monopolize him. She was a wise, witty and warmly affectionate companion and he loved her more each day and let her see that he did. She basked in Dan's attentive tenderness, his wonderful vitality and *joie de vivre*. He was the perfect companion. She chased him out at night after dinner in Monte Carlo to dance the night away under the stars with the myriad of young flappers who seemed in perpetual giggling pursuit of the tall handsome man. He flashed his teeth at them and joined their gay abandon for a few hours but seemed indifferent to their individual charms. She introduced him to the Ballet Russe de Monte Carlo. He was dazzled by Nijinski in *Spectre de la Rose* and *L'Après Midi d'un Faun*; found Stravinski's music jarring, unfamiliar, disturbing but exciting; allowed Deirdre to educate him to a better awareness of the art; and, meeting Diaghilev, Nijinski and Nijinska at soirées, concealed his astonishment at their flamboyant personalities and exotic clothes. They reminded him of peacocks, forever drawing attention to themselves.

He became accustomed to grand hotels, to the first-class treatment Lady Deirdre Tandy-Cullaine took for granted, as her right. Idly drinking tea to the sound of sweet violins in the palm courts of the hotels, high-ceilinged with gigantic sparkling chandeliers, dancing at night in the ballrooms under the stars or even more dazzling chandeliers, soon all of it became second nature to him. He responded ardently to the life Deirdre introduced him to. He became used to caviar and champagne, *foie gras* and oysters, truffles and pheasant, *boeuf en croûte* and *marrons glacés*. He learned about fine wines and brandy and he appreciated all the new entertainments: the magic of the theatre in Paris; of opera in La Scala, Milan; of escorting Deirdre in a landau to the d'Este Gardens in Rome. They listened to Mozart in Salzburg and danced to the strains of the waltz in Vienna. Dan held Deirdre's hand in Demel's, eating their famous cakes and drinking chocolate. They picnicked in the Vienna woods on a cold autumn day and spent the afternoon admiring the horses at the Spanish Riding School. They never reached London. Although Deirdre planned to be there for the Season, she suddenly became curiously reluctant about going and, in any event, they were having such an enchanting time dallying elsewhere it was of no importance.

He loved to share his thoughts and feelings with her, and his reactions to new sensations. Their relationship flowered beneath the blue skies of France and Italy and, without the tension of sex or the lunatic emotional turmoil of 'being in love', they could relax and grow in each other's love. They laughed a great deal. She taught him about music and painting. They travelled through the dreaming, terra-cotta coloured, sun-drenched towns of Tuscany and she was entranced by the wonder on his face as they explored Siena, Verona, Padua and, most of all, Florence. His soul yearned to be a painter with Guido di Pietro in the fifteenth century and walk the cobbled streets to the cloisters, listening to the bells of the churches ring on the hot dusty mornings, sharing the joyful austerity and learning of the monastic life, and painting those wonderful sensuous nuns who were both mistress and model to Fillipo Lippi, chastity vows or no. But then on a still night in Venice, as the gondolas rested on the calm water, their reflections blending with the mirrored, crumbling mansions bordering the canals, a tenor's voice singing a serenade to a wistful tune on a mandolin, or listening to the orchestra outside Florian's whilst drinking their coffee after a superb dinner, he would change his mind and dream of being Casanova, and chuckle over his exploits, and ask Deirdre about Vivaldi.

It was all so new and exciting and he was very greedy. He learned to differentiate between the pretentious and the tasteful, the shocking, the outrageous and the merely vulgar. The days and evenings folded slowly into and over each other. Life

235

had grace and style, it lacked the anxiety engendered by the need to work in order to survive. It held promise, it beckoned, it entranced with the munificence of its gifts. It revealed itself to Dan and Deirdre, and the more they showed their appreciation the more abundantly life showered on them its delights.

Chapter

36

WHEN Dan returned a year later it was to a Dublin as changed as he was. The political situation had altered drastically. Ireland was now a free state, albeit divided. Ulster remained under British rule, but the south was a Republic and the flag Conor had helped put up at the Post Office in 1916 was now flying over Dublin Castle. The British were gone from Dublin and Ireland had her own Parliament. Dan's heart soared at the possibilities, now, for free enterprise for the Irish businessman. If only, he thought, his father had lived he could have been a politician, like many of Eire's erstwhile freedom fighters. But his father was dead, and Dan knew that he could not give up the life he had been introduced to, so something had to be done. But what? He had no patience; he was not prepared to wait. Aunt Deirdre had promised much without being specific, and Dan found himself back in Mount Street with only her promise of seeing him at Slievelea in the autumn, when the house would be ready for the Tandy-Cullaines to move in, to look forward to. She herself had returned to Park Lane after their journeying and he missed her sorely. Mount Street seemed vulgar and pitiable to him now, and his life appallingly dull and petty.

The first thing he noticed on returning home was the linoleum in the hall. That had once been a source of pride as an enormous improvement on the Foley Place entrance, naked as the day the floor was laid, but now his feet were used to Persian carpets and the shiny stuff revolted him. He had become used to a fine quality of life and had lived in elegant style. Suddenly to find himself back in Mount Street proved too much for Dan's now cosseted equilibrium. He became as tense as a violin string and as intractable as a cat with fleas.

Spotty was no help. His gormless astonishment at his friend's sophisticated new image drove Dan to distraction so he was in no mood to be civil when Spotty told him he had fixed up a business appointment for him in Mooney's pub.

'There's a man wants to see you. Says only you'll do. Talks of big money, Dan, real big.'

'Yerra, sure, what does anyone in this benighted town know of big money? I ask you?'

Dan thought he might as well go though he had no stomach for this type of business just yet. The squalid interior of Mooney's appalled him. He was too fresh from the sights and sounds of the plushy side of European travel to adjust easily to Mooney's snug. On the other hand, he was eaten up with an anxiety that unless he found a way to make an enormous amount of money, the style of life which had become irresistible to him in one short year might be lost to him for ever. He had confided as much to Spotty, with whom he shared his feelings, expecting nothing back. And to Spotty it was as if Dan were speaking in a foreign language. Spotty had hero-worshipped his friend before he went away, but since his return Dan had assumed the status of a god in Spotty's mind. Also Dan had promised Spotty the flat when his fortunes improved, although Spotty could not imagine how Dan could want any more than he already had. The Mount Street flat was heaven to Spotty Devlin. Nothing promised by the priests in the Pro-Cathedral sounded half as good to Spotty as the plush splendour of the first-floor flat in Mount Street. He simply couldn't understand Dan's disenchantment with it.

'Jasus, it's gorgeous, Dan.'

'It's horrible, Spotty, quite hideous. When I make more money, which I *must* soon, you can have it.'

'Gawney Mac, Dan, do you mean it? Jasus, Mary and Joseph, that'd be the day! Sure, Dan, yer a right man yerself. Thanks a ton.'

Spotty thereupon gave his undivided attention to the problem of Dan's advancement with an ardour that amused and at the same time irritated Dan. Spotty's desire for the flat caused him to work harder on the knotty question of Dan's finances than he had ever done before in his life. He pricked up his ears and listened, chatted people up, lived, breathed, dreamed about ploys and plots that smelt of money without knowing what was important and what was not. Stolen goods or political intrigue, he followed up clues on both, but always the rewards were minimal or the undertaking too dangerous, the chances of being caught too high. Dan certainly had no intention of ending up like his father, in prison.

At last Spotty heard on the grapevine of something big for a Foley Place man, who had to be trustworthy beyond all else, and he went immediately to Dan. Spotty then went himself to reconnoitre, meeting a man called Foxey Finnegan, a little man, nearly a dwarf, a man with eyes that worked separately, one that turned circles in his head and one that twitched. It turned Spotty's stomach to look him in the face. He had a tick under one of the eyes, the eye that twitched, and a wart on his jaw. He seemed overcome by a powerful fear, constantly looked over his shoulder, and was incapable of sitting still. Spotty felt he was onto something: the fellow's palpable fear indicated that. So Dan agreed reluctantly to meet 'this apology of a man', as Spotty called him.

And so it was that they walked through the sunlit streets of the city to Mooney's. A dry, dusty breeze aggravated their thirst and they were glad to reach the pub where the atmosphere was as dark and damp as the streets outside had been arid, bright and hot. The people inside blended with the sepia-coloured interior. They too were wearing browns, tans, chocolate and black, tones echoed everywhere except in the shafts of muted light that slanted through the opaque engraved windows. Dan was the only oddity there. He looked like a hummingbird in a nest of sparrows, tall and proud, dressed fashionably, his hair stylishly cut, his nails manicured. Among the riff-raff of a crowd, where each gained comfort from the anonymity of being indistinguishable from the next man, Dan was a rarity, therefore suspicious.

Spotty saw Foxey at the table, the same table that Conor had sat at years before with Lefty Leary. It was the most secluded table in the pub and chosen for that reason by those holding conversations and not wishing to be overheard.

The introductions were affected, Spotty sitting silently, looking intently from one man to the other as they spoke. At first Foxey wanted him to leave, and it gratified Spotty that Dan refused, calling him his trusted friend and 'confidant', whatever

239

that might mean, and saying he was his 'right-hand man'. Drinks were ordered. The talk ran to and fro, full of ambiguities and half-suggestions and allegories. For a long time neither Spotty nor Dan could make head or tail of exactly what was afoot. Dan, however, was excited, for there was something about the ugly little man that suggested this was a big job indeed.

When Foxey was decorated with a moustache of froth from his second pint, and Dan had lit a cigar, the latter said, 'Well now, isn't it time that we got down to specifics?'

'Yes, yes, sir, indeed an' it is. Yes, sir!'

'Well, come on then. What exactly do ye want?'

'Put it this way, sir, the Party at the top is very high up indeed, the cream of the milk, ye might say, and this Party owns a nice site, such a cosy place for him to set up his business.'

'Where is the site?'

'Well, it's in Dorset Street.' Foxey was reluctant to name names and give exact locations; the words whistled through his teeth.

Dan said, 'Look, man, I'm not a bloody mind-reader, what do you expect me to do? Guess what this is all about?'

'Now, hold yer whist, don't get excited. Now. Listen. Where is Dorset Street? Where?'

'Round the corner up to the north of O'Connell Street. Why?' (Sackville Street had changed its name to be called after one of Ireland's great heroes and Dan hoped for a Casey Street to follow; after all, his da was one of Ireland's martyrs.)

'Well, now, can you think of its proximity?'

'What the devil do you mean? Proximity to what?'

'Ah no, proximity to *where*?' The little man finished his pint triumphantly.

Dan tried to keep his patience as Foxey banged down the empty glass and added, 'And then the new contraptions!'

'What contraptions?' Dan asked, bewildered at the turn the conversation had taken.

Spotty said, 'Motor cars. He's talkin' about motor cars. Those things.'

Foxey nodded, then jerked his head sideways at Spotty and said with a malicious gleam in his eyes, 'Maybe he's the one who should do the job?'

Dan looked at him contemptuously. 'We don't even know

what the job is yet and if you think I'm going to sit here for the next week and drag the information out of you, you're making a big mistake.'

'Ah no, sir, simmer down, simmer down. I'm gettin' to that. Now listen. The contraption is the motor car, the site is Dorset Street, the business the Party is interested in is a garage. Now are ye gettin' the picture?'

Dan said, 'No. No, I'm not.'

'Jasus, man, are ye thick or somethin'? What about another pint? No bird ever flew on wan wing, eh? eh?'

Drinks were purchased and when the three were settled again Foxey sighed. 'I suppose I better spell it out,' he said.

Dan nodded.

'Can't you guess what might bother the Party? Can't you see?' and as both Spotty and Dan shook their heads he sighed again and said, 'Well, I'll give you another hint.'

'If you don't get to the point soon I'll throttle you.' Dan was getting angry. He was beginning to think the whole thing was a waste of time.

'I'll tell you who the Party is, then. Lord Lewis. A young whippersnapper of an English earl. Lord Jasper Lewis.'

Suddenly everything became clear to Dan, clear as day. He nodded. 'Foley Place,' he said.

Foxey slapped his thigh with his hand in an ecstasy of delight. 'Right, right. Mind you, I've said nuthin'.'

Spotty looked from one to the other, nonplussed.

'It's an obstacle, ye see.'

Dan said, 'Yes, I see.'

'The man wants someone to be very creative with petroleum.'

Dan nodded. Spotty's head turned from man to man as they spoke, puzzlement written all over his face.

'And the money?' Dan said.

'Ah well now. C'mere.' Dan leaned forward and Foxey whispered in his ear. The amount was so large that Dan didn't notice the mingled odours of bad breath, unwashed body and stale booze that emanated ripely from Foxey.

'Ye see, he's payin' largely for silence and efficiency.' The two men nodded and Foxey continued, 'An' Foley Place is an embarrassment.'

'It's where me mam lives,' Spotty said and both men turned to stare at him, then as if by mutual consent they rose and

241

shook hands. It all ended so suddenly that Spotty had to run to catch up with Dan as he left the pub.

'What are ye goin' to do, Dan, what?' he cried plaintively, as he blinked his eyes in the sunlight, and trotted along beside Dan as he usually did, beside and slightly behind. He could see that Dan was excited; there were two spots of pink on his cheeks, and his eyes glittered in the sun.

'What are ye goin' to do?' he cried again like a child asking a parent and dreading to hear the answer.

'Didn't you hear him, Spotty? They're offering a fortune. Half now, half when the job's done. Young Lewis wants to have more than the family title, you know, Spotty. Our landlords. The Lewis's of Barra Bawn out of London own half of the tenements in Dublin. Well, now they are going into business, no less. Garage. Think of the money to be made. Out of cars, Spotty, cars, the transport of the future. Janey Mac, Spotty, he'll clean up.' Dan's acquired cultivated accent had disappeared. 'Thing is, Foley Place is right behind the property he owns on Dorset Street. He needs the space. Foxey is right. Foley Place is an embarrassment.'

'But what are ye goin' to do, Dan?' Spotty's voice was hysterical and Dan laughed.

'Don't worry, Spotty. It will be all right, I promise you, no one will be hurt. I'm going to burn down Foley Place, that's what I'm going to do.'

Spotty was very unhappy and apprehensive about the whole undertaking. Dan was excited and stimulated. He saw no problem. He knew none of the families in Foley Place would suffer; the last thing Lord Lewis wanted was a scandal. That would defeat the purpose.

At a subsequent meeting with Foxey, same time, same place, and guaranteed to be their last, the money changed hands, and Foxey, now more inclined to be loquacious, told Dan that Lord Lewis had the largest insurance imaginable with Lloyd's of London. They had no reason to be suspicious; they had dealt with the Lewis's for years. The families now living in Foley Place would get little houses out in Santry, nice new little places, and there should be no tears shed over that. Spotty, however, didn't think it would be that simple, and Dan, secretly feeling it might be more difficult than it had first appeared, got cross with Spotty.

242

They were walking down O'Connell Street one day and had reached the river when, as he turned to admonish Spotty, Dan spotted Jessica Klein crossing the bridge. She looked lovely with the breeze ruffling her jetty locks and moulding her light cotton dress against her body. Dan rushed over to her, calling her name. Spotty screwed up his face, remembering the lady's fury the last time they had met, for he had not seen her, after all, during Dan's absence. He fully expected her to clout Dan one, but there was Dan lifting her up in his arms and spinning her round so that her hat flew off. Spotty gave it chase, wondering for the millionth time at the contrariness of fate with regard to Dan Casey. Anyone else he knew got what they asked for, while Dan seemed to receive only smiles and never the deserved rebuke. Perhaps after all the Foley Place business would work out well for Dan. Everything else seemed to.

Dan was hugging and kissing Jessica and she was laughing and blushing.

'Sure I thought you'd gone for good, Dan Casey. Leaving me to pine away and die!'

'Yes, an' you the picture of life. I've never seen you look so lovely, Jessica me darlin'. Let me see your finger,' he looked for a ring. 'Are the men of Dublin blind or thick or what that none of them have asked for that little hand?'

Jessica tossed her head. 'Oh, it's not for the want of askin', Dan Casey, that my hand is bare, but sure wasn't I looking for a replica of yourself in the men and there isn't one to match you in the whole city. What about yourself? Is there a Mrs Casey, may I ask?'

'Not on your life, Jessica. In the length and breadth of Europe there wasn't a woman to match you, love,' and, as he said it glibly, he realized it was true. 'Will you come to the flat on Sunday for old time's sake and we'll talk, maybe?'

She grabbed her hat from Spotty and pulled it on, her cheeks flushed, her eyes sparkling.

'Sure I will. Try and stop me. And I hope talking won't be the whole of it,' and she ran across the bridge and disappeared into her father's shop.

Spotty and Dan walked home in silence, each pursuing their own thoughts. Dan was elated. Here was a way out of his difficulties, a delicate mission to be sure, but he was going to succeed and he was not going to allow anything or anybody to

243

stop him. How the people in Foley Place felt he neither knew nor cared. He had a plan and he intended to put it into action, the sooner the better.

Dan got Spotty Devlin to tell his mam that Lord Lewis intended to get rid of them. His mam informed the neighbour-hood, frightening the Foley Place dwellers half to death that Lord Lewis was going to scare them into leaving, he was going to frighten them, cut off their water supply, infest the district with rats, get bully-boys around to terrorize them so that they would have to leave.

There was truth in these rumours. It had been suggested. But Lord Lewis was greedy, and there would be no insurance if that particular plan succeeded. That they would have nowhere to go was a lie, Spotty told them; hadn't Dan Casey come to their rescue? He had taken up their cause with Lord Lewis, whom he had met on his travels, and he had insisted that they be rehoused. Things were not one hundred per cent ready but soon would be. At the end of the day, Dan came down and answered all their questions. He was greeted as a hero and people cried out, 'God bless you, Dan Casey,' and he smiled his charming smile and was once more amazed at the gullibility of the masses.

His mother, however, did not respond to his ready words. When he paid her a duty visit he became uncomfortable under her direct gaze and the irony in her eyes. He guessed he did not fool her, but did not want to enter into a discussion with her about it, so he left as quickly as he could after a cup of tea and returned to Mount Street, elated and astonished at how easy it all was.

Foley Place the next morning was a hive of activity. Dan had provided barrows and carts, and furniture and worldly goods were stacked up high and there was a party atmosphere in the place. It was surprising how few possessions people had and how relieved they seemed to be leaving the only home most of them had ever known. Neighbours laughed and joked and drank pints of porter. The sun helped to make it seem like a holiday and the fact that Dan had provided free drinks all round added to the gaiety. Spotty was the only bad-tempered one among the crowd. He was furious with Dan and he hated what they were up to although he couldn't put his finger on exactly what irri-tated him. True, the families, his own included, would be better off, more comfortable, but nevertheless the whole business smacked of crime and made him feel uncomfortable.

Some people were staying with friends, some with relatives, some were camping under the stars on the Santry Road until their new homes were ready. Everyone looked forward to a better future. 'There's a great day coming an' no mistake.'

Dan walked around a deserted Foley Place that evening making sure everyone had left. Memories flooded back as his feet made their lonely sound on the pavement. He saw his silent parents sitting on either side of the fire. Spotty and himself coming home with the barrow. He thought of the dark, foul-smelling hallways, the rickety stairs, the constant cacophony of noise, the drunken arguments. In the silence of the night his rage for the poverty of the place surged in him and he felt a great tide of joy engulf him as he left a petrol-soaked rag in each house. The end of an era, the end of poverty for him, the end of the struggle, the end of the smells, the feel, the degradation of the poor. Dan Casey lit a match.

There was no fear in his heart as he walked down the burning street. He knew he was on his way, that nothing would stop him now. He had no fear that the fire would get out of control, that he would be found out, that anything at all would go wrong. He felt protected, lucky, successful. Above all, he felt the beginning had arrived, not the end.

He remembered the song Molly Devlin used to sing:

Over the rainbow, far away,
We'll take the kids on a holiday,
Say goodbye backstreet morning, bye-bye.
Goodbye backstreet morning in the pouring rain,
Goodbye coldwater tower, goodbye crowded train.

Dan Casey threw back his head and laughed.

245

Chapter
37

JESSICA went out of the bright sunshine into the cool gloom of her father's shop. He looked up and nodded his head towards the window.

'So I see! The cavalier is back! The father has returned! So now what? Hugs and kisses again, I suppose, and nothing said?'

'Oh hush, Father! Where is Alexander?'

'And where would he be? Upstairs with Martha, your mother.'

'Thank you, Papa. Oh thank you.' She knew her face was flushed with joy and her eyes shining like stars. She knew her father could read her like a book and in any event she was beyond dissimulation. Besides, she understood well the little game they played. She was aware that her father was only too happy that she remained in the family home; the last thing he wanted was to lose her, but he had to pretend to be shocked at the situation between herself and Dan Casey, whereas secretly he rejoiced.

For herself, she knew full well she could not possess the man. She could only have him by letting him go. By always offering him love, by maintaining the wonderfully humorous rapport they had with each other, and by leaving him free, she would keep him for at least some of the time, but she knew that at the first sign of a trap he would be gone for ever and she would never see him again. That was why she had made up her mind never to tell him of the existence of their child. He felt completely free and unfettered with her and that was how she intended to keep it. She could not bear to lose him. She had resigned herself to the fact that she was a one-man woman, more by circumstance than by choice. Perhaps in the exotic places through which he had travelled Big Dan Caseys were ten a penny, but not in Dublin. There was not his like, Jessica reflected, in the length and breadth of Ireland, and if she could have just part of him she would settle for that. No one, she thought, would ever possess all of him. Too much of his energy went into work and dreams. He was constantly chasing another goal. What would happen when he ran out of goals? she wondered. He would send for her, hopefully.

She had mapped out her life and was content with the plan she had made for it. She would live here with her father and mother and help them, both in the shop and at home. She was learning the business and had become adept at dealing with people. As her parents grew older, she would naturally take over more and more, and eventually the business would be hers, then Alexander's. But that was the future, a long way into the future. They would never want and Alexander would be protected. Her father, partly to get her away from the gossip and partly because he wanted the best for her, had sent her into the deep green land of Cork to friends for the last months of her pregnancy and for Alexander's birth. The friends were farmers and eternally grateful to Hymie for his generosity. He had given them a loan on their meagre goods, which consisted primarily of a grandfather clock, a wedding ring and a gold watch chain and pocket watch. The loan had enabled them to start as farmers, and a good harvest had brought them in enough to repay him. But they had never forgotten his kindness and always urged him to think of them as friends. They were delighted to help Jessica who, they were told, was a widow, and in the heart of the country, surrounded by peace and beauty, Alexander was born. Jessica had been so happy there that they urged her to stay and she remained with them for the first six months of Alexander's life.

Alexander! She doted on Dan Casey's son. He had become the centre of the house, the heart of the home. The Kleins had always been a loving family and Alexander completed it and gave it a new dimension, taking away the shades of anxiety about Jessica's future, her departure to a new home with a man she would marry, for, now, how could that be? Women with illegitimate children did not marry. So she would remain with them and they would pour out their love on her laughing son and rejoice.

247

Jessica planned to be there for Dan Casey whenever he needed her. She would bring him joy and laughter and love with no ties, no recriminations. She knew he would marry politically, for money, for advancement, and she knew that would cause her pain, but she also knew that she would never show it. He would never know, and so would always come back to her. There was only one thing necessary to her plan and that was an apartment where she and Dan would be together. She knew how it would be decorated and she knew it would not be Mount Street. Spotty could have Mount Street and welcome. She decided to look for a place and get it in her own name. She could not tell her father about it; it would be too much for him to cope with. The delicate balance of their whole world could be shaken by indelicate handling of the situation. Her father could not know of her plan. If he were told the whole of it, he would perforce have to disapprove, take a moral stand against it, otherwise he could not live with himself. So, although he would be aware she was seeing Dan, she did not discuss the situation with her father, so that he was not made uncomfortable in any way. She would bear the whole moral responsibility.

Dan got his money, Jessica got her love-nest, and the Sunday assignations began once more. But Dan had changed, Jessica realized, in some good ways and some bad. He was not so sharply greedy, so fiercely eager for gratification as he had been before he went away. He was now much more determined to grasp everything life had to offer, to plunder every sensation and experience. He had lost a lot of the innocent enjoyment of discovery and now seemed intent on refinement, with a curious snobbery in respect of what was 'done' and 'not done'.

'Ah sure, who cares about that?' Jessica queried.

'I do.' Dan now rarely justified his ideas or demands; he was acquiring the habit of command.

'But here in bed, just the two of us. Sure who's to see if you shave or not?'

'I see. It matters to me,' was all the explanation she got, but she learned. She was determined to keep up with him. She soon saw he appreciated a certain delicacy she introduced into their intercourse. He liked it that she did not shout out her joy so much now, that she stopped using certain ribald words that used to arouse him to frantic excitement in the old days, but now had

248

the reverse effect. She was careful in her vocabulary and in providing him with a far more genteel ambience than ever before. She found the new regime a bore, and she felt a lot of the fun they had had in other days was missing, but her *idée fixe* was to please him totally and in this she succeeded. They no longer, to her regret, threw off their clothes and fell on the bed in an orgy of sexual passion. She would greet him in a peignoir of satin trimmed with lace, or silk trimmed with swan's down. She would serve him tea out of a silver pot and chat with him about his week, for all the world, Jessica thought, like a diligent wife.

The apartment was in Haddington Road and had a large bay window. A small table was placed in the curve of the window and they sat there, one on each side on elegant Regency chairs until Dan went into the dressing room. It was a tiny room off the main one which had previously been a dining alcove, but Jessica felt it would serve her better and suit Dan's newly acquired delicate sensibilities as a place to disrobe and attend to whatever toilet they needed in private. She would await his return sitting at the window, looking at the pattern of the lace curtains that shielded them from the street; and, when he came back into the room in his expensive Italian dressing gown, he would lead her to the bed for all the world as if she were a new bride. They would sit, one on either side, and remove their wraps, slide in, roll over and meet in the centre, arms entwining. She had to work hard to keep from giggling. She sometimes felt he was rehearsing, the whole procedure having a formality and ritual about it. His lovemaking was as ardent and satisfying as it had always been, and it was an effort for her to curtail her raptures. But she was so aware of each nuance of pleasure or irritation that she could adapt immediately and remove any moment of annoyance for him.

The summer passed. The weather was glorious. Dublin was washed every night by drifts of soft bright rain, and every morning the sun pierced the pale pink clouds and shone over the city, smudging the sharp edges, disguising the hardship of the poor and giving the place an unaccustomed glamour. It illuminated the great gaping hole that had been Foley Place and the hideous modern buildings, including the garage, that were growing up so quickly around Dorset Street. Dan did not think of Foley Place at all. He was too busy wondering why he felt so

249

little joy in life. He was in wonderful health, Jessica was a delightful mistress and, most important of all, he had money, and the money he had was making more money. How he came by it was of no consequence to him now, but why he felt so frustrated he could not think. He had a lot of what he had yearned, worked and prayed for, and was on his way to acquiring much more. So he could not account for these feelings of irritation and discontent.

Then one day a letter arrived in Mount Street. Spotty gave it to Dan. The envelope was of thick parchment and Dan felt a surge of excitement as he opened it. It was an engraved invitation.

LADY DEIRDRE TANDY-CULLAINE
Requests the pleasure of the company
of
MR DANIEL CASEY
at a Ball on the 4th September, 1924
at 9 o'clock
at
SLIEVELEA
CO. WICKLOW

Formal Dress   R.S.V.P.

His heart stood still and then started to beat ten to the dozen, and for the first time in weeks he felt elation and excitement course through his body, sharpen his senses and give him the charge of energy he so loved to feel. The flavour of life had changed; now there was an aim, a goal. He had a wonderful event to look forward to, the days sped past and at night he slept without moving. Jessica was alarmed. Tuned to his every mood, she was apprehensive about the change in him, and it took all her skill not to ask the cause of his elation. If he had wanted her to know he would have confided in her, so she did not risk his displeasure by asking.

She often wondered what he did, who he saw when she was not with him. There could even be another woman, she thought, but knew instantly that this was not so. Not yet. And so she enjoyed him while she could and put her heart and soul into pleasing him.

Chapter

38

DEIRDRE had come home to Slievelea at the end of August. She brought Edward, Letticia and Livia with her. There had been staff there all during August preparing for their arrival. Painters had painted, dustsheets had been removed, floor surfaces polished till they shone; gardeners had worked at full stretch to perfect the grounds, windows had been cleaned, linen aired and starched. Maids bustled, cooks ordered, butlers oversaw and stocked and kept work going at a pitch foreign to the Irish character. Deirdre had brought Bates with her and Mrs Bundy, the cook from Park Lane, but she employed an Irish housekeeper, a formidable woman by the name of Finoula Malloy, called Malloy by the rest of the servants in Slievelea. She was excellent at her job, but kept her distance from the others, particularly the 'foreign wans' as she called the English members of staff. When the family arrived she treated them all with equal severity and detachment except for Livia who won her heart and undying devotion with one glance of her big violet eyes.

Livia was at first intimidated by the house. Used to the cosy intimacy of her Chelsea home, the sheer size of Slievelea made her feel like a pea rattling around in a large pod. But not for long. Soon it seemed to her that she was opening out like a flower to the first rays of the sun. She straightened up and moved into the bigger space, taking it over, not allowing it to dominate her, and developing a surer grace of movement and gesture.

Deirdre watched her fondly. Livia reminded her grandmother of herself at that age, so full of life and energy and spontaneous laughter. Sometimes Deirdre thought the girl's high spirits were nervy, almost over-exuberant. The child seemed as highly strung as a thoroughbred.

Livia was not the great beauty Deirdre had been and still was. Livia was magically pretty. She had ankles and wrists as narrow as a fawn, a cleft in the tip of her short nose, her grandmother's great sapphire eyes, a body as slim as a gazelle; in fact there was something very deer-like in her whole appearance. She wore her hair short and straight like a red-gold cap on her head, and it was as smooth and soft as satin. Her little chin was pointed and the head balanced on a long and graceful neck. She is exquisite, Deirdre thought, all innocence and grace and horribly in fashion with her boyish figure and nervous slenderness.

Deirdre hugged herself and dwelt lovingly on her plan. She had put a lot of time and work and money into it and it must succeed. She would not allow it to fail. She had spent a fortune. She had hustled, cajoled and bullied a very reluctant Edward and an apprehensive Letticia away from the security and familiarity of the Chelsea house to this alien soil for their daughter's coming-out party when they had not seriously considered travelling further than Park Lane. Letticia was nervous of Irish savages, gunmen and terrorists who, Deirdre should remember, had murdered Lord Rennett. Edward would miss his clubs and his entertainment; there was no sophisticated society in Wicklow, after all. They quite sensibly argued that neither Deirdre nor they or, for that matter, poor little Livia herself knew anyone in Wicklow. Deirdre brushed aside such considerations, being quite adamant about her course of action, and eventually threatened to refuse to pay Edward's debts if they did not 'pander to an old woman's whim'. Letticia shivered when she caught the wicked smile in Deirdre's eyes as she said this, and knew her mother-in-law was capable of reducing Edward to penury to get her own way. So they agreed.

The girl herself caused Deirdre no moment of worry. She was quite perfect. She could see them together. What a couple they would make. She, Deirdre Tandy-Cullaine, could have in her seventy-fifth year everything she wanted in life, and give Dan Casey all *his* heart could desire. She never doubted for a moment that Dan would fall in love with Livia, or that Livia would fall for Dan. The last month in Ireland had not worried her; Dan was not going to rush into a misalliance. The difficulty had been keeping him 'on ice', as she phrased it, during their

252

year of travel. Dan Casey was irresistible to women. She had seen it countless times all over Europe. Her one worry had been that he would be carried away by some *grande passion*, so she had promptly whisked him away from any danger before the worst could happen. Many a hopeful mamma or randy countess had run up against Deirdre's invisible guardianship of Dan for Livia. As for Dan's feelings, Livia was an extraordinarily pretty and graceful young girl in the full beauty of her dawning sexuality, half-awake, half-asleep, like a princess awaiting a prince's kiss. In those dreamy violet eyes Dan would surely drown. She would also represent to him wealth, power, prestige and, above all, breeding. How could Dan Casey resist such an aphrodisiac! She laughed to herself. No, they would fall, and she would have him in the family, which was what she wanted with all her heart.

The nearer the great day approached the more beautiful Slievelea became. The late summer roses drowned the senses in a perfume so overpowering that it was dispersed only when the breeze blew in from the sea. Livia loved to wander in the rose garden, sitting dreaming on the stone bench, her grandmother's favourite, listening to the splash, splash of the fountain, and watching the water cascade down the fat, naked cherub. She could drowse there, a book by Mrs Radcliffe held loosely in her long white fingers, watching the birds taking cooling dips in the water, fluttering their wings. She felt enchanted and drunk on the scent, wrapping the tranquillity of Slievelea round her like an invisible cloak. She rejoiced in the sensation of letting her horse gallop through the soft green hills and dales, she whose only experience of riding had been a sedate trot in Rotten Row. She wallowed in the luxury of swimming in the clean, slate-grey sea, challenging the cold water with her firm young body.

An air of feverish excitement infected the servants and even Malloy lost some of her severity. Letticia was caught up in the flutter of feminine anticipation and was thoroughly enjoying herself, much to her own surprise. She found at Slievelea that with management, meals and general organization taken out of her hands all her defects of character seemed magically to disappear. Instead of being blamed for untidiness, no sooner had she left her room in its usual chaos than it was tidied by invisible hands. She didn't have to *do* anything, and with all the responsibility removed she too blossomed and became more serene.

The only fly in the ointment had been Livia's dress for the big occasion. Letticia envisaged her daughter romantically festooned in frills and lace, and pointed to the portrait of Deirdre in her coming-out dress as a perfect model; but Deirdre thought they could prettify Livia too much, and Dan admired elegance. So she suggested a white satin sheath cut on the bias to show off Livia's slim figure and allow the child, she said, to be a little modern. The argument passed to and fro for days, taken up and laid down like a book or a piece of tapestry.

'You don't want to make her look old before her time,' Letticia would say out of the blue and apropos of nothing, and everyone knew at once what she was talking about.

'I was the perfect shape for my day, just as Livia is for hers,' Deirdre said. 'My dress suited my shape and this will show off Livia's to perfection.'

Livia herself decided the question by choosing her grandmother's design. The idea for the type of dress needed and the measurements were sent off to Mr Molyneux in Paris and eventually the gown arrived. At the fitting a generously inclined Letticia admitted Deirdre had been right.

Livia remained calm and curiously detached from the hectic activity. She had had a warm and loving family around her all her life and although she was indulged she was not spoilt. She had the sunny, contented disposition of a person who has never had to be fretful or apprehensive about anything, who has never had anything to dread. This gave her a confidence in herself and a complete lack of introspection which in one so young was delightful. How she would react when clouds appeared on her horizon was something Deirdre speculated about. She sensed the core of high tension within the girl and wondered sometimes what would happen if it were ever activated. Although Deirdre liked to think the girl was a Rennett, she was nevertheless her mother's daughter.

Livia had been brought up in the old-fashioned belief that a girl prepares for marriage, that it is her purpose in life, the ultimate in achievement. You make your husband happy and comfortable, you provide him with children. Letticia had impressed upon her daughter how important this was. Only too aware of her failure in her mother-in-law's eyes, she was determined Livia would not have a similar problem when she married, though how Livia could achieve this at her mother's command was never explained. Edward epitomized men in general for Livia and as he was jolly and kind, loving and not at all intimidating, she had no apprehensions about the opposite sex. As a blonde, violet-eyed little girl she had been cooed over, admired, and told how pretty she was by all and sundry, so that she accepted the fact of her good looks and was not in the least concerned. She was a very fortunate young lady, and she knew that too. But this summer she had for the first time felt emotions entirely foreign to her and her nerves were sharpened. Her reactions became tense and acute, and she realized she could be as nervy as her mother if she allowed herself. This was a big surprise. She came to understand how sheltered she had been and how little she knew herself. She was not alarmed, however; she was merely interested and she knew she had all the time in the world to explore her own emotions. Some day, some time, she would look within, but not yet.

She used the pause in time to wait, holding her breath as she stood on tiptoe before the curtain was raised on the second act of her life. It was as if she had prior knowledge that something wonderful was just about to happen, that over the edge of her world an overwhelming event was about to take place. She awaited its coming eagerly, inwardly full of heart-stopping excitement, but outwardly calm. She spent a lot of time alone exploring the estate, sitting beside warm grey stone walls, picking at the emerald lichen, gathering buttercups in the waist-high ferns at the side of the cobalt-blue lake, staring at her reflection in the calm waters. She let her mother and grandmother fuss about the details, whether the flower arrangements should be predominantly pink or would white be too wishy-washy? Funereal even! Was it too late to use oysters for a stuffing, would they bring a Negro pianist from London to play some jazz or would such modernity be too much for the older members of Wicklow society? Well, the ball was not for the older members, Deirdre pointed out to Letticia, who sometimes drove her mad with her incessant anxiety about conforming and not conforming.

'Oh dear, I do so hate being shocked,' she would say. 'It's the time we live in. Young people today have no modesty at all. My mother would turn in her grave.'

'Silly old hen, of course she would,' Deirdre thought, but did not say, her lips tightening into a fine line. She wondered if

255

Letticia had ever been truly young — or old, for that matter.

Edward wanted Chinese lanterns in the trees, all the fashion in London he had heard. 'Ball in Grosvenor ... whole Square twinkling ... topping show.'

Deirdre agreed. She remembered the fairy lights looking so delicately beautiful on the night of the ball when her father died. His death, she thought ironically, had been caused, however indirectly, by the father of the man she now hoped would marry her grand-daughter.

Deirdre did not attempt to contact Dan beyond sending him an invitation, content to leave matters entirely alone now, and to wait to see what the evening of the 4th would bring.

Chapter

39

THE day brought a fury of last-minute preparations. The family picnicked by the sea in their own little cove, and Livia swam in one of those outrageous new bathing costumes while Letticia squeezed her eyes closed and hugged her knees in an agony of embarrassment at the sight. The day was languidly long, the sense of waiting, anticipating, unbearable. Everyone was silent. Edward smoked his cigar, Letticia watched her mother-in-law apprehensively. Deirdre was testy and crotchety with everyone, even Livia, and was cross with herself for being so. Livia gave herself over to the physical pleasure of the sea and the sun and the sharp salt waves. She relaxed in the total wellbeing of her healthy young body. They were all relieved when it was time to return to the house.

Slievelea lit up at eight o'clock, and the stars came out, although it was not dark. They decorated the sky, blinking down on the Chinese lanterns swaying in the slight agitation of the air stirring the trees. The orchestra played a mixture of the old and new, dressed in white tuxedos and fronted by the Negro pianist and singer, who amazed and delighted and was not considered shocking at all.

Carriages and motor cars started arriving. Deirdre, Edward and Letticia stood in the entrance under the many-faceted drops of the graceful Russian ormolu and crystal chandelier, greeting the guests as they arrived. The Rowleys and the Vestrys were there, and the Blackwaters and Lord Jeffries' scatter-brained grandson, who had seen Livia and lusted after her in the most obvious and ill-bred way. He had a tall friend with him and when Deirdre saw this friend for some reason her heart missed a beat. What was it about him that reminded her of something bad, an evil dream? She tried to dismiss her foolish sense of fear. Music filled the great hall, couples greeted each other with laughter and squeals of glee, waiters served cocktails and glasses were held by their delicate stems between long, manicured fingers. Yet in the midst of the festive air of gaiety and good will it was as if a ghost had passed over Deirdre's grave. Then she straightened her back, lifted her chin and brushed the ghost away. She looked at the man, the stranger, again. He was very tall and very elegant, older than Jonathan Jeffries; he must be in his mid-thirties, she surmised. An odd friend for young Jonathan, but the lad was a wrong-un, as Edward would say. She held out her hand as they approached. The stranger's height was remarkable. Slim and beautifully groomed, his face was severe, his cheekbones high, his black hair clustered tight on his head like a cap, growing long at the sides. He wore a moustache and though he tried hard he could not disguise the ice-cold eyes, the lethal eyes of a man with no pity. He bent low, kissing her hand, and she shivered again, then told herself she was over-excited and carried away with the evening's emotional quality.

'My friend Diramuid Holland,' Jonathan Jeffries murmured and moved on, and Deirdre turned to the other arrivals.

Yes, it was true that she was feeling emotional. Memories of the past could not but flow back. She was dressed in black chiffon, diamonds at her throat, her white hair piled high on her head, looking regal and slightly forbidding. How different I look tonight, she mused, from that girl who long ago had just such a party here in this very place. Was it her imagination or was the music more hectic, the gaiety more superficial, the drinking and eating greedier? Or was it her old age? She looked at Letticia, a wedding cake of pink frills, decorated in bows of satin, her chubby face glowing with a mixture of fear and excitement, and she remembered her views and murmured, 'Hurrrrumph.' Edward looked at her sharply, then his attention was claimed by the arriving guests, who seemed to Deirdre to be the same people who had come here that Christmas many moons ago, such was the resemblance to their grandparents.

Well, the young can black-bottom the night away, she thought, I wish them well. 'Oh, be still my heart,' she whispered to herself as she saw Dan Casey arrive, run up the steps and come into the hall. As the butler took his coat, she nodded to the band leader and the music changed to a waltz. She lifted her hand in a tiny wave to Malloy, who was in the gallery looking over the iron-wrought balustrade down into the hall, awaiting the signal to go and fetch Miss Livia.

Deirdre's eyes shone bright as the stars outside in expectation. The next ten minutes would bring the success or failure of her plans. The excitement within her was almost unbearable. She turned to greet Dan Casey. The man looked good enough to eat, she thought, and remembered fleetingly the first moments of her awareness of his father as a different band played a different tune in this same place fifty years ago. She remembered her bouffant lace dress, the frills around her shoulders, as she floated down the stairs, so eagerly, so ready for life. Then she had seen Conor. Her guests then seemed pale shadows compared to the vivid, brighter, more brittle people here now. How positive Dan's presence was, tall, broad, immaculate in his white tie and tails, his rakish grin splitting his tanned face, those cornflower blue eyes sparkling with wit and life. He was laughing at her as usual and setting her heart knocking at her ribs like a seventeen-year-old.

'You are a witch, Aunt, a witch!' He was smiling up at her as he kissed her hand. 'Remember the first time I did this?'

'Yes, of course I do,' she replied, her heart ceasing its knocking and melting within her like butter in the sun. 'Why do you say I'm a witch?'

'Why? Because you become more beautiful every time I see you. I've missed you so, dear Aunt. You'll never know.'

'And I you. But wait.' She laid a hand on his arm.

Livia had appeared at the top of the stairs, a golden girl, sheathed in white satin, slender as a wand, light as thistle as she glided down the stairs. And just as Deirdre had planned it, as she knew it would be, Livia saw Dan. She was halfway down the stairs when her eyes fell on him. They opened wide and she stopped for a heartbeat, then delight flooded her face and she smiled at him and him alone, a smile full of welcome and promise.

Dan was straightening up from kissing Deirdre's hand when Livia swam into his vision and the smile died and expressions of wonder, disbelief, hope and fear chased each other in quick succession across his face. Then he relaxed and purposefully left

259

Deirdre to greet Livia as she reached the foot of the stairs. Taking her hand he led her into the lush music, into the dance, into his arms, and the die was cast.

Why then, Deirdre wondered afterwards, did she feel so let down, so old, so ill-humoured? Was it because there had been no Dan Casey for her, only sheepish Anthony Tandy-Cullaine? She made Letticia cry by asking her if she had intended looking like the Chelsea Flower Show or whether it had been an accident. She told Edward to dance with her, then walked away from him halfway through, complaining that an elephant could do better and her feet were not walnuts waiting to be cracked. She had thought that this would be her finest hour and yet she felt angry, resentful and distinctly out of sorts, and was wildly irritated with her feelings.

She watched Livia and Dan, two stunning creatures in the first moments of falling in love, and realized how bitterly she envied them their feelings, their freedom to express themselves. How deprived she had always felt that the man she had wasted so many years on, the servant-father of this man who danced with her lovely grand-daughter, had been unsuitable. That fate had decreed that she would have to settle for second best. Or did she bring her own fate about by clinging to a girlish memory all those years? Why, oh why, had it all come about this way? She felt someone's eyes on her, and looking across the room saw the tall stranger, the man introduced to her by Jonathan Jeffries — what was his name? Oh yes, Diramuid Holland — leaning gracefully against the mantelpiece, looking at her as if he could see into her soul. Their glances held for a moment and it was she who withdrew her gaze first. Moving away, she retreated to the relative quiet of the music room.

She sat in the window in the semi-dark. A branch of candles glimmered on the buhl bureau. She looked out over the lawns, quiet and sleeping in the lavender twilight. A full moon had come out and hung gleaming over the gentle swell of the earth, putting the Chinese lanterns to shame. They really were not very nice, she decided, more suitable to Monte Carlo than Slievelea. Her own fairy lights had been prettier, subtler, more magical. Oh dear, she was getting old!

She heard the band strike up a Charleston and a chorus of young voices shout 'Boop-boop-eh-doop' in a break in the beat, and their laughter sounded like the cackle of geese to her. She thought for a moment, as she sat at the window, that she saw Siobain hurrying down the drive to her, to fix her hair, to help her undress, to talk her to sleep. Dear loving, undemanding, warm, giving Siobain. Why had she never told her maid how much she loved her? Why hadn't she known she would miss her so much? There was no Siobain. It was a trick of the light. There was no Mamma and Papa. There was no Conor, and not even Anthony Tandy-Cullaine. All, all were rotting away beneath the earth.

She sighed, wondering what place she had here with the young whose pulsating music did not suit her old-fashioned sense of harmony, and for a moment she thought she would burst into tears, but then a hand gently rested on her shoulder and she started in surprise and looked up into Dan's face. He looked into the violet eyes, full of unshed tears, and recognized the pain there, the unfulfilled longing. He pressed her frail shoulder and let his arm fall around it.

'Oh my dear, how very wonderful you are.' He bent and kissed her brow. 'I know how you feel,' he said, 'I love you too. Thank you for tonight, for Livia. She is all I have ever looked for in a woman ... a wife. You knew. I will of course apply formally.'

She saw he was blushing, that for once Dan Casey was not master of a situation. But he said, 'Shush,' as she started to speak, 'don't say anything. You are a witch, a fairy godmother. No, more, much more. You have given me the world, dearest Aunt. Be peaceful for me. I'm really yours, you know,' and he left the room.

She sat a long time after he had gone, then made her way upstairs through the laughter, the noise of the conversation, the hectic beat of the Charleston and the popping of the champagne corks. She called her maid to her, a wee bit of a Wicklow girl called Mary, and she sighed again for Siobain. This little scrap was scared to death of her. She thought, how I wish you were here now, Siobain. I wonder what you would make of all this. I believe you would be shocked rigid! And Deirdre chuckled, and the little maid's fingers fumbled in fright with the tiny buttons on her dress.

Still, you too would fall under your grandson's spell, like all of us, she thought, and said aloud, 'Don't fuss, Mary, I'll not eat you.' She undressed slowly with Mary's help and got into bed.

261

She kept a candle lit beside her and, dismissing Mary, thought about dying, and decided against it tonight, then recalled the touch of Dan's hand on her shoulder and his lovely, kindly words. She took a deep breath and, feeling at peace and happy for the first time that day, fell into a deep, untroubled sleep.

Chapter

40

LIVIA fell totally in love with Dan Casey and never, after the meeting, so cleverly contrived by her grandmother, was she ever to be free of tension. The tidal wave of emotion his mere presence induced in her overwhelmed her. She had never had to cope with such strong feelings before. In Chelsea with her father and mother, their well-bred friends and equally well-bred children, her strongest emotions had been small frustrations and little storms in teacups; her mother's nervous vapours had tended to amuse Livia, who did not understand them. The people she met, the boys who were children of her parents' friends, were all feeble compared to this man. For this was a man, a masculine man the like of which she had never dealt with before, a man she could no more twist round her little finger than she could a wild beast. All the other men in her life seemed pussycats to his tiger, and she was terrified of him. She was pinned down by her fascination with the inherent danger of him, like a butterfly pinned to a board. In her estimation, Dan Casey could not be controlled; this man would dominate. The thought frightened and bewitched, weakened and challenged her all at the same time. She felt Dan's veneer of sophistication was only skin deep and she was scared yet fatally attracted to what lay beneath. She was out of control and she could not confide in anyone. She was scared to death and she did not know what to do about it. If this was falling in love, she was suddenly beginning to understand the power of the emotions she had read about in the novels she loved, emotions that led to murder, war and rape.

She realized from the beginning that this man would take

some keeping, and like Jessica Klein she decided on a plan. Her plan worked as well as Jessica's but at enormous cost to herself.

From the first moment that their eyes had met and he took charge of her and she knew she was lost for ever, Livia adopted, at first unconsciously, as a defence mechanism, and later quite deliberately, the role of the inscrutable female. Instead of answering questions, and thereby betraying her ignorance, she simply shook her head and smiled seductively and looked mysterious. She played her role well, and Dan was baffled and fascinated by this apparently cool, ultra-sophisticated woman who always held something back. He never realized that what she held back was fear. He never realized how scared she was — scared of his finding out what an ordinary, boring little miss she really was, scared of failing him, scared of not understanding this fascinating, strange, masculine creature, scared of losing him.

If she had but known it, Dan was equally apprehensive about disappointing her, of failing her. He loved her as much as he was capable of feeling love. She represented to him the personification of his dream and she was his ideal woman. He was proud of her, and found her marvellous and mysterious, and he courted her very correctly, never doubting the outcome.

He played tennis at Slievelea, took tea on the lawn during the long, golden, late summer afternoons when the heavy bees fell on the sugar lumps, drunk with honey, and the whole riotous abandoned glut of full-blown roses scented every breeze, drowning him in their perfume. The young people, with faces gently beaded with sweat, lay on the lawn sipping Earl Grey tea and biting cucumber sandwiches and scones, shading their faces with straw boaters, their whites tired after their game of tennis, their eyes screwed up against the huge orange sun, and their exhausted conversation more and more monosyllabic. Dan was uncomfortable with the others and usually sat with Deirdre. His body seemed large and ungainly to him compared with their slight, angular frames, and he was much more comfortable dancing with Livia than playing tennis. He was not good at games, and whilst on the dance floor he was graceful, on a tennis court he became clumsy. And he wanted to win. He hated to lose. He wanted to show off to the insolent young men but they beat him easily and carelessly and he hated it, though he kept his feelings concealed and laughed with them at his inept playing. Only Deirdre saw, and they joked about it together; only Deirdre understood. When he danced he knew he was graceful. He and Livia danced at night to the saxophone and the trumpet and the jazz piano. They swayed in each other's arms to the new romantic music, and one night in the music room at Slievelea in the candlelight he asked Livia to marry him.

She stood with her back to him, her cap of gold hair shining in the pellucid rays of the moon that slanted through the French windows and bleached the sky silver. He saw her back stiffen, and for one horrifying moment he thought she would refuse. Then she turned and stretching out her hands to him she said, 'I'd love to marry you, Dan.'

He took her hands in his and kissed her. It was a gentle, restrained kiss, soft lips on soft lips, and as Dan drew his face away Livia had an almost uncontrollable urge to pull his face back to her and devour his mouth hungrily. But instead she smiled sweetly and calmly at him and said, 'Let's tell Grandma.'

He laughed, 'I think she already knows,' and Livia felt again the deep surge of jealousy she always felt when those two were together. She knew it was absurd to be envious of a woman of seventy-five but, unreasonably, she was. Sometimes she ached to lay down the whole burden of these frightening emotions and find some oasis of peace, to take time off from the world for ten minutes, but that might mean losing Dan and she would prefer to lose her life.

The next few weeks were a continuous round of gaiety and celebration. A huge engagement party was given at Slievelea. Once again the Rowleys and the Vestrys, the Blackwaters and the Jeffries and their chums arrived and drank the fine French champagne and danced the night away. Livia wore a calf-length beaded sheath that barely touched her hips. Its crystal beads sparkled and twinkled as she danced and on her silken head she wore a Juliet cap with diamond crystal drops hanging on her milk-white forehead. She looked fragile enough to break and pride swelled in Dan's heart, making him want to hold her all evening. But he did not dare, so fearful was he that his passion might be aroused and he might crush this delicate wand of a girl and have her turn away from him or, worse, laugh at his gaucherie.

At that party, too, the tall elegant figure of Diramuid

Holland lingered — always apart, always alone, with his cold eyes sliding away from Dan whenever their glances met.

Jessica Klein read about the engagement in the papers. She was taking care of the shop while her father was out looking at the contents of the house of an old lady who had died and whose children wanted to divvy up as soon as possible. Jessica's mother was upstairs with Alexander and the sound of her voice floated down to the girl as she stood frozen to the spot in the dim light of the cluttered shop. Martha was singing:

> Sleep my little one, sleep,
> Fond vision I keep,
> Lie warm in thy nest,
> By moonbeams caressed.

Her voice was old and cracked but full of the sweetness of tenderness.

The overhead lamp, necessary in the shop even on the sunniest day, caught the sparkle of the tiny diamonds, rubies, emeralds, zircons and precious stones, the hocked gold rings under the glass top of the case. Pathetic tokens discarded and forgotten. It shone on the brasses and the coppers, on the aged, tawdry remnants of others' lives, but Jessica's attention was riveted on the rings. It would not be this kind of a ring Livia Tandy-Cullaine would wear. That was her name . . . Livia.

Jessica knew what she had to do. Nothing! She knew full well that that was the answer. Nothing! Nothing, nothing, nothing! The most difficult thing of all. Know nothing, pretend that nothing had happened. How could she manage it? she wondered. Her body felt like a stone, a cold statue, her stomach felt sick, and her heart felt as though it had cracked in two. But there was nothing she could do. All she could pray was that he would continue his visits to her apartment. If he did, she would bind him to her by her indifference to changing events, to the fact that come hell or high water she was constant.

He came. The following Sunday he was there and he found her warm and loving as usual. Afterwards, before he left for Mount Street, she brought him a brandy as usual. He delayed his return home, the flat having become increasingly repugnant to him. He sat for ages in front of the fire in the graceful

266

pleasant room, sipping a drink, talking to her, running a hand over her masses of black hair, twining curls around his finger as she sat on the floor beside him, her head on his knee.

'When will you be married, Dan?' she asked suddenly. Careful now, careful she told herself. She had decided to speak to him lightly about it. She was so afraid that he would leave her and never come back. She wanted him to know there were no ties, that he could always come here to her, without obligation, that she would never seek to impinge on his other life. She wanted him to know there would never be tears here, or jealousy. She wanted to be a habit, a haven for him always.

'How did you know that?' he asked, somewhat sharply. Now she's going to be difficult, Goddamn it, he thought and smiled down at her, the smile she least liked, the smile that he used to charm deliberately.

'Oh, I can read Dan Casey, you know, I'm not a total ignoramus.'

'Sure. I never thought you were.'

'I know you didn't, dear man. I hope she's good enough for you?' She smiled up at him, her face innocent of any expression save genuine interest. He was surprised and it threw him off balance. The smile disappeared and he found himself answering honestly.

'I'm not sure, Jess, that I'm good enough for her. Sometimes I'm scared.'

'You, Dan, scared? Whyever?'

'It's frightening, Jessica, when you think of it. Slievelea. The house my grandfather was a servant in — not even house servant, but gate man, gamekeeper, jack-of-all-trades. My grandmother was Lady Deirdre Tandy-Cullaine's maid, my father was her servant, and here I am marrying the daughter of the house. I'll be master here, in Slievelea, Aunt Deirdre says. Her son, Edward, is a gambler and not to be trusted to manage things. He's a nice old boy and I think a bit afraid of me, but he has no interest in Slievelea. He wants to spend most of his time in London, in Tattersall's and Crockford's and White's, the gentlemen's gaming clubs, Jess. He doesn't run too high and it doesn't cost Aunt Deirdre, that is Lady Tandy-Cullaine, too much income to cover him, but she says he's most unsuitable as a squire for Slievelea. He's quite happy about it all himself, says he can't wait to get back to Chelsea. It's all going to be mine.

I'm a kid from Foley Place, and you can't get any lower than that, and I'm going to be Lord of the Manor at Slievelea and why should I be afraid? Tell me why? I can do it standing on my head. I love it. But Livia is something else, Jess. She's so beautiful, so sophisticated, so cool and poised. Sometimes I look at her and I'm almost afraid to touch her. Oh Jess, I shouldn't be talking to you. It's such a relief though ...'

'Of course you should. Isn't that what I'm for, you eejit? From now until the end of time, Dan Casey, I expect you to bring your troubles, your fears to me! This place is the place for you to come whenever anything is bothering you. It's away from all the world, the world of work and money and family and responsibility, and when any of these things gets a bit wearying, you can come here to me. My arms will always be open to you, my sympathy and understanding always yours.'

He looked down into the passionate face resting on his knee and took it between his hands and gently kissed the mouth.

'Do you mean that? I thought you would be angry.'

'And why would I be? I'm not greedy, Dan, I just want my small piece of you. I'm content with that. No one can have all of anyone. The businessman, the husband, the other people you are, all belong to others. I'm happy with the lover, my dear, dear man.'

He felt like a schoolboy let off detention. The scene, the tantrum, never happened, the secret did not have to be kept. He felt totally at peace, and relaxed into it, counting himself a lucky man.

'And remember, Dan, Foley Place is no more. They tell me it doesn't exist any longer. Neither does the Daniel Casey who used to live there.'

He caught her eye. She was smiling mischievously at him. Did she suspect something? Know something? He doubted it. Yet ... and yet ... But it didn't really matter, his secrets were safe with her. He sighed contentedly and, sipping his brandy, peacefully closed his eyes.

He did not see the strain on her face then, when she knew he was no longer looking at her. It had taken every fibre of her being not to scream at him, shout, tell him he must marry her, her, Jessica Klein, that no one would ever love him as much as she did, that he must give up this hateful, cold, upper-class bitch he was going to marry. But she wanted to keep him. There would never be anyone else for her, so her feelings could not be expressed, her emotions had to be firmly held in check. He would never know how much the effort had cost her.

Chapter

41

THE wedding was one of the biggest Dublin had ever seen. Both Dan and Livia were Roman Catholics and although neither practised the religion with any fervour or fidelity the church ceremony was held in the Pro-Cathedral. As he arrived, Dan had a sudden vision of himself standing on this very spot all those years ago, a tattered, snotty-nosed, under-sized little gurrier stealing Da McCabe's barrow as the old man ricocheted off the Archbishop's car and he and Spotty Devlin ran hell-for-leather for Foley Place and the welcoming haven of the slums.

That had been the beginning of his climb to fortune, of his becoming the man he now was, in the position he now was: an elegant, well-spoken bridegroom, impeccably dressed, stepping out of a Dusenberg with his best man, Diramuid Holland, at his side, entering the Pro-Cathedral to marry a lord's daughter, one that was more beautiful than a rose in May. God, how far I have travelled, he thought, and shivered superstitiously, thinking of what might have been, and paradoxically smiling nostalgically for the excitement of those days.

The tall, unsmiling man at his side took his arm and they ran up the broad steps of the church together. He had chosen Diramuid Holland as his best man because he was the only socially acceptable man he knew well. It had never occurred to Spotty that he should be best man, which was just as well as Dan had left his old friend far behind. It had not even entered Dan's head to ask him to the wedding; he had assumed Spotty would be out of his depth. He did not ask his own mother either. She would be uncomfortable, he told himself, and hastily put it out of his mind. That was another world, more foreign to

270

him now than Paris or Rome, and he did not want to remember it or be reminded of it. So, there was no one at all from his side at the wedding. There were enough Rennetts and Tandy-Cullaines, Rowleys, Jeffries and Vestrys to make up for the lack of Caseys, and Deirdre and Livia seemed bent on smoothing his way for him, making sure he did not suffer an embarrassing moment, and no one was allowed to notice his lack of family. Diramuid had cultivated Dan's friendship. An adventurer and a gambler, he nevertheless had the manners of a gentleman and money he could only have acquired outside the law. Such was Dan's summing up of his new friend, whom he neither trusted nor respected but with whom he felt easy and relaxed. The man's American accent, his tales of his travels down the Mississippi on river boats, the fights, the excitement, the names of exotic places like New Orleans all interested Dan. He knew that some day he might explore the New World across the mighty Atlantic, and this man could be a great help. They had the same kind of approach to business. Why Diramuid should have courted his good will he could well imagine. The new master of Slievelea could open many doors for an adventurer.

The ceremony passed for Dan in an unreal haze. Livia floated up the aisle looking like a vision in a dream, a swan on a lake in the moonlight, he thought. She seemed totally unreal to him and he went through the ritual mechanically. It all seemed to be happening to someone else. He felt as if he were outside the proceedings, looking down on himself, watching this stranger perform in a play. He felt very much as if he was the small Dan Casey with his nose pressed to the windows of the happenings of the great, condemned always to be on the outside looking in. He tried to shake off the feelings of otherness but could not. He placed the ring on Livia's finger, he said the responses, he heard Bach played on the organ as they left the church. He kissed Livia and she snuggled up to him in the car, and he felt as if he were not there and his voice came from far away.

Slievelea smiled on them and he still moved as if in a dream. Letticia wept over him, Edward got drunk and Diramuid stood tall and dark and remote, apart from the crowd, gazing at him cynically from across the room.

The photographs were taken, the cake cut, the endless speeches were over and they were in the car again, in different clothes on their way to Kingstown. It was not until he found

271

himself alone with Livia that the two persons he had seemed to be merged and he became totally himself again.

There was no orgasm for Livia that night, nor for many years to come. Dan treated his virgin bride with such tender respect, such gentle concern, that she remained unfulfilled and frustrated. She could not tell him about it although she ached to be allowed to lose some restraint, to abandon herself to him. It always seemed inappropriate in the face of his courteous respect. She adored him, his smell, his body, every muscle and curve of him, but she thought he would be shocked if he knew. She had so many thoughts that made her blush, and she thought perhaps she was unusual, that she should not desire such things, that there was something evil in her or at least abnormal, so she added guilt to fear. But no one guessed what lay beneath the cool, blonde beauty, the calm untroubled brow, the serene smile, the tranquil movements.

Now a seasoned traveller, Dan proudly showed Livia Europe, but the novelty soon wore off. It lacked the spice it had had for him when Deirdre was with him. He did not realize that he would always be a product of his environment, of Foley Place and his parents, his upbringing. He had entered this new world full of light burdened with the dark drabness of his childhood. No amount of instruction by Deirdre could really have changed him at the deepest level. Oh, she had taught him how to behave in polite society, and she had taught him how to converse and hide his true thoughts behind his handsome and charming exterior. She had taught him what it was fashionable to like and what was considered pretentious or vulgar. And he played the game well. He convinced everyone and even sometimes himself. The cultural veneer was thin, although strangely he had natural good taste, an instinctive nose for the best, the most beautiful, the most expensive. It was his reaction to the world of art and architecture, of music and literature that was at odds with the circle of people he moved within. He came, saw, assimilated swiftly, moved on, or wanted to, as quickly as possible to the next thing, the next experience, or he wanted to acquire it for himself. Deep down Dan remained the primitive, hungry little gurrier full of fear. He never really gave himself over to the enjoyment of the music, the theatre, the beautiful buildings and paintings, the travel, the watering places, the leisure that filled the lives of the *haut monde*. He could not relax into, rest in this new world and enjoy the ambience. He worried constantly that it would suddenly disappear because really he did not deserve it, or he would be found out for the ignoramus he was.

Livia seemed a passive audience and asked no questions, showed no desire to pursue topics and pathways to discovery. Nevertheless, he was in love with her in his way and happy. She was everything he had ever dreamed of in a wife and she completed him. Neither of them was unaware of the impact they made when they were seen together at the opera, the ballet, dining, dancing or, more particularly, descending the grand staircases of the best hotels. People gasped at their beauty, made room for them as if it was their due; pathways were miraculously cleared as people parted like the Red Sea to let them pass. But Dan was soon impatient to go home. He spoke about it to Livia in Maxim's in Paris one night.

'But of course we'll go home,' she said eagerly, forgetting that she was speaking of Slievelea and not of Chelsea. For a second she yearned for the childhood she had left behind, for the careless, untroubled days in that lovely warm untidy house. Then she threw back her head in a gesture curiously reminiscent of her grandmother and took his hands in her own.

'Of course we'll go to Slievelea. I've plundered the shops of Paris and Rome. I've acquired five extra cases, you know! It's time we went before I bankrupt you!' she teased.

He loved her like this, a restless exciting flame. He danced with her, and all the men in the room envied him. They drank more champagne than usual and when he made love to her she cried out fiercely and startled him, so he thought perhaps he had hurt her and withdrew from her body, promising himself he would be more gentle with her in future. He kissed her tenderly, telling her he loved her, and fell asleep unknowingly leaving her weeping into her pillow, aching for the fulfilment that had slipped away seconds too soon.

They were back in Ireland for Christmas 1926. Edward and Letticia had returned to their contented domestic bliss in Chelsea. Deirdre had Slievelea looking wonderful. She had put a big Christmas tree in the hall. There was holly and mistletoe and huge log fires smelling of pine in all the grates. Deirdre was delighted to have them home and Dan delighted to be there. He drew confidence and security from Deirdre; she gave him strength. Only Livia felt isolated, apart, the odd one out. The

273

other two were so frank, so open, and it was quite impossible for her to be equally honest — she just did not know how. The others did not seem to realize that she had left all her friends in Chelsea, that she had no girl friends around to share her secrets with. She was alone in a world where she was a total stranger, without the maturity to know what to do.

The months passed and she waited for her period to stop. She had decided she would become pregnant immediately, but she did not. She couldn't understand it. The women of Ireland were breeding like rabbits and there was no sign of her starting. The humiliation was awful! People asked. They said she was too thin. She prayed and began to go to Mass regularly.

Diramuid Holland seemed to be around Slievelea a lot these days, and he and Dan were talking about Dan's proposed visit to America. Her grandmother did not like Diramuid, Livia noted, which was odd for she usually loved good-looking men. Livia herself hardly registered his presence, so preoccupied was she with her own problems.

One night, coming down to dinner in a scarlet dress that marked her out from the background like a flame in a dark night, she was sure Diramuid saw her but he continued to speak to Dan, pretending not to notice her slowly descending the stairs.

'Lucky man, a wife like Livia and a mistress like Jessica Klein ... God, man, you should thank your stars.'

Livia froze for a moment, ice cold with shock. Dan was still in the library, and Diramuid had spoken over his shoulder. She heard Dan laugh. He did not contradict Diramuid. He just laughed his big contented laugh, the laugh of a man well pleased with himself, and Livia thought she would die. But no one would have guessed. She paused a moment on the stairs, to give herself time to recover, and to ensure that Dan remained unaware she had heard the remark. Diramuid, she knew, meant her to hear. He could see the hem of her scarlet dress from where he stood in the hall. But that night she appeared serene and tranquil as usual, and she saw Diramuid looking at her speculatively, wondering perhaps if she could be a little deaf, or stupid. She wondered why he had wanted to hurt her, then stopped thinking about him. She would have to get pregnant, she must have Dan's child. Everything would be all right then. The terrible tension, the guilt, this pain would go if only she became pregnant.

But she did not. Time passed and her period still came regular as clockwork. People stopped asking her for news and Deirdre became worried about her. She was too thin and she had a fine-drawn tension that had become noticeable. Deirdre thought and worried about the cause. She couldn't understand any woman living with Dan and not being happy and contented, but she had never understood or tried to understand Livia. Perhaps it was because Dan had plunged into his business and was often away in Dublin or London, she thought. She left it for the moment but resolved to keep a closer eye on her grand-daughter.

Livia became obsessed by Jessica. Her dreams were haunted by images of the other woman who appeared sometimes tall and blonde, sometimes voluptuous and dark, or seductive and red-haired. Often she looked like the women in the Hogarth paintings, the bawds, the whores, the prostitutes, and Livia's delicate soul shrank from the thought of Dan coming to her after contact with such a woman. In the end she did the only thing she could think of doing: she went to Diramuid Holland.

One evening, after a dinner party at Slievelea, the men rose, some of them to play backgammon or cards, some to smoke a cigar in the library, and some to sit with the ladies in the music room, play the phonograph and talk about the latest movies.

Livia laid her hand on Diramuid's arm and whispered in his ear, 'I want to talk to you a moment — please.'

He nodded discreetly and followed her out onto the terrace. They could hear the sea pounding in the distance and, nearer, 'Blue Moon' tinkling from the music room. In the indigo sky a full moon hung over the trees, veiled occasionally by rushing clouds.

There was an awkward silence. The tall man stood leaning against a column, his face closed and remote. Inside he was in a fever of excited anticipation. He waited for Livia to speak first. Looking at her through eyes half-closed against the smoke of his cigar, he could see her tension. The small chin was quivering, the eyelashes blinked rapidly, and she kept biting her rouged bottom lip.

At last she could bear it no longer.

'Who is this woman you say is Dan's mistress?' she blurted out.

'What? Dan's mistress? I don't know what you mean. I never said . . .'

275

But she had whipped round on him, facing him fiercely and almost spitting at him, 'Don't play games with me, Diramuid. I heard you say it to Dan that evening, and he didn't deny it. You *know* I heard it. You meant me to!'

Diramuid tried once again. 'I don't know what you are talking about.'

Livia shrugged and turned to go indoors. 'Very well. Then there's nothing more to be said.'

He caught her arm as she passed him. 'All right, I did say it! But not to be overheard. I would never do that.'

She pulled her arm away and looked at him contemptuously. 'You needn't bother to lie. Who is this Jessica Klein? I want to . . . I thought I would like to . . .'

'See her?' he said. He could see the agony Livia was in, how her pride was violated by having to speak to him like this. He could see a small purple bruise rising under the lip rouge on her mouth where she had bitten it. He almost felt sorry for her — she was not a Casey and she had done nothing to him or his. But no! He hardened his heart. It was her sort who kept him in penury, her sort who did not understand the insecurity, the fear, the terror of poverty. Besides, what hurt her, hurt Dan Casey. He continued.

'It's very easy. Her father owns a shop on the quays — just across from the Halfpenny Bridge on Ormonde Quay. She's there most days. I'll take you, if you like.' This last was going too far. She stopped him.

'That won't be necessary. Thank you, Diramuid.' She almost choked on the words.

He smiled mirthlessly. He had made progress.

'Shall we join the others?' she said. Her eyes were full of tears, but her head was held high and she took his arm as they left the cold terrace and went into the warmth and the sound of bright music and laughter.

The next morning Livia drove the Pierce-Arrow into Dublin. Diramuid, guessing she would not, could not wait, concealed himself on the other side of the graceful footbridge in the narrow arched passage that led to the Halfpenny Bridge.

From there he could see anyone entering or leaving the Klein shop. He saw her, wrapped in furs, jump out of the glamorous car Dan had bought her, leaving it in the middle of the road where it caused quite a traffic jam, and enter the shop.

Livia bought a small garnet necklace from the old man behind the counter. He was so gentle and so sympathetic that she nearly burst into tears. A child was singing somewhere out in the back of the shop and the clocks within started to chime the hour. The old Jew ruefully shrugged his shoulders and apologized for the burst of noise when the door opened and Jessica bounded in. Livia knew it was her at once and she felt hopeless and despairing at the sight of her husband's mistress. She did not know what she had expected: a cheap little floosie, a common little tart, that was what she had tried to think, but not this voluptuous woman, beautiful, seductive and full of vitality. She brought warmth and excitement into the dark shop by her mere presence there. Livia pushed past the radiant woman who was greeting her father and rushed out of the shop, forgetting to take the necklace.

Diramuid had crossed the bridge quickly and had seen Jessica Klein coming down Ormonde Quay and entering the shop five minutes after Livia. He saw Livia leave in a hurry and he went into the shop. Hymie Klein said, 'That woman who has just left! Catch her! She forgot her necklace.'

Jessica picked it up. 'I'll run after her,' she said.

Diramuid took the necklace from Jessica. They did not know him for though he had heard about Jessica from Dan they had never met. But he was well dressed and well spoken, so they did not demur when he said, 'No, give it to me. She's a friend of mine. I'll give it to her,' and he hurried out after Livia. He stopped with the box in his hand calling out, 'My dear, my dear, you forgot,' and the door closed behind him. Jessica went upstairs to tend Alexander, and Hymie went back to his sums and figures. Livia drove away unconscious of Diramuid's presence on the quays. He slipped down a side street and vanished into the rain.

It was raining. The whole world seemed to be weeping. The rain swept the city and Livia drove about in it for a long time. She could not think properly. Her brain was muddled and confused. She turned the car back to Wicklow and drove wildly, not looking where she was going, and both she and the car ended up in a ditch. At least there were no broken bones but Livia was in a bad state of shock. A local farmer found her and sensibly did not move her, but fetched a doctor.

She awoke in a hospital bed with a nun bending over her and

she thought for a moment she was back at school in the convent. Then she became frightened and thought about Dan and losing him, Dan going away because she was not full of vitality like her grandmother or that girl, Jessica Klein, and because she could not give him a child. She began to scream. The screaming alternated with catatonic silences. They told Dan she was highly strung, that she suffered from nerves, that she was ill with a very common disorder brought about by a *crise de nerfs* and curable with time, patience and loving care. Dan couldn't understand it at all, but he blamed himself. He was sure he had somehow, however unconsciously, driven her to this by his uncouth, crass personality. Something in him was not gentle enough for this finely nurtured and fragile woman.

When Dan brought her back from the hospital he treated her like a piece of breakable china. Livia misunderstood his attitude for one of remoteness, his solicitude for lack of passion. So when Deirdre suggested his taking her to Italy for a complete break, she was pleased. She would get him away from Jessica Klein, away from Deirdre, his absorbing work, his cruel friend Diramuid, and she would have him all to herself. She would work a miracle, she would somehow forget that other woman. Perhaps she might even succeed in getting pregnant.

Dan gave in gracefully to the suggestion when he saw how pleased Livia was with the idea. He had urgent business in Berlin and hoped to go there, but Livia's health was more important to him. He was extremely puzzled by her. Her restlessness distressed him and there was a tension between them that he could not understand at all.

He spoke to Jessica about it, but unfortunately Jessica's generosity was not magnanimous enough to include hints on how to keep his wife happy. She had a pretty good idea of the problem: she believed that Livia had fallen for his virility but that Dan was treating her with an overwhelming respect, and that was not what poor Livia really wanted. She drew the line at giving Dan this advice: your wife needs a good roll in the hay, no holds barred. No, even though she sometimes felt guilty, she could not bring herself to solve that particular problem. The situation suited her, and she allowed him to talk about it and, indeed, anything that troubled him, all the things she knew he should talk to his wife about but would not.

Dan's relationship with Jessica was very comfortable. In the warm, seductive atmosphere of the room in Haddington Road, they were far more like a happily married couple than Dan and Livia ever were at Slievelea. Jessica had put on weight, but it suited her. Her relaxed speech and manner untied the knot of tension he often didn't notice had been there until, with the help of her ministrations, he felt his whole body unclench, and a great flood of peace pour over him. In this room time stood still and he was more comfortable there than anywhere else in the world. His troubles, his preoccupations and anxieties were left at her doorstop, and they were easy together.

His lovemaking had reverted to the natural bawdiness of his pre-Livia days, something for which Jessica was very grateful. She had worked out for herself that he had been rehearsing for his virgin bride, quite mistakenly she thought, imagining a restrained passion would be suitable for Livia. It was with great relief that one evening he simply let himself go and they ended up in a mutual burst of abandoned ardour, removing, in Jessica's opinion, the only important impediment to their total contentment.

Jessica would sit at his feet sipping chocolate, like a beautiful, voluptuous madonna. She resembled Raphael's *La Fornarina* which he had seen in Rome and which struck him at the time as so like her — the sloping milky white shoulders, the plump arms, the rounded breasts and stomach, the gentle enigmatic Jewish smile. Her soft body, half revealed in the laces and satins of her carelessly draped peignoir, the way she slid her fingers round her breast and tilted the nipple towards his lips, drove him wild. His knees would go weak as she slid her fingers up his thighs, and the things she said to him aroused him, till full to bursting he would have to come again and again. She said he filled her, she felt him within her like a leaping trout, no, no, a salmon she said, a trout was not big enough, strong enough. She held him within her, opening and closing her body around him like a sea anemone. She said he was a sword of pleasure, a stallion full of power. She locked her body to his, crying out in pleasure, the prolonged spasms of rippling, darting orgasm driving her to whisper more and yet more wildly seductive spurs to his amorous inventiveness until they lay replete in each other's arms, idly caressing the organs of their pleasure, the instruments of their eroticism until, aroused yet again, they would drown in each other.

Yes, Jessica was pleased at the state of things, happy for them to remain just so. She was very upset and hurt beyond belief at the news that he was taking Livia to Italy, but she did not let him see. She smiled and wished them both a happy trip, said she hoped Livia's condition would improve under the blue Italian skies and that he would be home soon. She said goodbye to him as casually as if he were returning at the weekend, waited until the door closed behind him, then broke two Sèvres vases she loved, and burst into a storm of weeping that would have alarmed Dan had he been there to see.

Chapter

42

LIVIA and Dan returned from Italy sooner than expected. Once again Dan had become restless and he itched to plunge himself into his business world. He thrived on the challenge and excitement that could only be derived from his presence in the arena. In Dublin Livia could not help but see the name Casey writ large everywhere. On van sides, on hoardings and against scaffolding, giant letters advertised Dan's construction company. From buying and selling Dan had branched out in all directions, most prominently in the construction business. Dublin was a bustling young capital city now and after the long and destructive road to freedom, houses and shops, factories and offices needed building and reconstruction. Dan Casey was there to do it. Dan intended to expand worldwide when the time was right. A war was coming in Europe, he was sure of that, and, biding his time in Ireland, Dan knew that inevitably the day would come when Europe too would need rebuilding. Until then his construction work and, less publicly, his sorties into arms dealing and the moving of money from place to place were bringing him great rivers of gold, enough to satisfy even his insecure soul.

Livia, truth to tell, was glad enough to get home too. She had missed the peace and serenity of Slievelea. Deirdre was very glad to have them home, for her world was complete with them there. Slievelea that May was more beautiful than ever before, Deirdre thought. She had found over the last few years that she was losing her vitality, slowing down, and curiously enough she did not mind. She felt more at peace than ever before. Edward, the dear boy, would never have Slievelea to gamble away, a fear she had had for many years. She knew he would not have meant to, but Edward was for ever finding himself in a fix and being entirely baffled as to how he had arrived at that point. Dan was in control and his business enterprises were flourishing and Slievelea was in the safest hands. She knew he loved the place as she did — differently perhaps, but with as much passion.

Deirdre felt herself growing closer to nature the older she became. She loved to walk over the land or sit in front of her favourite view, painting it in a leisurely fashion. She had taken up painting and enjoyed it enormously, producing strangely tender, wistful watercolours, lovely but, she knew, not brilliant. Time passed, slowly, gracefully. The lilac trees perfumed the air that May, their mauve, purple and white bunches of blossom weighing down the slender branches. The huge crimson rhododendrons massed against the stable walls and flanked the driveway, holding the eye with their gaudy grandeur. The roses ... oh, the roses. She wandered through the rose garden feeling the velvet leaves, plucking off the dead flowers and marvelling at the colours and variety of the Slievelea blooms.

The land was veiled in blue, and the green of the meadows and hedges swam through it hazily. The mountains were patched with golden gorse and purple heather and the water around Slievelea had never seemed more mysterious to Deirdre. The sea sounded far away even when she walked on the shore and the waves moved like huge beasts heaving and stretching in a cloak of silver foam. The little river jingled along through the wood, its pools of purple and slate grey boarded by fern, rushes, shamrock and watercress.

She spent time everywhere, in every nook and cranny of Slievelea, each tree, each flower, the mountains and the valleys, the sea and the woods were etched on her mind, clear and focused, as if they would be preserved for ever. In her heart she was saying goodbye and, although she knew it was foolish, she wanted to imprint each beloved grouping of tree and flower, water and grass, hedge and ditch, brick and moss on her memory to take with her wherever she was going. She felt no sadness, only the inevitability of death, and, as for most of the things in her life, she prepared for it.

She eventually tackled the lake. She had avoided it since her return to Slievelea. She had not been down through the woods to the lake since the night her father died, and her talk with Conor later. She had often paused on her walks through the woods as she looked for lily of the valley or the tiny wild violets that grew around the base of the oak and elm and ash to look down towards the glimmer of blue in the distance. The azure sky reflected itself in the still waters, and it would beckon her through the trees, peeping at her seductively, inviting her to its side by revealing little glimpses of its shifting beauty. She had found it impossible to make her feet take that path, and her mind shied away from the recollection of events that could still cause tears to fill her eyes and pain to flood her heart.

Eventually she knew she could not die peacefully without facing that particular arena of emotion, facing the memories and laying them to rest. So one sunny May morning she purposefully headed through the woods, treading on the carpet of bluebells and crushing them beneath her feet. Her hands were clenched tight and her heart thumped against her rib cage as she came out from the shadow of the trees into the clearing, and the shores of the lake spread out before her. She let out her breath, realizing she had been holding it as tensely as she had gripped her fists.

It was so beautiful and peaceful, she thought. The waters danced as the tiny gold darts from the sun glanced off the wavelets and twinkled and sparkled like sequins on the lavender surface. The gazebo on the island out in the middle had the fairy tale quality of the ballet sets she had seen in Monte Carlo. It was blurred in a haze as if veiled by enchantment. And the memories flooded back, an onslaught of the past: her father, dead on her lap, the white of her dress splashed with the scarlet of his blood; Siobain's dear face, her arms open to comfort, always to comfort; Conor, unheeding, not realizing the passion she felt for him, and later, that beauty soured, the ordinariness of the man she had chosen to love for half a lifetime revealed.

She shuddered. There seemed to her no reality in the substance of all the years she had spent in Park Lane; they had the quality of a dream. She felt weak and vulnerable and unloosed sobs pained her throat as she gazed her fill of the magical scene. She stood still for a long time, feeling she had reached the end of something, that a curtain was drawing down over her vision. Then out of the curve of the trees on the opposite shore came a boatman in a punt. He stood tall, black clad, gaunt against the

283

pastel surroundings. She felt the pain pierce her heart like an arrow or a sword. As the man poled the boat nearer and nearer she saw it was Diramuid, and suddenly she knew who he was, who he had reminded her of; and with that knowledge she knew why he was here.

He saw her on the bank and lifted his hand and waved, and as she sank to the ground, stabbed by the second thrust of agony, she knew she could not die now, not here like her father at the feet of the descendant of the man who murdered him. Somehow she would have to find the strength to live long enough to warn Dan.

Dan sat beside her bed and looked tenderly upon the woman who had given him so much and who was now dying. He held the fragile bony little hand in his large warm strong one and wished she could receive some of his strength through the tips of his fingers. The face on the pillow was drawn in pain, the skin stretched tightly over the bones. He looked at the purity of structure, and reflected that Livia had exactly the same nose, cheekbones, chin and brow, and would some day in all possibility look like this. Yet in motion Livia was quite unlike this woman. As Deirdre raised the fine colourless lashes from her cheeks he was startled by the vividness and brilliance of the violet eyes that looked at him urgently.

'Listen Dan, listen to me.' She needed all her strength to speak, he could see the superhuman effort she was making. 'I've something to tell ... important.'

'Dearest Aunt. Calmly. Gently. There is time. Don't get upset and you will make it easier.' He saw a tiny tear slide from the corner of her eye into the white hair at her temple, and he patted her hands gently. She nodded and took a deep breath. Her eyes were anxious, he saw, restless in her pale face.

'What is troubling you, dear?'

'Dan, do you remember me telling you about your father and the man who killed mine?' He nodded. 'Well, Diramuid is one of them. A relation, I would think the grandson of the man who shot ... He is so like ... Something in the way he moves, the turn of the head ... the ...' She was becoming agitated and Dan stroked her forehead and gently hushed her.

'If you say it then I know you are right. There is no need to go on. I will take care of it, dearest Aunt. Now that I know who he is you need not fear. No harm will come to any of us, or to Slievelea.'

She smiled happily. Relief flooded her face and the tension was smoothed away.

'You always understand,' she said.

'You are so good to me,' he said.

'We are good to each other, dearest boy.'

'Oh, Aunt, it was love at first sight.'

She chuckled delightedly. 'You're sending me to my Maker with wicked thoughts in my head.' He laughed with her but his throat was full of pain. It was the last conversation they had.

Deirdre lay in the dear familiar room flooded with memories. Perhaps it was because the sun filled the room with golden light that none of her memories seemed unhappy. She saw herself as a young girl all those years ago, yet it seemed like yesterday, in her first long ball gown, it had been so pretty, and Siobain dressing her. Her mother's face as she gave her her fan and the walk down the stairs towards the three men who would influence her whole life: her dearly beloved father; the calm, good, dull man, Anthony Tandy-Cullaine; and the servant, Conor, who would never realize how much she loved him, but whom she forgave freely now, and thanked for the gift of his son, Big Dan Casey, who had lit up her last years and given them an unexpected glory and fulfilment.

Dan found her lying peacefully and he knew she was dead. He stood in the pink and gold room struggling with his emotions, then knelt by the bed and wept. He wept for his loss, for all the inexplicable yearning in his heart that she alone could soothe and tame. He knew life would never be as complete for him again and he wept as the last vestige of the child in him flew out of the window. Now he was truly master and he wished just for this moment that it was not so.

285

Chapter

43

THE gambling world in Europe that Diramuid Holland born Mulholland inhabited was a night-time one — a world of high-ceilinged rooms and charged nerves. The rich needed gamblers like Diramuid. They invited him to their parties, private and semi-private, and asked him to dinner, graciously including him in their conversation. But there was always the game afterwards, and a thin line separating the great families and those that were incorporated in their lives simply for their entertainment value. They were with them but not of them. Diramuid and his like were insecure, finely balanced between affluence and penury. One evening's bad luck, insignificant to the hosts, could put Diramuid into an untenable and dangerous position. Tailors and landladies did not wait for the likes of Holland. He had lopped off the Mul and called himself Holland when he came to Europe, not because the name was unwieldy, but for two purposes: firstly he thought it was a more attractive name and secondly he did not want to alert the Caseys when he met them, as he had determined to do. For his grandfather was Declan Mulholland.

Colleen Devlin had left Foley Place in 1868 with her baby Liam, child of Declan Mulholland, in her arms and no possessions save the clothes on her back.

The flight to America, the land of opportunity, promised some hope, offered some tiny ray of optimism for the future for the more energetic of the Devlin tribe. But there they had found themselves not on streets paved with gold, but in worse straits, coming from Foley Place to the Bronx, from one kind of poverty to another, even more desperate life, made harder because they were alien and far from their own kind.

Colleen had not really been in any condition to begin the hazardous journey in the first place. She had been frightened of the sea, frightened of strangers and frightened of change, so the whole experience had been a nightmare. She had never been out of Foley Place in her life. She met a Pole, Andrej Polyevenski, and he cared for her. He was a big, gentle giant of a man, and in the cramped prison in the bowels of the ship he made her and the baby a space, gave her his coat to sit on, and his bundle to lean on, his food to share, held her head when she vomited and bathed her forehead when the place became an airless, fetid sweatshop. She did not understand his language and his English was impossible, but his kindness was heart-warming and she leant on his physical strength, depending on his masculine authority. She mistook his size and kind heart for character and purpose. She made a grave misjudgement, for Andrej was the gentle, slightly retarded son of a woodcutter and this was all he knew. There were no forests in New York and he was not bright enough to make the transition from country yokel to city slicker.

Andrej was petrified from the first moment of their arrival in America. Far from leading them to decent accommodation as Colleen had hopefully expected, he proved useless and they had crammed themselves in with the Devlins who had emigrated every so often from Ireland to New York and had ended up in the Irish Catholic Bronx, Hell's Kitchen, in the hope of work and an end to struggle. Andrej clung to Colleen's skirts like a child. He froze in front of the traffic, pinned to the centre of the road, impervious in his panic to the yells and curses of the drivers. He was terrified of the permanent noise, his soul shrank in the concrete jungle, yearning for the stillness of the forest, the grandeur of the trees.

Colleen had merely changed one slum for another. In Foley Place they had lived at a slower pace; they had had less than here, but it was familiar, it was home. Here she was frightened. There were rats in the garbage and the noise hurt her head. They were surrounded by foreigners who spoke strange languages. The teeming tenement where they mucked in with the other Devlins was more crowded than they could have dreamed. The alley they lived in was squeezed between giant buildings. Washing hung out across the street, waving like tattered flags in the breeze. It dripped on the pavement and ran in little rivers where the children played hopscotch, barefoot and ugly with poverty. It was always dark there, for the sun could find no entry between the tall buildings. It was hot as the fires of hell in the summer and cold as the grave in winter. Colleen had never experienced such extremes before, and hope died, optimism faded, tired resignation took her by the hand as day dragged into day, an endless dreary acceptance of hopelessness. Liam was her only relief, her only joy, and the stories she brought from Ireland, her home, which in retrospect seemed a much rosier place. The sentimentality of looking back blurred and softened the past's sharp edges and highlighted its injustices.

When Colleen arrived sick and exhausted at Ellis Island she carried Liam in her arms and the story of the Mulhollands in her heart. She was bitterly resentful that Declan had not married her and legitimized Liam. She blamed the Casey family for this and everything that sprang from it: Andrej's uselessness, their poverty, the fact that they were strangers in a strange land, all, all she believed were caused by the Casey tribe. She had heard Declan whisper it into her ear often enough as he rode her body to their mutual fulfilment, whispering the poisoned words of hate, sex words, exciting dirty words that aroused them both and stimulated their lovemaking, cursing the Caseys and promising revenge. It was a horror story she told and retold her son, tending the tale like a garden full of poisoned flowers, belladonna, deadly nightshade. She whispered the litany of the Caseys' brutality to the Mulholland family to her son until he knew the tale by heart.

Liam grew like his father Declan, a wild, intense child and man. The saga of the Mulhollands was the cornerstone of his fantasy world, which was the cornerstone of his life. He lived in his head, on his unsavoury dreams. They were his pride, his identity. He was to pass the story to his son Diramuid, polished, hardened, diamond-bright with hatred; his heritage, his legacy. He had nothing else to give him.

Colleen was worn out from work and bearing children, for she and Andrej had many. Some died at birth, some before; some lived, were sickly and gave up the struggle early; some lived, survived, thrived; little street urchins, tough and hardy as the rats that infested the garbage thrown about the alleys and the sidewalk.

Liam went his own way. He despised Andrej and thought he had a destiny unlike others. He did not know what it was, but he was a Mulholland of Barra Bawn and somehow, some way, something would change the course of his life.

Nothing did. Andrej died. Eventually, as the law of averages decreed, a car hit him as he stood frozen to the spot, petrified by the oncoming vehicle. His mangled body was taken to the city morgue and Colleen unemotionally identified him and resumed her life as if nothing had happened, which in a way was true. Andrej had long since lost his identity for her. He had no reality, no real substance. He had become a shade, a lingering shadow on the periphery of her mind.

When Liam married the woman his mother had picked out for him, his cousin Kathleen Devlin, she moved in with Colleen and the fleeting Mulholland children, who scuttled in and out, strange beings from another planet, speaking another language, the language of the street. Kathleen Devlin was an energetic, down-to-earth little woman and she set her heart on escape from the hellhole to where the grass was abundant and green and the willow drooped its branches into the water. Her dream was just as fierce as Liam's, but she was the strong one, the realistic one, and what she wanted she usually got. Her aims were not high. She did not mind hard, demeaning work, she did not mind her husband's wild and unrealistic dreams. She liked his broody dark good looks, the black curls on him and his long lean body. Meanwhile she bided her time. Secretly she had been saving her cents, her nickels and dimes, and the day arrived when she had enough for a train journey.

Diramuid was thirteen years old when his mother at last escaped the hated concrete of New York, and taking Liam and her son, hoping to better their situation, left the city for the softer, sweeter air of Carolina. The destination was an arbitrary one, chosen because the first train at the right price had been going there. And it was south. South to sun and mellow climates, south to green fields, trees and empty land rolling to the horizon.

She found herself a job as maid in the employ of a fairly wealthy Carolina family in Hillsborough. The de Venturans came originally from France during one of the many Republics, having survived the revolution. Negroes had won their freedom, much to the disgust of the de Venturans, and the Irish replaced them in service. The de Venturans had one child, a thoroughly spoiled daughter called Felice, and it was one of Kathleen's duties to look after her. Mrs Mulholland wore a very smart uniform and worked from dawn till dusk for a pittance, but she never complained. To Diramuid's contempt she seemed only too grateful for the opportunity of being a virtual slave, though she thought she was lucky and sang as she worked. Diramuid could not understand the gratitude she felt to the family. He thought her wages were an insult, and he burned with anger at the unfairness of the situation.

Kathleen was content, but Diramuid's head was filled with stories of Ireland. Liam remorselessly cultivated his own obsession in his son. In the climate of his son's mind this was an easy task, and so the hatred was handed down, father to son, the tale of Ireland's lust for revenge manifest perfectly in these two. Only this was not a thirst for freedom, this had refined itself into a personal vendetta, the discontented shifting the blame for their condition onto someone else.

Diramuid did not like country life. He missed the city. He was a nocturnal animal and was always attracted to the bright lights and the mystery and secrecy of the night. He hated school and avoided it as much as possible. As he grew older he became more and more handsome, but his face was cold, his eyes hard. Love had no place in his life; indeed he did not understand it. He did not love his mother though he was fiercely partisan and took her side, defending her when the need arose, or he imagined it did. He was passionately attached to Liam, locked with him in a mutual hatred of the Casey family which was food for his soul, nourishment for his mind and an aim for the future. It was their dream, their goal, that Diramuid would somehow return to the motherland and avenge the wrongs done to their family, all the pain caused by the Caseys.

Diramuid fled Hillsborough the day Felice de Venturan turned her greedy eyes on his strong body. Her demand that he make love to her the way she had seen him make love to a servant struck terror in his heart and he knew that whether he agreed or refused she would never forgive him. So he left, saying no goodbyes, determined to become rich and reach Ireland, where he would right all the wrongs that had brought down his family.

As he crossed America, Diramuid learned many things. He

290

learned that with his inherited dark good looks he could excite women, and this aptitude he was to use whenever he could for his advancement, coldly and deliberately. He learned that dealing with the rich and famous, the powerful and the important, needs great caution. He learned to leave town one jump ahead of the sheriff, that discretion is the better part of valour and that he who runs away lives to fight another day. For his life was a fight.

He headed for New York, finding that the only way he could make money was by his wits. The world he was most at home in was the world of crooks and shady deals, of hoodlums and gangsters. He frequented pool halls. He became a gambler, a good one. His cold, unrevealing face, his icy control of his nerves, his unemotional temperament, stood him in good stead, though he never managed the big time, or won the jackpot. He was often within smelling distance, tantalized and frustrated. His bitterness and resentment grew, unleashed, held secretly within him, thriving like fungus in a damp dark place.

On reaching New York he found that Colleen had died. Her prop for living had gone with Liam's leaving and she had simply given up.

Diramuid travelled the length and breadth of America. Wherever the dice rolled and the cards were shuffled he was there, always managing to slither away when the going got rough or the places he was in were raided. He was a loner; men were nervous of him, women desired him, but he trusted neither and formed no ties anywhere. The dream in his head was the same dream that had given purpose to his forebears: the spur of revenge. He plotted and saved to go to Europe; the Riviera, London and Paris beckoned. In the meantime he waited very patiently.

He was in Chicago when news reached him that Liam was dying and wanted to see him. The wind that blew in off Lake Michigan was not any colder than Diramuid's heart. Riddled with anger that he was now to lose the only companion he had ever been able to talk to, the only person he trusted, he packed his few belongings and took the train to the place he had once called home.

It was after ten when Diramuid arrived and Kathleen was not in the little clapboard house his parents lived in. He was shocked by his father's appearance. The old man was a wreck. Grey, he seemed, all grey. Dirt-grey face, grey singlet, grey skin

291

and grey stubble. The two men talked, and it was of only one thing. They had been shut away from the light by their obsession, shut away from the sun and from life in the sun.

'You mustn't let your mother see you,' Liam said. 'She's never forgiven you for leaving without a word.'

Diramuid shook his head. His face was closed. He rocked in the wicker chair, backwards, forwards.

Liam lay on the bed eaten up with physical neglect, smoking cigarette after cigarette. The air was as grey as he was and the moonlight slatted its rays through the old wooden venetian blinds. Time ticked by. Diramuid wiped his face with a fine linen handkerchief. It was one of his affectations, a spotless white handkerchief; another was a fine Havana cigar. Men knew him by these trademarks.

Liam began. In Barra Bawn near Skibbereen the Caseys had betrayed the Mulhollands . . . He told how Rory was buried alive in an open grave, wedged in with the cold dead bodies of his family and how by God's miracle he had escaped to the west and had married there a faithless bitch, who gave him his beloved son Declan. How he had come to believe that God had charged him with a mission of revenge. How Rory and his son Declan had hunted down their quarry over the land to Dublin's fair city. How in Wicklow, on the vast estates of the Rennetts (Lord they were, Great Ones) at Slievelea they had found the Casey brood under the protection of the Foreign Master. How then the Caseys had done away with Declan and sent Conor Casey, Irish patriot and hero no less! to murder the poor ould Rory who lay in his bed helpless in the dead of night, in Foley Place. The old man had disappeared and his body had never been found. These men, Liam's father and grandfather, had no grave, no resting place. There was no headstone to weep over, no plot of land dedicated to their memory. It was as if they had never lived, had never existed, and didn't Conor Casey, hero and patriot no less, live in the dead man's room from then on! Oh they knew, the Devlins, knew about it all. Did the Caseys think they were eejits then that they couldn't see, couldn't guess? Yerra it was as plain as the nose on yer face. Oh, it was a story to wring tears from a stone! He chanted the history, honed by time, warped, one-sided, spewed forth in a singsong voice, and Diramuid nodded, the familiar words repeated in his brain and fuelling the hatred in his heart.

When the tirade was over the old man pushed himself up on his elbows. 'Get them,' he whispered fiercely, his breath smelling foul on Diramuid's face. Diramuid did not mind. This too was part of the evil. He nodded.

'Get them, the Caseys. They are to blame for this. It's their fault we lost our own bit of land in Mother Ireland. It's their fault my clan have no resting place. It's their fault me mam never married. It's their fault I am a bastard and me mam had to leave her native shores and settle with a no-account Polak. It's their fault you have to roam the world carving out a living by your wits, while they, they . . .' he spluttered, grey spittle on his nicotine-stained mouth, twin spots of red on his cheeks, the first sign of colour on him since Diramuid had arrived. He shook with rage, his body trembling till Diramuid became frightened that his fury would carry him away, that the old man would have apoplexy and die on the spot. But he recovered.

'Lookee here, lookee what I found. One of the cousins sent it. Lookee.'

He leaned over the side of the bed, his grey singlet streaked with sweat, his skin slippery and yellow.

Beside a chamber pot full of urine a paper lay. A newspaper. It was curling with use, well thumbed.

'I hid it. She would say I was being morbid. What does she know?' Diramuid nodded. He and his father had always understood each other. 'Lookee here.' Liam pointed a yellow-nailed, birdlike finger at a faded picture on the front of the newspaper. It showed a handsome smiling man, crombie-coated, the belt carelessly tied at the waist, a fedora hat perched rakishly on his thick dark hair. White teeth revealed in a dazzling smile. He had his foot on the running board of a Dusenberg and the caption read: 'Successful Irish business man Daniel Casey has formed yet another company, this time in the construction business. "Dublin needs rebuilding," Mr Casey is quoted as saying, "and we are the people to do it. Irish business for the Irish."'

Diramuid's eyes narrowed. This then was the enemy. He was glad he at last knew what Dan Casey looked like. He hated him even more now that he had seen him. He was handsome, successful and obviously rich. Now he was diminished in Diramuid's mind, had lost his enormous shadowy intangibility and become flesh and blood, a man with a body and face as other men. He nodded to his father.

'I'll get him,' he said. 'Never fear, I'll get him.'

The old man looked into his son's eyes. He found the response there that he craved. He nodded.

'That man ruined my life,' he said. 'My mother was left manless by that family and I was illegitimate and fatherless all the days of my life. Because of that I was emasculated, my spirit burdened by the unavenged voices of my father and grandfather. You'll have to do something about it all, Diramuid. End it for once and for all. Put our family out of their torment. If you promise to avenge the wrongs done to our family by the Caseys I'll die in peace.'

Diramuid's black eyes glowed. He felt full of vigour and excitement. 'Yes. Yes. You can die in peace. I'll avenge our family, never fear.'

Although there was no sound, no warning, Liam suddenly cocked his head sideways. 'Ye better go, your mam's coming. And remember everything I've told you, Diramuid. You must avenge us. Now go .... go.'

Diramuid escaped before his mother returned. Now he was a man possessed. He began cheating, determined to raise his passage and more, to cover his expenses for a time. By dint of luck, feverish application and determination he raised enough, and began his pilgrimage. He travelled halfway across the world to meet the family that had destroyed his, the man he blamed for all his misfortunes.

Dublin yielded up the information that Dan Casey was in Europe with Lady Tandy-Cullaine. Ay, it was true he was a rich man, though not as rich as the Tandy-Cullaines who were outclassed only by the royal family in England itself. He listened, assimilated all the information he could get and followed Dan and Deirdre. On the Riviera he pursued his profession. He did not see the beauty of the ice-blue sea or the waving palms, but he was provided with the first sight of his enemy.

He did well in Monte Carlo, and seemed to be on a winning streak, but he knew better than to celebrate the fact or relax. Therein lay ruin. Winning streaks were inevitably followed by heavy losses. The bitch goddess luck was very contrary. He took no chances.

One night in the casino, it happened. He heard the familiar name whispered. 'Casey ....' 'Dan Casey ...' 'Lady Tandy-Cullaine.' 'Casey ... Casey ... Casey.'

He thought for a moment it was his imagination, that the name he had lived with so long sounded in his ears alone. Then, as he saw heads turn, his heart stopped its steady beat and he realized the tall handsome man with the aristocratic old lady on his arm was his family's long-time enemy. He felt a rush of triumph such as he had never felt before. He wanted to laugh, sing, dance immoderately. No wine he had ever had had given him such a feeling of exhilaration.

The couple moved away. Dan looked momentarily over his shoulder and caught the bright black eyes of the tall, dark gambler. Diramuid bowed to him, smiling at him. Dan looked puzzled for a moment, then returned the bow with an incline of his head. The old woman turned also and looked at him. Diramuid repeated his gesture to her and she nodded, then turned to Dan, who inclined his head, bending down to her to hear what she whispered. The watching gambler saw Dan shake his head and the woman shrug her shoulders. Then Dan straightened and waved to someone slightly to Diramuid's left. He glanced around swiftly and saw a red-haired woman just as she lowered her arm, which had obviously returned Dan Casey's wave. He looked back and saw the couple continuing on their way, leaving him hugging himself with glee. At last, at last he had seen his enemy's face in the flesh.

He was a wild man that night. He won a great deal of money, and he knew he had to have a woman. As he was about to leave the tables someone spoke to him, the red-haired woman who had waved to Dan Casey. He had been subconsciously aware of her near him, losing money with careless abandon throughout the evening.

'Do you know him then? Dan Casey?' she was asking.

'A little,' he shrugged. 'Do you?'

'Oh yes.' She nodded very emphatically, 'Oh yes, indeed.'

Something in the way she spoke gave him the distinct impression that she did not like Casey. He looked at her more closely. She was a pretty woman, in her late twenties he guessed. She had a mop of flaming curls, bobbed below the ears and parted to one side. It was a glorious mixture of autumn colours, vibrant and vivid, and it seemed to take all the colour out of the woman's skin to feed its flame. She was very pale, with light green eyes, old-gold lashes and brows, and soft coral lips. She wore a green silk dress which revealed the opulent

295

curves of her breasts. His eyes rested on her lips and his desire grew. She sensed it, and smiled at him impishly, wrinkling her nose.

'I'm not crazy about Dan Casey,' she said. 'I'm not one of his vast army of sycophants. Every woman on the Riviera is after him, but he only has eyes for the old biddy you saw him with.'

'Why? I wonder why?'

'I can tell you if you really want to know.' She smiled up at him under the golden curtain of her lashes.

'I do. Oh, I do!' he said. 'Will you have . . . I would love you to have supper with me.'

'Oh yes, of course.' Diramuid had an uncomfortable feeling she was laughing at him, but he often felt that about women, and he pushed the feeling away.

'I'll collect you in half an hour then.'

She smiled. 'Yes, at the Hotel de Paris, room twenty-three.'

She stood up and as she pulled the green silk down and smoothed it over her thighs he saw that she was nearly as tall as he. She smiled once more into his eyes and, holding her silver clutch bag shoulder high, she swished between the tables and chairs and out of sight.

She was waiting for him half an hour later in the pale blue Louis Quinze bedroom. She was naked, and all the hair on her body was red-gold. Round and tall and avid she came to him. When they had satisfied each other they lay side by side, smoking in the gleam of the bedside lamp.

She laughed suddenly and said in a mock upper-class English accent, 'I'm Caroline Vestry, by the way. What's your name?'

'Diramuid Holland.'

She squealed, 'Ah, you're Irish. With a name like that you just have to be.'

'Yes, I am. But I've lived in America all my life.'

'That accounts for the accent. Why do you hate Dan Casey?'

'I . . . you were the one who said you didn't like him.'

'Oh, I know and I don't. He's conceited and *nouveau riche*, and a peasant. He thinks he's God's gift to the world and he has Aunt Deirdre in such a muddle she doesn't know whether she's coming or going.'

'Aunt Deirdre?'

'Well, she's not really my aunt. She's our neighbour in Wicklow in Ireland. I've known her all my life. We stay with her

296

for the Season in Park Lane.' He looked puzzled. 'Park Lane in London,' she explained. 'My father is one of her oldest friends. I used to be Caroline Jeffries. Then I married Charles Vestry. We all live near each other, though Aunt Deirdre has lived in London for the last ages. She's coming home now, to open up Slievelea, and Dan Casey is never out of her sight. What do you think he wants from her? My husband needs her help to keep Mount Rivers, our home, going, but he'll never get it if she goes on being besotted with that, that, charlatan!'

Normally Diramuid hated this post-coital chit-chat that some women seemed to go in for, but not this time. She was feeding him the inside information he sought, so he would let her be as loquacious as she wanted.

She shook her curls and turned to him. Her soft mouth was bruised from his kissing and her eyes were cloudy with passion. 'All this means nothing to you. I'm sorry. I've been boring. Worst crime there is.'

'On the contrary. I'm as, shall we say, interested in Dan Casey as you are. Oh, no, no, no, no. You don't bore me in the least. You excite me. That's what you do, you excite me.'

She closed the gap between them, curling her legs round his, stretching them apart, fitting herself onto him. She was obsessed by the size of him. She had never known a man so big and the resultant pleasure made her greedy. But he was furious.

'Not that way! No!' he cried and pushed her over on her back.

'Like this,' he said, 'like this.'

She gave up the fight, gave in to the pleasure, closed her eyes and let Diramuid bring her to wild orgasm again. Then, too tired to talk any more, she drifted away into sleep.

Diramuid remained awake however and smoked cigarette after cigarette until dawn edged through the cracks where the curtains met the windows. He rose and bathed. He grimaced as he donned his soiled evening clothes. He felt resentment flare. Dan Casey would not have to rely on one crumpled suit. But this morning hope burned high. This morning was not all black. The tide was turning. His star was in the ascendancy, his time was coming.

He left the room without a backward glance at the girl. He knew just what he would do. He had listened very well. He remembered what she had said about Mount Rivers.

He took his time getting to Ireland, to Wicklow. He introduced himself to the Jeffries as a friend of the Vestrys of Mount Rivers. He met Jonathan Jeffries, a wild, easily influenced young fool who fell for the dangerous charm of this visitor from the States and who quickly became his slave. Diramuid believed that at last he was on the right road!

When Dan came home Diramuid nearly lost patience, for there was a long wait before he could get any news of his enemy. Then an invitation to a ball at Slievelea arrived at the Jeffries and as he was a house guest at Usher Castle he was naturally included.

The size of Slievelea intimidated him, while its beauty amazed him and added fuel to the fire of his hatred. He saw Dan and Livia fall in love, and he marked it well, hardly able to contain his bitterness. It poisoned him for weeks after the ball and for a while his task daunted him. How could he pit himself against this man, who did not have to scratch a living from society, did not have to pander to people and was not insecure about his welcome? How could he understand a run of bad luck when your cuffs began to fray and you put shoe polish on the shiny parts of your dinner jacket? How could he know the thousand slights tolerated with the ingratiating smile of the inferior, when others, more important, went first, were catered for, cosseted and looked after, leaving him pretending he did not care? All his petty hatreds were coalesced into one big hatred of the man Dan Casey, and it became his only entertainment to dream up schemes of revenge on the Casey family, plans for the destruction of Dan Casey himself. He found it easy to become a friend of Dan's. Dan liked people around him, and Diramuid was persistent. Soon he found himself playing cards and backgammon with Dan, and he was on the guest list at Slievelea. His own tumultuous feelings kept him at a distance from the others, but he did not see it that way. It was they who were excluding him from their bonhomie and his hatred grew apace. Then in the course of his constant prying into Dan's affairs he had found out about Jessica Klein.

PART FOUR

Chapter

44

DAN Casey, old and dying, sat at the window and smiled. He remembered Deirdre and as usual the thought of her filled him with joy even now. He remembered the day she had died, and that glorious sunny day when all the birds of Dublin, Wicklow and Wexford had joined together to sing her funeral oration. He knew too that no one at the graveside really cared that much about her although they were dutifully sniffing into their hankies. Letticia had never liked her, and nor had Livia, except when she was very young and biddable. Letticia had always been terrified of her mother-in-law, and Edward had been afraid of her and behaved to her as a recalcitrant child. Only he had appreciated and loved her proud spirit.

Well, Aunt Deirdre, he thought, wherever you are I'll be joining you soon. So many dead, he thought. He could not remember now exactly when his mother had died, but it was soon after Deirdre, and her funeral had been massive. He chuckled, remembering, and felt the pain again. Would he never be free of pain, the constant nagging? he wondered, and he knew he would not. The end of this pain was the end of life.

It had been a farce, his mother's funeral, he thought, a lot of Republicans showing off, and himself helping the whole thing along so that he could cash in on the notoriety and forge lasting ties with the politicans for whom a connection with the erstwhile freedom fighters was *de rigueur*. He decided to have a drink and pulled the bell rope. Devlin came in, Spotty Devlin's son, whom he had rescued from Mountjoy Jail where he was incarcerated not for political crimes but for petty larceny. The Devlins were all the same, he thought, losers. This man's son

301

was now mixed up in the I.R.A. and being trained somewhere in Libya. Training to be a target, Dan mused wryly. Bloody silly thing to do. Never could see the point of it myself, and he laughed silently now as he remembered himself standing to attention beside his mother's coffin pretending to a patriotism he did not feel, had never felt.

But I would die for Slievelea, he thought, I would lay down my life for this place. Deirdre had known that.

'A whiskey, Devlin.'

'You know what the doctor said.'

'Yes, I do. I'm dying.'

'Yerra, never say so, sir.'

'Shut up, Devlin. I'm dying. So what possible difference can a whiskey or two make?'

'Well, if you lay down the law, like that ...'

'Yes, I do and hop to it, man.'

Devlin obeyed and Big Dan returned to his memories.

Things had never been the same after Deirdre's death. Nothing again was ever as clear cut, as uncomplicated, as simple. Deirdre had left all the vast reservoir of the Rennett wealth to Dan in trust to use at his discretion during his lifetime but dependent on the fact that he remained married to Livia. It was a loose arrangement and gave him almost limitless power. The money would revert to Livia at his death; if they divorced or separated, it was to be left to their children. If they died without issue, or if their children should die before them, the money would go to Letticia and Edward, and if they too had passed away the estate would revert to distant French cousins.

So for Dan's lifetime, provided he remained married to Livia, he had the use of the Rennett fortune for the upkeep of Slievelea. He was scrupulously honest in his accounting of the estate and never tried to take advantage of his power to channel money into his business. In fact, he was never in need of extra funds, so he was not put to the test. However, it rendered him vastly wealthy, as his home, all its appointments, the servants' salaries, the food, the upkeep of the grounds, the horses, grooms, and so on were all paid for out of Rennett money, whilst his own enormous profits were independent and his to do with as he wished. He saved a great deal and ploughed the money into sure-fire ventures, never risking failure by involving himself in dubious projects. He bought works of art and rare objects for Slievelea, investing wisely, asking Livia's advice and taking it. It gave him joy to contribute from his own pocket to the precious contents of Slievelea.

He built a swimming pool, bought Livia emeralds, sapphires and diamonds, opened accounts for her with the great fashion houses, Jaques Fath, and Balenciaga, and bought her rare furs, all with his own money. He was very rich, but he could not rest. He had to work harder, make more and more to satisfy his desperate need, his insecurity, his fear that it would all vanish if ever he sat back to enjoy it.

And so he made the years after Deirdre's death tough in spite of all she had left him. He spent them fighting. Not that Dan had ever gone to war. When he spoke for neutrality and against Ireland becoming involved in British aggression, he was not in fact really interested in peace. He was mainly concerned with what was best for his business interests in America and Germany. He himself had no intention of donning a uniform to die. In fact, armament in Germany was crucial to his investments. No, his fighting had been to increase his fortune and to keep it.

He and Livia were very happy together. They spent a lot of time in America. That country suited him exactly. He loved the hustling, the rough justice, the endless opportunity, the cutting of corners in business, the proud assertion that men had risen from the gutter to become millionaires. He loved the aggressive lack of moral niceties in much of the business conducted there, and he identified with the ruthless pursuit of fame and fortune indigenous to the young country. Here you did not have to have an Earl or Countess in the family or a coat of arms or a public school education to be a member of society. He and his beautiful wife were welcomed everywhere and were the toast of the town. They dined in the Algonquin and in Jack and Charlie's 21 Club, socialized with the Vanderbilts at the Savoy, ate lunch at Le Pavillon, drank bootleg gin and made friends with gangsters and film stars. It was all such fun, and though they were both fired with an inner restlessness, as was the society they found themselves in, they were wrapped in their great love for each other and were unhappy apart.

Dan had seen the crash coming in 1928 and pulled out just in time. On subsequent visits to the U.S.A. he called the tune.

303

Many of his friends were bankrupt, ruined in the slump that followed. He was a power, not just a rich visitor from Ireland but a man to court and cultivate. He became richer and richer, and he could not pause for fear someone would sneak up behind him and take it away from him. The crash in the States had frightened him and he did not sleep soundly for months after. If it could happen there and to some of his most solvent friends, it could happen to him. From the time Deirdre died he trusted no one, and one way or another got rid of all his enemies, or those out to defeat him, and the first person to go was Diramuid Holland.

He had put Deirdre's warning to the back of his mind until the two funerals were over. But he watched Diramuid closely. The man had almost become a member of the family over the years since he and Livia had met and married, and Dan had grown to like him. He liked the recklessness in him, his whippet-lean body and austere, geometrical face. He liked the air of menace and indifference to others' opinions that Diramuid showed by his confident, unapologetic manner. He had the careless grace of a panther and a ruthlessness like his own, Dan thought.

He trusted Deirdre's instinct totally, but eventually began to wonder if perhaps the old lady had become fanciful in the week before her death. Then something occurred that proved she had been right.

Dan was not a man to be in any way curious about his wife's personal belongings. He was not given to jealousy or its attendant prying. He had no interest whatever in his wife's possessions so it was quite by chance that he found the letter.

He had come in unexpectedly to their room one day and Livia, who was reclining on the chaise longue, pushed something behind the cushions. He thought nothing of it. Livia was in one of her states, he realized. He had come to accept and live with her periods of tension and was glad that they were few and far between. They did not worry him at all except that when she was in the grip of nervous irritability she herself seemed so unhappy, and he would have done anything in the world to prevent that. They had moved into Deirdre's room at Slievelea, which was the biggest and sunniest room with the prettiest view, and the chaise Livia sat on was the one he had often shared with Deirdre while she told him about the then, to him, unknown world.

As she sat on the chaise longue Livia was painting her toe-
nails a bright cerise. She wore a Japanese silk kimono which was
loosely tied at the waist and she was smoking a cigarette. He
could see the small firm, wine-tipped breasts and the curve of
her pinkly white flat belly as she leaned over her long, slim legs.

They were going to dine with the Jeffries. W.B. Yeats had
promised to be there. Not that Dan cared at all for poetry, but
the Jeffries were powerful people and where there was power
Dan Casey liked to be.

He had come to ask Livia if she had seen the cufflinks she
had given him for Christmas. She waved her feet about to dry
her nail lacquer, giggled and said he had left them last night in
her dressing room — didn't he remember? She went to get
them. Dan went over to the chaise, running his hand over the
brocade, remembering Deirdre for a moment. He saw the envelope sticking out, a white triangle against the rose material.
Idle curiosity made him pull it out before he was really conscious
of what he was doing, and he saw Diramuid's handwriting.
There was a small packet in the envelope, a jeweller's box which
he immediately identified as one of Hymie Klein's velvet boxes
with his name in gold letters on the satin inside. The box was
open and a pretty, fragile little Victorian necklace nestled on
the cotton wool within. Dan was too amazed to jump to con-
clusions. He read the envelope, which simply said, Mrs Daniel
Casey. There was nothing else so he looked behind the cushion
and found two much-handled torn sheets of notepaper.

Dear Livia,
      had your best interests at heart, so I thought,
    you had left this trinket you had
    his shop, I would take this opportunity
    you from the bottom of my heart
    that you had visited Hymie
    about Dan's mistress Jessica
    only say that I am deeply

    does not realize how lucky he
    for his behaviour to you, and if
    you on that score, just say the word.

that I was the innocent harbinger of bad news
such great esteem

Very sincerely,
Diramuid.

Dan was angrier than he had ever been in his life before. It was all so patently obvious. The letter was a travesty and Livia would see that. Poor dear Livia. No wonder she was in a state and had been distressed for so long, fighting her knowledge of his infidelity, concealing from him the fact that she knew, never reproaching him, never chiding him about the other woman.

He called her. She came in laughing. She wore the flame silk beaded dress, her slim hips barely touching the material as she walked. She dropped the cufflinks in his lap, but he stood up and pulled her into his arms. It was as if for the first time, and as he looked down at this slender, pretty woman with Deirdre's large, violet eyes, now full of wistful yearning, his heart filled with so much love for her that he drew in his breath sharply as he held her.

'Oh my darling, my own darling. Oh, how you must have suffered! Why didn't you tell me?'

At first she didn't know what he meant, then she saw the letter in his hands. 'I was afraid. I thought I would lose you.'

'Lose me! Oh my darling, darling girl! Jessica is an old flame I still see, that's all. She's from my past, a link I have never broken. But I will. If it upsets you I will never see her again, I promise you, never. You'll never worry again. Promise me?'

'Oh Dan, I've been in such a mess. I've been so frightened.'

'Well, it's all right now. Everything is over now.'

He suddenly desired her desperately. He was wiping the tears from her cheeks, and her love for him, her pliability, her great yearning eyes aroused him. She read his eyes and putting her hand on his chest held him off.

'Oh Dan, wait — mustn't now. The Jeffries said dinner prompt, and my lips ... Look.' She pointed to the shiny crimson coat of carefully applied lip rouge. 'Later, my love, later. Promise?'

He kissed her cheek, smelling her exotic perfume and the dusting of powder on her face and shoulders.

'I promise, my love,' he said.

That night at the Jeffries Dan Casey took Diramuid Holland for every penny he had. The men played blackjack after dinner. The game was usually casual and good-natured. Tonight, however, all the men there realized that Dan Casey was out to get Diramuid Holland. And he did. The men wondered what Diramuid had done to merit such ruthless revenge. There was no other word for it.

Diramuid himself was cold and clammy with fear as he saw for the first time the killer instinct in his opponent. Dan did it with charm and grace and icy intent. Diramuid had the most horrible sinking feeling in his stomach, and fear ate at his confidence as the chance to win or at least split even receded. Eventually he stood up. The room was grey with smoke and dull lights lit the table, so small, so vital, the cards looking up innocently. Yet thereon lay Diramuid's whole life.

'Gentlemen, I cannot proceed,' he said with as much nonchalance as he could muster.

'Why not, old boy?' Dan's smile was wide but his eyes were cold. 'I'll cover you. Come on. It's a great game. Only a fool or a coward would quit now.' He pulled Diramuid back into his chair and the ruined man had no option but to continue. Dan proceeded to wipe out Diramuid. He saw his life savings, every penny he had, disappear. He found himself piling up hundreds and hundreds of pounds' worth of debts to Dan Casey without being able to extricate himself.

Jonathan Jeffries said afterwards that it was very bad form. 'Both of them were like fanatics and really at each other's throat, not at all gentlemanly. And when Holland was ready to concede, to give up, Big Dan Casey wouldn't let him! Kept him at it long past the point of discretion. Well, Holland is all washed up now, I believe. Into Big Dan for thousands. Now he's scarpered. Left the country. Disappeared with his tail between his legs. Mind you, can't think of anyone who'll shed tears over that! But what on earth can he have done to Big Dan, that's what I ask myself?' And Jeffries dismissed from his mind the man he had himself admired until Diramuid's humiliation.

Livia lay that night waiting for Dan, but he didn't come home until dawn.

He did not give up Jessica Klein, although when he had

promised he had really meant to. It seemed unnecessary afterwards. Livia trusted him; she would not believe anything Diramuid Holland said, if the man ever dared to show his face at Slievelea again. She would always take Dan's word against the word of the gambler. So Jessica remained in his life.

As he sipped his forbidden drink, Big Dan Casey remembered Diramuid and said to himself smugly, 'But I got you in the end, you bastard, I got you.'

Chapter

45

DIRAMUID watched the shores of Ireland disappear in a mist. The boat he was on was no better than a cattle boat. He thought of the homes of the people he had just left. He thought of Slievelea, of the warmth of its blazing fires, the welcome of the starry lights greeting you as you came up the drive on a dark night. He thought of the deep soft chairs, the comfortable beds and *objets d'art*, and he ground his teeth in rage. He never once blamed himself. And as his forebears had done, he vowed again to get his own back on the Caseys. He forgot that the Caseys always won.

Ten years elapsed before Diramuid came back to the fair shores of Ireland. The years had not been good to him. His luck had run out. No amount of persistence could effect his re-entry into the fashionable European gambling fraternity without capital. Besides, he was hampered by the decline of his clothes. He looked sadly shabby now and could not raise the money to refurbish his depleted wardrobe. He tried Edward Tandy-Cullaine but was sent away with a flea in his ear. Edward's own run of luck put him out of sympathy with any hard-luck story, and he was not a generous giver anyway. He needed every penny he could get for his own game. "Sides which, fellas shouldn't gamble if they can't afford it,' he said to Letticia, who nodded her head in complete agreement and thanked her dear Father in Heaven for the millionth time that her dear darling pudding couldn't get his hands on their capital and had to cover his debts out of his own generous allowance.

Diramuid's luck went from bad to worse. To increase his bitterness, the news from Ireland chronicled Dan Casey's increasing success. As the owner of Slievelea, with a successful marriage and secure business interests all over Europe and America, Dan Casey did not have to scrabble for his daily existence.

War was coming to Europe. Diramuid had an alarming spell in Berlin, where he nearly ended up in a Nazi jail for cardsharping. He finally decided that the only thing to do was to play his trump card — Alexander. He had promised himself not to use it until in extremes. Well, that was now!

He would have preferred to go to Dan in a more prosperous condition. He hated the humiliation of looking so obviously a beggar. It was not how he had played the scene in his head. In his dream, he was as rich as Croesus and he was destroying a cowering Dan with the news that he knew he had an illegitimate son by his beloved Jessica. He knew what it would do to Livia if she found out and if anything happened between Dan and Livia, Dan would have to leave Slievelea; and Diramuid knew from his years as Dan's friend that Dan Casey could not bear that.

Dan would not see him. Diramuid couldn't stand it. He was furious. All his attempts to get to the big man were thwarted. In his frustration he turned to Spotty.

Spotty now lived in the Mount Street flat he had coveted. Dan's gift to Spotty had earned him Spotty's total devotion. He had always admired Dan; Dan was his hero, and what Diramuid did not understand was that Spotty, far from coveting Dan's position of power and wealth, was terrified by the magnitude of his old friend's enterprises and hoped and prayed that Dan would not demand more of him than he was capable of giving. Dan understood this and kept Spotty busy, amply rewarded and happy doing the kind of work he was good at — organizing deliveries and shipments, overseeing crating and packaging, keeping the peace on building sites, and a hundred other tasks where he was involved in getting the best out of a bunch of men determined to do the least work for the largest pay. He had a way with these people and achieved spectacular results, averting strikes, earning Dan's gratitude and settling comfortably into a life which was as luxurious as his limited ambition could aspire to. He had the flat of his dreams, Dan's *bijou* residence in Mount Street, and he had married a brassy, big-bosomed barmaid from Mooney's who kept him laughing and loving, well

310

fed and at peace. Spotty secretly felt sorry for Dan, whose wife's slender, high-strung beauty seemed to him a very bad bargain indeed, compared to his Tillie's luscious charms.

Diramuid sought out Spotty and began to pour poison in Spotty's ear, assuming that anyone who had started neck and neck with Dan Casey and had been left so far behind could only harbour resentment and hate. It did not take Spotty long to figure out that this man had it in for Dan. So he reported back to his friend, who decided the time had come to have a talk with Diramuid.

The meeting was in Dan's office in Dawson Street, Dublin. Diramuid sat in the leather chair reserved for visitors. He showed distinct signs of seediness, Dan thought. He sucked on his Havana cigar, a long bronze cheroot clamped between his fine white teeth, and his cold eyes were narrowed as he looked at the man he hated. He had no idea that Spotty had said anything to Dan, for that kind of loyalty was outside his ken. His mass of hostile emotions lay concealed behind his bland, enigmatic, poker-player's face, only his eyes giving any indication of his true feelings. But Dan sensed his inner turmoil, and his eye fell on the man's long, pale hand lying with careless grace along the smooth mahogany-coloured leather arm of the chair. He looked across the street at the Mansion House, and thought of his father, the great Irish patriot, Conor Casey, while Diramuid studied the hunting prints on the wall. Dan let the silence drag on. He could feel Diramuid's uneasiness grow. At last Diramuid could stand it no longer and broke the silence.

'So. It's good to see you again, Dan. I miss our games.'

'Do you?' Dan's voice was extremely friendly, but he was waiting. Let Diramuid talk.

'Yes, indeed. How is your family? Well, I trust?'

'Extremely well. Well, now. You wanted to see me?'

'Indeed I did.'

'May I ask what about?'

'Yes, I'll tell you. Look Dan, this is difficult. For some reason you had it in for me.'

Dan looked blankly at Diramuid, who continued, 'That last night, the last night I saw you, at the Jeffries'. You took me for every penny, and you did it deliberately. I don't know why.'

'Don't you?' Dan's voice was casual, calm.

'No, I don't.' Diramuid was bluffing it out; he sounded like a

311

man justifiably aggrieved. 'No, Dan. And I must tell you that you deprived me of my livelihood. You must have known you were doing that. For me to be left with no float . . .'

Dan shifted in his seat. He looked levelly at the other man. 'You know, Diramuid, that is your profession, after all. Every time you play you take the risk of losing. Don't you?' his voice was politely inquiring. Diramuid controlled his mounting anger.

'I want you to help me now,' he said.

'How and why?'

'Give me a float. Return some of the money you took from me that night.'

Dan burst out laughing. 'You have a nerve, Diramuid, I'll say that for you. Why on earth should I?'

Diramuid said, 'Otherwise I'll have to tell Livia about your son.' He saw Dan's face and knew he'd hit a nerve. He didn't know he'd signed his own death warrant. He did know a moment's triumph as he saw Dan's bewilderment. Dan didn't know! He hadn't known about Alexander! This was worth travelling across the world for, this was worth losing all for, this was indeed a sweet revenge — the sight of Dan Casey totally shaken.

'My what?'

'Your son. Alexander Klein — or Casey, I suppose.'

It took all Dan's control not to hit him, kill him then and there, but he held on, breathing evenly, calming himself, counting in his head, one, two, three, four . . . He counted up to thirty before Diramuid spoke again, but in that count Dan was in command of himself again.

'I thought you knew.'

'Oh, I did. I knew. I'm just shocked that you know. How did you find out?'

Diramuid knew he was lying, that he hadn't known, but he found himself almost believing Dan.

'Jessica Klein has no interest in anyone but you, never ever has, everyone knows that. She has a child. The boy, Alexander, although he looks like her, is very like you too. It was easy to deduct.'

'Ah! I see.' Dan steeled himself to look with clear eyes into the cold eyes of the man opposite. He controlled himself, went to the cabinet across the room and took out a large cut-glass decanter. He held it towards Diramuid and raised his eyebrows in inquiry. He did not trust himself to speak, though his face was impassive and calm.

Diramuid nodded. Dan poured the whiskey into two heavy-bottomed glasses. He handed Diramuid his, carefully making sure their hands did not touch. He sat down once more behind his desk.

'Diramuid, let us never mention that subject again.' He held up his hand as Diramuid started to protest. 'Hear me out. I have some business to attend to in the United States. I would like you to come with me. You are discreet and I want someone with me who knows the south. I have never been there. You told me once you spent some time there. True?'

Diramuid nodded. He was trying to work out what was happening, how he should react. He had not expected this invitation at all.

'Well then, it occurs to me you are just the man I need. You said you knew Virginia?'

Diramuid nodded again.

'Fine then. I'm interested in some horseflesh there. Do you agree to accompany me?' Dan sought the correct words. 'The assignment will of course carry a fee, and all your expenses will be paid. My associates travel first class. I like them to be relaxed and free from any unnecessary worries except about their work.'

Diramuid's mouth was dry as dust. It was an offer he could not refuse, did not want to refuse. To travel in Dan Casey's entourage was to travel in luxury, to work with him was to start at the top. He had an intense moment of struggle as the subversive thought came to him that Dan Casey's friendship could be much more useful to him than his hate, but simultaneously he realized that it was too late to change his own deep-seated, well-nourished loathing of the man. He would accept and see what opportunities for destroying his enemy came his way.

'It's very kind of you, Dan. I'd be happy to be of service.'

'But no mention of the other business.' Dan could not bring himself to even utter the word 'son'. 'If you ever speak of that to me or anyone else it will be the end of you. Understand? I must impress on you that I do not wish Mrs Casey to be troubled with this piece of information. Otherwise there is no question of your accompanying me to America. But if you come you will find the financial rewards more than adequate. You'll be paid well and there will be stock bonuses.'

Diramuid nodded, trying to conceal his triumph. He had found Dan's Achilles heel. He had infinite power over the man he hated and it had a good feel to it. He could take his revenge slowly, savouring every moment. He saw Dan glance at him and he knew Dan had read his thoughts. Dan nodded and rose. He went to the back of the room, and pushing aside a print of the hunt in full cry, he revealed a safe. From the safe he took a wad of notes. Relocking it and replacing the print he came back to the desk and dropped the money in front of Diramuid.

'This should see you through meanwhile. Now go,' he said.

Diramuid did not hesitate. He grabbed the bundle of money and after giving Dan the ironic bow he had used all those years ago in Monte Carlo when he had first set eyes on his enemy, he left the room.

He found himself in Dawson Street a thoroughly confused man. He tried to work out what had been said, how much Dan knew, whether in fact Dan was as surprised as he had thought him. The jubilation suddenly left him. He could feel no triumph, no joy. Yet he had seen Dan Casey squirm. Or had he? Of course he had! He had a blackmail weapon he could hold over Dan's head for ever, a weapon that would cause his adversary pain and insecurity. Dan would know now how it felt to feel threatened, to know that your security could be destroyed by another's whim. Oh yes, the tables had been turned all right. Then why did he feel so let down, why did the sweet taste of revenge vanish so quickly, leaving only unanswered questions, questions, questions?

Dan took Diramuid with him to New York. He had contacted the powerful Gambelino family, with whom he had had dealings there, and for whom he had done a good turn by taking American dollars to Sicily through illegal channels. Dan neither knew nor cared about what became of the laundered money. What he did know was how to ingratiate himself with these powerful people, and by doing them favours he had built up credit with the family which could be drawn on when needed. He was calling in his marker now.

One night he asked Diramuid to meet him in Union Square at the corner of 14th Street. Diramuid was early for his appointment. As usual his mind was in ferment. The lights around Union Square were brilliant, gaudy as paste jewellery. They winked in the puddles on the sidewalk and were reflected in the

314

slanting rain. He felt elated and sure of himself. He had enjoyed this American trip. Being close to Big Dan lent excitement to his life. It delighted Diramuid when Big Dan took him into his confidence, told him little secrets, confided in him. He had Big Dan. Big Dan was in his, Diramuid's, power. Big Dan trusted him. Oh, it was a grand feeling. He could scarcely contain the magnitude of his satisfaction as he turned into Phillie's Place and ordered a coffee.

As he sipped the hot liquid he reviewed alternative methods of revenge. He played with ideas, discarding this plot for another. It was his favourite pastime. He sat at the counter and watched the slow trail of traffic jams. Cars and people were blurred with the rain washing Phillie's plate-glass front. It was silent inside, the roar of the traffic only intruding when someone entered or left. It was steamy and warm, a 'greasy spoon', and Diramuid was surprised again at how at home he felt in places like this, much more at home than under the chandeliers of the rich. There he felt at odds with the world, looking for slights, resenting people on sight. Here he was cocooned, warmly at peace. He smiled. He sat alone over his coffee and smoked a cigar, solitary and isolated until it was time for him to leave.

He turned up his collar and went outside. The rain was pelting down. He stood waiting for the car to come and pick him up. Big Dan had explained the exact place where he should wait. He was a very precise man, Big Dan. Diramuid felt good. The coffee was warm inside him. Then a thought flashed across his mind, so appalling, so devastating that he drew in a quick breath as if in pain and banished the thought as quickly as he could. But it returned, the thought that when he had accomplished this task, this administration of justice to the figurehead of the perpetrators of so many crimes to his family, that when this was done, there would be nothing left for him to do, nothing left for him to live for. The main purpose of his life would be gone and all else would be meaningless.

He saw the car as it came round the corner. He was walking towards it when a fedora-hatted man leaned out and shot him with deadly accuracy. The car accelerated and was driven swiftly away before anyone noticed what was happening. Anyone except Diramuid. In those seconds it all became terrifyingly clear. He had underestimated Dan Casey. His family had always

315

done that. He was filled with such hatred that death came as a release from torment. He fell in a pool of blood. His last thought was, 'I tried, Da. I tried.'

As Diramuid Holland died, Dan was dining at Sardi's with Livia and Otto Preminger, whom he had met in Germany. They drank Manhattans and talked of how much money was needed to back a film Preminger wanted to make of the play they had just seen on Broadway. Gino Gambelino sat with them, a big cigar in his mouth.

No one missed Diramuid. He seemed to have no family, no close friends. At any rate the story Dan had concocted never had to be told because no one ever asked what had become of Diramuid Holland. Dan felt it had been worth the danger involved in juggling the money. He never minded paying for favours and this favour was one he had long dreamed about. The night Diramuid died he felt he had cause to celebrate and no bad dreams troubled his sleep. He had waited long and patiently for the sweet moment of revenge and he was relieved it could be managed so discreetly with the help of this good Sicilian family.

Dan decided not to ask Jessica about Alexander, her son. He decided that she obviously did not want him to know or she would have told him, so the best thing to do was to keep mum about the whole business. He obviously could not acknowledge Alexander as his legitimate heir without irretrievably damaging if not destroying his relationship with Livia.

Livia would ask him to leave Slievelea. That was inevitable. He believed that if she ever found out about Jessica and Alexander she would of a certainty banish him. To be cast out of Slievelea was something he could not bear. The house, his life there, the position it gave him in the eyes of the world whether people liked him or not was irreplaceable. There was no way of reproducing the glamour of Slievelea anywhere else. Sometimes Dan thought he loved the place more than anyone or anything in his life. And to Dan, Slievelea was synonymous with Livia. She went with it and without her he was an exile. Her happiness was his deepest concern and her very reason might be jeopardized by the publicizing of the fact of Dan's illegitimate son. No, it must never be known, and it appeared that Jessica felt similarly about the whole business.

316

He felt a surge of rage whenever he thought of this alien human being he had sired but not known of until now. He hated the idea of Jessica's son and he did not know why. He knew only that he did not want a son by Jessica Klein; his aspirations were too bourgeois to accommodate illegitimacy, it smacked too much of Foley Place and the darkness and shame of his own birth. It terrified him that this boy was a replica of himself, conceived out of wedlock, out of the social sphere he now moved in, out of Slievelea and out of his control. He would have been brought up by Hymie with Jewish customs and Jewish beliefs. Dan was not anti-Semitic, far from it, but it was an alien culture and he was a narrow-minded man when it came to his family. He wanted everything ordered, above board, accountable. Dan realized he did not want to know about Alexander so he buried the knowledge of his son's existence deep. He put it firmly at the back of his brain into the compartment reserved for things he did not want to dwell on. These things included Foley Place, Da McCabe and the barrow, his mother, the fire in Foley Place, Livia's past unhappiness, the letter, and, so deeply buried that he rarely gave it a thought, Diramuid's death on the corner of Union Square and 14th Street.

Chapter

46

SHORTLY after their return from America Dan went to Berlin. He had an appointment with Dr Goebbels about an arms deal that he was arranging. The Krupps' family business could not keep pace with the Führer's demands for more and yet more weapons and armaments. Dan could manage, with the help of his 'friends' in the U.S.A. and with little danger to himself, to satisfy the greed of the German high command. They relied on Dan to organize shipments from America. Of course the American government would be kept well out of the affair; Dan was, after all, a businessman operating out of Dublin, and his American connections were discreetly handled.

When he arrived, that November in 1938, the National Socialists were full of fury and self-righteousness, spurred to a heightened hatred of the Jews by the events of Crystal Night.

The meeting with Dr Goebbels in Friederichstrasse was a great success, although it had begun inauspiciously. Goebbels was a skinny little man with a limp and receding hair, and he was clearly intimidated by the appearance of this tall, attractive man with abundant greying hair. He was ill at ease until he had scurried round behind his vast desk, where beneath the giant portrait of the Führer on the wall behind him, inevitably flanked by the two long flags of the Weimar, he regained his composure and an overwhelming sense of his own importance. He did not stand beside Dan Casey again, always managing to remain seated until his guest had left the room, or to fall so far behind or walk so far ahead that no comparison could be made.

The little man's office was impressive even to Dan. There were priceless tapestries on the walls and a glorious Russian chandelier hung from the ceiling. The room was a vast, echoing place with tall windows casting silver-grey shafts of light slanting sideways over the highly polished floor.

'It is our Embassy in Paris,' he said to Dan. 'This scum of a German Jew has shot and mortally wounded our Third Secretary. The full responsibility lies with the infamous underground activities of Jewish propaganda. This is helped, Herr Casey, by your, ah, old enemy, the British. We have, don't you see, to do something. Our glorious Reich must not be contaminated in this way. So, ah, a clean-up of our city is, regrettably, in progress now. An example must be made. It is very sad that your welcome in Germany should be, eh, poisoned by this Jewish element. They, you see, permeate everything if they are so permitted.'

Dan shrugged. German internal politics were not his concern except insofar as they affected the Casey interests.

Dr Goebbels spread his hands and shrugged, imitating Dan's gesture. 'The Weimar will not tolerate it,' he said. 'It is too much. And the rest of Europe too should beware the Jews. They should look to the economy and they will inevitably find a Rockefeller, a Rothschild, a Goldenblum behind the money holding it tightly in their fists. But they will not listen, the other governments. We, the enlightened ones in the Third Reich, are aware of the worldwide Jewish conspiracy. We deplore it, and it must ... they must be dealt with. Only the Third Reich has the courage to act.'

Dan Casey listened as the little man waxed eloquent. He gave the impression of charming agreement and therefore was a great success. All arrangements were satisfactorily concluded, and the doctor dismissed his guest. He shook hands with Dan, stretching across the desk so that Dan had to lean forward.

'It is concluded, Herr Casey. We pay you a lot of money, but we are generous, we can afford to be. I will see you at dinner. We have planned a visit to the Grand Opera House here. We hope you will be entertained. Let us see if we cannot eradicate any unpleasant, ah, impressions caused by these inferior people. Most regrettable for you, Herr Casey. But they are everywhere, insidious, taking over the cultures of our lands. It must be stopped. Do you not see?'

Dan shrugged again.

'We will meet at dinner, Herr Casey. *Guten Abend.*' And the interview was over.

Dinner was formal, courtesy the keystone of the meal. Everyone's manners were perfect, polished and under control. No one raised any controversial topic at all. No one spoke of any other country, of world affairs, of art, except with regard to what was happening in the Third Reich. There were no women present. Everyone listened with great attention when Dr Goebbels spoke. All the men wore uniform: black, blue, belted, brass buttons gleaming, burnished boots shining like coals, the broad red band on the left arm decorated with the swastika. After dinner they donned long, smooth leather coats, black and sleek as satin, shining and luxurious, and a white silk scarf knotted at the throat.

His escort to the opera had a small, close-cropped blond head and eyes ice-blue, cold as marbles. He was very neat. The opera was, of course, Wagner. Large ladies with round, glorious voices and big men sounding of trumpets and brass created a magnificent cacophony of sound, of triumph, of victory, soul-stirring, rousing. Dan was very excited by the display, by the audience and by the performance. Rows upon rows of perfectly uniformed men and beautiful, opulent women, bejewelled and gorgeous, applauded the singers. Dr Goebbels was there with a pair of Valkyries, statuesque blondes with vacant faces. What impressed Dan was the feeling of power that filled the place almost to suffocation. These people felt themselves to be perfect, they were unequivocally right, they basked in their own glory, they were gods.

After the opera the tall Oberleutnant took him and others in the group to a brothel where a woman sang, 'Ich liebe dich' in boots and a black corset, her breasts bare, her face tired, dispirited, joyless, and Dan was courteously offered his pick of the girls.

Not because he wanted to, but because he did not want to offend, he chose the least tarted-up female there, a gretchen, a country girl, and taking her up to her room asked her to talk to him and smoke with him instead of making love.

'Why not? Am I not to your taste? Then why choose me?'

'I don't wish for sex with anyone at all,' he said.

'A boy, perhaps? Although it is frowned on by the Party. But you are English. Englishmen like each other in bed.'

He sighed. 'I am not English. I am Irish.'

She shrugged. 'The same.'

'What is your name?' he asked.

'Lotti,' she said. 'I am a good German — the best. I'm Bavarian. Like the Führer. Why don't you like me?' she asked coquettishly. 'Wouldn't you like a little *bumsen*?'

'No. You are beautiful, Lotti, but I, well, I love someone, someone at home, and I don't want ...'

'It should not matter. It would be a change.'

He thought of Jessica and Livia and how he had never ever wanted anyone else in his life. He needed no change, and he wondered if he were odd and realized he didn't care.

'No, Lotti, we'll talk.'

'But you are a beautiful man. You are very dark and you have such white skin.' Then a thought struck her and she shuddered. 'Not *Jude*? Not Jew?'

'Oh no.'

'That is good. The Jews are filth. Pigs.' She ran her tongue round her mouth and spat.

'Why do you say that, Lotti? Has a Jew been unkind to you?'

'*Ja, ja*. I would not be here if it were not for the Jews. They poison our country, they bring greed and pollution to our race.' He stopped listening. The girl was reciting propaganda without understanding what she was talking about. It was a convenient channel for her resentment. He thought of Jessica and Hymie. Hymie behind his counter, his kind old eyes smiling as he slipped an extra shilling to the woman who was selling her precious wedding ring, and his shrewd bargaining with the gambler who wanted a lot more for his gold watch or tie pin than it was strictly worth. An ordinary man with the same instincts that Dan and most men had. A kind man. And Jessica in the glow of the firelight after love, her face smooth and blue-veined, her hair a halo of black curls, her lips swollen with kissing, and he shook a little as he thought of Alexander, their son. He had tried to bury Alexander, the thought of him, the fact of him. He did not want to dwell on the reality of him, but here and now, he realized, in this country, at this time, that little family, his son, would be doomed. Just as his father Conor had hated all the English, every man, jack, babe and mother of them, so these people here hated Jews. It was insanity, he thought. People were people. Some good, some bad, some beautiful, some ugly. What was the point of lumping a group of them all together under one banner and alienating them from their brothers for an ideal? It

321

was an idea he had always rejected. He remembered Deirdre's voice. 'Leave the patriots to fight battles in Dublin's fair city, and you and I will talk in peace here, Dan,' and he smiled. Personal vendettas he could understand, casualties in the struggle for power, but where did it stop? Surely this man Hitler was the ultimate example of a power-mad climb to the top? He let nothing stand in his way, not the burnt offerings of his fellow human beings, not the screams of a race. But was he, Dan Casey, in his small way so very unlike him? He shuddered at the thought. But at least I am not blinkered by delusions of patriotism, he thought. I am doing it for myself.

He smelt the preparation for war in Berlin, the electric air of power in the streets emanating particularly from the army. The hard, grey cobbled roads, the shuttered grey houses, and the cold grey sky were a neutral background for the huge red flags, white circle at the centre, with the black swastika sitting in the middle. They decorated the buildings, hung everywhere. Phalanxes of troops marched beneath these, kicking their boots waist high, uniforms shiny and black as ink in the pale sunlight. He saw the terror-permeated scuffles in doorways, the little groups of Jews, brutalized by troops, violence disguised as authority, something smart and righteous. Arrested, hustled to prison, their rights ignored, ceasing to be citizens in their own land, overnight the Jews became aliens.

It reminded him of the Tans in Dublin those long years ago, of boots marching up a dark street, the banging on the door, the windows shutting, curtains closing, the scurry as bystanders fled the menace. At the ultimate violence, the shots in the night, or the agonized cries, the isolated scream of pain, people turned over in their beds and thanked God for a respite, that this time it was someone else, or congratulated themselves that they were on the right side and safe from the terror in the night. Dan shut his mind to the comparisons with Dublin and the grim little scenes he was accidentally privy to.

He shook himself free of the oppressive gloom he felt in Germany. The climate here had had the uncomfortable effect of forcing him to face truths that he usually made sure to avoid at all costs. He was glad to leave Germany the next day.

Jessica was overwhelmed by his ardour on his return. He could not wait to make love to her and he held her to him as if he could never let her go. She was curious as to the reason but too sensible to ask. She simply responded to his mood as usual and made the most of his excessive desire for her while it lasted.

However, soon after his return from Berlin, in 1938, Dan took Livia to Italy and Jessica was once more left alone.

Dan wanted to investigate the business opportunities and examine the political climate in Italy, in Mussolini's back garden. Despite his hidden disapproval of fascism he was anxious to get on the bandwagon and make the most of the opportunities afforded by the war that was clearly coming. Or someone else will do it, he thought, placating his conscience.

Dan was also worried about Livia's health. Burningly restless, she smoked incessantly, sometimes not finishing one cigarette before she lit another. She slept badly and was thin as a reed, her eyes enormous in her little face. She tried very hard to be gay and entertaining for Dan, but he knew she was acting and he felt confused and anxious about her behaviour. He constantly wondered why she could not relax when he was doing all in his power to attend to her comfort. He made love to her more gently than ever, leaving her nerves screaming and her body aching for fulfilment.

Murmurs of war were reaching a new pitch in Europe when Dan and Livia paid their visit to Italy. They settled in Venice, staying in the Gritti Palace. The city's sad decay and decadent air suited their edgy mood. They spent their days roaming around the town, gazing at paintings, buying lace and glass. Dan was tired. He had been working too hard, Livia said, and he smiled wanly, the spirit missing from his anxious eyes. He could not shake off the feeling that they were in a dream. It seemed to him that a miasma of uneasiness pervaded Europe. She was waiting, holding her breath, marking time. People laughed too loudly, pursued pleasure too intently, rode a merry-go-round of high nervous gaiety and blind indulgence. They were not thinking, Dan believed.

Oh, it was different that year with you, he thought as he remembered being there with Deirdre, the elegant leisurely life with her, the slow process of time then, the resting in and enjoyment of the moment. That was all changed and his wife seemed to embody the speedy nervousness of the time they were living through. In any event, whenever he was away, except for that one year with Deirdre, he longed to be home and felt restless until he could return to Slievelea.

The weather was grey and misty except for an orange ball of sun that hung without rays over the lagoon and gave St Mark's and the Doge's Palace the appearance of an enchanted city from the *Arabian Nights*. Dan was right to worry about Livia. She was very near the edge of a *crise de nerfs*, feeling as taut as a violin string, unable to find a moment's rest. Even at night, tired out after a long day, no peace came.

The big idea came to Livia one night while she was sitting outside Florian's. At first it appalled her; the thought was too bizarre, and she dismissed it. Then, more and more, it crept back into her mind, to tantalize and titillate her.

It was Dan's and Livia's custom to drink their after-dinner coffee in the Piazza San Marco and listen to the orchestra. They naturally favoured Florian's, and they would sit out under the stars and watch the world go by. Venice spread herself out before them like an old courtesan, her tawdry finery crumbling into ruins, the barbaric splendour of the cathedral squatting in front of them. But the ever-present, aggressive and self-confident gangs of Mussolini's *Fascisti* were alarming, and it was almost impossible to feel peaceful in company with their noisy presence, their strutting arrogance. Livia, preoccupied with the pros and cons of her plan, was only marginally aware of their function, and the implication of their ebullient mood was lost on her. Dan, however, was aware of the political situation and made up his mind to finalize the Berlin armaments deals before the trouble came to a head. It was one of the most lucrative deals of his career and he was beginning to find it irksome dallying here with a highly strung wife who was obviously not enjoying herself when in fact he wanted to intensify his work with the German connection.

The more Livia thought about her plan the more it seemed the answer to all their problems.

One night as the waiter put the coffee in front of her she raised her hand to take a cigarette and knocked his arm at the moment of his placing the cup on the table. The coffee spilled all over her dress. The waiter was very distressed and hurried off to fetch a cloth. She begged him not to trouble. It was an accident. Dan told him to forget it and, dropping some lire on the table, took Livia's arm and led her back to the Gritti Palace. It was his practice to see her to her room and then have a stroll

324

around the waterfront, after which he usually stopped and had a brandy before he joined her in their suite. He said the nightly promenade helped to clear his mind and put him in the mood for sleep.

In her room, Livia turned over the idea. She had seen how that waiter always tried to serve them, how he obviously admired her, was smitten by her. In common with most Italian males, he was constantly assessing women in general, on the ready for an amorous adventure. She was realistic enough to realize that when she no longer frequented Florian's he would find another *amorata*, but in the meantime he could cast doe eyes on her, sigh over her, and flirt the moment Dan's back was turned. This suited her purpose exactly. The last thing she wanted was trouble in the future. A casual encounter in a hotel in Venice ... it would be of no account. He was very good looking, she thought, as almost all Italian youths were. His face was out of a Raphael painting.

She knew that what she was planning would place her in unfamiliar territory, outside accepted behaviour, but the alternative had become unendurable. She knew that if she had to go on as she was now she would lose her reason. If she lost her mind, she would inevitably lose Dan. She would propel him into the arms of Jessica Klein. The mere thought drove her to distraction, and she could see that her abstracted behaviour irritated Dan. She determined to put her plan into action.

That night Dan took a stroll along the Grand Canal. On impulse he booked a gondola, its slow, rocking motion soothing his tension, as he idly admired the buildings they passed, murmuring the beautiful, rolling names Deirdre had taught him: Ca'D'Oro, Ca'Pesaro, Santa Maria de Nazareth, San Geremia, the Fondaco dei Turchi, the Fabbriche Nuove di Rialto, Fabbrichi Vecchie di Rialto to the Rialto Bridge, and on, and on. He said the names aloud, using the resonant Italian inflections and sounds to the delight of the gondolier, who joined in the litany, laughing proudly. Arriving back at the room he found Livia fast asleep, the peaceful sleep of a child, her cheeks flushed, her lips slightly open and smiling. He was surprised and glad. Perhaps Venice was curing her, he thought.

It was, but for reasons that would have stunned Dan. While her husband had walked through the Venetian dusk and glided down the Grand Canal murmuring the enchanted names of the *casas* that flanked her crumbling walls and laughing with the gondolier, Livia had taken the Italian waiter to her room. Fear had taken away her inhibitions and the feeling that at any moment Dan might come back had both excited and frightened her. It had lent an intensity and speed to the whole procedure, with a total absence of foreplay that took the Italian's breath away and made him boast to his friends that the English milady was the hottest woman he had ever been with. Because she was in command and because she was the aggressor, she lost any reticence and she reached a climax on the rug in front of the fireplace in the bedroom with half her clothes still on during the first moments of her encounter with the Italian. He was bewildered by her voraciousness, her greed for his body. She could not believe the sensation and to his alarm wanted it again. 'At once,' she said, bewildering him. 'And quickly,' she cried. However, he managed it, and felt very rewarded by the magnitude of her orgasm; he had not realized he was capable of giving such pleasure. He didn't mind too much the speed with which she hurried him from the room, so much a success she made him feel.

'What a lover I am,' he said to himself, nearly colliding with her husband in the lobby.

It continued for a week. Each evening he would serve their coffee and after Dan had taken Livia to her room and left for his walk, the waiter would rush up to her and they would fall upon each other, she issuing greedy commands like a demented sergeant major. 'There. No, there! Yes, Yes! Oh yes! Now ... now ... now there, yes! There ... now, now!' and they would consummate their passion in seconds. At the end of the week Dan and Livia left and he never saw them again, but he often bored his friends with his boasts about this sexy Inglese who looked as cool as cucumber but was a tigress in bed.

On the last day she said to him, 'By the way, what is your name? I never asked you.'

He said, 'Alain, Alain Castinetto. My mother is French, my father Italian. It makes me a better lover, no?'

'The best,' she said and kissed his cheek. It was the only time she ever kissed him.

Livia went home to Slievelea radiant, serene, tranquil and pregnant. She told Dan one night when they were driving back from an evening with the Jeffries. The dinner had been a glittering affair. The Vestrys had been there, Caroline bright and sharp as glass. The other guests were strangers to Dan, a poet, two actors and a French intellectual. The French intellectual had loved Caroline and they conversed in French a lot of the time, while the poet and the two actors kept up a brilliant repartee, tossing the crystal ball of conversation back and forth across the table. Only Dan felt left out. He understood most of what was said but could not join in the complicated badinage. He could not manage the light, elegant phrases that tripped so easily from their tongues. He felt clumsy and clod-hopping, a pheasant among peacocks.

He drove the car through rain which was wrapping a mantle of grey over the trees and fields. The headlights of the car picked up the shadowy beeches pressing forward in the wind. It was warm in the car, a cocooned shelter from the inclement weather. The protection of the rich from the elements, Dan thought, congratulating himself, his discomfiture gone in a flash. I have achieved this, I have clawed my way here, into this richly equipped car, whispering its way through the dark and the rain, my slim, elegant, well-bred wife beside me, on my way home, to my home, to Slievelea. He felt a surge of triumphant joy course through his body, a charge of energetic intoxication that had nothing to do with the wine he had drunk at dinner.

Livia was nervous. She had tried to tell Dan her news several times since their return, but each time at the last moment her courage failed. She believed that by telling him she would make the child his.

'Dan. Darling. I'm pregnant.'

Dan said, 'What, Livia? This damn rain. I can't see a thing. What, my love?'

He had heard her but he needed a second before he could produce the correct responses. What kind of man am I, he thought, when my wife tells me she is having a baby and all I feel is fear and apprehension?

Livia repeated her statement. 'I'm pregnant, Dan.'

He glanced towards her and saw her radiant little face turned to him, full of anxiety. There was a pleading in her eyes and her mouth trembled. He felt a flood of overwhelming love for her engulf him. He stopped the car, took her in his arms and kissed her hair. He knew what to say now, how to behave. This was Livia's gift to him. He would not let her down by seeming ungrateful. He would rather have had things go on exactly as they were, but she must never know that.

'Oh my darling, how wonderful!' He kissed her hair again, then cupped her face in his hands. 'Oh Livia, aren't you the pearl of a wife now?'

He smiled at her and all the tension and anxiety disappeared from her face. For a moment he held her close in his arms in the warmth of the car, listening to the deluge beating on the windows, then he started the engine and they drove through the rain back to Slievelea, Livia wrapped in her happiness, certain that what she had done was right, Dan praying, for no reason that he could fathom, that the baby might be a girl.

Livia bloomed in pregnancy and lived in a state of blissful expectation. She had found the key to her sexuality in that week in Venice, and bit by tiny bit she used her new-found knowledge to encourage Dan to treat her less like a china doll and more like a woman. It was a slow process and sometimes tested her patience, but Dan must not realize what she was doing or he might turn away in horror, she thought. Dan felt pregnancy had brought out the woman in her, and her more ardent responses to him surprised but pleased him.

Letticia and Edward arrived in Wicklow for the birth, and Aisling was born in the big bedroom at Slievelea, relatively easily, on a glorious, sunny day. Dan reacted in just the way Livia had hoped he would. He was completely bowled over by the baby, fell in love with her as quickly as he had fallen for her mother, he said, and doted on the tiny, fragile, helpless bundle. In fact he was as proud as he could be of the baby and more enamoured of Livia than ever before. They gave a huge christening party at Slievelea a month after the birth. They called the baby Aisling and her godparents were Caroline and Charles Vestry.

Chapter

47

THE magic of Aisling's childhood was something she never really recovered from. In the green countryside around Slievelea she lived in an enchanted world of Irish folklore while the guns roared across Europe, bombs annihilated the culture of centuries, and civilized men and women blasted each other to kingdom come. The Chaplinesque figure who terrorized Europe and whose paranoid shrieks ricocheted across the Continent was not heard in this peaceful backwater.

Dan was, for Aisling, the perfect father, just as Livia was the perfect mother. To the little girl, they were a fairy-tale couple and she basked in their love for each other and for herself. Dan's love for Livia and her ardent response to him was obvious to her. Laughter filled her home, her heart, and her mother and father and she were mutually wrapped in a circle of happy intimacy.

Aisling was protected and cosseted and as she grew up in the company of the local children, the wonder of the world she lived in held only happy revelations. She led her gang of followers, children of the staff and from the nearby village, of whom she was undisputed leader, down the lanes through the jade mist on a wet day and the purple mist on a dry one. They climbed the trees, swung on the wide iron gates to the fields, chewing the juicy grass, and meandered along the narrow boreens, picking buttercups and blackberries or chestnuts and acorns.

They often walked to the old forge on the Wicklow Road, Aisling, in her flower-print puff-sleeved summer dress with smocking at the waist and piqué collar, leading a small group of village children. They would stand in the doorway of the forge, the mouth of hell, and watch the activity within, fascinated and enthralled. The forge had a heart of flame in Aisling's vivid imagination. It was the home of giants, of ogres, of Fafner, of Prometheus, and it reverberated with the sounds of the glorious 'Anvil Chorus' that she listened to entranced on Big Dan's record player. The blacksmith, bronze-bodied from heat and dirt, muscles rippling, hammered rhythmically in his leather apron and black trousers, throwing his huge shadow on the wall, his powerful strokes making the sparks fly under the heavy impact of metal on metal.

Standing hand in hand, quiet in the sunlit lane, they would peer into the interior, trying to make out the outline of the 'ouldest man in the world' as he was known, as people told it. Blind Danny sat in the corner, his eyes milk-white, his gnarled ould hands twisted like the branches of the giant chestnut in the bluebell woods, grasping a shillelagh. Some said he was a Fir Bolg, a man from the dim mists of time, forgotten by God, and left to guard the treasure that was hidden during the 'troubles'. Many had tried to find out if the legend were true, that a rich elegant lady, cloaked against the night, sympathetic to the Cause, had come fleeing from the Brits to Blind Danny's forge from the Wicklow hills and left him her jewels and a bag of gold sovereigns to care for. They were hidden, some said, under a stone deep in the heart of the forge, but the only man who had tried to find out the truth of the story had put the heart across himself at finding himself staring into the milk-white orbs, translucent in the darkness, of Blind Danny himself, sitting there in the forge in the deep of the night. The man, Liam O'Doherty by name, a poacher and a chancer, a dodgy customer an' no mistake, said he nearly died of fright an' could it be true that the blacksmith was older than time and had sat in that place unmoving from when it was a cave or a palace hung with the singing shields of warriors?

Aisling and her companions had heard these stories, which filled them with excitement and fear. They would peer intently into the forge, and when their eyes became accustomed to the darkness within they would stare at the old man wrapped in the glowing shadows of the place. He was a magic mystery to the children. To Aisling the story was a romantic fantasy, one of the wondrous tales of Ireland that were half real to her, mixed into the fabric of her being.

330

Other times they bicycled in the opposite direction, away from Dublin, and turning down a lane not half a mile from the southern boundaries of Slievelea they would stop at Annie 'Clackity' Halligan's cottage and sweet shop. Clackity was a vast woman, three times the size of Bunty, her sturdy daughter and Slievelea's cook, as wide as she was tall, and when she laughed, which was all the time, she wobbled like one of her daughter's jellies.

She fed them cinnamon buns and home-made loganberry jam, and when they handed over their two pennies and piped up, 'A farthing's worth of those, and a ha'penny worth of those, an' a ha'penny worth of those, and a farthing's worth of those,' she would shift the ill-fitting false teeth around in her mouth and, making the castanet sound that gave her her nickname, she would make cones of newspaper and fill them with bull's-eyes, aniseed balls, liquorice allsorts, acid drops, butter-balls or toffees. They got six sweets for a halfpenny, three for a farthing. They stood in the little fly-filled shop, watching the insects' death struggles on the sticky piece of orange-coloured flypaper hanging from the ceiling. Clackity Halligan would stand on tip-toe and dig her fat hand into the tall glass jars full of sweets and count out the correct number. Then she would put the rest of the sweets back into the jar and wipe her hands on her floral apron and fill the little newspaper cones with the sweets, a separate cone for each variety. She also sold ham, cut on a machine that sang to and fro with a fearful shining guillotine blade, smoothly shaving thin pink slices. She sold tomatoes and home-made bread, Lyon's tea, rationed, and Jacob's biscuits in tins with glass lids. She served them in fistfuls too and when she patted the children's cheeks they could smell the biscuity-sweet scent from her sticky fingers.

She dreamed of having a little money-container that ran up on a wire rope when you pulled it, to a waiting cashier, who popped the change in the container and sent it reeling back to you below. She had seen such a contraption in a shop in Wicklow town and had coveted it ever since. Meantime she had to make do with a tea caddy under the counter stuffed with six-pences, shillings, threepenny pieces and the odd pound note.

Dan took Aisling riding in front of him on his big black stallion and fishing with him in the trout stream early in the morning when the dew starred the grass and the violets still had their eyes shut. The cobwebs stretched across the hedges, holding the silver drops of moisture tentatively on silken skeins, shuddering and falling eventually in a rainbow splash. Aisling hated the cobwebs when they caught her face or hair, but she loved everything else in nature and was joyously at one with the rhythm of her world.

Dan adored her. He loved her fearlessness. She swam like a fish; she sat her horse like a huntress; she played tennis like a champion; she was strong and brave. She was, he thought, very like Deirdre, the young Deirdre he had never known, the Deirdre who had fallen in love with Conor, his father. And she was beautiful. More beautiful than Livia, and, indeed, if one could judge from the portrait, more lovely even than her great-grandmother. She grew apace, heedless of her own beauty, loving and lovely, happily contented with the sweetness of life.

Gone were the days of French chefs and English butlers at Slievelea. With the two world wars the remaining international staff had, in dribs and drabs, returned to their native lands. Home they went to fight a war and Slievelea settled into a comfortable Irish regime. The food, with Bunty Halligan as cook, was superb, but not at all sophisticated. They ate salmon, lobster, Dublin Bay prawns and freshwater trout from the stream at Slievelea, roast beef and lamb in season and, when they could get it, rabbit and hare. The days of meat or fish *en croûte*, of *vacherin*, *bavarois*, *dauphinesse*, *au vin* and so on were over and Dan was happier that way. He loved the taste of simply cooked food although Deirdre had done her best to wean him onto gourmet sauces and exotic delicacies.

There was no real shortage at Slievelea during the war. Of course bananas, oranges and other such foreign fruit and products vanished, and there was no sugar, but who cared when they had their own heather-honey and thick Kerry cream? Tea and coffee were rationed and Livia called tea 'black gold dust', which pleased Aisling's aesthetic sensibilities.

The great house shone, polished with beeswax and Silvo and Brasso, silver and bronze shining and wood gleaming. The rooms were full of Livia's flowers, which she arranged with careless grace, singing now as she did so. The stylized elegance and formality of Deirdre's day were over. The servants were excellent in all respects but one: they would not be rushed. It all happened in the fullness of time, they said, and in the heel of the hunt wasn't it better so? It took the fluster out of life, Bunty Halligan said. It certainly had a beneficial effect on Dan and Livia, for they fell in with the slowed-down pace and gave themselves an opportunity to rest in their happiness.

The war raged on. At Slievelea no sound of gunfire was ever heard, no bombs defaced the beauty of the place, no siren shriek ever shattered the peaceful sleepers in the night. The war years were an oasis of peace in the lives of Aisling, Dan and Livia. Dan said that the Irish had made up their minds that there should be no more wars on her fair green land. Her gentle body would not be raped again. No more, they vowed, would men slay each other in her fields and streets; no more would the blood of her sons be shed in her name. The Republic would be pacifist, would be neutral. Five hundred years of conflict and oppression were enough. In freedom and peace they would mend their lovely country, tend her, soothe her tired spirit, nurture her and watch her grow. Let those who felt strongly about the conflict in Europe enlist in the British Army, Navy and Airforce, and many did, many would. But not here. Ireland was sick of it, sick unto death. So Slievelea lay tranquil under the misty purple hills, content, at peace.

Dan had made a fortune out of his deals in Europe, and now that was over. There were endless opportunities still for speculation but for the moment and for the first time in his life Dan gave himself some sort of rest. Of course there was business to be transacted in the U.S.A. and he kept his mob connections there and in Sicily. Sicily was playing a vital part in the war. Partisans were helping the Allies to escape, and Dan, at a safe distance, had a finger in the pie. As usual he cared little about the ideologies involved; he was only interested in the building of the Casey empire. He also knew that when the war was over, just as in 1918 Ireland had needed to be rebuilt, so Europe would have use for his construction company. Yes, he would be ready. But his constant scrabble for work, his total preoccupation and obsession with it, ceased for a time and he became a family man *par excellence*. There was a new warmth, a deeper love between husband and wife, and Livia grew more beautiful as edges were smoothed away and laugh lines appeared. She gave up smoking and began to age a little, tranquilly, and Dan loved her late blooming.

Then Livia became pregnant again. Her pregnancy was an

anxious time for them all. She was, of course, old for child-bearing. Her pregnancy came as a surprise, and not an altogether pleasant one. She was confused by the contrariness of her emotions. She had believed for so long that to bear Dan's child would be the ultimate achievement of her life. The reality proved different. They were so happy together, Aisling, Dan and herself, and David's arrival seemed an intrusion on that content. Her pregnancy was difficult. Her nerves returned. She could not fathom why. Aisling, despite the secret of her conception, had arrived in sunshine, joyfully celebrated. David arrived, and was to live, in shadows, in tension, apprehension and deep unexplained anxiety.

David was born in 1947. Aisling was thrilled at his arrival and with a wonderful generosity welcomed him with no feelings of jealousy or emotional displacement. She treated him like a living doll and loved him with all her heart. Aisling also loved her mother. It was often the child that soothed the high-strung woman and charmed her into relaxation during and after her pregnancy. And she adored her handsome father, followed him everywhere and asked him questions which if he could not answer they looked up together in the encyclopaedias in the library at Slievelea.

As David grew older he tagged along behind Aisling wherever she went. His father was irritated by him. David took after his mother and what Dan could excuse in his wife he could not tolerate in his son. David was a nervous, timid boy, a dreamer, a poet. He often lost himself in some imaginary world of fantasy which made him look stupid and Dan would long to shake the boy out of his daydreaming. Often it was Aisling who averted trouble for David. She diverted Dan's attention and saved her brother many a dressing-down. In the summer they swam in the cove whether the weather was good or bad. On cold days they went blue and had goose-pimples and purple lips, and the tips of her fingers went crêpe-like. Aisling adored the huge grey breakers; the cold, salty waves made her feel clean and vital and alive. On hot days they explored the rock pools and lay in the ferns, and Aisling told David tales of Fin McCool and Maeve and the Fir Bolg and the Tuata de Dannan and the magical land of Tir na nOige where no one grew old, but remained for ever young.

'But it's sad, David,' she told him, 'they never laughed there and they never cried.'

The sound of laughter echoed in Slievelea. The pounding of children's feet up and down the stairs, the tennis rackets and footballs scattered about, cricket bats and scooters, bikes and fishing tackle, wet swimsuits discarded, maids scolding, bursts of tears over bloody gravel-torn knees, all filled Slievelea with a family warmth, softening the old house like its mistress, making it more human, more comfortable, less intimidating and grand.

The cook and the housekeeper were surprised and shocked to hear Mr Casey chasing Miss Aisling up the grand staircase and falling in a heap near the top, shrieking with laughter.

'Got you, Ash, got you!' he would shout and Aisling would weep with laughter helplessly, convulsed with joyous mirth, and bury her face in his tweed jacket.

'Oh Pappy, Pappy, you cheated ... you took the stairs two at a time, you did, you did, you did!'

Dan gave the children piggybacks round the table in the dining room and Sheilagh, one of the maids, closed her eyes in agony in case he banged into the priceless crystal and smashed it. But he didn't seem to care. There was hide-and-seek through the house and through the grounds in the spring and summer, and Livia hiding treats all around Slievelea at Halloween. They played blind man's buff, and got scared half to death at unexpected bumps and sudden touchings when they thought no one was near. There was bob-apple in the great hall, biting great succulent bites, hands tied behind backs, and hurting noses as they pushed the apples floating in a barrel, water in their nostrils trying not to laugh because on pain of sin they could not touch the fruit against the side. There were Christmases in the snow, and Big Dan as Santa Claus creeping into their rooms, and they would tiptoe down at the crack of dawn to see what was under the enormous starry tree decorated with fairy lights saved from long ago when Great-Grandmamma was a girl and danced the night away here, wearing pearls in her hair and carrying a fan. It was a wonderful, carefree time.

Aisling was always to remember her first grown-up dinner party. It marked the first moment of her awareness that life was not all it seemed, and that smiles and laughter often hid complex emotions. Not that anything spectacular happened; there was no drama, no quarrel or discord, and it was that very fact that made it a difficult and confusing experience.

335

It was summer at Slievelea and a hot one. She was fifteen and David six. They found it difficult to sleep and there seemed no air in the world, not even from the sea. Then one afternoon on the lawn at tea in the cooling shadow of the giant chestnut, her mother said, 'Aisling, would you like to come down to dinner with Pappy and me and our guests tonight?'

Her father flashed a smile at her. 'For a treat,' he said.

Aisling was sick with excitement. Her face flushed and she slung back the hammock she was swaying in idly and slid out, running over to her mother under the tree.

'Oh may I? May I? May I?' she cried.

'Darling, darling! It's too hot . . . Oh, don't rush about so.'

Her mother wore a cool, sleeveless, ice-green linen dress with white piqué lapels low across her still boyish breasts, and she pushed up her hair on the back of her neck. Aisling could see the soft damp curve of her mother's hair, and the tiny bobbles of her vertebrae down the bend of her slender neck. Her mother's skin was white and soft, and she dabbed it with her handkerchief. Her fingers were slim as flower stalks and her wrists small and graceful.

Big Dan had his Panama over his eyes. His throat was bare and brown and very thick to Aisling's eyes. She could see the hair on his chest, where it began, and it frightened her a little. She always felt a delicious thrill of fear at certain aspects of her father's masculinity. His size and strength made her feel weak and feminine, but challenged her too in some strange way that she did not understand.

He pushed back his hat, and his blue eyes, navy now in the shadow of the chestnut, twinkled at her. 'Would you like to, poppet?' he asked.

'Yes, yes, yes, yes, Pappy, yes!'

'My, my, all this excitement over a dinner party! It'll be very dull, my dove . . . very. Grown-up and boring.'

'I don't care, Pappy. It'll be my first ever dinner party.' Then a thought struck her and she cried in consternation, 'Oh what, oh what shall I wear? Oh dear, I've got nothing, nothing!'

Big Dan threw back his head and roared with laughter. She could see his strong white teeth. There were some gold fillings at the back. His face seemed to her as if under a microscope. She noticed for the first time the dark stubbly shadows around his jaw and cheeks, the thickness of his eyebrows and lashes, and the grey in his blue-black hair. The pores of his skin were magnified and the veins at his temples blue under his tan. He was so handsome, she thought, so handsome and strong, and her mother so fragile and delicate, and she imagined how beautiful they would be naked together. Then, horrified at the thought, she raised her eyes from her parents and stared at the shimmering hills, the sloping lawns. The plump figure of Sheilagh, black uniform immaculate, white apron stiff and starched, hurried from the house to clear away the tea things.

Dan rose and stretched. There were damp patches under the arms of his short-sleeved fine cotton shirt.

'Ah well, I'll leave the burning question of what you'll wear to you and your mother, poppet. I have some business to attend to. I'll see you later.'

He seemed very brisk, and Aisling saw that her mother was suddenly pale.

'Is Devlin about, Sheilagh?'

'Yes, Mr Casey.'

Livia turned round swiftly. Her neck almost snapped, Aisling thought, with the tension of the movement. There was a pink stain on the white skin of her throat and cheek. 'You're not going into Dublin now? Not in this heat?'

Dan laughed carelessly, ''Fraid so, my love. Business.'

There was a final ring to the tone of his voice. It was dismissive and brooked no debate. Aisling felt something in the air, a shiver of tension, a razor-blade of division, an unexplained atmosphere of unease. She felt suddenly like bursting into tears but didn't know why.

Then it was all gone. Her mother shrugged, her face calm. Her father ruffled Aisling's hair and bent to kiss her mother tenderly on her lips, a gentle butterfly kiss, and Aisling decided she had imagined something and was cross with herself. She knew she would keep the picture of her father's soft touch on her mother's lips for ever in her heart.

The shadow of the tree was lengthening and her mother smiled up at her. 'Well, well, well, what shall you wear, my pretty princess?'

'Oh, Mummy, I've nothing, nothing, nothing!' Aisling sounded despairing, and then she saw that Sheilagh was convulsed with silent laughter and her mother was smiling behind her hand.

337

'Ah well. But we've been busy, eh Sheilagh?'

Aisling was puzzled and impatient. 'What? Oh, what's going on?' she cried.

Sheilagh had to put the silver tray down and gasp for breath.

'Oh Sheilagh! Sheilagh, what is it?' Aisling's voice was high and sharp. 'What's the secret? Please. What is it?'

Livia was aware of the near hysteria in her daughter's voice and she said soothingly, 'It's just that Sheilagh and I have kept your new dress a secret.'

'My new dress! Oh, Mummy!'

'Yes, my pet. We smuggled it into your room. Or rather, Sheilagh did while we had tea. I imagine you managed to do that, Sheilagh?'

The maid nodded emphatically, her face bright red and damp with sweat and excitement and tears of laughter.

Livia said, 'We thought we would just let you discover it yourself when you went upstairs. But now I've spoiled it. I've told you. Only I can't bear to see you upset.'

'It's so pretty, miss. Yerra, it's like a fairy tale.'

Aisling was racing across the lawn. The house, silvery-grey in the sun, was cool indoors. She passed her father on the wide staircase. He looked fresh in a light cream linen suit. She streaked past him and flung open the door of her room.

The dress was laid out, beautifully arranged on her bed. There was a pair of fine crêpe de Chine camiknickers, silk stockings, a lacy suspender belt, and the dress.

Aisling put her hands to her mouth and stared at the creation on the bed. It was everything she had ever dreamed of. It was rose-white, silk and strapless, draped across the bosom and billowing out from a tiny waist.

When she put it on she was frightened at the change in her appearance. The girl in the mirror was a stranger to her and she felt ill at ease with her. She was a beautiful, remote adult, someone Aisling did not know, was not sure she wanted to know. But she was beautiful, even Aisling could see that, and she was not at all sure that she was happy about it. Just at this moment she wanted with all her heart to be like Camilla Vestry, a little plump, a little plain.

Aisling later remembered the strangest things about that evening. She could never remember greeting the guests, or going into dinner, but she remembered pleating the crushed silk

338

material between her fingers while the older people talked. She could see clearly the dining room, with dim, golden pools of light cast by the candles on the faces of the guests, on the pictures on the walls. She loved those pictures: Canaletto etchings of Venetian scenes her romantic soul could wander through: a Tiepolo pen and ink study of a boy, his head seeming alive in the candle flame, smiling and winking conspiratorially at her.

The huge flower arrangement in the middle of the long table, the crystal, the silver, the white napery all made her feel sleepy and special and privileged to be sitting here on her father's right and opposite Caroline Vestry, her friend's mother, voluptuous in gold, her red hair vying with the burning logs in the fireplace.

There were twelve guests. Her father often looked down the table at her mother, who sat facing him at the other end. Their glances met sometimes to confirm, sometimes silently to question a remark made by someone at the table. Her mother looked beautiful in her cream moiré taffeta strapless gown, at her throat the diamonds and emeralds Dan had given her. Caroline Vestry wore no jewellery. She was the only one who didn't. All the other women were ablaze with gems and even Aisling wore Great-Grandmother Deirdre's pearls.

The talk around the table was confusing to her. The men and the women did not speak directly to each other much; rather, each sex spoke to its own kind, and they communicated thoughts and feelings that sometimes had nothing to do with what they actually said. They did not like the fact that Aisling was there, there was an edginess in their acknowledgement of her that upset her and made her feel a stranger in her own home, at her own table, yet no one was anything other than exquisitely polite to her. But she knew.

Kevin Rowley, a young man of about twenty-six, was saying, 'The north ... the bloody north ...'

'Apt description, blood.'

'Let the British worry about the north,' Jonathan Jeffries said. 'It's their problem. They created it. Let them sort it out.'

Someone else said. 'Oh, come on. It's not that simple. The northerners chose themselves to remain under British rule. You can't lay the blame completely at Britain's door.'

But Jonathan Jeffries was adamant. Aisling thought he had had a little too much to drink.

'That's what I say. It's their *problem*. Never mind *blame*. It's *their* problem.'

Kevin Rowley said quietly, 'Exactly, Jonathan. Quite.' But he doesn't mean a word of it, Aisling thought. 'Fine. But the south will always feel mutilated until Ireland is made whole.'

Jonathan said, 'The northerners *chose* to remain under British rule. Social Security, Welfare State, all that. Let them have it, I say. They wanted it that way. Let them have it.'

Young Kevin Rowley smiled, but Aisling could see he was angry.

'But it's not fair. All that wealth. Oh, England gave us back the heart and soul of our country when she gave us the south, but she kept the purse strings by keeping the north.'

Then Big Dan spoke and everyone listened, not because they wanted to but because it was polite, the correct thing to do, Aisling saw, feeling astonishment mount as she realized that there were some people there who actually did not like her father.

'The north was rich, but it is rapidly declining. Cotton mills and ships made it a gold mine. However, cotton is now mass-produced in Asia and South America, and shipbuilding has been declining since the thirties. Even the launching of the *Queen Mary* was a sop to public opinion. It gets worse every day. The north will get poorer and poorer, and with poverty will come violence. Then if she's our responsibility she'll be a hell of a burden. No, let Britain keep her.'

Through this conversation Aisling could hear her mother's soft voice, 'Yes, I love the longer skirts. They are so pretty, and I'm afraid at my age short skirts would not be at all elegant.'

'Oh Livia, you'd look lovely in anything,' the fat, good-humoured Anna Jeffries said. But there was a hint of envy in her voice, a flash of jealousy in her eyes. 'I love nylon. It's great not to have to worry about the ironing.'

Livia wrinkled her nose. 'No, I hate it. Really I do. I loathe synthetic fabrics. I deplore the fact that good taste seems on the wane.'

'But the new things are so labour saving, so practical.'

Livia shook her head. 'I know, and I cannot argue against that. But it's sad, so sad to see beautiful things go.' Aisling was acutely aware of the feel of her underwear, soft as a whisper under her gown. 'Everything now is disposable,' her mother was saying. She picked up her Georgian silver fork. 'Look at this.

It's so beautiful. But now they will persuade us to replace it with plastic.'

'Ah, but it helps the poorer people, does it not, Livia?' Caroline smiled down the table at her hostess, her eyes glittering maliciously. 'But that is not your problem. *You* will never have to buy nylon underwear in Madam Nora's in O'Connell Street, now will you?'

Everyone appeared a little embarrassed and Charles Vestry, her handsome husband, said hurriedly, 'Livia, come, come. You have brought quite a few appalling — that is, in my humble opinion — paintings which can only be described as "good taste on the wane".'

Aisling realized that Charles, like herself, had followed two conversations at the same time, but he had given no indication of that till now.

Livia laughed. 'Touché, Charles. You have me there. Nevertheless, they *are* works of art.'

Aisling remembered her mother's painstaking explanations of the more obscure works, and although Aisling had not paid much attention at the time, she was well aware of how passionately her mother felt. She was therefore amazed at how lightly she spoke, how good-humouredly she parried the taunt about her taste.

Dan had frowned at Caroline, whose cheeks were flushed, and now he said, 'Well, I don't understand the Kandinsky, but I love the Barlach bronze. It's warm and round and lovely.'

'You hate the Juan Gris,' Livia pouted.

And Dan finished, 'But I love, love, love the Monet. It's the colours of Slievelea.'

Charles shrugged. 'Monet can hardly be lumped with the others,' he said.

Nellie Gorman said, 'Andrew bought a Picasso blue. It's much nicer than the new stuff he's painting which, like you, Livia, I think is awful and modern.'

'Well,' Livia hesitated, 'I didn't exactly say *that*.'

'Has anyone seen Michael and Hilton's new play at the Gate?'

The conversation became general. They ate as they talked, smoked salmon with Bunty Halligan's crumbly brown bread, followed by rack of lamb with peas and glazed carrots and little roast potatoes. Fresh mint sauce accompanied it and then came

Bunty's summer pudding, a mouthwatering affair of soft mixed red fruit, blackcurrants, redcurrants, raspberries and blackberries made into a pudding with soft white bread, meringue and cream, and although the women made feeble protests about their waistlines, Aisling noted that it did not prevent them having a second helping. Then they had some cheese and drank coffee with chocolate truffles.

As they finished their coffee Dan leaned over to his daughter and covered her folded fists with his big hand. 'This little lady goes to bed, eh, Livia?'

'Yes. She looks tired,' Livia said.

The attention of the group around the table suddenly focused on Aisling. She was aware of the guarded eyes scrutinizing her and she blushed.

Charles Vestry cleared his throat. 'Are you set for a game, Dan?' he asked.

'Yes, why not? There are at least three of us.'

'Pity Holland is not here. He really was a good player to have around. Where did he vanish to, Dan?'

Aisling saw the malice in Charles's eyes and heard the falsely casual timbre of his voice as she felt her father's hand tighten over hers in an oddly fierce grip. He laughed lightly. 'Search me. I've no idea. Come along, poppet. Bedtime.'

He kissed her and she went with the ladies to her mother's dressing room and bathroom, where like a flock of tropical birds they repaired make-up, redid hair, squeaked and squealed and gossiped. Aisling, suddenly tired beyond belief, curled up on Dan and Livia's big bed. She could hear the sound of Dan's favourite recording of Hutch floating up the stairs. It was the last thing she heard before she fell asleep.

She could never make up her mind whether she had enjoyed that first adult late-night party or not. There was something intimidating about the grown-ups' attitudes to each other, something antagonistic and competitive. Everyone seemed firmly entrenched in their own opinion and though they gave in gracefully enough in argument you could see in their eyes that they had not really conceded an inch. It was not what they said, it was what they didn't say that was anathema to Aisling, even though she was so young. The nuances beneath the casual remarks, the inferences underlying the exchanges were part of a game that in all her life Aisling would find unplayable. She

342

began to understand that she could never be completely secure again. The man who had tossed her into the air, who she was confidently sure would catch her, was not as black and white as he seemed. There were ambiguities, undercurrents lurking which she would never be allowed to understand. Her father took his first tiny step down from his pedestal that night.

His attitude to David caused the next, bigger, step. One night, a year later, when David was about seven, the house was awakened by screaming. Aisling knew it was her brother, and pulling on her dressing gown she ran down the passage to his room. She found Dan and Livia in the corridor and a whey-faced David, shaking and sobbing now.

Dan's face was red with anger, his voice dripping with contempt. 'There's no one there,' he said, 'no one! There's no such thing as ghosts, you little fool. For heaven's sake pull yourself together, David! Do you want to be a coward or a man?'

'Oh please, Dan, don't badger him so. He's only a child. A little boy!' Livia was crying softly and tried to cuddle her son, but Dan put her firmly, gently away.

'No, Livia. He has to learn. He's got to be brave. Have you ever seen your sister snivelling like that?' Dan said to the cowering boy and gave him a shake. 'Have you?'

'N-n-no, F-father,' David stuttered between sobs.

'Look at you. Stuttering "n-n-no f-f-father". Cringing and scared like a sissy. Stop it at once!'

He shook his head and David, whose sobs had ceased but who could not control his sharp intakes of breath, the aftermath of his crying, wiped his sleeve along his snotty red nose. In disgust Dan pushed his son's arm away from his face. 'Look at you,' he said contemptuously. 'Look at you. Sissy-boy!'

David's face was blotched red and white from his crying, his nose dripping, his cheeks wet. His head jerked sideways with the hard, staccato intakes of breath that tore through his slight frame.

'Go to bed,' Dan commanded, once more preventing Livia from holding her son. He put his arm round his wife and steered her back to their room below. She looked over her shoulder but Dan said firmly. 'No, Livia, he's got to learn.'

Aisling pulled her sobbing brother into his room. She tucked him up in his little bed and soothed the damp hair away from his forehead.

'What was it all about, old fella?' she asked. 'Tell me.'

'Oh Ash, Ash. I thought I saw a ghost. I was going down to the lav and there was this white thing, this figure at the other end of the corridor. I screamed. I saw it, I did, I swear, I saw it.'

Aisling thought. Then she laughed.

'Ash, don't laugh. I was so scared. I saw it. I did.'

Aisling put her arms round him. 'That was you you saw. Yourself. You in the mirror. In the mirror on the back of the linen room door. It must have been open. When it's open it goes right back and you can see yourself in the mirror. The ghost was you in your white jammies, dolt! Oh, Dave, Dave, I love you.' She was laughing and crying a little as she hugged him. 'Don't cry any more. Pappy didn't mean it. He's an old bear sometimes.'

'Never with you, Ash. It's only with me. And I don't mean to do anything wrong, really I don't'. He gazed at her earnestly, his eyes enormous in his pinched little face.

'Oh, I know that. Mummy knows that. Just don't pay any attention, Dave.'

'Sometimes, Ash, I wish I wasn't here at all. Sometimes, Ash, I'm *not*. I'm somewhere else entirely. I don't know what's the matter with me. Help me, Ash ... please help me.'

She hugged him close again. 'I will. I promise I will. Cross my heart. Never fear. Now go to sleep.'

He lay on the damp pillow when she had gone, staring at the white moon through the window. It was the moonlight, he realized, that had shone on his own reflection, tricking him into thinking he saw a ghost.

'Tricky,' he said to the moon, 'trick-ey. Moonlight ... moonbeam. I wish I was. I could slide into other people's rooms, and into the dark woods and no one could catch me. No one at all.' He lay wide-eyed, staring through the window. It was morning before he slept.

Chapter

48

ALEXANDER had asked Jessica many times about his father. It had started after Martha had died. It was natural for him to be curious, but Jessica and Hymie refused to give him any information whatsoever on the subject. They were very worried that he would find out and were alarmed at the thought of what he might do if he once discovered the truth. They were also aware that he was very likely to ferret out anything he wanted to know. He was extremely clever and had a mania for pursuing knowledge; Hymie remarked that he could be a detective, like Humphrey Bogart in the movies. Hymie had become a dedicated film fan since his wife's death and often left Jessica in charge of the shop while he went to the little cinema called the Grand Central at the top of the quays in O'Connell Street. There he contentedly crossed his hands over his stomach and watched Frederick March in *Les Misérables*, fought with Tyrone Powers in *The Black Swan* and desired in the purest possible way the peekaboo beauty of Veronica Lake.

Alexander wanted to be an artist. All his life he had drawn and painted; everywhere he went his long slender hands were busy with pencils and paper, sketching continuously. He helped Hymie in the shop, but he was hopeless. He forgot what he was supposed to do and would become fascinated by a face, the arrangement of light, the beauty of an ageing hand, and breaking off the conversation he would rush to his pad and begin to scribble. There was no point in scolding him; he would smile and carry right on with his drawing. He was impervious to anger, he simply ignored it until it had passed. He just continued drawing, painting, sketching. Hymie could tell he was very good, but he did not know how good.

'You have to have that something extra to be an artist, Alexander. You have to have magic.'

'Yes, Grandfather, but how can I find out? My teachers here say I'm a genius, but what do they know? No one here knows enough about it.'

His dark eyes would flash, full of intensity and passion. He was a tall slim boy, full of fire and darkly Judaic in his looks, with his mother's sculptured bone structure and his father's brilliant smile. The obvious thing then for Jessica and Hymie was to send him to Paris to study. This seemed a perfect solution to their problem as well as being the very best thing for Alexander. Jessica missed him very much and Hymie missed him more.

Jessica's whole life revolved around the evenings or afternoons with Dan, and she had always worried in case Dan found out about his son. She knew it would complicate things unendurably for him and she was pretty sure he would not be pleased. The embarrassment he might feel about the ambiguity of Alexander's position, especially now that he had a legitimate son, might cool or even spoil forever the wonderful relationship they had, a relationship that grew in richness and tenderness as the years passed. So, although she loved her son, his presence was a constant worry to her and it was a great relief when he went to France.

Alexander loved Paris. The war was over but there were still heart-breaking reminders of it. He painted the ruins, the faces of the war-weary people, the refugees, the homeless, the greed, the resignation, the acceptance. He painted the carnival atmosphere of freedom, the frantic fear that there would be no tomorrow so 'let's cram it all in now, at once'. He painted with a passion and flair that irritated his teachers, who had not yet come to terms with modern art, and who wanted him to conform to some school, any school. Everyone was painting like Mondrian and Klee and Rothko, Jackson Pollock was making a splash and Alexander did not fit into these new forms at all. The wit had gone with Miró, Magritte and Max Ernst, and the dream-like beauty of a romantic world dusted in magic had seen its last days depicted by Monet, Van Gogh, Manet and Renoir. The satirical edge was exchanged for geometric abstractions, but this was not Alexander Klein's style. His painting was uniquely his own. He painted elongated figures of suffering against a jazz party, the outsider always lonely, always looking on, never joining the gaiety, and the gaiety itself had an hysterical edge. The teachers and their opinions did not really impinge on Alexander's inner self. He was never at the mercy of their criticism. He applied it when he agreed with it; he took from them what they could helpfully offer and paid no attention to the rest. He did the things all the other students did, and he was very popular, but never one of the gang. There was a preoccupation about him that often irritated his friends, an absent-mindedness, an aloofness. He had a room in the Montana and spent the evenings he was not working in the Deux Magots or the Café des Flores where he drank endless coffees, sipped a Pernod and had continuing arguments and discussions, and watched the world go by.

He liked to eat alone at the Brasserie Lipp, studying faces, watching the human comedy play itself out.

He fell in love with Juliette Greco, from a distance, discussed art with Picasso and existentialism with Cocteau and Sartre.

There was some good-humoured joking about his age and the fact that he still called himself a student.

'I hope to be one all my life,' he parried, for deep within Alexander was a sureness of thought and feeling that ran contrary to popular beliefs and current ideas; unlike his peers, he knew exactly what he wanted and was determined to pursue it.

When the conversations began to bore and became repetitive, and the faces became over-familiar, he decided to move on. He had benefited enormously from his stay in Paris and decided that Italy was the next obvious choice. But first he planned a visit to Dublin.

Jessica was delighted with him. From her years with Dan she had learned to hold her tongue and suspend judgement and above all not to comment on things she did not understand. She had learned the art of the noncommittal but sympathetic nod. She listened to her tall handsome intense son chattering on about painting and the importance of the Eiffel Tower and the automobile in the development of abstract art; of his gods, Braque and Cézanne, of technique and perspective and the relative merits of oil and water. She liked his work, understood the pain and anguish he caught on canvas and the intense bitterness of the juxtapositioning of revelry and death, of poverty and merrymaking, of escape from the unbearable into

347

the unthinking world of booze and jazz.

She was glad, too, he was not staying long. The vitality of his presence in the tiny shop on the quays and his steady stream of questions with regard to his origins disturbed the even tenor of her days.

Alexander had faced up to the realities of life. He felt he was an interpreter, a reporter. He had always felt a little apart, different, and he was perfectly happy to be that way. He could not understand why his mother did not tell him who his father was. He would not condemn her, or even care if it was a labourer, a passing salesman or a soldier on the town. He tried to imagine what was the cause of her reticence and was unable to fathom it. Eventually he decided to do some detective work. He did not like spying on his mother but he felt justified.

Everything in the shop was above reproach and yielded no information at all. One thing, however, aroused his suspicion and at first he did not think it had anything to do with him. His mother received a couple of telephone calls a week and after each call she dressed herself up, her eyes sparkling, her cheeks glowing, and left the shop not to return till late and sometimes not till morning. Alexander realized that this had been going on as long as he could remember and he had never questioned it. He had accepted it as part of normal routine and only now that he had started to pry did it suddenly seem extremely odd.

He started to follow her. It was incredibly easy. He saw her enter the house in Haddington Road with her own key, and decided to hang about for a while. He soon found a friendly informant in the occupant of the ground-floor flat who had come out to empty her rubbish and fell, hook, line and sinker, for Alexander's smile and twinkling eyes.

'Isn't it a grand day now?' she saucily opened the conversation, a bold invitation in her eyes.

Katie O'Callaghan was a forty-year-old widow who spent most of her life at the pictures. She was lonely and she had delusions about her beauty, which she felt was remarkable. The rest of the world did not quite see Katie the way she saw herself, but that did not worry her. She had enormous confidence in herself and copied the film stars she most admired, Linda Darnell and Paulette Goddard, though Hedy Lamarr in White Cargo was certainly the bee's knees as far as seductiveness went. She based her behaviour on their flirtation with the camera, batting her heavily mascaraed eyelashes, pursing her lips coated with 'Purple Passion' lipstick, sashaying along swinging her hips in her too tight skirt, and leaning forward to reveal her cleavage whenever she got the opportunity. She was in fact quite pretty and had the Dubliner's good-humoured fatalistic outlook on life in general.

She had spent many hours fantasizing and planning to entice Big Dan Casey away from that woman who was too old for him. She ignored her own age; she felt twenty and thought that with the make-up she looked it. She often hung about the house, inside or out, lying in wait for Big Dan, hoping that one day one of those encounters that happened in every Joan Crawford movie she had ever seen would happen to her. She was eternally optimistic.

Alexander grasped the essence of her character almost at once and fell into conversation with her, accepted her offer of a cup of tea and encouraged her to talk, which she did at length and without too much prompting. She told him all about Jessica Klein, a pretty woman, but past it now, she would have thought, and Dan Casey, the richest and handsomest man in all Ireland, God bless him. She told him about Slievelea and Livia. She admired Alexander's thick dark hair and ran her fingers through it as she poured a second cup. She told him his teeth were like Cary Grant's, his smile Errol Flynn's, and that he was the spit image of Gregory Peck in *Gentleman's Agreement*. She unbuttoned the top button of her low-cut blouse, then threw caution to the winds and undid the next two. Alexander sighed in his amused fashion, gave in to the inevitable, responded to her kiss and they ended up on her duck-feather quilt, passionately smothering each other. Alexander had never attached too much importance to sex. He appeased his sexual appetite when the opportunity arose, and it often arose; there had been no lack of bedfellows in Paris. Still, the situation was not without its humorous side, he thought, looking at the ceiling where his mother and his father were probably indulging in the same sport as he was below. He kissed Katie tenderly, and left at 3 a.m. promising to return, a promise both of them knew he would not keep. But Katie was well satisfied. She had had an adventure that even Bette Davies would not be ashamed of!

Alexander waited for the rest of the night in the church porch opposite the house but it was morning when Dan Casey emerged. He looked at his father. He was indeed a handsome man, he thought, and he was obviously rich. The car, a Mercedes, was sleek, the interior leather and wood, polished and shining with an expensive sheen. Alexander guessed it was not his only car, but he did not mind, was not worried about all this. It was of no consequence to him whether his father was rich or poor. Money as such was meaningless to him. His art was his preoccupation. His mother and grandfather had more than enough to supply him with what he needed. He had his creature comforts. They enabled him the luxury of travel whilst he pursued his chosen profession. All he needed was his curiosity allayed, then he could put the whole thing out of his mind and get back to his painting. His curiosity was based on his interest in his antecedents and how he had come to exist with his soul-searching talent, his looks, his intellect. He did not intend to disrupt his mother's life. If she needed to keep it all secret, that was fine by him. He found the fact that she had been with the same man for so long, obviously loving him for all those years, endearing and somehow touching. He decided, though, to have a look at Slievelea. The way Katie had spoken of it had made him curious.

'It's the most beautiful house in Ireland,' she had said. 'They say that the Caseys went there as servants during the Great Famine, and Lord Rennett, the great-grandfather of Livia Casey, took them in and they near to death itself. But money doesn't buy everything, oh no! Livia Casey nearly went out of her mind on account of she couldn't have any children. Now she has two, so I suppose it's all right. I dunno though, sometimes I envy her, the beautiful house, servants, money, oh and all those clothes.' Her eyes drifted involuntarily to the meagre contents of the heavy wardrobe at the bottom of the bed. 'And then again when I have a fella like you in me arms, and the sun is shining outside, an' I've fifty quid in the bank and I'm going to see *Affair in Trinidad* with Rita Hayworth and Glenn Ford, well, I wouldn't change places with a millionaire, an' that's the truth, so give us a kiss. One of your shut-eyed ones, an' leave off talkin' for a while.'

The day before he was to leave for Italy he took the train to Bray. He walked from the station, asking directions as he went. The sky was blue and the lanes drowsed in the sun. Gnats and tiny insects pestered Alexander as he walked along, carrying his jacket, his shirt sleeves rolled up, mopping his brow with his handkerchief. He did not want to use the main entrance so he skirted a field, climbed a gate, and walked through the long grasses in the general direction of Slievelea. He felt a great desire to lie down in the field and go to sleep, but he pressed on. Suddenly the field gave way to a wood full of bluebells. The trees he had been making towards were not a single row marking a boundary as he had thought, but a group of elms that opened out and revealed oaks, ash, glorious copper beeches, and the sycamores, surrounded at their base by a carpet of azure flowers. The trees gradually became more massed, but always enough apart to allow shafts of brilliant sunlight to fall through. As he penetrated deeper he could feel the stillness and peace of the place descend on his soul. He lost all sense of time, bemused and fascinated by the play of light on the hundreds of shades of green the trembling leaves revealed. He had never thought there could be so many variations of one colour. 'I've never really seen the country,' he thought. 'It's always been Dublin or Paris, city streets, concrete; it's the hectic life led there I've really looked at. This is something quite different, secret, quiet, shy.' His eyes were registering the shapes and texture of the leaves, the stout bark, the slim, gently curving branches when, caught in a beam of dazzling golden light, he saw a girl. He was aware of her presence for minutes before he stopped and caught his breath. She was the most beautiful creature he had ever seen, standing barefoot on the grass, the bluebells all around her feet, in her light summer dress, a delicate sea-green voile, her long straight hair hanging down her back. She looked unearthly, like a dryad or a nymph, a creature of the woods or of the sea. She was totally unaware that he was there and she seemed so still that after a long five minutes of immobility he wondered if indeed she was a mythical creature or a figment of his imagination.

Then like a fawn she turned her head sharply as if listening, aware of danger. He quickly stepped behind a tree. She heard the movement in the wood; her slim body tensed and she turned her face towards him again, but could not see him, hidden as he was in the thick foliage. Then she walked away with such grace of movement that it seemed as if she were listening to some music she alone heard. He watched her move from him through the wood, shadows dappling her dress and

351

the sun catching the fine gold sheen of her hair until she vanished from sight, leaving him shaken as if he had been in a tempest.

Alexander walked back to the station in a daze, no longer intent on seeing his father's home. He took the next train back to Dublin, and once on it he tried to capture on paper the likeness of the young goddess. He carried a sketching pad and pencil with him everywhere but he could not get even a remotely similar face and body down on the page. In the wood it had seemed all movement and light and shade. On the cold white paper it lacked life and he was frustrated. He was touched and overwhelmed by the beauty of the girl and the magic of the moment they had shared, although she had been ignorant of his presence ... or had she? She had been conscious of something. He longed to return and find her, but his tickets to Italy were purchased and the date could not be changed without a lot of trouble, so he shrugged his shoulders and left the next morning. It would be almost exactly a year before he saw Aisling again.

Chapter

49

WHEN Aisling was launched on Society in Ireland she met a curious fear. She could not understand it. Girls with not half her beauty were constantly in demand whilst she had to rely on her mother's procuring the feeble descendants of the Jeffries, the Rowleys, the Blackwaters *et al* to escort her to the hunt balls, the parties, the races, the R.D.S., clubs like Kilcrony, where one ate and danced to the strains of 'La Vie en Rose' and sambaed to 'South American Joe'.

She was humiliated and hurt. She did not understand that her beauty frightened the boys and her father's vast wealth frankly terrified them. She had not developed an aggression or a bravado that would have seen her through. Coming as she had from the enchanted protected world of her childhood into the false animation of the cocktail party and the riotous strident bacchanalia of the hunt ball, she was unprepared and completely confused. She looked cool and sophisticated but inside she was terrified. She was ill prepared for pain after the unclouded days of her childhood. All those golden days were suddenly over and womanhood was beginning, but nothing had intimated that her life might change; the undertones of her first adult dinner party had alarmed her but not taught her what to expect. Livia hesitantly imparted the 'facts of life' to her daughter, but she had never spoken to her of the thousand pains of adulthood, of facing up to life on its own unfair terms; for that she was totally unequipped. And Big Dan, laughing, had simply promised to marry her when she grew up. Now, it seemed to her overnight, she was an adult. She had to dress correctly for all occasions, no more spending half the day in her riding gear. She

353

had to walk gracefully and not run, sit still and listen, participate in conversations, dance and flirt and drink champagne. The last made her tipsy, but gave her the courage to talk to boys. She was very bad at it. She had no defence against their banter and the cattiness of the girls. Her friend, Camilla Vestry, was saucy with the fellows they danced and played tennis with, and was a huge success, and yet she was not nearly as pretty as Aisling. It was all bewildering and even frightening. Aisling spent a very uncomfortable year in Wicklow and Dublin trying to pretend she was enjoying herself with the round of parties and dances, when at heart she was sick with apprehension. Perhaps she had no sex appeal, the thing it was currently most important to have. Perhaps she was boring and dull. She certainly felt like that most of the time. Would no one ever ask her to dance? And when they did the stilted conversation that followed sent her partners fleeing from her as quickly as they could. No one was as rich and successful as Big Dan Casey, so they resented his daughter, for how could they show off to such an heiress as this? She suffered terribly and was unconsoled by the fact that none of the young men appealed to her in the least. It took her a long time to realize that she was just that bit too beautiful, just that bit too rich. Beauty was a curse, she thought. Perhaps it would not have mattered if she had been poor, if she had grown up in the hurly-burly of neighbourhood life, joined the local tennis and swimming clubs that the other girls frequented, where they developed a joshing, teasing, flirtatious relationship with all the young men they met there. But Slievelea had its own swimming pool, and its own tennis courts. Yes, it was a bad time for Aisling. And for her brother, who was not happy either.

The nervous, highly-strung David tried to please his father and, to do him justice, Big Dan tried as hard to be a loving father to his son. However, Big Dan's idea of educating David was mainly to try to toughen him up, to chastise him when he showed weakness, to urge him to be strong and brave, good at sport or in a fight. Dan could not see that intellectual pursuits might really benefit the heir to Slievelea, that David was exactly like his mother both physically and temperamentally, and he wondered for the millionth time why Aisling was not the boy and David the female.

Livia was aware that all was not well at Slievelea. Her heart

354

bled for her daughter and her son and she wondered again why she seemed to attract disaster, why nothing ever went as easily for her as it seemed to do for other women. She lived quietly with her quandaries and never gave an inkling that there was anything disagreeable on her mind, but inside the anxiety gnawed. It was to nurture the cancer that killed her.

Livia was still uncertain of herself and her ultimate hold on Dan. Aware once more of his continued liaison with Jessica Klein, who must be quite old by now, she thought, she was afraid of her own inability to keep Dan happy and content. She had realized exactly what he was doing when he took to going into Dublin of an afternoon.

She had always loved his faults as well as his good points, his ruthlessness, his single-mindedness and his sometimes lack of sensitive understanding as well as his beauty, his generosity, his loving kindness and loyalty, his wit and laughter. It was no use criticizing Dan to Livia; it was no use pointing out his dodgy deals, his involvement with the Nazi regime in Germany, his association with the Gambelino family in New York. None of this disturbed Livia's opinion of or love for her husband. It was her fate to love him, for better or worse, as she had promised in the marriage ceremony. He was the one person in the world for her, the only man she had ever loved or desired. Beside him all other men in the world paled into insignificance. With him even a bad day seemed good and sweet. But she wanted all of him, that was her problem. And she obeyed him. So, she was of no use to her children; she exerted no control over them and left it all to Dan, never interfering with his decisions. She succumbed to the belief that Dan knew best, that he must be right. David needed discipline, Dan said, so they would send him to England, to Ampleforth, a good Catholic school. Livia knew the reputation of the college was excellent, but she was loath to send her son so far away. Dan, however, was adamant. It would be the making of the boy, he said. The child could not be allowed to moon about reading in corners.

David did not want to go away. He was scared silly to leave home. Dan resisted all pleas that he change his mind. He wanted David at that school primarily because he believed it was the done thing. A gentleman sent his son to public school and therefore it was the right and proper thing to do. He would not listen to debates or discussions about it.

David cried on Aisling's shoulder. 'I don't want to go, Ash. All those boys together. I want to stay with you and Mummy. Oh, Ash, I don't want to go!'

'Don't worry, old fella. It'll be all right,' she whispered.

'No, it won't, Ash,' he said calmly. 'It'll never be all right. Father hates me. He always has. He always will. I can never be what he wants me to be. I can never do what he wants me to do. There's nothing I can do about it, nothing at all.'

'No, David, you're wrong. Pappy does love you. I know he does. It's just that he loves to ride and swim and he's tough, and, well he doesn't understand you. You're too different.'

'Oh, I know I'm not like him. I only wish I were. I do so want to please him.'

But nothing about David pleased Dan.

'Where did we go wrong with the boy, Livia?' he asked. 'Aisling is not like that. She's fine and brave and fearless. David's a little coward.'

Livia's heart shrank within her. It was not the first time he had made the comparison. Oh God, she prayed, never let Dan find out she's not his. Only David is. Only poor little David. Oh God, let him never know. She fought the fear, knowing the chances were that he would never find out, constantly re-assuring herself of this as a pain started deep within her, a small isolated pain, a suggestion.

Aisling would always remember that unhappy coming-out year; the misery of her brother; her mother's tension; the deprecating remarks about her father overheard at parties and dances; her own lack of confidence; the gauche mistakes, the battered pride; the heartache and the fear.

It was at a party in Dublin given by her father that Aisling was 'discovered' quite by accident. An English film director was looking for a leading lady for a costume drama he was making with the financial backing of one of Dan's American friends. Stunned by Aisling's natural beauty, the two men persuaded her to go to Elstree for a film test, then swiftly signed her up.

Aisling was launched in the film world as Aisling Andrews, both because her employers felt her own name was too ordinary and because they did not want to be accused of nepotism; Dan was putting up a lot of money for the film. She enjoyed making it, for it was fun, but she seemed to spend an awful lot of time posing for glamour stills and not in front of the camera. In the film world in London she became just another beauty among many. As one of the Rank starlets she was praised, courted, petted and cosseted, and all because of her face and figure, not for herself. She felt more like a commodity than a person. No one even seemed interested in whether she could act. All they wanted from her were the pouts, poses, alluring postures, to bring in the paying customers. Even with Dan she felt part of an investment rather than his beloved daughter and friend. He constantly showed her off, as if she were Prince of Darkness, his black stallion.

When at last the filming was over and the film successfully released, Aisling went to Italy for a holiday and a rest.

Almost exactly a year had passed since Alexander had arrived in Italy. He had dallied in the environs of Tuscany for many a long golden day before finally arriving in Florence, taking up residence and beginning his study. He found a whole new world of art in the city of the Renaissance. The jagged edges of his work became tempered, influenced by a place where art treasures were created before the acceleration of time forced painters to a more frenetic form of expression. His work never became tranquil, but it attained new depths, and tragedy replaced a tendency to pathos. His work grew stronger, more virile as he himself became more mature and confident.

He spent mornings working and he usually lunched with a group of American or Italian fellow students, then in the afternoon, in the time left before the city shut down, he haunted the Pitti Palace, the Uffizi Gallery and the Medici-Riccardi Palace and the Bargello. He spent long hours in the churches: Santa Maria Novella, where the marvellous Masaccio fresco depicted the Holy Trinity; Santa Croce and the Taddeo Gaddi Crucifixion and the Giottos; and the mighty Michaelangelo's tomb. There was so much to see and study, and every day, crossing the Ponte Vecchio on his way to and from the city, he thanked his stars for his good luck and the richness of life in this warm, terra cotta-coloured town.

Then one day he saw Aisling. She was sitting in a long low white MG sports job as gleaming and as sleek as the girl in it. The car was stuck in a traffic jam on the Piazza Lorenzo. He was with a group of four other students, all Italian, who were making their way to the Medici Chapels to have yet another look at the details of Gozzoli's 'Voyage of the Three Kings'. They were talking and arguing and laughing, pushing each other in a friendly tactile Italian way as they walked along. A cacophony of blasts on various car horns filled the air with impatience and Aisling was pressing the silver disc at the centre of her wheel with as much irritability as everyone else. Her long blonde hair blew across her face and she kept drawing it back and away only to have it flutter like a golden flag in the breeze again. Alexander broke from the group and ran to her car and sat on the bonnet.

'What the hell do you think you are doing?' she asked with astonishment, keeping her hand on the horn, stabbing at it angrily and leaving the hair to blow across her face in golden strands.

'Yerra sure what's a nice Wick-el-eh girl like you doin' in a place like this?' he replied.

His Italian friends had approached the car in the narrow street and were egging him on with shouts and whistles, thoroughly enjoying the situation and showing a typical Italianate approval of her beauty.

Alexander enjoyed the look of bewilderment on her face as she heard the Dublin accent he had exaggerated for the occasion. The cars in front started to move and instantly from the pile-up behind Aisling an impatient blaring filled the street with an even higher density of noise than usual. Alexander stayed put on the bonnet.

'Will you get off this car immediately, whoever you are?'

'Alexander Klein is my name, and I will when you promise to meet me in the Boboli Gardens at the Fountain of the Ocean at five o'clock this evening.'

'All right, all right,' she said, curious about this man who spoke in the language of home and knew she came from Wicklow, and irritated by the impatience behind her as men leaned out of cars and screamed invective at her.

'Promise?' he insisted.

'Promise.' She smiled at him, making his heart leap within him. His four Italian friends cheered and he jumped off the car. She turned and stuck her fingers in the air at the drivers behind her, and was gone.

When he saw her crossing the grassy verge that evening, the fountain spray veiling her from clear sight, he remembered the girl in the woods and thought again of her as a nymph, a dryad. She put her hand trustingly in his and smiled up at him. They stood there, both a little weak-kneed, smiling mistily; then they laughed together and started to run as if they had received a charge of energy. They talked, they walked through the beautiful gardens, they ate, they drank coffee and wine. In a trattoria opposite the gardens she forked *tagliatelle verdi* covered in a light butter sauce and he gently pushed the odd straggling strand of pasta into her mouth. She bit into strawberries he had dipped into cream and held to her temptingly. She dipped her finger in the cream and sucked it off and he lit her Gauloise and she smiled at him in the flame light.

They talked and were silent with each other and comfortable, as if they had known each other for years, and yet the excitement of the brand new, the unknown, was there too.

Aisling thought that all her life had led to this moment. All the happiness of her childhood at Slievelea and all the misery of her young womanhood had led to this resting place: Alexander Klein. Without question, without logic or reason she deposited her faith, trust and heart with him instantly, and knew it would be all right. And he looked at this woman who was the apparition he had seen in the wood, a reality now, flesh and blood, and he knew a moment of terror before the magnitude of his feelings. This was not another adventure, an *affaire de coeur*, entered into with curiosity and a plan of escape in case it did not work out. There would be no escape here and he paused for a moment on the threshold of commitment, knowing nevertheless that he had no choice but to follow his heart.

He told her about himself; his hopes, ambitions, his art.

'I thought you were the tutor,' she said.

'Oh, no. I'm a perennial student.'

'My name is Aisling Andrews,' she said.

'The film star?'

'The same,' she laughed, then searched his face anxiously, vulnerable suddenly, at his mercy if the attraction should be her fame. He covered her hand with his, shaking his head and smiling, for he divined her thought and wanted to reassure her. She did not take her eyes from his face, exploring it, getting to know it, longing to be familiar with it, and when he smiled she was struck with a foreknowledge of it.

'I've seen you smile before,' she said.

'And I you. But, go on. Tell me.'

'Well, the fact is I was "discovered" at a party in the Shelbourne.'

'The dear old Shelbourne. I used to go there with my mother and have afternoon tea in that room on the right. You know?' She nodded. 'Little sandwiches of pink salmon. Scones and éclairs bursting with cream. Tea in a silver pot. I'd forgotten about it, that place. We sat on a big sofa covered in pale chintz and thought we were very grand. Oh, we were not poor at all. Comfortable but careful, my grandfather used to say.'

'What does he do? Your grandfather?'

'He owns the pawnbroker and jeweller shop on the quays. "Hymie Klein. Honest Business Done Here." It's a Jewish business. A little gold mine.'

It was his turn to look wary, to watch carefully for a reaction, but she simply smiled into his eyes and nodded as he had done.

Then he said, 'Sorry. Go on. I keep interrupting. Tell me.'

'Oh yes. Well, at this party there was a director who was looking for someone to play in a movie, a terrible one, a romance called *The Lady from Vauxhall*, because Phyllis Calvert and Margaret Lockwood couldn't do it. He saw me there, this director, quite liked me and gave me the part. My Lady Hester de Vere. I wore a black patch under my eye,' she pointed, 'here, and I whipped my link-boy!' The dimples danced around her mouth.

She's so young, he thought, and her eyes pleaded with him not to think her too frivolous, a fool, not to despise her because she was a film star and he was so serious, intelligent, an artist, a painter.

He told her more about his painting, joking again about being rather a mature student. But he did not seem so to her. She was used to her father's friends and the only men she had met in her entire life, other than the boys at home in Wicklow, were the actors in the film, all of whom had seemed ancient to her, and the director, backers and producer, who appeared even more decrepit. Alexander was young in his manner, slim and quick, and he painted. It fired her imagination, it excited her beyond anything and it made her cautious. She made up her mind not to tell him about her rich father, not to reveal too much of that side of her life. She had found a man who had shaken her to the very core of her being and she was not going

360

to risk losing him. She had no intention of revealing to this art student that Slievelea was her home, the Casey millions her heritage. In any event his views, she discovered, were radical. He talked at length about the exploitation of the poor by the rich. He spoke of Adler and Jung. He talked of Mao Tse-tung and Schopenhauer, and Aisling listened, enthralled. She had never had such a conversation, heard such talk, from anyone, nor been so mentally stimulated, had such exciting new avenues of thought to explore. She kept wanting to touch him, his hair, the back of his hand as it lay on the table, to curl her fingers round his wrist, touch the hollow of his throat. She was fascinated by his erudition, the quickness of his mind.

They sat in the trattoria all evening and into the night. The *patrone* gave up on them indulgently. He was not so old that he did not remember what it was like to be young and in love. Besides, they had eyes only for each other. It was no use clearing the table; they simpled ordered another *cappuccino*. It was no use giving them the bill; they left it on the table until the *signor*'s sleeve brushed it off as he reached over to touch the *signorina*'s hand, and it fluttered unheeded on the floor. The *patrone* nodded his flat head and left them to it. *Amore* ... it was a madness, and it was a waste of time trying to make contact with anyone suffering from its early symptoms. Nevertheless, he kept a sharp eye on them, for he had no intention of allowing them to become so absent-minded that they forgot the bill.

'How did you know I was Irish, when you saw me in the car?'

'I recognized you at once. I've seen you before.'

She thought he meant in a film magazine or a newspaper.

'I saw you once in a wood in Wicklow — exactly a year ago, as a matter of fact.'

'Oh!' she was startled.

'Near Slievelea. I was there to ... I was visiting.'

'Do you know anyone in Slievelea, or thereabouts?' she asked warily.

'Not really,' he said. He was fiddling with a box of matches.

He gave her a cigarette, then looked at her quickly.

'Do you know Dan Casey?' he asked. He struck a match and gave her a light. She steadied herself and blew out the smoke, screening her face, playing for time.

'Rich geezer, filthy rich bastard, actually. Owns a ...'

She cut him short, 'Yes, I know him. Why?'

'Thought you might.'

'He was one of the backers of our film,' she said.

'Well, it's people like him who should be shot,' he said. 'All Ireland knows how he helped the Germans arm themselves, how he provided them with the instruments to annihilate half my race.' Alexander had by now learned too much about Dan to retain his early indifference to the man.

'Please don't let's talk about it just now,' Aisling said.

He could see she was distressed. He was cross with himself for his outburst, realizing that it was instigated as much by hurt at his father's total indifference to his existence as by horror at Dan's lack of scruples in business.

Aisling felt pain, as she always did when people were nasty about Dan. They often were, she thought. Was it jealousy? she wondered. Certainly not in Alexander's case. No, his was probably a social, a political judgement.

He leaned across the table and gently stroked her hair. His hand travelled over the silken strands and rested on her cheek. Neither of them breathed for a moment. They looked at each other vulnerably, wide-eyed, their feelings clearly mirrored in each other's eyes, and Aisling turned her face into his hand and kissed the palm. They left soon afterwards and the *patrone* sighed with relief and a little regret. Alexander walked her back to her hotel. He was startled by the opulence of the place and she quickly said, 'The studios are paying,' then, 'Good night, Alexander.'

'I'll pick you up tomorrow at nine. We'll go to Fiesole for a picnic.'

She nodded, touched his cheek and was gone.

She had barely reached her room, pulling off her shoes and twirling about hugging herself, when the phone rang.

'I love you, Aisling Andrews,' he said.

'I love you, Alexander Klein.'

'Goodnight, *cara*.'

'Goodnight.'

The phone clicked and went dead.

The days that followed were summer days full of the wonder of discovery. They picnicked in Fiesole, high on its hill overlooking the whole Florentine valley with its warm, terra cotta roofs. They strolled hand in hand around the cloisters of San Barnardino in the little church of San Francesco, dropping a

362

coin in the well. Alexander picked a stem of bougainvillaea and tucked it behind her ear. He took her on his little Vespa all around the city of Florence, and drove her car to Pisa, Verona and Siena. They gazed hand in hand at the glory of Michaelangelo's Palastrina Pieta. They preferred the great 'unfinished' dramatic creations that flanked the sides of the corridor leading to the famous David rather than that classical perfection. In Siena he introduced her to Duccio, the town's most respected artist. He introduced her to Giotto, Masaccio and Brunelleschi. They sat in the Boboli Gardens eating slabs of pizza and talked about art, and Aisling felt life was a glorious adventure, and all the flooding joy she had felt in her childhood in Slievelea that she had thought gone with adolescence returned a hundredfold. She felt she could not absorb enough of the beauty of nature and the knowledge of the magnificent art treasures revealed to her and illuminated by Alexander.

She asked questions, delighted in his instructive answers, felt young and feminine and dependent on him, trusting his charge of her, his male taking over, his dominance. She adored him and, worshipping this man, she discarded her past. The Florentine sun shot its rays to meet the paler sun of her Slievelea childhood, and meeting they eradicated the painful betwixt and between part of her life. Alexander had restored her to the serene content, the wellbeing, the joyous celebration of life that had been her daily state all through her childhood at Slievelea. All was well with the world once more.

She listened raptly to his talk and the chatter of his friends, for sometimes they were joined by his fellow students over a cappuccino or an espresso, and the old arguments about the relative superiority of this or that artist were debated heatedly. She loved being quiet in his company as she had with her father before she had matured and grown. She transferred some of her wide-eyed unquestioning acceptance of her father's views to Alexander. His opinions became hers, and she would nod her head emphatically when he spoke. She knew nothing about art, or little compared to him, and having no opinion saw everything through his eyes. He took charge of her and she was glad to allow him to. They kissed tenderly; their fingers touched and felt. They took their time. Each moment they spent together was precious, isolated from time as it affected the real world. He always delivered her back to the hotel, touching her lips with his in a gentle brush as soft as a feather's and leaving her with, 'I love you, *cara*.'

'I love you too,' she would say, and run into the hotel to await his call. He always phoned her from the post office on his way home, and the conversation was always the same.

She was content to leave the unfolding of their relationship in his hands. Each day their knowledge of each other progressed, their love grew, and she knew he would know when it was ready for fulfilment. This was too important to rush. This was the most overwhelming thing that had ever happened to her and she knew the same was true for him. They stood at the edge of their passion, expectant and preparing.

One day, sitting in a crowd of students with him, talking and smoking, Aisling suddenly remembered when she had felt like this before. Tea under the chestnut at Slievelea. Livia cool in white linen and her father in his flannels. The silver pot on the table, the half-eaten sandwiches, the Hammersely cups and saucers with the scattered violets printed on them and the tiny gold rim. The vase of white lilacs in the centre and the glorious sea smell advancing and retreating as the breeze blew. The crumbled fruit on the plates. Where was David? She couldn't recall, but she did remember the coolness of the breeze on her warm cheeks and the golden and bronze rays of the sun setting behind the Wicklow mountains. A bird sang, Livia yawned, and the maid came to clear the table. She had suddenly been filled with an overwhelming rush of love for Slievelea, for nature, for life, and for Dan. She had jumped up and, going behind her father's chair, had thrown her arms round him, hugging him and kissing the top of his head.

She felt like that now, and she excused herself and went to the '*Signore*'. When she returned to the table the argument still raged fiercely; arms were waving, cigarettes were stubbed out half smoked, voices were raised in emphatic liquid Italian. She stood behind Alexander, draped her arms quietly, gracefully round him and, duplicating the action with her father, she hugged him, kissing the top of his head. He patted her bare arm and looked up at her.

'We go to Taormina at the weekend,' he said, and she hugged him tighter. She knew the time had come when they would make love.

Chapter

50

TAORMINA in Sicily lies on the extreme south-east fringe of the Monti Peloritani, before the deep Alcantara Valley separates them from the volcanic mass of the beautiful, dangerous Etna. It is a balcony, this little Eden, this village halfway between the great single smoking mountain and the blue-green waves of the Ionian sea. It is never really cold there, and the air is full of the scent of tropical flowers. The slopes are heavy with vines, the wine from which is the nectar of the gods. To the right of this jewel of a village stands the Greco-Roman Theatre, the ruin blending with the landscape. Arches, columns, sea and sky form a single scene of vast, composite beauty. Taormina was to remain Aisling's most beautiful memory, the place where she reached a happiness she never dreamed possible, a happiness too intense to last. It was as if in that place everything came to fruition, reached a peak of perfection that never again in her life was possible.

They took a small house halfway between the little town and the sea. Etna reached to the skies above them and at their feet and before their eyes the view spread out, a gorgeous display for lovers. The sea was aquamarine or cobalt blue depending on the tides and winds. The air in Taormina was soft as baby's breath; the silver sun, platinum in the day, cast a sparkling myriad of tiny stars across the bay to wink and blink radiantly in shimmering beams, and at night was an amber bronze ball cloaking the sea in a blanket of gold. The colours of the flowers, the bougainvillaea, jasmine and fuschia, splashed the curving hillside in a riot of colour. The lemon and orange groves, the vines trailing their tendrils across the hillside, almost blinded the eyes with

365

their dazzling colour, stunning the senses with the sweetness of their scent.

Their house was cool and paved with flagstones. A fountain splashed in the tiny courtyard and an olive tree gave them shade. The walls were rough stone and whitewashed, and there was a makeshift shower but no bath. The furniture was simple and sparse, but old and heavy, seventeenth century, carved, the wood polished with beeswax and time. The bed was big with a thick woven creamy-white cotton coverlet and heavy starched sheets smelling of lavender and lemon verbena.

Aisling wore a dirndl skirt and peasant blouse and flat sandals on her brown feet and went shopping in the village. They ate hot bread and cheese, fat red beef tomatoes, onions and salami, fettucini and tagliatelle with parmesan, melons and oranges, pears and cherries. They drank the local wine and swam in the sea and stopped out at night to sit under the brightly coloured umbrellas at a table on the tiny straggling Corso Umberto I where they would watch the world go by, eating ice cream and drinking *cappuccino*. Then, with a million diamond-bright stars to guide them, home they would walk arm in arm down the hill, to drop their clothes on the marble floor, and fall into bed and each other's arms.

Their lovemaking had an intensity neither of them understood. It was as if each time they made love might be their last. At first Alexander was almost afraid of the perfection of Aisling's naked body, but his desire and love for her overcame his fear and he led her gently into the knowledge of intercourse with a passion that she returned with fiery abandon. Each loved the other's body; each grew to love their own through knowledge of the other's. Aisling became aware of how much pleasure her breasts, her fingers, her mouth and that warm home between her legs, which ached for him to enter and fill with his love, were capable of giving. They spent long hours within each other, greedy for each other, besotted with the smell, the taste, the excitement of their discovery of each other. Then they would swim again, and stroll around the hillside, or pay a visit to the Greco-Roman Theatre.

Sometimes Aisling would go to Mass in the cathedral in the Piazza Municipio, summoned by the bells. She would cover her head with a mantilla, a small triangle of white lace embroidered with silver thread, and kneel as the padre muttered the Latin in

366

a monotone, assisted by two wicked-faced scrubbed little boys who coughed and scratched and got the giggles when the old priest's back was turned. Alexander went with her. He could not be a moment apart from her, and although the service seemed meaningless and almost blasphemous to him, he was enchanted by the triptych by Antonio Giuffre of the Visitation of Mary to Elizabeth, and St Joseph and Nachariah whose exquisitely simple faces, and the golds, bronzes and crimson colours of their robes mesmerized him into contented study.

His eyes would travel from the contemplation of the dazzling Renaissance faces and rest on his beloved, her hair gleaming under the snowy lace, her head resting against the rose-marble pillar, her exquisite profile raised in thanksgiving to a god he could not understand. It did not seem profane to Aisling to thank the Jesus she was familiar with for her present happiness. It seemed to her that everything in nature, the creation of the Father in Heaven, her body and her love were in total harmony in a paean of praise and joyful celebration. So she thanked and was grateful to an almost superstitious point, practising a few pagan methods of winning luck along with her Christian worship.

They dined out sometimes and listened to a guitarist playing music that filled the evening air with aching sadness or exuberant gaiety.

One day as they strolled through the village they saw a man walking up the steep hill ahead of them. He wore a camel coat and fedora although the day was very hot. He carried a silver-topped malacca cane and wore pigskin gloves and black patent shoes. He stopped before each shop and the *patrone* would come out and kiss his hand 'as if he were a bishop', Aisling whispered to Alexander. They stood watching the man's progress down the cobbled street. He took off his glove each time and put it back on again, and they saw that on one finger he wore a large diamond ring. The proprietor would then give an envelope or package to one of the two men who walked slightly behind him on either side. The men looked like guards; Alexander was almost sure they carried guns under their jackets. They had shifty eyes that darted here and there and seemed constantly to be searching the upper storeys of the houses and the hills for something. They had unpleasant expressions and were enormous bulls of men and no one greeted them. One of the men had a scar that ran down from his forehead across his right eye and down his cheek to his mouth. In its path it had pulled the eye out of shape and distorted the mouth.

'*Buono giorno*, Signor Gambelino,' the shopkeepers said.

'Mafiosi,' Alexander whispered to Aisling, and she shivered.

'Come on, let's go,' she cried, and they turned off the Corso Umberto I, to go down the steps to the fishmonger to buy some fresh giant prawns caught at dawn that morning. Aisling would cook them over an open flame, and they would scald their fingers eating them and laugh together. He would toss the salad, and they would get a little tipsy on wine and love and the drowning velvet beauty of the night. Then they would go inside to the cool bedroom and languidly make love. Their passion, knowing no bounds, would rouse them to ecstasies until their bodies, tranquil at last, would fall into a deep, dreamless and quiet sleep.

Chapter

51

DAN had no intention of allowing Aisling to wander alone and unattended through Europe. His friends on the staff of the hotel in Florence were asked to keep a strict watch over her and to let him know if anything untoward happened. When the hotel phoned to say Miss Aisling Andrews was leaving next morning for Sicily he asked innocently enough who she was going with, if anybody.

'Why, the Irish *signor*, of course. The one she spent all her time with here in Florence.'

'What Irish *signor* was that?'

Dan tried in vain to keep his voice patient though the line was crackling and the voice kept receding, only to become clear again.

'The Irish *signor* who was an art student.'

'And who, pray, was that? His name?'

The manager was sorry, he did not know, he could certainly try to find out in the morning. Of course he would be discreet. Of course he understood Signor Casey. He was a papa too ... Yes, he would telephone Signor Casey and give him the information he requested, if he could discover the *signor*'s name.

'Ah, but they were in love,' he said. 'It was so beautiful to see.'

The following morning Devlin brought Dan the post on a silver salver as usual and there was a letter in Aisling's handwriting postmarked *Firenze*.

The sun came streaming into the room, glancing on silver and glass. The white damask tablecloth hid the high gloss of the mahogany table but the room was filled with the warm smell of

369

polish. Sheilagh must have been at work early, he thought, and decided a word of praise would be in order.

Livia was still not down. She had been sleeping later and later recently, he mused, as he drank his orange juice at the window. The lawn was like green velvet and the sculpture of Diana the Huntress that he had recently purchased looked imposing and pagan standing on its pedestal near the giant chestnut where, weather permitting, they would have tea this afternoon. He speculated again on why this last acquisition did not satisfy the eternal unappeased longings within him. He seemed sometimes to be chasing his own tail. No matter how hard he tried to stop, to slow up, it seemed impossible. There was a demon driving him. Other friends in business took time to enjoy, to holiday, to have pleasure, but not he. It was not that he didn't want to. Often he listened with envy to a colleague describing a pleasure trip, but since the magic year he had spent with Aunt Deirdre and those wonderful years when Aisling was small he had never been able to relax and enjoy himself. There was this urgency within that never let him rest, this feeling that he might miss something, that some evil genius would deprive him of everything with one stroke. That this was impossible his reason told him, but it was an ever-present fear within him, giving him no real rest.

He helped himself to a piece of crispy bacon, some scrambled eggs from under their silver lids, some kidneys from a chafing dish, hooked his finger in the toast rack and set down the food in his place at the breakfast table. He poured himself some coffee and slit open Aisling's envelope with a silver letter opener.

Dearest Pappy, darling Mummy,
You cannot imagine how happy I am, and I know you'll be happy for me.

He smiled fondly.

I've found a man, a marvellous man and I'm going to marry him! Oh, he doesn't know that yet, but he will ask me and I'll say, 'Yes, yes, yes.' Oh, Daddy, I love him *so* much. I know he is only a student, but he is the most wonderful painter. He is a genius! Please don't let that influence you. I assure you he is very respectable, and you must make up your mind to love him, because I do. His name is Alexander Klein ... don't you think that's distinguished?

The letter went on but Dan didn't read any more; he couldn't see the page. Livia had come into the room and he didn't see her. He sat there at the table, his face ashen.

Livia, who had become increasingly aware of the agonizing pain which came and went without warning, and left her shaken and afraid, was preoccupied with trying not to allow anyone to notice how ill she was, but even she saw vaguely that something was amiss with Dan. She asked him was there anything the matter and he replied that it was nothing, a piece of bad news about business that he could easily set to rights with a couple of calls, and no, thank you, he did not want to finish his breakfast, he would take some hot coffee to his study and get those calls out of the way. She was too full of pain to argue. She did not have the strength to pursue the subject, to ask him to share it with her. She just let him go. She was overcome with a desire to put her head on her arms and weep, but she made a valiant effort, controlled herself and wearily lifted the cup to her lips. She had asked Father O'Brien to come and see her this afternoon. She hoped she would be well enough for the visit. She thought perhaps in their conversation she might find some surcease from the agitation in her mind. She drank her coffee and sighed.

Dan stood a moment in the doorway, the steaming cup of coffee in his hand, irresolute, hesitating. He had a sudden inexplicable urge to confide in Livia, to tell her the truth, but as soon as the thought came he discarded it. He could not afford the luxury, he would not hurt Livia that much. How could he tell her and lose Slievelea? Oh God, he had been right always to think of Alexander as a threat, although up to now he had feared him only in connection with Livia. Now the serpent had turned to sting him through his daughter. He looked at Livia's bowed head mutely for a moment, then squared his shoulders and left the room. He called Sicily. He spoke at length to his friends. They were good friends. They owed him. He explained his problem and said, 'I want him removed from the scene ... removed, do you hear? I want her to think he's dead. He's not

371

to be eliminated. It must just appear so. Understand? I leave all the details to you.'

He felt a moment of triumph. Alexander would be pushed out of his life, out of all their lives. No longer a threat, no longer a danger to him. He could truly forget about him now. He need not lurk on the periphery of Dan's mind any more.

But in the heat of the moment Dan had done as he always did. He had given no thought to Jessica, to Aisling. It was not his custom when he took a decision to consider others' feelings until it was too late. Now a cold hand gripped his heart and he shuddered, his body momentarily out of control.

'Jesus God, Jessica!' he thought. 'Jesus God, Jessica.'

For a moment he was tempted to call Sicily again. But no. He pulled himself together. No weakness now. He would explain to Jessica. Next week. She had no way of finding out. He would tell her that Alexander was not harmed, was not dead. He squirmed in his seat, pushing away fear, dread, alarm as he thought of his beloved mistress. Eventually he stilled the tumult as he had done a thousand times before. It would be all right. Everything always was.

His coffee was cold. He sipped it, then grimaced, and rising from his desk pulled the bell rope. He turned as the door opened and Devlin came in. Devlin thought suddenly how old Dan looked, not so big any more ... He seemed to have shrunk.

'Bring me some fresh coffee please, Devlin. Oh, and tell Sheilagh Miss Aisling will be coming home. See her room is prepared.'

Chapter

52

THE fire crackled in the wide, deep grate, the smell of the sweet wood scenting the room. Father O'Brien and Livia were sitting in the library. There were books from floor to ceiling, amber colours, mellow bronze, deep mahogany, and the golden patina from the fire and single lit lamp over all, most of all Livia, held captive in the glow, her beauty luminous in the deep shadow of the winged chair she sat in.

The silver tea pot stood on a silver tray beside her with all the accoutrements, the wafer-thin china, the minute almond biscuits, the sugar basin with delicate little tongs, the tiny jug of milk and thinly sliced lemon glistening in its own juice.

She had divined his desire for something else and gave him a whiskey in a thick tumbler without being asked. He was not a heavy drinker, but the fine China tea served at Slievelea did not satisfy his palate, used as he was to the darker Indian beverage served in thick mugs, hot and strong, at the presbytery.

Father O'Brien looked at the beautiful woman opposite him. Thin, he thought, too thin. Ah well, sure that was the fashion these days and wasn't it odd indeed? You only had to look at the changing face of Mary Mother over the centuries, from the ethereal Raphaels and Michaelangelos to Linda Darnell, no less, in full Hollywood glory, all lollipop lips, uplift bra, peroxide curls and dimples. On at the Savoy Cinema she was, and everyone in Dublin City enamoured of her. Sure, how in the name of all the Saints could Mary be peroxide blonde an' she a Jewess from the East? Sure, the human race was as eejity as the second-form boys in St Michael's, he often thought. His own favourite was the Murillo Virgin, reproductions of which hung in his living room and over his bed, and before which he prayed, on his knees, night and morning.

He had been a priest now for a long time. He had officiated at Livia's and Dan's wedding, baptized Aisling and David and looked after the souls of all the parishioners around and in Slievelea. Confession, Canon Keane had told him years ago, made you an alcoholic or a wisely tolerant man, and for Father O'Brien it was the latter. Full of a deep compassion for the human frailty of his flock, his pale blue eyes twinkled deep in the tanned creases of his face, and his beetle bushy eyebrows were constantly slightly raised as if in query. He had a ready laugh that sprang from his belly and it was often heard of a morning in the cool hushed chapel as the congregation waited for Mass to begin. Father O'Brien's great bellow would boom through the peaceful place making the drowsy congregation jump and smile and nod to each other, as one would over a baby, 'Ah sure, it's only himself', and the chapel would be full of smiles when their priest entered in his vestments carrying the gold chalice, a freckled altar boy before him swinging a censer.

Mrs Casey was speaking to him. She wore a soft burgundy wool dress with pearls at the throat. Her finger seemed too thin to support the square diamond ring that glittered in the saffron light of the fire.

'Father O'Brien, I'm going to die.'

He laughed, embarrassed. 'Ah sure now, aren't we all?' he said, cursing the banality of the remark that came out before he could stop himself. But this woman always rendered him a little tongue-tied.

'No, no, Father. I am. I'm quite resigned. How long it will take I don't know. I'm very tired, you see. Too tired to struggle any more.'

Father O'Brien nodded, and said nothing. She was one who would have made life an uphill climb, he thought. One of the ones whose personality stood between themselves and their own happiness. Why did some people make life such a problem? he wondered.

'Do you remember, Father, a long time ago, my confession?'

Father O'Brien sat back in the wide chair and shook his head.

'My dear lady. Remember a confession? Why, I hear hundreds every day . . . and yours . . .?'

'No. No, Father.' She sounded impatient, then controlled

374

herself. The white skin on her forehead was beaded with sweat, shining like marble in the dim light. 'No. This was an important one. About my, my, misconduct.' She choked a little over the words. 'My misconduct,' she said more firmly, 'in Italy ... and ... the result.'

He remembered at once.

'Ah now, ye must not worry about that.' The poor woman was probably worrying about the fate of her immortal soul and she convinced she was about to die. 'Sure ye confessed it and I'm sure ye repented long ago.'

She said tartly, 'No, Father, I did not. I never regretted it for a moment, neither the deed nor the result.'

Father O'Brien blinked, wondering what would come next. He was a simple man and he was becoming confused.

'Well, I'm sure the good Lord will overlook ...'

'Father O'Brien, at this point I don't much care whether the good Lord overlooks or not. I'm not worried about it at all. I suppose the good Lord to be a kinder, more forgiving person than I am, and if He finds it impossible to forgive my little sins then I'm not at all sure I want to spend eternity in his company.' She looked up at him, her eyes suddenly filling with tears. They looked enormous in the firelight, black-rimmed and glittering.

'I want you, Father ... I give you permission to break the seal of that particular confession, to tell my daughter Aisling ... to tell her the facts, whatever you deem necessary, if ever you feel you should do so. I mean, if circumstances arise ... if you think it advisable ...'

'Ah, yes, yes, dear Mrs Casey, I understand.' Father O'Brien heaved a sigh of relief. At last he knew what was expected of him. He could relax. 'I understand, dear lady. Rest assured, I'll carry out your wishes. Only, though, if it causes no problems to anyone else.'

'Oh, Father, that goes without saying.'

'Don't fret, dear lady, don't fret. I've got your meaning entirely.' He smiled reassuringly into her eyes. She looked calmer, the tension eased from her face.

'Good,' she said. 'Then I'll leave it with you.'

He sipped his drink, at ease now. The light of the room wavered and glowed on the face of the beautiful woman opposite him.

She said, 'You are a dear, good man. You have always been kind to me and mine. You are surely beloved of your boss.' She gave him a dazzling smile, a smile that took his breath away. He blushed and laughed. She looked into the fire and continued more seriously, 'I suppose now I should regret my sin ... my infidelity, but, Father, I don't. I can't. You see, all my married life I have loved my husband so much, and I've never been able to regret anything that brought him happiness, brought us closer together, and Aisling did that.'

She remembered the first painful years when her body had yearned for him and how frustrated she had been. After the birth of her daughter things had gradually improved, as little by little she had led him down the sensuous avenues of her body to the fulfilment she had always yearned for. Aisling had been the indirect cause of that, but she could hardly tell this holy man about that.

'She brought him, and me, a lot of joy. She lit up Slievelea. She was an enchanted child, but then ... then ...' Livia sighed, 'then she grew up. People became jealous. They were unkind to her. You understand.'

He nodded. Indeed he knew. He had watched, unable to help as Aisling uncomprehendingly puzzled over her friends' nastiness, and he had tried to explain that she was too beautiful, too rich. Such a generous, open, trusting spirit as Aisling's could only survive in a plainer package. Her great beauty and wealth left her wide open to rejection and the thousand cruelties that society can inflict on the unprotected.

'Oh, my dear Mrs Casey, indeed'n I know.'

'Well, then, perhaps some day she'll need your help.'

'It'll be there for her, never fear.'

'I hope she'll meet someone to love her as much as I love Dan. If I've committed a grave sin, Father, it must be the one of covetousness. Or is it possessiveness? Is God jealous, do you think, when we love someone so much we make ourselves ill from wanting to possess their very souls?'

'No. No. God is not jealous, dear lady. We do it to ourselves. It's lack of trust. He wants us to trust love, not to try to cage it. Caged things die. Set free, they live and grow.'

She looked up at him, surprised for a moment, then nodded again. One of her cheeks was red from the fire. It made her look feverish.

376

'Are you all right?' he asked.

'Yes, dear friend. How wise you are. It would have been so much better if I had set Dan free, been content with the part of him that was mine. But I wanted all of him.' She shrugged.

'I've had more happiness than most, Father. When I think of it, all those years of content. The ball here when we met, Dan and I. Ah, the magic of it. The fun we had in New York. Those days were so hectic, so exciting.' She leaned forward, her pearls catching the light from the fire, rich cream on the deep-toned velvet. 'But my happiness was at its peak, became supreme, because of my infidelity. Aisling, the days of her childhood — Dan and his girls, as he called us here in Slievelea during the war. All Europe, Father, in a bloodbath and I supremely content in the bosom of my family because of a sin. Can you explain that to me?'

He shook his head and said, 'No, I cannot. Sure, how could I? I don't presume to judge. God waits till we are dead to do that. An' sometimes I think he'll quiz us not on what we think of as sins, not on the big, passionate things, but the little cruelties, the poison darts, the casual unkindnesses. Maybe. I don't know.'

They were silent, the atmosphere in the room one of tranquillity. When the priest rose to leave, Livia's eyes were closed, her head resting on the palm of her hand, and she was deeply asleep.

Chapter

53

AISLING and Alexander did their usual things that day. Rising late, the hot sun high in the clear blue sky as they untangled themselves, golden limb from golden limb, and laughing heedlessly donned bathing suits. Slinging towels round their necks they raced down to the sea for their 'dunking', as they called it. A busy road crossed the rocky incline, and Alexander cautiously pulled Aisling back, restraining her from darting across through the traffic.

'Oh, don't be foolish, darling,' he cried as she tried to run away from him. 'One of those Vespas ...'

'Oh, you old fuddy-duddy,' she laughed, giving him the slip. Lightly as a dancer, quick as lightning, she evaded a van and the dreaded motorbike and reached the other side safely. She jumped up and down, making faces at him.

He was cross when he got over to him but she ran from him again down the small winding pathway to the sea. Then she slipped and fell and had to hang on to a post stuck beside the steps at the last incline, and she was laughing and crying at the same time when he reached her. He licked the grazed knee and she made a feeble attempt at a joke, like a child, he thought, putting on a brave front, then her face crumbled and she began to cry in earnest.

'I got a fright!' she sobbed and he held her in his arms, comforting her there on the steps while the people going to the beach tried to circumvent them.

'Well, you deserved to,' he said and pulled her to her feet.

Smiling radiantly at him through her tears she said, 'You were worried though, weren't you?'

He looked back at her, his gaze level.

'Yes,' he said, and added, 'Do you think that's fair?'

She looked at him sadly and hung her head. 'No,' she said. 'No.'

'*Scuse.*'

'*Scuse.*'

'*Prego, Signor.*'

'*Prego.*'

'*Prego, Signorina.*'

The crowd clambered past them to the sea.

After their swim, their bodies glowing from a rough buffeting from the waves, they had lunch halfway up the mountainside at the little trattoria that perched overlooking the sea, and ate sea bass and salad and drank a bottle of light white wine. Then drowsy with sun and sea and food they climbed home, falling into bed. They made love, the sunlight shining through the slats in the blinds, striping their bodies dark and light, slipping around in patterns as they moved. They made love slowly, tenderly, their bodies aching from all the love they had made over all the days they had been there. Their bodies fitted together perfectly now; they knew each other's nerve endings and pleasure spots, and they aroused each other and reached their long climax of love with a crying of ecstasy and unbearably sweet sensation. They lay replete, still panting a little, and Alexander saw that Aisling had tears in her eyes.

'Oh my darling,' he began.

'I'm sorry, *cara*. I'm sorry I worried you. Oh, I'm so sorry.'

'It's all right, my love, all right. It doesn't matter now. Not now.'

'No, it's me. I mustn't do it again. I'm so afraid of losing you. That this, this wonder is all a dream that will vanish, disappear.'

'It won't, Aisling, my darling. I promise it won't.' He folded her in his arms. Their bodies were sticky with sweat.

'You'll still love me when I'm old?'

'Oh, Aisling, love ...'

'No, when I'm ugly ... it's not just my ...'

'No. No, *cara*. You know better than that.' He knew her fear of being loved simply for her looks. 'You know how much I appreciate your beauty, *cara*,' he said. 'I'm lucky to love someone so lovely, so perfect. But it's yourself I love most. The spirit of you, the soul of you. What makes you laugh and cry, which, by the way, you always seem to do at the same time.'

'In Tir na nOige, the land where one is always young, you can do neither.'

'Poor forever young!'

'Will you love me when I'm old?'

'Probably more than I do now, though I can't imagine that. My mother is old but she is still loved very much indeed.'

'By your father?'

He nodded.

'You never talk of him.'

'He is not important. You are my love. Never doubt me again.'

'Oh, I won't. And I don't think I doubt you. Myself perhaps a little. I'm afraid it will all end. It's so good, so beautiful.'

'No, it will never end. You are the most loved woman on earth. Say it.'

'I can't,' she giggled. 'I can't.'

'Go on, do. You can. I am the most loved woman on earth ... say it to please me.'

She took a deep breath and said tremulously, 'I am the most loved woman on earth.'

He kissed her gently. 'Believe it,' he said. 'Now I need a dunking. Last in is a ...'

Aisling started to laugh, 'No, no, that's not fair! My swimsuit is more difficult.' Her voice rose in a wail.

'Come on,' he cried and ran out of the door.

She heard the shots. She paid them no heed. She thought it was a car backfiring, if she thought at all. Then suddenly she froze as still as she had been in the wood when Alexander first saw her. Her heart seemed to stop too and her flesh was covered with goose pimples, and an icy shiver coursed over her skin. She stood immobile for a moment in the room, then her eyes widened and she ran to the door. Alexander lay there in the sun. He was dead, she was sure of that. His chest was covered in blood, his face twisted sideways, cheek on the gravel, so awkward. She stood looking at him in her bathing suit, the towel in her hands, shivering, shivering. A bird sang and somewhere someone laughed. She fell on her knees beside him and mopped the blood with the towel. She lifted the inert body tenderly in her arms and held him to her breast, soothing his hair and kissing his cold pale forehead.

'There, there, my love,' she crooned as if to a hurt child.

380

'There, there, now.' Then the awful moans of grief broke from her, the agony stabbing again and again as she wailed out her loss to the blue sky. The cry reverberated down over all the years of Aisling's life.

Chapter

54

THE ambulance bumped and bounced over the stony road. It was travelling too fast, but no one was going to complain about that. A private plane awaiting them at Palermo would transport the patient to a boat that was taking a leisurely journey to the Panama Canal. It was allowed no further. Many boats of dubious reputation and engaged in very doubtful pursuits were registered in Panama. No one asked questions. From there the patient would be flown to South America, to Brazil or Mexico, where so many who wanted to disappear vanished without trace.

The men in the ambulance did not know this. Two of them, hard-faced and nervous, sat on one side. One of them had a scar that ran down from his forehead across the right eye and down the cheek to the mouth, distorting the face horribly. A white-clad doctor fussed with a stethoscope and oxygen over the body on the stretcher.

'He's all right, I hope?' the scarred man asked the doctor.

'If anything happens to him, we don't get paid,' the other one said, flicking the barrel of his gun round and round in his agitation.

'Don't worry, he'll live,' the doctor said.

The men spoke in Sicilian dialect, the doctor in Italian. He had been horrified at Aisling's display of grief. No one had warned him of that. After he had given her a shot and she had been removed, the body of Arnando Ferrara, a young fisherman, had been substituted for this stranger lying on the stretcher, put in the second ambulance, and was even now speeding to the morgue, where he would be hastily incarcerated in a coffin, to be buried tomorrow on the hibiscus-bright mountainside. The paperwork would easily be arranged and officially stamped, and the girl, so heavily sedated and too shocked to react with any rationality, would be out of it all for at least twenty-four hours. Poor girl. The doctor sighed. Her grief had been so tragic, so raw. At all events his debt to 'the family' was paid, and now he could look forward to a fashionable career in Rome. Money and success awaited him. This was a small price to pay, he thought, and turned his attention to the young man on the stretcher. What had he done, who had he offended, he wondered, to deserve this treatment? The doctor hazarded a guess that some powerful man somewhere objected to his daughter's liaison with this handsome man lying pale-faced and bullet-ridden below him. Ah, Romeo and Juliet once again, in a modern context, perhaps the most common of human tragedies. Parents disapproving of their daughter's choice, young love, high passions. *Dia mia*, how wonderful to be young and to suffer so! The Italian doctor remembered his own ill-fated teenaged romance with Bianca, a Sicilian farm girl who had bewitched him one summer long ago. Bianca, black-eyed, deep-bosomed, glancing over her brown shoulder at him as she picked the grapes on his father's summer *casa* in Taormina, and he shuddered delicately with relief that his father had broken his heart for six long months and cured him of the infatuation. There was no place for Bianca at the side of Dottore Guiseppe Chiarelli in the Via Veneto in Rome, or at the other end of the dinner table at the fashionable parties he would give as he climbed the ladder of success made smooth for him by 'the family' in return for the 'favour' he was performing for them now. *Ecco* . . . the boy would recover. Those gorillas could relax, they would be paid. If only he could put the face of that girl out of his mind, and forget the agony of her cries echoing over the mountain and the azure sea.

Chapter

55

AISLING spent twenty-four hours in hospital, doped, in a sub-conscious nightmare world where she ran, ran, ran down a slippery slope and Alexander after her. She skidded and cut her knees and called his name but he was nowhere. She was in a vast arid place with the landscape of the moon and she cried out, 'You promised, you promised, you promised,' but her voice echoed in the wilderness. Two nurses, large peasant women who spoke no English, stayed with her all the time and through the police inquiry. They injected her whenever she showed signs of stress. They took her in a big black car with smoked windows to the airport and she was put on a plane in the charge of a pretty air hostess. The hostess treated her as if she were insane or an invalid, and she was both, she thought. A deadly calm overcame her, a coldness like the endless cold of the dead.

She flew into Collinstown in Dublin and her plane was met by Dan. They drove along the lanes to Slievelea, the car saluted by the labourers passing by.

Aisling knew Dan had been responsible in some way for the tragedy, but could not for the life of her imagine why. How she knew he had something to do with it she couldn't work out; she simply was certain that he had. She had heard the convers-ations, the rumours about Dan and 'the family', the Mafiosi, and she had made the connection. All her love for her father had turned to hate. She felt betrayed, abandoned, totally numbed by grief and shock, and all she wanted was her mother. But Livia, Dan told her, horrified by the agony and loathing in her eyes, was dying. He was afraid of her, this woman in the car — she was untouchable, removed from life, separate, wrapped

384

in her loneliness. In a dream, Aisling sat beside her father in the limousine driven by Devlin. She neither saw nor heard the greetings of the labourers, nor noticed the dear familiar countryside unrolling before her. Since Alexander's death, all through the police inquiry that she knew was a mockery, and which was miraculously terminated by two phone calls, one from the States, and curiously enough one from Wicklow, Ireland, all through the hasty funeral and the journey home she had been in acute physical pain, as if every part of her body had been tortured. Now she was icy calm and full of hate. She felt nauseous when she looked at her father. She could not bear the smell of his skin and hair, once so dear to her, now so abhorrent.

She said calmly to him, 'You killed him. I know you did, so I don't want any arguments. You had him murdered. I've heard about you, but I never believed what people said. I used to stand up for you. Oh, what a little fool I must have seemed. How people must have laughed at my innocence! I heard rumours about Foley Place, and people said Diramuid Holland went off with you and never came back. They say you helped the Nazis and you have connections in the underworld. But Alexander ... What's he ever done?'

Dan did not reply. He couldn't. He was in pain, in such agony that he ached to be drunk or dead. He had never felt like this before. He was a lion with the venom of a poisoned thorn in his system, constantly aware of the pain, the agonizing irritation, not understanding how it had happened, what had gone wrong. He knew dimly that he had always feared Alexander, always resented his existence, this alien child, this part of himself that was not in his control. He knew too that he was scandalized by the fact of Aisling's love affair with her brother. He felt in some remote way that he had over-reacted in his method of removing Alexander from Aisling's life, but it had seemed at the time, in the urgency of the situation, and indeed now, the only thing to do. Knowing his daughter, he knew that death was the only thing that would separate her from someone she loved. But. But. But.

Deep down the suspicion gnawed at him that perhaps his motives were not as pure as he pretended. When he reassured himself that his action was, if precipitate, at least well-intentioned, preventing incest, he was uncomfortably aware

385

that that was not the whole truth. For the first time in his life he became doubtful about the validity of some of his decisions, and he knew he would have to still these voices, bury them, for that way madness lay. He wished he could explain to this cold adult in the car beside him the why of it, but he knew he never could. She would tell Livia. He knew his daughter's fierce honesty. He had always known that Livia would ask him to leave Slievelea, expel him from paradise, if she ever found out about Alexander. He would never tolerate that. Now Livia was dying, and it was important that she had a peaceful death. And afterwards? He knew it was too late to repair the damage. His daughter, no matter how valid his excuses, no matter that Alexander was her brother, would never forgive him. Their relationship was beyond repair. Too late. Too late. The saddest words in the English language.

Aisling's voice broke in on his thoughts. Her voice was colder than a pebble in a mountain pool.

'I'm going away, Pappy. I'm leaving Slievelea and I'm never coming back. I never want to see you again.'

'You don't know, Aisling, you don't know.'

'Well, tell me then.'

'I can't.'

'You've destroyed my life, Pappy. I don't care about anything any more. I don't think I ever will.' She turned and looked at him and he flinched away from her look. 'Don't destroy David's life too. Please don't do that. You are going to be very lonely, you know, when Mummy dies.'

Jessica Klein got the news of Alexander's death and burial in Taormina from his friends in Florence. Within two days they phoned her and when they spoke of Aisling Andrews she knew exactly what had happened, that Dan had known about his son after all, and had now coldly disposed of him, and in one fell swoop Dan lost everyone he had loved and who had loved him. She grieved in her room over the shop and no sound was heard. Hymie guessed too what had transpired and he was shaken with a great inward anger. There was nothing they could do and Jessica set her face implacably against Dan. She would never go to Haddington Road again. Katie O'Callaghan could have whatever was there, and whatever was left of Big Dan Casey. She had always coveted him, Jessica knew; well, she could have

386

him now. Jessica wanted no part of him any more. She and Hymie went to Taormina. They stood in the hot sun, listening to the violent singing of the thrush. Holding hands they wept over the little stone marking Alexander's grave. They planted a cherry tree there and hoped it would shield his spirit. Then they went home to Dublin to the little shop on the quays and a great silence fell.

Chapter

56

LIVIA died three days after Aisling's return. Aisling had been shocked by her appearance when she arrived home. It seemed that after all those years of self-control Livia had just let go, and her decline was speedy. She seemed to be trying to tell Aisling something, but somehow couldn't manage it. Dan had aged too, Aisling thought dispassionately. He was an old man now.

Livia had indeed given up. The struggle suddenly seemed so trivial now. Dan would have loved her anyway. He wanted Slievelea and without her he could not have it. Even so she knew that in his fashion he had loved her better than that. He admired all I represented, she thought, and shifted in her agony. She would be glad when it was over. Perhaps she had tried too hard. Perhaps she need not have suffered so much all these years. It seemed to her as if she had been struggling upstream since the day of her meeting with Dan. It had been wonderful, but oh such a strain. If she had threatened to leave him would he have given up his mistress? He had certainly meant to the day he found the letter. Perhaps she should have pressed home her advantage. But she might have lost Dan by doing so. It was too late now. The enormous struggle to keep Big Dan Casey was over. Had it been worth it? Would it have been better to be like her grandmother, Deirdre Rennett, who sighed when she said she had never known real love?

Oh yes, it had been worth it, she thought, even though she knew that Dan had murdered his own son. She had been wrong about his needing children. She need not have worried. She need not have worried about so many things! He had kept Alexander away from Slievelea, away from his heritage, away from himself. He had shown no interest in the boy at all. She had been profoundly happy when she had found this out. She had been shaken to the core at the discovery that he had a son and her nerves had let her down. Did Dan really think such a thing could be kept from her? Over the years, against her will, she had sometimes visited the shop on the quays. She had seen the child — divined the rest. But then she had discovered that he never saw the boy, never took any interest in him at all. It was amazing. And he did not like poor David one little bit. She thought about David. She remembered his bad reports from Blackrock College, where they couldn't understand an Irish boy who was not happy to play rugby. But David was an exception, and Dan derided him for his difference. Now at Ampleforth it was not any better but at least he was away from Big Dan. What would David do without her? How would he survive? Poor little scrap.

She wished she had the energy to arrange things, to talk to Dan. Not that it would do any good. All her life with him she had known that though she had loved him, out in society in the world of parties and business, Big Dan was hated. He was rich, he was powerful and he could make or break you. People had cause to fear him and where there is fear there is dislike. Few people, she thought, love their benefactors. Well, his family hated him now. She didn't. She never could. But she was dying. Soon she would be gone, and he would be left with Jessica's hatred, with Aisling's hatred, with David's fear. There would be no one left to love Big Dan.

She had known immediately she had read Aisling's letter from Florence what had happened, what Dan had thought. But it was not true. Only she knew that and it was too late now. She did not really care, she only knew it was probably her fault, but she was too tired, in too much pain, and anyhow the damage could not be undone. She should tell Aisling though, Aisling should know. She hoped Father O'Brien would tell her. It was funny, really, she thought, funny that everyone was blaming everyone else, and it was all her fault, hers and Alain's, who knew nothing whatsoever about any of it. Where was he now? she wondered. Killed in the war? Probably. The waiter's face floated into her head, clear as a film close-up. Alain, Alain, she thought, at last I know what it's all about. An enormous surge of pain filled her body like a tidal wave, engulfing her. She tried to scream, but no sound came out. Dan held her hand but she could not feel it, neither his, nor her own. The pain exploded and she said, quite clearly, 'Alain, Alain ... at last,' and died.

David came home for his mother's funeral. Aisling held him in her arms as he cried helplessly.

'Oh Ash, Ash, I'm so unhappy,' he sobbed, his frail body shaking in her arms.

'I know, David. I know,' she whispered.

He was small for his age, frail, slim, with the face of a Walt Disney animal, huge wide eyes, a *retroussé* nose that gave other boys ammunition for teasing, teeth slightly forward, and a small quivering chin. He looked woebegone and lost, and Aisling noticed that Dan did not come near him. They stood in the little churchyard where Siobain and Michael were buried and where Deirdre and Lord and Lady Rennett rested. The sun was shining and everything was lushly green, the whole world bathed in light. The aged plump little couple, Livia's parents, her grandparents, hardly known to anyone, stood together. Edward had his arm round Letticia, gently patting her shoulder. Aisling stood beside Dan and David stood opposite, on the other side of the grave. The Jeffries, the Vestrys, the Rowleys and the Blackwaters were there, all the families from the county, come to pay their last respects. A lot of Dan's business acquaintances from Dublin had come. Their black clothes looked incongruous in the perfect sunny day.

Aisling could not cry. Her heart lay like a stone within her. Even the hatred she felt towards Dan was abated. She was too numb to feel anything. Father O'Brien droned on, his white surplice billowing in the breeze. 'Ashes to ashes, dust to dust.' That was all that was left of Alexander, of that beautiful living body that she had held in her arms ... once the worms had done their job. Her body would never be at peace again, she thought, without him close to her, without him a hair's breadth away. 'He leadeth me to green pastures,' the priest intoned. There were green pastures all around them. The trees were heavy with a million leaves.

Beside the little church Aisling watched as the first sod of earth hit the coffin. Dan stumbled beside her. He would have fallen if she had not caught his arm. He was trembling. She could feel the bone under her fingers. His arm seemed frail somehow, as if the sinew and muscle had dissolved and the healthy hardness gone. She held him up, feeling sorry for him in a dispassionate way. Poor old man, she thought. Poor old Dan. She looked at him for the first time since she had spoken to him in the car on the way from the airport. His face looked grey and old. He turned his eyes towards her. They were full of anguish.

'Why? Why? Why did she say Alain?' he said, and shook his head as if to shake away the torment in his brain. 'Why?' he said, looking at the coffin where David had dropped a single rose. Aisling smiled, and did not answer. He was in pain. It was enough. And she was glad.

Dan went to Haddington Road several times to see Jessica to explain to her, but she never came. At last he realized that she was not going to come ever again and then he knew that he had known she wouldn't. A great fear and loneliness engulfed him. He sat alone in the room, so full of her personality, her perfume, her warmth, a room full of the echoing sounds of past laughter, shared confidence, mutual passion. He sat remembering, his hands clasped, his hat held loosely between them. Sounds from the street drifted in, muted. The cry of the paper boy, 'Herril-er-Mail, Herril-er-Mail'. The chanting of children skipping, 'I met Molly Tansey an' she told me this.'

He remembered Molly Devlin's sweet voice singing:

Over the rainbow, far away,
We'll take the kids on a holiday,
Say goodbye backstreet morning, bye-bye . . .

It all reminded him of Foley Place and his lost childhood, the days of innocent happiness, unclouded by anxiety and full of love he had never had. The Devlins had had it. He remembered Spotty's ugly little mug lit up with a kind of protective love as he shrugged and obeyed his mother's sharp call, 'Get up here, Spotty, or I'll knock yer block off.'

He and Livia had gifted it all to Aisling and David, no matter how they might balk at his ruthless ways, his apparent heartlessness. Livia herself had been gently bred in that cosy cluttered house in Chelsea, surrounded by love and warmth and laughter, as had Jessica with Hymie and Martha in the shop on the quays.

Only he, he alone, unloved, unwanted, an anxious little boy, acquiring, stealing, procuring anything he could in order to escape, knew the vast loneliness of the child who never was allowed to be just that, a child. He had grappled with life and won, and all in order to escape the coldness, the lack of affection, the smells, the sounds, the daily grind of poverty.

Waves of shivering shook his large frame, and to his horror tears slid down his cheeks. Big Dan Casey had never for a moment in his life felt self-pity, yet now it engulfed him.

Why did he feel so desolate? He told himself it was Livia's death. Shock. But he knew it was more than that. His life had suddenly changed. Aisling was irretrievably lost to him. David he could never really reach. He wished he knew a little more about his son, how he felt, what he thought, but it was unlikely, he realized, that David would ever confide in him now, no matter how hard Dan tried to repair the damage. He knew that even if he told Aisling the truth it would probably make no difference, for she too had lost confidence in him. And now where was Jessica, his anchor, his mainstay through all the black days of his life? Only she had the power to console him. He ached to bury his head in her ample bosom, hold her as close as he could in his arms, drown with her in passion, escape from his loneliness and his despair.

Why did he feel this anguish? He shook his head, bewildered, and it was then he felt the tears. He brushed his cheek with his hand. He looked at his wet fingers. He could not remember ever crying before in his life, except when Deirdre died. Oh God, if only she were here now. She would have understood; she was the only one he had been truly himself with.

Jessica had found out! She thought Alexander dead. It was the only reason she did not come. Nothing else would prevent her. So he had lost her too. Why had he ever imagined he could keep her after what he had done? He wondered at his own stupidity. He had become accustomed to disregarding totally the effect of his actions on others. She thought he did not know about Alexander. Well, now she would realize he did and she would hate him for what he had done. Dear God, she believed that her son was dead. He bent his head lower and a tearing sob shook his body, a ragged, awkward, discordant cry was wrenched from his soul, howling out into the emptiness. He shuddered and covered his face with his hands as the tempest tore through him, leaving him wet, limp, sobbing. A stranger

392

would have thought him an old man sitting there in the dark, alone weeping.

Hymie Klein was bent over his account books in the dim, mote-filled shaft of sunlight that shone through his shop window and rested on the dusty ledgers and his gnarled, wood-rough hand as he scratched and scribbled with his nib-pen. The bell on the door made him look up and his breath caught in his throat as he recognized the visitor as Dan Casey. He stood in the doorway, his back to the light. It was the only time Hymie had ever seen him dishevelled, his steel-grey hair tousled, his clothes awry. Hymie rose to his feet.

'Get out. Get out of here ...' He could hardly speak and his old limbs shook as if in fever.

'I must speak with Jessica. I must.'

'You must nothing. Get out or I'll have the Gardi take you from here and I only would to God ... *Oi vay ist mir* ... they could hang you.'

'Listen to me!' Dan shouted wildly, then he looked away from Hymie to the door behind the counter. Jessica stood there framed in the soft light spilling from the inside room. There was a step up into the room and standing on it gave her a height that made her look tall and formidable. She wore black, her face a stark white mask framed in her black hair. Her eyes were hollow caverns of despair and her mouth had lost the warm seductive curve Dan so loved and was set in a hard straight line that gave her an unaccustomed severity. She looked at him and her hatred reached across the room and touched him and made him recoil.

Seconds, minutes passed, freezing the trio in the shadowy light of the dusty room. When Jessica spoke her voice was calm, controlled.

'Get out of our house and never enter it again,' she said. 'How dare you upset my father like this?'

Dan opened his mouth to speak but she said, 'I curse the day we ever set eyes on you, Dan Casey.'

'Listen to me. Alexander is not dead.'

There was another, longer, silence. Jessica gasped for breath a few times and old Hymie's eyes filled with tears. After unbearable minutes, his sobs broke and the air was rent with their pitiable sound.

'Listen,' Dan said again. 'Alexander is in Brazil. He is alive and well. I had to do it, don't you see? Aisling is his sister. She is my daughter. They became lovers ... It's monstrous. It's obscene.'

'Oh Dan, Dan! You stupid fool. Must you always be so paranoid? Must you always solve things dramatically? Will you never trust reason? Moderation?'

'You talk of reason! Moderation! He is her brother, for God's sake.'

'I know. But it could have been arranged.'

'It was. I arranged it. She thinks he is dead. She'll have to relegate him to the past. She'll have to forget.'

Jessica said coldly, 'You've always hated men, Dan. You judge them all by your own behaviour. Have you ever thought about it? You have no men friends. Unless you like to count poor little Spotty Devlin whom you have always treated like dirt under your foot. You know, I didn't find it too hard to believe that you had killed Alexander. I think even now you wouldn't mind if he were dead. No, Dan, it's women you like. You kept us very close, the women in your life. Me, Livia and Aisling. You were jealous of anyone at all near us. Well, now you've lost us all.'

'I have money here for tickets for you both to go to Alexander. As much as you want. Money to pay for your flights in first-class comfort ...'

'Money, Dan, always money. One day you'll be left alone with your money. I hope it comforts and consoles you in the long reaches of the night when the black dog sits on your shoulders and you're alone.'

She turned and went to her father, putting her arms round the dazed old man.

'Keep your money and go, Dan. Leave here. We'll get our own tickets. All I want from you, now and forever, is his address. That's all. We'll make our own arrangements. Now go.'

He stood, isolated, excluded now from their company, the warmth of Jessica's love, a love he had taken for granted, and he felt the chill. He turned and went out into the bustle of the street, and he realized that he had left for ever in that little shop one of the best and most beautiful parts of his life.

Aisling left Slievelea with her grandparents after the funeral. Edward and Letticia were in their eighties. They had turned into a scatty Dickensian little couple, dressed in the outmoded fashion of a bygone era. Letticia had become extremely plump with old age but her soft golden curls had kept their colour, or lack of it, and she wore them pinned up on her head as coyly as when she was eighteen. Edward was now vast in size, and dressed eccentrically in velvet jackets, flowing jabots, yellow socks and check trousers. He sported a cloak and was as devotedly in love with his wife as ever, if not more so. They were a delightful, doddery old couple, finishing each other's sentences, totally in tune with each other and full of a sweetness and grace of character that created a restful atmosphere, soothing to Aisling. They still lived in the house in Chelsea and were delighted to have Aisling there. She loved the comfortable untidiness in which they lived and their gentleness, almost timidity, and consideration were a balm to her shattered nerves and bruised spirits. She let them simply look after her for a while. They did not know what had happened other than that Livia had died. They felt sure that there was more to Aisling's grief than that, but did not press her to find out. The death of their daughter grieved them but did not overwhelm them; they had always been sufficient unto each other.

Aisling was restless. After a few weeks of their caring for her she decided to get a flat on her own. Edward and Letticia were both sorry to see her go but relieved to have the house to themselves again, to be able to relax and potter about in their own way and not to have to concern themselves with visitors. Edward still had his gambling nights and his clubs were still there ... Crockford's, White's. Life had hardly changed for them at all.

Aisling found herself a flat in Paulton Square off the King's Road. She went to see her agent, Paul Dixon, who had been sending out SOS signals for her. *The Lady from Vauxhall* had made her a star and she was in demand; the time was right to cash in on its success, and a lot of people had been interested in using her. Paul got her a role in another period film, playing exactly the same sort of part. She threw herself into her work and made two more romantic swashbuckling movies before she noticed a change coming over the film scene. The sixties had arrived and the times suited Aisling down to the ground. She was invited to parties where she inevitably had too much to drink, but heigh-ho, man-oh-man, what the hell! She became permissive with society, had many lovers, some of whose names she did not know, or remember, and she numbered kings and princes among her admirers. She had two abortions and smoked hash and grass and as a result of dropping a lot of acid she had a bad trip. In fact life became a series of bad trips.

She had raised her skirts to just below her crotch and stripped for her first modern movie, *The Ragdoll*, a tale about a girl like herself, beautiful, successful, a model in films who gets hooked on alcohol and pills and ends up slashing her wrists. She won an award for her performance, was seen topless in Cannes at the Festival and took a trip to Hollywood in case she won the Oscar she was nominated for, but did not, flew back to England and could not remember the visit at all. She had functioned in a black-out. And it was all meaningless. She told herself she was experiencing life. She was cool. She was hip. But her heart was empty and cold and her body felt used and second-hand and she knew deep inside herself something had broken; the mainspring had cracked that day on the hillside in Taormina.

Chapter

57

'SHE is your sister, Alexander.'

The words hung in the air, uttered now, said.

Jessica sat fanning herself as the heat shrouded her like a blanket, making movement exhausting and reducing energy to the minimum.

Alexander's voyage to this tropical island had been arduous. He had spent that time on board ship drugged, in a haze of nightmarish half-dreams. On arrival he was dumped in the hospital in Rio. Hymie and Jessica had followed him to Brazil, without thought, leaving their beloved little home and shop behind them in the pursuit of Alexander. They had rescued him from the hospital. Alexander remembered little of his time there or of the voyage and now, recovered from his physical wounds, demanded an explanation of all the events that had brought him here, desperately determined to follow his love, to find her again. The terrible words had had to be said. 'She is your sister, Alexander.'

They had searched for a place to bring Alexander, a secluded, quiet place, and this island off the coast of Brazil seemed the perfect answer. It satisfied their requirements and there was a house available immediately. So in this place, this house on the beach, expensive, luxurious even, they had settled with Alexander, happy to spend Hymie's carefully saved money on her resurrected son. But, thought Jessica, they were like souls in limbo, pinned to the scorching sands by the sun, like butter-flies pinned to a collector's board. She had nothing to do but remember. There was nothing here to take her mind off all that had happened not only to Alexander, but to her. The only man

397

she had ever loved had betrayed their love so brutally that she was numb with the shock of it. Dan Casey had not only broken Alexander's heart but had smashed hers into smithereens as well. The enormous tidal wave of her love for him had turned to an equally deep hate.

Her thoughts were constantly lingering on the past. She knew full well that she had seduced Dan and that never in his life had he made promises to her. You either loved or hated Dan Casey, few were indifferent to him. Well, now she hated him. But he asked for neither love nor hate, seeming to remain indifferent until people made up their minds which emotion they decided to inflict on him. He had never allowed himself to be vulnerable. He never asked. He took, and took only what he knew would be freely given. He never asked, for fear of rejection. Even Livia had been handed to him by Deirdre, she thought. No, Dan had never risked rejection, he had never dared. Dan had put all his faith and all his security, emotional as well as financial, in the acquisition of power and money. Well, that was all he was left with now.

Meanwhile, if only this merciless sun would stop beating down, remorseless as death. The heat, dear God, the heat. Ireland, beloved motherland. How Jessica's heart yearned to rest there a moment in her ferny mountain glens, to listen to the whisper of her streams, the wild raging of her stone-grey seas, the peaceful tranquillity of her emerald fields and weeping woods, the cheerful cry of Dublin's well-loved streets. Here the wine-coloured ocean pounded the sands, and the sand was golden as the rising sun. The fruit was obscenely ripe. Yes, you could say it was paradise, but not for Jessica. Her soul wept for her homeland and all that lay dear there, not least her youth. Dan had taken that. It had all been his.

Had Dan never thought about how she would feel to have her own son's life torn apart? No, no, of course not, he never had, he never would. He reacted as usual, swiftly, mercilessly, when he or his family were threatened.

And now he had made her home a place she could not go. She knew she would never, could never return to Dublin, her loved home, her spiritual nirvana, where she had always felt complete, at one with herself.

'She's what? She's my . . . what?'

Jessica looked at her son, her eyes full of mournful sadness.

398

'Your sister, Alexander,' she said.

She watched his face. It was such a sensitive face, she thought. The fine bones were easy to see beneath the white skin, the nostrils delicate, the edges of his mouth vulnerable and tender. Why was it the gentle ones that were destroyed? she wondered, and supposed it was the price you paid for a loving soul, a sensitive mind, an ardent disposition. Big Dan had none of those qualities, she knew, yet she had loved him. Alexander was the product of the great, the only passion of her life. How could she love a man so devoid of those qualities she most admired? She shrugged mentally. Love knew no reason, obeyed no laws. If people only loved the good, the innocent, the human race would have died out long since. Dan, like his daughter, had that incredible physical beauty that made people lose their rationality. It put them above the rest of mankind, isolating them, bestowing on them a licence to disregard the rules by which lesser mortals played the game of life. Beauty in such magnitude was dangerous, and she thought probably a curse on the ones who possessed it. The fairy tales were wrong. Cinderella and the Sleeping Beauty should have been plain little girls who lived happily ever after, for the beautiful ones rarely did.

She watched the incredulous face of her son, his expression as realization dawned.

He had been hard to control once they found him in the hospital in Rio, but he had been too weak to put up much resistance. Getting him here had been difficult, but they had managed, she and Hymie. It had all been very hard on her father, going so far from home and from everything precious to them both. His little world on the Dublin quays was all he ever cared about. He loved it and was part of it and it part of him; the shop was an extension of himself. The setting was perfect for him, and he was diminished without it. They were strangers in a strange land, and the sun burned their tender skins as it beat down on them, drying up their souls. They thirsted for Ireland as a man dying in the desert thirsts for water.

Alexander had been difficult — no, impossible — but sick and therefore manageable. Now he was better. Today, for the first time, he was up and hungry again and explanations could no longer be delayed.

She spoke the fatal words without preamble, for she knew his

399

patience would not stretch to cope with preparations.

'Aisling is your sister.'

She did not know what to expect of him, but she was ready, alert for all eventualities. His face expressed bewilderment, outrage, agony, sheer disbelief, then a dawning of truth, and agony again. The silence was profound. It seemed to Jessica like eternity. Then she started speaking, slowly, hesitantly at first, but gaining in assurance as she progressed. She told him the story of her life. She was searingly honest, leaving nothing out, including her own culpability. She told him patiently that she had pursued Big Dan and seduced him. She said that many times she could have left him, perhaps married another, but that she had stuck as close as a burr to a land girl's petticoat even when he married another and even when Livia found out about it and she knew it caused Dan's wife great pain. She explained to Alexander how she concealed the fact of him from his father, who she knew would be furious with her, but that he had obviously found out in any event, and true to form, ignored it, burying it as she knew only too well he did all unpalatable facts that could cause him pain and hurt his legitimate family. She spared herself nothing, and when the sun dipped and died, leaving total velvet blackness picked out with stars, she finished and silence fell again.

Alexander, she realized, had said nothing. Not even when she had explained about Aisling, Dan's besotted love for her and the changing of her name for the movies. He said nothing. Nothing at all. She could not see his face in the sudden darkness that had fallen from the sky like a cloak. Then she felt his hands on her shoulders. At his touch she felt a stinging behind her eyes. Her body dissolved into tears, tears held back for so long, now unstoppable. He held her close, and Hymie, coming into the room, a frail old man, joined them and put his loving arms about them both.

When the storm was over, Alexander gently disentangled himself and left the house. They saw him cross the verandah, a shadow, insubstantial in the night.

They did not see him for a week. When he returned he looked older and the gentleness had left his face. He brought with him equipment for painting, all the paraphernalia of his art, and he started working as if possessed by a demon.

Alexander's work became touched with genius. What he put

400

on canvas scalded the viewer, could not be ignored, forced Jessica to draw in her breath and tears to sting in her eyes. What he put on canvas was his soul and it saved his reason.

PART FIVE

Chapter

58

AISLING Al-Mulla received the news that her father was dying on her return from lunch at the Olden. She had planned to go skiing but the weather had turned tricky and a high wind had blown up, closing the Wasserngrat. So she had come back to her chalet for a lazy afternoon. The news had sent her straight to the gin bottle. Hassan, the major-domo, had, as usual, already thought of everything. He had bought her a ticket for the little train that would take her to Geneva and had booked her flight from there to Dublin. He had also given instructions to Annie, her maid, to pack for Ireland. Annie's eyes had lit up at the prospect of home, but her mistress informed her that she intended to travel alone.

Life had sped past, travelled fleet of foot from year to year. It had not been too bad really, if she was honest. It had been very happy these last years, since the birth of her daughter.

She had married Ali because he was a kind and loving man who asked little of her and counted himself lucky to be her husband. She was a good wife, beautiful, poised, his most cherished possession. The fact that he was rich, richer than her father, helped too to insulate her against 'the slings and arrows of outrageous fortune'. His money kept her in the manner to which she was accustomed.

As the first agony of her loss, the sharpness of immediacy, passed by and the years lengthened, she became accustomed to the emptiness at the bottom of her heart. There was so much else in life; her husband, then her daughter, her life in New York, Gstaad and France, all combined to pour balm on her wound and heal it, or at the very least soothe the hurt.

Her life became less frenetic after the first bout of abandon Alexander's death engendered. On the whole and in the fullness of time, Aisling's pain slept and her life was tolerably happy and fulfilling.

Now the news of Big Dan's imminent death had ripped the cover from the wound, and thoughts and pain suppressed for years came clamouring back to drive her once more to seek temporary anaesthesia. She had drunk very little during the years since Samantha was born. She had thought seldom of her father, for the memory of him was deeply buried too, but now the unavoidable news of him drove her back to the bottle.

While Annie packed, Aisling poured her second gin and wondered why she felt so panicky.

You're going to die, Big Dan Casey, at last, and I should be filled with joy but I'm not.

Unbidden memories of the sunny days of her childhood drifted through her mind — days when Big Dan had been God and her mother a fairy queen. She could see herself being lifted up high, her father's strong hands holding her safely. She could smell the clean, fragrant smell of her father's skin, feel the rough tweed of his jacket on her cheek. She could see his strong white teeth as he laughed. He was always laughing in those memories and he made her mother laugh too. She pushed the thoughts away. She had refused to indulge in these reminiscences for a long, long time, but, even as she shook her head, they flashed back through her mind like photographs in an album ... the lawns at Slievelea, the table spread for tea under the chestnut and her mother's small tussle with the breeze to keep down the edges of the damask tablecloth. There had always been a slight, cooling wind at Slievelea, even on the hottest day, which frisked around and made tea something of a battle. As Aisling remembered the wind, she also remembered swimming and how, until she had found the Mediterranean, she had always associated bathing with shivering and goose pimples. Swimming meant wild waves crashing on the pebbly beach of their cove, her teeth chattering in her head, and a wild joy in her heart. She thought of Mamma and Pappy holding hands as they returned to the house, of her brother David with his wet hair plastered to his head, his nose red and his lips blue. For a moment, she felt again the contentment within the group of them as if all they had to look forward to were endless days of love and laughter. Tears filled her eyes and she swallowed her gin. Sad to remember. So sad. Especially as David, floating around the drug scene in London, had cut himself off from her; seemed lost to her for the moment.

Refilling her glass, she went upstairs to her room to dress for the journey home. In the bath the memory of Alexander came crashing in on her. The previous recollections had opened the firmly shut door for this last, most painful one.

She leaned back and the pain exploded in her heart, as if her heart had burst, and her head throbbed as tiny darts of pain pierced her temples. It was always the same when she thought of Alexander, so she tried very hard not to, and had succeeded ninety-five per cent of the time in obliterating every memory of him from her daily life. Now it flowed over her, the dark lava of her unhappiness at the memory of him. My whole life would have been different with him, she thought. I wouldn't have had to live half a life. That's what I am, half alive, semi comatose. Since Alexander died I have been half dead. I don't feel things the way I did when I was with him. Then everything was so important, every Goddamned thing so terribly important. She shook her head and a sob caught in her throat, so painful it caused her to squeeze her eyes together tightly.

She had hoped for so much from her marriage with Ali. She had shut her mind firmly on the painfully sentimental memories of Slievelea, her father, the agony of Alexander, and bravely, courageously she had begun a new life with him, and then Samantha. It had nearly worked. She tried. God knew she tried. She desperately wanted the marriage to succeed, to be a good mother, to enjoy life. She wanted more than anything to be like her memories of her mother and father, to have what they had had. She wanted that peace and happiness, that content that comes with fulfilment, but that kind of happiness eluded her. Sometimes she held it for moments in time. An afternoon in the park with Samantha, the child's laughing face turned to her, the wide eyes full of trust, the little pink fist thrust confidently into her hand, and her heart would fill with an overwhelming joy, and she would say to herself, this is it, this is how it should be all the time. But it wasn't. Perhaps I ask for too much, she thought. Perhaps with Alexander I had more than I deserve.

Tears slid down her cheeks, splashing into the bath. She shook her head again. This simply would not do. She pulled the

407

plug and turned on the icy shower. She gasped at the shock of the cold water pummelling her body. She took it only for a moment, braced against the water, then she wrapped herself in a fluffy towel and patted her glowing body dry. She went into the dressing room, dropping the towel on the floor as she left the bathroom. The mirrored closets reflected her perfection from every angle. She was still so very beautiful. There was not a flaw to be seen in the long slim legs, the forward-jutting hips, the narrow waist and perfect twin mounds which were her breasts, small, firm, cherry-tipped, the sloped shoulders, the neck proud and long. The skin covering the perfect bones was a glowing gold, smooth as satin and as yet unlined. She shook her hair out of the bath cap — hair that was long, thick, all shades of blonde, natural, full of sunshine.

Aisling had often wondered if her frozen feelings had preserved her youth. I am like the Sleeping Beauty and time shall not touch me, she thought, but no perfect prince will ever awaken me. Sad.

She slipped into a pair of satin Janet Raegar knickers and pulled on her beige leather Gianni Versace pants. Her pure silk café-au-lait shirt, hand-made for her by James Drew, and her Valentino cashmere coat completed her outfit.

Hassan took her cases to the car and drove her to the station. Her eyes were distant and unfocused. She did not see that the mountains looked like huge mounds of icing sugar scattered with pavé diamonds glittering in the sun. The little train squealed and groaned down the mountains past Sanaan, Rougemont and Chateaux D'Oex with its pretty little church on the hill. Houses hung with icicles flew past the windows unseen; white veils of snow drifted across the mountain tops and powdery plumes wafted from the rock crevices; black firs rose from the soft white mounds; trickling brooks and waterfalls fed frozen lakes shining like ancient mirrors. The church spires rising in each town did not dominate the view, as they did in most European cities, because the mountains rising in majesty could not be dominated. The lace of the leafless trees and the forests were dappled with snow as if for an over-romantic Christmas card. All passed unseen. She had opened the floodgates and there was no stopping the tide of memories that blinded her eyes with a mist of tears. Unseen too were Montbovon, and the mountain with its head in the clouds, Les

Sciernes, with the earth sliding away steeply down to the valley below. Massed perpendicular ranks of grey trees wrapped in white blankets, the sun slanting on some far-off valley, flew by. The sloping roofs of chalets with wood packed under the eaves for the winter fires and icicles hanging like steel followed. Then they came to Allières and under the bridges into the darkness, the wheels grinding loudly, and outside were the uniforms of a crowd of skiers, ski-suits red, blue, white, with earmuffs, knitted hats with bobbles, and boots like the men on the moon. The laughing healthy crowd jostled onto the train, their breath in cold clouds steaming the window, but she did not notice them.

Only once did Aisling look out of the window and see, actually register, the village nestled under a blanket of snow on the mountain whose top was hidden in a pearl-grey mist. The whole scene was etched in black and grey and white except where a sunray peeped from behind a dove-grey cloud to flood a slope and turn it rose. Alexander would have painted that scene, she thought, how he would have loved it, and a sob caught in her throat and she angrily brushed a tear away, stood up and went into the dining car to order a brandy. As she drank, she resumed her sightless gaze through the window, not even noticing the change from unrelieved black and white landscape to the green of grass and the red of brick as Chernaus, Fontanivent and Montreux were reached.

At Montreux she changed trains, porters, always her willing slaves, resetting her luggage on the larger and more sophisticated express to Geneva. She passed through Vevey, Calley, and Vilette, its shimmering lakeside close enough to the train for passengers to be able to see its gentle movement. Lausanne and finally Geneva. She took a taxi from the station to the airport and now she waited, flicking through a magazine, fidgety because the flights were not called and she had to keep her eyes on the board. Then there it was, her Aer Lingus flight to Dublin.

Sitting on the plane, alarms and panics shot through her body like notes on an out-of-tune violin. She had not told Ali! How could she have forgotten that, for Christ's sake? He would be distracted with worry if he could not reach her tonight. He called her every evening. She reassured herself that Hassan would let him know, but that did not excuse her forgetfulness, her lack of consideration.

Their lives were as tailored and as organized as an efficiently run office. They went to France in the summer and Christmas was spent in Gstaad. Ali, Samantha and Aisling arrived on 21 December from New York, and Ali and Samantha returned, the former to his business commitments, the latter to nanny and school, on 1 February. As the high season in Gstaad began on that date, Aisling always stayed on for a couple of weeks before returning to New York and her family. Every night of their separation Ali phoned, and Aisling spoke to Samantha at the weekend as the time difference made it difficult to speak during the week.

Aisling never went to Slievelea. No, never Slievelea. But now, dear God, the panic rose, now she was on her way. Although she had not been back, Big Dan and her home had always been in the background, lurking on the edge of her mind. Always there. But now, oh my God! She was on her way to see Big Dan die! An era was over. It was like the end of the world, the rock of Gibraltar sinking into the sea, Napoleon slipping away on Elba, the dinosaurs howling in the scorched world. This man who had, except during her time with Alexander, been part of her thoughts and feelings in love and hatred, omnipresent every moment of her life since the day she was born, was making his exit, leaving her forever.

The pain made her shudder. It had to be got rid of. This fluttering in her stomach, this tension in her chest, could not be endured. She reached up and pressed the button over her head and ordered a large brandy.

Chapter

59

DEVLIN was at Dublin Airport to meet Aisling's plane from Switzerland. She seemed remote to him, as if she were not really there. Also, he thought she was a bit sloshed. But then, begod, hadn't she got good reason to be?

I can't see him, Aisling thought, I can't see my father. Dear God, after all this time. How shall I feel? What shall I say? I need a drink. And as the car started towards Slievelea she told Devlin to stop at the Gresham Hotel in O'Connell Street. She knew he was surprised and probably disapproving but she did not care. She felt as if she were suffocating and she had to get out of the car, escape.

She went into the lounge of the hotel and sat down at a table. The pianist was playing 'Some Enchanted Evening' and priests with their families and visitors from the country were having afternoon tea. The rattle of china mingling with the piano music and the gentle resonance of Irish voices unnerved her, disarmed her, made her feel a child again.

The waiter asked her pleasure. She ordered a brandy, a large one. He winked understandingly at her and went to get it. Devlin would be getting impatient, but she wasn't going to worry about him.

She remembered how people used to whisper about Big Dan Casey. 'He's very dangerous,' they said, 'not a man to cross.' She was going to have to face him at last. How did she feel? So very nervous. Relieved, too, as if she always knew this day would come and she was glad now that it was here, but terrified of facing up to it.

She picked up the brandy, but clumsily missed the stem of the bulbous glass and let it drop. It smashed to bits, the dis-

411

cordant sound of breaking glass causing a sudden silence in the room as people turned their heads to look.

'Why, Lord bless my soul, it's Miss Casey. Mrs? Oh, God blessus, I don't remember. Aisling, isn't it?'

'Please go away, Father O'Brien. I really don't want to talk to you now.'

'Yerra girl, now that's no way to talk to a man of the cloth.'

Father O'Brien spoke lightly, but looking into Aisling's unfocused eyes he decided she was drunk and in a mess. He sat down at the table beside her and covered her hand with his big ham-fist.

'What's the matter, allana?' he asked.

Whether it was the real concern in his voice or the drinks she had had or the fact that she was home again, Aisling never really knew, but she burst into tears, bawling loudly as if she were a child again and had cut her knee. Father O'Brien soothed her, stroking her hand as one does a child's and speaking gently with paternal reassurance.

Several ladies sipping their tea stopped gossiping and stared at her, cups held in mid-air.

A sibilant whisper sounded through the room.

'Isn't that Aisling Andrews?'

'Aisling Andrews . . .'

'Is she all right . . . looks odd to me.'

The pianist, Péggy Dell, turned around to see what the competition was. A couple of waiters giggled, well aware of the cause of the commotion: 'Ah sure, God bless her, wasn't she pissed as a fiddler's bitch, the creature.'

A small girl with ringlets who was stuffing a chocolate éclair into her mouth paused in mid-gulp and asked her mother loudly, 'What's the matter wid the lady, Mam? What?'

Father O'Brien decided it was time to get Aisling out of the public room and, taking her by the hand, said, 'Come with me, young lady, and stop that howling.'

To his surprise, she instantly obeyed and Devlin was astonished to see her emerge from the Gresham Hotel into O'Connell Street holding the hand of the priest and hopping quick as a flash into one of the rows of taxis parked before the hotel. He slammed his hands on the wheel of the Mercedes, then shrugged. 'Yerra sure there's going to be trouble, no matter what,' he said to himself, 'an' mebbe I'll get off easier if I tell him she's gone off with Father O'Brien than if I have to bring her home pissed as a newt.'

In the end, after much cogitation, Devlin chose the coward's way out and phoned Slievelea, leaving a message with Sheilagh that Miss Aisling was with Father O'Brien and would be home in the fullness of time.

Father O'Brien's room in the priest's house next to the church on the Wicklow Road was a cosy little room. A coal fire burned merrily in the grate and the beloved print of the Murillo Virgin smiled above it. A clock ticked on the mantelpiece, which was cluttered with a brass replica of the Eiffel Tower, a blue-and-white Virgin under a glass dome from Lourdes, a framed picture of his aged parents, a pipe rack and a framed scroll of the Pontiff, signed and inscribed to 'Father O'Brien, faithful follower of Christ'. There was a bottle of Paddy on the sideboard and glasses but the priest did not go near them. Instead he asked his housekeeper, Mrs Venebles, to bring them some biscuits and lots of hot coffee.

Seating Aisling in the Vranlon-covered chair, he settled himself in his mock-leather one. It was cracking a bit on the seat and at the point where he rested his head, but, bless the Lord, it was comfortable as a mother's lap.

He waited patiently, looking at the woman opposite him. Beautiful ... too beautiful, he thought, just like her mother, and desperately unhappy. He remembered his promise to Livia very well. He felt the time might have come to fulfil that last request. It was obvious the girl was troubled, in pain and instinctively he felt sure that this was the moment to divulge the truth. The truth was always best, he thought. Surely God had sent her to the Gresham today.

Aisling stared into the fire. It was warm here. It was good to hear the soft Irish voice of the priest fall like spring rain on her parched soul. To mourn a lover for so long was unreasonable of her, she knew, but she did. Oh, how she did.

When the coffee arrived, the priest poured the steaming black liquid into a mug and handed it to her. She sipped it gratefully. It warmed her. He offered her a biscuit. She shook her head, but he insisted and she gave in to his gentle bullying.

After a moment's pause, while she nibbled, he leaned back in his chair and said softly, 'Can you tell me, acushla, what has you in this state?'

413

Aisling looked at him. Then she said, 'I'm unhappy so I drink. I drink because I'm unhappy. That simple.'

'No, Aisling, it's not that simple. Why are you unhappy?'

'Father, all I've ever been is beautiful. It's all people see. It's all they care about. I'm Aisling Andrews, film star, to be stared at, gawped at, whispered about. Didn't you hear them at the hotel? Of course you did. They don't care how I feel, how I think. I'm identified with that image on the screen in the cinema. I'm a symbol to them. I'm not a person. I'm beautiful and must always appear so, so that they can stare ... stare ... stare.'

'You don't have to act if it makes you unhappy. I thought you retired when your daughter was born? You see, Aisling, I do know a little bit about it. I'm one of those people who see you on the screen, and all I feel for you is concern and love.'

She shook her head impatiently. 'It's not only that, Father. It's being beautiful. Before I ever acted, girls, my friends even, hated me, or were jealous. Boys were scared of me. I was never ordinary. I do so want to be.'

'Ah, come now, Aisling. You work at it, you know you do. You must, to look like that.'

Aisling smiled for the first time.

'Oh yes, Father, you're right, I work bloody hard at it. I'm afraid, you see, that it's all I've got. I have beauty treatments at Elizabeth Arden. I am massaged and waxed at the Sanctuary. I go to dance classes where I keep my body in perfect condition. See how agile I am? I play tennis in the summer in Antibes and ski in the winter at Gstaad. I dress in Valentino and Gianni Versace, Yves St Laurent and Perry Ellis. I eat yoghurt and fruit for lunch when I'm alone. Oh yes, Father, I work at it. You are right. But, you see, I think sometimes that if I lost my beauty there would be nothing there, just a big empty hole, an emptiness.'

'That's not so, Aisling, and you know it.'

'No, Father, I don't. It's how I feel.'

'You are afraid.'

'Of what?'

'Deep in your heart, Aisling, you have always wanted to run away from responsibility, to escape back into the uncomplicated world of childhood. Remember, I've known you all your life. In a way that was probably why you chose acting as a career. And

414

it was partly, if not wholly, your father's fault. He kept your childhood so apart, so protected. He shielded you from life instead of teaching you how to cope with it. I remember often telling him so, but he wouldn't listen and your mother only ever did what he asked. She obeyed him in all things. Ah, she was a grand woman, a fine and loyal woman, your mother. Dignified and graceful. That was why . . .'

He faltered a moment, then said, 'We grow through pain, Aisling. If we allow ourselves. If we don't we become warped and bitter. Sour. Don't let it happen to you. You see, Aisling, happiness lies in us or nowhere. Happiness does not lie in another person.'

She interrupted angrily. 'No, Father O'Brien. Oh no. You are very wrong, indeed you are. It's a sad, sad story. No doubt you may find it excessively silly. No, that's not fair of me. Forgive me. But listen. I was in love once. The man filled my heart, my soul, my body, my life. But he was not suitable for Aisling *Casey*. Not suitable for a *Casey*. So my father had him shot. Does that sound melodramatic to you?'

The priest shook his head. Confession had made him cognizant of the fact that there was no such thing as melodrama, only life. The wildness, the unpredictability, the idiosyncrasy of people's behaviour had long since ceased to amaze him. 'No. Indeed no.' he said.

Aisling continued, 'I've never stopped bleeding since. Oh, I know all the answers you would give, but I've tried praying, I've tried everything, and nothing, nothing works. I don't want to be unhappy. I desperately want to love my husband and my child with all my heart and soul, but always, always Alexander stands between them and everything, everybody, life, and me.'

Father O'Brien looked at the beautiful face that was nakedly exposing her anguish. The chin quivered, the tears were just held back, the eyes were dilated with pain. He cleared his throat and said, 'Have some more coffee, Aisling. I want you completely sober for what I've got to tell you. 'Tis too important for you to get muddled in the facts.'

She could not imagine what he was talking about, but she was glad of his company, glad of the delay. She was so frightened of facing her father, frightened of having no control of her emotions. She looked around the little room. The walls were covered in an appalling wallpaper patterned in orange and

415

rusty brown. There was an overhead bulb, bright and hardly shielded by a plastic shade covered in red roses. Yet the room emanated a peace and warmth soothing to Aisling's troubled spirit. In the silence a shudder shook her frame and she sighed. At last Father O'Brien spoke.

'Your mother spoke to me before she died. She had told me something many years before in confession and she asked me to tell you if ever I thought it should be told and I do now, Aisling — I don't know why, but I do and I trust my instincts — they're God given.' He paused.

She looked at him, uncomprehending, confused, and he had a moment's doubt about the advisability of giving such a stupendous piece of information to so obviously disturbed a human being. But it was too late. Her eyes had a new intent look.

'My mother? Confession? What do you mean, Father?'

He took a deep breath and fixed his eyes on the sweet, familiar and consoling face of the Madonna.

'Just this, my child. Your mother confessed long, long ago to the sin of adultery. She confessed that you were the result of that sin and not your father's daughter.' He heard her gasp and the jarring sound as she banged her mug down on the table, but he kept his eyes on the Virgin's face, drawing strength from it.

'She stressed she loved only your father, but she wanted a child more than anything and none were, ah, forthcoming, so she planned to conceive, and she chose someone called Alain for no other reason than to get pregnant. I don't think she ever regretted her sin.' The priest shook his head. 'But, well, that is none of our business. We leave all that to the mercy of the good Lord. In any event, she said that I should tell you if it ever seemed necessary. Big Dan knows nothing of this, my child, and I think your mother wished to keep him in ignorance. It was simply you she thought might need to know, as I said.'

Much later, as he watched Aisling tuck into a plate of bacon and eggs prepared for her by Mrs Venebles, Father O'Brien sent up a prayer of gratitude to the Virgin. Surely it was a good thing he had done this day. Sure he only had to look at the change in the woman opposite him as she gobbled up her food with a hearty appetite to know that what he had done was right and proper. The good Lord surely moved in mysterious ways.

What he did not know were Aisling's thoughts as, suddenly ravenous, she wolfed down her meal.

416

'I've got him,' she thought triumphantly. 'At last I've got him.'

Father O'Brien drove Aisling to Slievelea. He did not speak to her during the drive and she was glad of the silence. The journey through the familiar lanes and roads of her childhood home moved her more than she could have imagined. The gate-house looked like a pile of grey stones as the car swung up the drive. She saw the chimneys rise, and the house, lights on to welcome her, appear in all its beauty and her heart leapt and tears filled her eyes. She blinked them back, and thanked the priest, saying goodbye to him at the door.

Dan had gone to bed. Sheilagh was the only servant about and she clucked and cooed over Miss Aisling as if she were still a child. Aisling thought that the whole Irish population tended to treat people as if they were children, invalids or halfwits. At any event of importance, weddings, deaths, home-comings or leavings, they adopted a conciliatory and paternal or maternal tone that consoled and yet irritated her beyond belief. But she reluctantly admitted to herself that at the moment she was grateful for Sheilagh's treating her as if she were seven again. She was in a highly emotional state. The overwhelming infor-mation received from Father O'Brien, added to the fact that she was home again at Slievelea, had left her feeling so tired that she fell asleep as soon as her head hit the pillow, leaving her no time to speculate on how she was going to use her newly acquired knowledge.

417

Chapter

60

AISLING was still in an emotional turmoil when she saw her father the next day.

She woke in her own bed. A little maid brought up her breakfast of scrambled eggs and toast, coffee and marmalade and home-made brown bread. They had remembered her favourite breakfast.

After a hot bath she went downstairs, geared to see her father, but the little maid said he was still resting and would see her in the afternoon. The day was wet and windy, the leaves soggy on the driveway. Aisling saw a man of about forty clearing them. He must be the gardener, she thought, he must be new. She put on a raincoat and boots and went for a walk. It was all the same. Nothing had changed. She walked through the blue-bell wood. There were no bluebells now. She remembered that Alexander had first seen her there, in this wood. She went on to the lake. The water looked jade green in the rain, which made little umbrella patterns on the surface. The gazebo was standing there as she remembered it, a theatre for David and herself when they were small. Oh the games they had played! Had all the days really been so long, so happy, so golden? One thing she knew beyond doubt was that for the first time in a long while she felt peaceful, she felt at rest. It was Slievelea. She realized how much an exile she had been away from this beloved house, these dearly familiar woods and paths. Slievelea. The beauty of it calmed her and stilled the fear and despair at the inner core of her being. She walked back to the house and, leaving the coat and boots in the cloakroom, went upstairs and towel-dried her hair.

She ate a solitary lunch in the dining room. It was excellent ... *foie gras*, toast, wild duck with limes, a cherry compote and almond tuiles, Stilton and coffee. Her father must have ordered it. As she ate, the past kept returning. Her mother's voice filled the air around her, and the gentle replies in that soft voice her father always used when he addressed her fell on her ears as if they were both in the room with her. The food, so carefully prepared, so beautifully cooked, tasted like dust in her mouth. As she finished her coffee the new young butler came in to tell her that Mr Casey was in the music room and would like to see her.

Her heart was knocking against her ribs as she crossed the hall. She opened the door and heard his voice for the first time since her mother's funeral. It was the same. Older perhaps but gentle, Irish, cultivated.

Dan looked at his daughter as she stood in the doorway. She wore a cream satin blouse and soft beige suede trousers. It was the satin against her skin that vividly, painfully reminded him of Livia. And Deirdre. The line of Rennett women, proud, beautiful, restless as the sea, each typical of her time: the deep-bosomed Victorian beauty, the flapper, and this long, lean, cool modern lady here before him. Between them they had given him everything he had ever coveted, and perhaps, he thought, we need an unfulfilled desire or two. He drew a deep breath, girding himself for this interview, preparing himself for whatever the outcome.

'Come in, my dear. Sit by me. There where I can see you. How very beautiful you are.'

I hate him, I hate him, she reminded herself, but obediently crossed the room and sat near him in front of the big log fire.

She did not look at her father. She stared instead into the fire as she had so often done in this room when she was small. She had often sat quiet as a little mouse on the hassock at her father's feet while he sipped his afternoon tea in the autumn or winter when it was too cold or rainy to have it outside. She had felt so secure then, so protected and safe, sheltered here against the cold and rain, at peace with the guardian of her security.

Now she said sadly, 'Is David here?'

'No. He did not reply to Devlin's call. We haven't heard from him at all. I never see my son now. There is never anyone here. The people are all gone and the house is ... is lonely and full of ghosts.'

419

There was an awkward pause. Aisling's tongue felt thick and unmanageable. With a knock at the door the little maid came in to build up the fire and lay the table for tea. She placed it near Aisling, covered it with a damask cloth and with unhurried, gentle movements she put out the china, still the same violet-strewn cups and saucers, with the silver tea pot and jug and sugar bowl. There were hot-buttered crumpets, barm-brack and toasted scones, but neither Dan nor Aisling had any appetite.

Big Dan spoke to the girl, and once more Aisling was aware of the softness in his voice, the consideration it held. 'Will you call the young whipper-snapper and get him to give me some of my medicine, my dear? It's not every day my daughter comes home and I'm a wee bit over-excited.'

She pulled the bell rope and the young butler came in. He did as Dan had asked, and Aisling remained quite still, staring into the fire. When he had gone Dan said, 'Aisling, won't you have any tea? I ordered all the things I thought you would like best. For breakfast. For lunch. For tea. Oh, my dear, I had so hoped you would enjoy it all. Well, never mind. Perhaps you would like a drink?'

He was trying so hard, she thought. She searched his voice for irony, but there was none. She realized that she had never heard her father's voice angry or sarcastic with her. Even that day in the limousine hers had been the sharp voice, the harsh intonation. She shook her head. 'No, thank you, Pappy.' She had made up her mind that she would be cold as ice. She had rehearsed the scene many times in her imagination. And here she was speaking as a polite obedient daughter. The habits of childhood are hard to break, she thought. As soon as I see this man I assume the role of the inferior bowing to a greater authority, a higher power. My father — but no, not my father at all.

'I suppose it is a shade early,' he said calmly.

'Not for me it isn't. I often have a drink at this time.'

She knew she sounded childishly silly and contrary, but she seemed to have no control over her tumultuous feelings or her tongue.

'Do you?' he said mildly. He sounded to her as if he had made up his mind to reveal nothing, to contain his feelings in an iron control, and this infuriated her. How dare he have such ascendancy over his feelings when she was so emotional? But it had always been so.

She bit her lip. 'Yes, Pappy, I do. I often need to drink.' She sounded truculent, she thought; a childish defiance reverberated through all she said and she couldn't help it.

'Why, Ash? Tell me why?'

'You know why, Pappy. Life is very hard to get through.'

'Life is a series of compromises.'

'Maybe for you, Pappy, but I only ever wanted one thing, Alexander, and you took him away. Why?'

'Alexander was your brother, Ash.'

'What?' She was stunned. There was silence in the room.

'I am dying, Ash. I want to make a sort of peace.'

'My brother . . . How could that be?'

'He was my son. His mother was the kindest, nicest woman in the world. She was my mistress long before I met your mother. She never told me about Alexander. I found out by accident. Aisling, I have done you a great wrong. I'm not denying that. I did the only thing I could think of doing then. I expect if it all happened again I would do the same thing. I'm not asking you to forgive me. I'm asking you to listen to my point of view . . . to know how I saw things.'

She heard him, the words that could have dispelled her hatred for him over the past years. She realized now, foolishly, he had thought he acted for her own good. She shook her head at his stupidity.

She decided to have the drink. She stood up and crossed to the table placed near her father and poured herself a John Jameson. She raised the bottle towards Dan, but he shook his head and she noticed for the first time how sick and old he looked. She was shocked out of her resentment by the complexity of her feelings at the sight of him. His hands trembled and the flesh hung loose on his face. He had huge pouches and lines of pain around the once beautiful eyes, now lacklustre and dull.

'You see, Ash, I was not brought up like you. I had to take what I wanted. I had to be ahead of most men, I had to act quickly, even violently, to get here, to get Slievelea. It was all I ever wanted, and I know now it was worth it. You all were. You, your mother, Jessica Klein. But I botched it somehow, and, Goddamnit, I don't know how. Don't judge me, Ash. I have been punished. I have no one now. I have been completely alone these last years. There is no one in the world, including yourself, who has any love for me, and I love you, my darling, with all my heart. I really thought at the time I did the things I did that it was the only way. To protect the ones I loved, to get, to keep Slievelea. But I destroyed everything. I don't know how I destroyed your mother. I loved her so much, Ash. But I did destroy her, and I don't understand it. David is like a stranger to me. I know how I ruined your life, yet I know too, Aisling, that there was for me no alternative, no option. I have been set on a course since the day that I was born and once on that pathway there seemed no way off. I've caused anguish to every person I have ever loved, except one. I mean your great-grandmother, Aunt Deirdre. She made all this possible. She gave me Slievelea.'

Old man, you are a fool, she thought.

And she said, 'You are a fool.'

His eyes blazed blue as ice, cold as the north wind. 'Don't sit in judgement on me, Aisling. From what lofty peak do you dare to condemn? I never craved your pardon, only your under-standing. You judge me from the viewpoint of a childhood cos-seted in this sanctuary of a house and the best education money could buy. You have been surrounded by lands that are open and spaces that are wide. You were fed on the fat of the land and clothed in fine silks and lace. You rode and swam, and when-ever you needed them you had the best doctors and dentists at your beck and call. Tutors you had to instil in you a love of music, literature, and the arts. You were warmly and fiercely loved, and you condemn the father who gave you all this. I grew up barefoot in a slum where cutthroats were the order of the day, where drunkenness and violence, dirt and decay were an intrinsic part of the pattern of life. No one loved me, kissed me, held me, tended my wounds, taught me, educated me. All I ever got was the rough justice of the alleys, the laws of the jungle. I was scarred by my loveless childhood but I never inflicted it on you. There was no love in my life until Jessica Klein entered it. There was no grace, no space, no beauty at all until Deirdre, that wonderful, magnificent woman, taught me the rudiments of gracious living. I had no family until your mother deigned to have me as a husband, and I failed with both my children because I did not know how to be a father. I had no way of knowing how to be. But I tried. I did my best for you. I did only what I thought was right.' The anger suddenly left him; the fierce outburst had exhausted him and he bowed his head before her. 'I said I was not asking for forgiveness, only understanding but ...' He paused, took a deep shuddering breath and said, 'I'm sorry. I shouldn't have ...'

She cried out in her love for him, in her need for his love, 'No, no, Pappy, no. I know. You gave me the happiest childhood imaginable. You gave me so much joy. Sometimes I forget. But then you did that terrible thing ...' She looked at the man she had tried to hate and she near burst with the well of love for him that flooded her heart. She tried to fight it, to stem its flow. Remember Alexander, remember Alexander. But the bonds this man had forged over the years and the habit of her loving him were strong, so very strong.

They sat speechlessly, the two of them, the clock ticking, taking comfort from this familiar atmosphere, the fire spitting and crackling, a log falling in a flurry of sparks. They sat apart, alone, isolated, wrapped in their own thoughts, but reaching out silently to each other over the painful gap of the years. They sat as the birds twittered excitedly outside, heralding rain, as the last leaves fell soggily tired from the trees, as the dogs barked and the house creaked a little and the wind from the sea rattled the French windows, where long, long ago a beautiful, aged woman had stood, her hand to her forehead to shield her eyes from the sun, and called out, 'Who is that?' to a recklessly handsome young man.

Eventually Dan raised his head. Aisling looked at him. His eyes were defencelessly full of tears and the vulnerability of the old.

'Oh, Pappy, are you all right?'

'I'm all right ... all right,' he whispered. He obviously had difficulty in speaking, his lips seemed numb.

'I love you,' he said. 'I don't deserve ... but I love you.'

Her sobs rose in her throat, a hard, tight little knot. She stretched out her arms to him, but he forestalled her.

'Sit down, Aisling, and listen. It's important.'

'Not any more, Pappy. We've said too much already, I'm tired and so full of conflicting feelings.'

'I know, but listen. Perhaps all is not lost entirely.'

She realized she had risen, but she obeyed, and sat down on the hassock at his feet.

'What is it, Pappy?'

She saw his eyes fill with tears, then he blinked and they vanished.

'Listen, Aisling. All my life I pursued power and money at the expense of human relationships. It is the price you pay. I have never had a friend. I don't know what friendship means. Your mother suffered. You suffered. Jessica suffered. David suffered . . . is suffering. Even my mother. I gave her a beaver coat, but I think she wanted my love. I didn't know how to break through her reserve. There was one moment when my father and I were close. One moment in our lives when I held him on the steps of the G.P.O. an' he just back from a spell in an English jail. I went on my way, pursuing my dreams, dreams of power and money. And I was ruthless. They were right, Aisling, when they said I did terrible things; but, Aisling, I did not kill Alexander.'

She looked at Big Dan in disbelief.

'I don't understand. I saw, I saw . . .'

'It was arranged that way, Aisling. You were supposed to think. But it wasn't so. I didn't do that. I knew he was your brother and I knew you were in love with each other. I was . . . horrified by incest. Frightened of it. I had to stop you both, and to find a way whereby you would not, could not see each other again. I did not trust you. I'm sorry. I judged you by my own ruthless standards. Jessica accused me of that once. In any event, Livia could not find out. It would have killed her and I would have lost Slievelea. But now I am appalled at my omnipotence. I think I thought I was God. Perhaps if I had not interfered, the truth would have come out. All of it. And you could have been happy. I don't know. It's easy to be wise after the event. All that I can tell you is that it was a put-up job and Alexander is . . . was safe.'

'Where is he?' she asked and joy flooded her being, warm as honey. 'Where is he?' she cried, a wave of sweet, suffocating excitement drenching her soul. 'Oh, where is he?'

'I don't know, Aisling. I really don't. He went to South America. I had him sent to Brazil. Jessica and Hymie followed him. That's all I know. They vanished out of my life forever. But why do you want to know? What use . . .?'

She drew in her breath. This was the time to strike if she wanted the revenge she had prayed for. This was the moment to tell the old man she was not his daughter. But she could not.

She could not do that to him. A long time ago, maybe, when the wound was still raw, but not now in this sweet moment of hope and joy.

'I'm sorry, Aisling,' he said feebly.

She laid her head on his knees, this old man who was not her father, and her hair made a covering of gold in the firelight. She knelt before him as if for a benediction, a blessing. Her heart sang for joy, for only she knew Alexander was not her brother.

Dan took a deep breath and expelled it slowly. He caressed his daughter's silky hair, running the strands through his fingers. Aisling was back. She did not hate him any more. He could die in peace now that he had mended things with Aisling. Livia, he mused, was entitled to her secrets. He would not let his sleep be disturbed any more by agonizing about who Alain was. Leave it all buried with her. In any event it was stupid to think for a moment that she had not loved him. Balance was restored. He gently ran his finger over the delicate edge of her ear, and he felt her smile under his sensitive touch.

It was all explained, what her father had done. Knowing Big Dan, it was his way. How could she expect otherwise? The man who fought his way out of the gutter to the top could not be expected to change his personality halfway there. Under his urbane, enchanting exterior Big Dan had always been part savage, fighting according to the laws of the jungle or, indeed, none at all.

He had done his best for her, for them all, by his lights. She loved him, she knew now, for better or worse she loved this man who was not her father but whom she would always think of as 'Pappy'.

She gathered him into her arms and felt how fragile he was. She desperately wanted to tell him the truth, that Alexander was not her brother, and that she would find him again and live with him. But she could not do that to him now.

She would find Alexander. She would search the globe, the four corners of the earth for her love.

'I love you, Pappy. I love you.'

He smiled at her through tears. He touched her face and enfolded her in a bear hug. She felt the strength of him back again, momentarily.

'I love you too, Ash. Thank you.'

She put her fingers on his lips. 'Shush,' she whispered.

425

A warm peace fell over the room, over the occupants bathed in the firelight's glow. Big Dan leaned back in his chair. The fierce pain had gone. He felt very tired but at one with life again. 'Slievelea, Slievelea,' he thought, 'you demanded a high old price indeed, but you were worth it, every moment.' He chuckled, looking at his daughter's lovely face in the firelight. Please God make her happy. Keep her happy.

She smiled back at him, her eyes golden in the glow from the coals. The peace and love in her face filled him with delight so acute that he laughed again and was surprised it did not hurt.

Aisling thought, he's alive, my love is alive. Alexander, Alexander, somewhere on this earth you live and breathe and I will find you. Oh my love, my love, I'll find you.'

It was evening. Dan sat quietly content at last. The past had been laid to rest by Aisling and himself this afternoon. There had not been pardon or forgiveness, but there had been reconciliation. They had laid the ghosts. Now he had Aisling with him in this his favourite room in Slievelea, his beloved home. She sat across from him, the firelight glowing on that beautiful, sad face. She was resting, recovering from the emotional turmoil of the day. Did she know, he wondered, that the only place she would ever find rest would be Slievelea?

Night fell on Slievelea. The silver moon hung motionless in the sky and the stars winked in slow motion. A leaf fell here and there and the dew settled on the emerald green grass. A rabbit scuttled under the bowl of a tree in the bluebell wood and all the birds slept. The spider spun a silken web and the waters in the lake sighed and moved. Deep within the bosom of the lake the bones of a skeleton shifted their position and settled more comfortably in their resting place.